THE RED DOOR

ALSO BY CHARLES TODD

THE
RED DOOR

Charles Todd

wm WILLIAM MORROW
An Imprint of HarperCollins*Publishers*

THE RED DOOR. Copyright © 2010 by Charles Todd. All rights reserved. Printed in the United States of America. No part of this book may be used or reproduced in any manner whatsoever without written permission except in the case of brief quotations embodied in critical articles and reviews. For information address HarperCollins Publishers, 10 East 53rd Street, New York, NY 10022.

HarperCollins books may be purchased for educational, business, or sales promotional use. For information please write: Special Markets Department, HarperCollins Publishers, 10 East 53rd Street, New York, NY 10022.

Library of Congress Cataloging-in-Publication Data
Todd, Charles.
   The red door / Charles Todd. — 1st ed.
     p.   cm.
   ISBN 978-0-06-172616-3 (hardcover)
   1. Rutledge, Ian (Fictitious character)—Fiction. 2. Police—England—Fiction. 3. World War, 1914–1918—England—Fiction. I. Title.
PS3570.O37R43   2010
813'.54—dc22
                                                        2009024160

ISBN 978-0-06-196979-9 (international edition)
10 11 12 13 14   OV/RRD   10 9 8 7 6 5 4 3 2

For Tony

We never got to run with the bulls in Pamplona, or see our names in lights or in the opening credits, or find a solution to all the problems of the Universe, but by God, we enjoyed talking about everything Life had to offer . . .

God bless the butterflies.

William Granger Teachey
    MAY 15, 1930–JULY 25, 2008

I

She stood in front of the cheval glass, the long mirror that Peter had given her on their second anniversary, and considered herself. Her hair had faded from shimmering English fair to almost the color of straw, and her face was lined from working in the vegetable beds throughout the war, though she'd worn a hat and gloves. Her skin, once like silk—he'd always told her that—was showing faint lines, and her eyes, though still very blue, stared back at her from some other woman's old face.

Four years—have I really aged that much in four years? she asked her image.

With a sigh she accepted the fact that she wouldn't see forty-four again. But he'd have aged too. Probably more than she had—war was no seaside picnic on a summer's afternoon.

That thought failed to cheer her. She wanted to see joy and surprise in his face when he came home at last. The war was finally over—the eleventh hour of the eleventh day of the eleventh month. Yesterday. It wouldn't be long now before he came striding over the hill and up the lane.

Surely they would send the men in France home quickly. It had been four long lonely unbearable years. Even the Army couldn't expect families to wait beyond a month—six weeks. It wasn't as if the Allies must occupy Germany. This was, after all, an armistice, not a surrender. The Germans would be as eager to go home as the British.

Peter was some years younger than she, for heaven's sake—though she'd never confessed to that, lying cheerfully about her age from the start. A man in his midthirties had no business going to fight in France. But of course he was a career soldier, fighting was what he did, in all the distant corners of the Empire. France was nearly next door; it would require only a Channel crossing and he'd be in Dover.

She had never gone with him to his various postings—Africa, China, India— to godforsaken towns whose names she could hardly remember, and so he'd bought her a map and hung it in the sitting room, where she could see it every day, with a pin in each place he'd stayed. It had brought him nearer. One year he had nearly died of malaria and couldn't come home on leave. That was the awful winter when Timmy died, and she had been there alone to do what had to be done. She had expected to lose Peter as well, sure that God was angry with her. But Peter had survived, and the loneliness had been worse than before, because there was no one in the cottage to talk to except for Jake.

He'd sent her small gifts from time to time: a sandalwood fan from Hong Kong, silk shawls from Benares, and cashmere ones from Kashmir. A lovely woolen one from New Zealand, soft and warm as a Welsh blanket. Lacey pillow slips from Goa, a painted bowl from Madeira, its flowers rampant in the loveliest colors. Thoughtful gifts, including that small but perfect ruby, set in a gold ring he'd brought back from Burma.

She had asked, on his next leave after Timmy's death, to go with him to his next posting, but he had held her close and told her that white women didn't survive in the African heat, and he'd resign his commission before he'd lose her. She had loved him for that, though she would have taken her chances, if he'd asked.

She had kept back a new dress to wear for his homecoming, and each day now she must wash her hair in good soap, rinsing it in hard-to-come-by lemon juice she had also saved for the occasion. She could see too that she needed a little rouge, only a very little so he wouldn't notice the new lines, thinking instead how well she looked.

She'd reread all his letters until they were as worn as her hands, and knew by heart every one of them. They lay in a rosewood box by her favorite chair, where she could touch them and feel his presence.

It occurred to her that she ought to do something—something so special that he'd always remember the day he came through the door and found her waiting. Something that would take his mind off *her*, and the changes he was sure to see first thing.

Another thought struck her. His letters had been fewer and the weeks between them longer in the past two years. And there had only been one this year. Was *he* concealing something? She had dreaded word that he was dead, even though he'd spent most of the war safely behind the lines at HQ. But men were wounded every day. Still, if anything terrible had happened to him, he would surely have told her—or asked the sister in charge of his ward to write to her if he couldn't. He would never keep a secret from her. *Never*. They had always been close and truthful with each other about the smallest thing. Well, of course not about the difference in their ages! He'd always lived a charmed life—he'd told her about the tiger hunt that went badly wrong, and the African warthog that had nearly got him, and the storm that had all but wrecked their troop ship in the middle of the Atlantic, the volcanic eruption in Java when he was trying to bring the natives to safety.

But even charms ran out after a while, didn't they?

His last letter had been written in early summer, telling her how enthusiastic the British were to have the Americans come into the fighting after long weeks of training. He'd told her that he'd soon be busy "mopping up."

The Hun can't last much longer now the Yanks are here. So, dear heart, don't worry. I've made it this far, and I'll make it home. You'll see!

But what if—?

She put the thought out of her mind even before it could frame itself. If anything had happened, surely someone would have come to tell her.

Instead she tried to think what she could do—what would cry welcome and love and hope, and show her gratitude for his safe return at last.

She gazed around the small bedroom, at the curtains she kept starched and crisp, at the floral pattern of the carpet and the matching rose coverlet on the bed. No, not here. Leave their room as he remembered it. She went down the stairs, walking through each room with new eyes, trying to see it as Peter might. There was neither the time nor the money to buy new things, and besides, how many times had Peter told her he liked to find himself in familiar surroundings, because they offered him safety and the sure sense that he was home.

Desperate, she went out to the gate, to see if she could fasten something there, a banner or ribbons. Not flags, flags had taken him off to war. And not flowers—there were none to be had at this time of year.

She turned to look at the house, neat and white and holding all her happiness, except for Timmy. She wouldn't change it for the world.

And then all at once she knew what she must do. It stared back at her with such force she wondered she hadn't thought about it before.

The next morning, she walked down to the village and bought a tin of paint and carried it home jubilantly.

That afternoon, as the sun came out from behind the clouds and the light breeze felt like early autumn again, she painted the faded gray front door a vibrant and glorious red.

2

Essex, Late May, 1920

There were Japanese lanterns strung high across the lawn, the paper ribbons tied between them lifting and fluttering with the evening breeze. The lanterns hadn't been necessary in the lingering dusk of a spring's night, but as the hour neared eleven, they came into their own, sparkling in the stream that ran by the foot of the lawns, adding a fairy-tale look to the façade of the old house and gleaming in the windowpanes, red, gold, and blue.

Most of the guests had gone home finally, leaving behind the usual detritus of a party. The plates had been stacked at the ends of the three tables for Dora to collect tomorrow, and a pile of table linen, like a miniature iceberg, stood out in the green sea of the grass.

I ought to move that, Walter Teller thought, *before the damp comes and ruins the lot.* But he stood where he was, looking toward the house, his back to the darkness beyond the stream.

"A penny for your thoughts," his brother said.

Walter had forgot that he was there. Peter had taken two of the chairs and brought them together so that he could rest his bad leg, sitting quietly as he often did when he was in grievous pain. Turning, Walter said, "Sorry?"

"You were miles away," Peter commented, lightly tapping his chair's leg with his cane.

"Birthdays remind me that I'm a year older," Walter lied.

"Any of that whisky left? My leg is being attacked by angry devils."

"Yes, I think so." He went to the drinks table, found a clean glass, and poured a measure of whisky into it.

"Thanks." Peter downed half of it in one swallow.

"You ought to be careful of that," Walter said, keeping his voice level, without judgment.

"So they tell me. Which is why I wait until I'm going up to bed. It helps me sleep." He shifted his leg, searching for comfort. "I should have gone back to London tonight, with Edwin. But I couldn't face bouncing about in the motorcar for hours on end. Cowardly of me, wasn't it?" he added wryly.

"Why? This is where the four of us grew up. You. Edwin. Leticia. Myself. It will always be home." But it was in fact Edwin's house. The eldest son's inheritance. He himself lived here because Edwin preferred London. It had been a thorn in his side for ten years, this kindness, but Jenny loved Witch Hazel Farm, and so he had said nothing. It was a small sacrifice to make for her sake.

"Jenny and I are going up to London tomorrow," he went on. "You and Susannah can come with us or stay on here for a few days." Walter considered his brother. The damaged leg was beyond repair. And there was no doubt his pain was real. Still, of late there were times when he had the feeling that Peter's nightly whisky dulled more than the ache of torn muscle and smashed nerves. "All's well between you and Susannah?" he asked lightly.

"Yes, of course it is," Peter answered testily. "Why shouldn't it be?"

"No idea, old man. Except that she was a little quiet this weekend."

Peter shifted under Walter's gaze. "We've been talking about adopting a child. She has. It's complicated."

Walter looked away. "I didn't intend to pry."

"No." Changing the subject, he said, "Is Harry looking forward to school? He doesn't say much about it."

"I expect he is. He knows his mother is against it. For her sake he doesn't dwell on it."

"Jenny's a marvelous mother. Edwin was saying as much the other day." Peter hesitated. "Harry's only just seven, you know. I don't see why you can't wait a year."

Walter turned on him, suddenly angry. In the light of the blue lantern above his head, his expression was almost baleful. "It's what Father wanted. Harry's the only heir, it's what's been arranged since the day he was born. You know that as well as I do."

Peter said gently, "Father has been dead these six years. Why are we still under his thumb?" When Walter didn't answer, he went on, "He got it all wrong, you know. The eldest son to the land—that's Edwin, and he's no farmer. The next son to the Army—that's me. And I hated it. The next son to the church. That's you. And you lasted barely a year in your first living. I think, truth be told, that you found you weren't cut out to convert the heathen savage, either."

It was too close to the mark. Only that morning Walter had received a letter from the Alcock Missionary Society, wanting to know when he would be ready to return to the field. That, and Harry, had haunted him all day.

Jenny called from the house, saving Walter from having to answer his brother.

"Yes, coming," he replied, and then to his brother he said, "I'll just put these candles out. Why don't you go on up to bed? You aren't going to find any peace until you do."

Peter reached for his cane and struggled to his feet. Walter caught one of the chairs he'd been using as it almost tipped over. Peter swore at his own clumsiness. Leaning heavily on his cane, he made his way across the lawn toward the house. And halfway there, he turned and said to his brother, "Things will look better tomorrow."

Walter nodded, then set about reaching into the colorful paper cages and pinching out the flame of each candle. As he came to the last of them, he stopped.

It was too bad, he thought, that life couldn't be snuffed out as easily as a candle flame.

Could a man will himself to die? He'd seen it happen more than once in West Africa but never really believed in it.

Now he wished he could.

His sister, Leticia, would call that arrant nonsense. After all, he didn't suffer in the same way that his brothers did. Not physical pain.

He could have borne that.

It was not knowing what to do that haunted him.

3

London, Late May, 1920

Before leaving the next morning to give evidence in a court case in Sheffield, Ian Rutledge had taken his sister, Frances, to dine at a new and popular restaurant. There they encountered friends just arriving as well and on the point of being shown to a table. They were invited to join the other party, and as new arrangements were made, Rutledge made certain that his own chair remained at what had become the head of a larger table. His claustrophobia after being buried alive when a shell blew up his salient in 1916 had never faded. Even four years later, he couldn't abide a crowded room or train, and something as ordinary as a chair in a corner, with others—even good friends—between him and the door could leave him shaken. Frances, unaware of her brother's irrational fear, was already enjoying herself, and he watched her flirt with Maryanne Browning's cousin, an attractive man named Geoffrey Blake. She had met him before, and as they caught up on events and old friends, Rutledge heard someone mention

Meredith Channing. He himself had called on Mrs. Channing not ten days earlier, to thank her for a recent kindness, only to find that she was away.

Now Blake was saying, "She's in Wales, I think."

And Barbara Westin turned to him, surprised. "Wales? I'd understood she was on her way to Norfolk."

Someone at the other end of the table put in, "Was it Norfolk?"

Frances said, "I don't think I've seen her in a fortnight. Longer . . ."

"Doesn't she visit her brother-in-law around this time of year?" Ellen Tyler asked.

"Brother-in-law?" Rutledge repeated.

"Yes, he lives in the north, I believe," Ellen replied. "He went back to Inverness at the end of the war. Apparently he was sufficiently recovered to travel."

"A back injury," Alfred Westin put in. "His ship was blown up and he held on to a lifeboat for two days before they were picked up. A brave man and a stubborn one. He was in hospital for seven months. But he's walking again, I heard, albeit with canes now. He was here in the spring, for the memorial concert."

Rutledge remembered: in early spring he'd spotted Meredith Channing trying to hail a cab just as a rainstorm broke, and he'd stopped to offer her a lift. She had said something about a concert. St. Martin-in-the-Fields.

"I'm surprised she hasn't married him," Ellen Tyler went on. "Her brother-in-law, I mean. He's been in love with her for ages."

"Speaking of love, have you seen the announcement of Constance Turner's engagement in the *Times*? I am so pleased for her. She deserves a little happiness." Barbara smiled. "But wouldn't you know—another flier."

Rutledge had known Constance Turner's husband. Medford Turner had died of severe burns in early 1916, after crashing at the Front. He'd been pulled from his aircraft by a French artillery company that had risked intense flames to get to him. Rutledge and his men had watched that dogfight, before both planes had disappeared down the line. He hadn't known it was Turner at the time, only that the English pilot had shown amazing skill.

Their orders were given to the waiter, and the conversation moved on.

Hamish, ever present at the back of his mind, said to Rutledge now, "Inverness is a verra' long way." The voice was deep, Scots, and inaudible to the other diners—a vestige of shell shock, guilt, and nightmares that had begun during the fierce battle of the Somme in July 1916. In the clinic, Dr. Fleming had called that voice the price of survival, but for Rutledge it had been a torment nearly beyond enduring.

Inverness might as well be on the other side of the world. Rutledge had made it a point since the war to avoid going into Scotland. And Hamish knew why. Even his one foray there, on official business, had not ended well. In truth, he'd nearly died, taking Hamish into the darkness with him.

At that same moment Frances turned to her brother with a question, and he had to bring his attention back to the present.

But after he'd dropped her at the house that had belonged to their parents, and driven on to his flat, he couldn't shut the words out of his mind: *Doesn't she visit her brother-in-law around this time of year? I'm surprised she hasn't married him. He's been in love with her for ages.*

Meredith Channing had never spoken—to him—of her family or her past. And he had been careful not to ask questions of others that might draw attention to either his ignorance or his interest. She was reserved, a poise almost unnatural in one so young. Rutledge suspected it had been the result of what she had seen and done in the war. Nor would she have cared to be discussed as she was tonight.

Hamish said, "She refuses to let hersel' feel anything."

Was that it? Something must have hurt her very badly. Or someone. The loss of her husband?

I'm surprised she hasn't married him . . . He's been in love with her for ages.

4

When the weekend was over, Walter Teller had dropped Peter and his wife, Susannah, at their house in Bolingbroke Street, and driven on to call on his banker. He conducted his business there, arranging for his son's school fees to be paid as they came due, and strode purposefully out the door of the bank and back to his motorcar, his thoughts moving ahead to the rest of the day's errands.

Those accomplished, he had only just reached the outskirts of London on his way home when his body failed him. Sweating profusely, he fought to see the road ahead through what seemed to be narrowing vision, and his limbs felt like lead, moving slowly, clumsily.

What the hell is wrong—?

He'd never felt this way before.

Am I dying?

He started to pull to the side of the road, out of the light traffic, and then thought better of it.

If I'm to die, I'd rather die at home. Not here, not in the middle of the street. I've survived everything else—malaria, dysentery, parasites. I can make it to Essex.

He drove with utmost concentration, his hands clenched on the wheel, forcing muscles that had no will of their own to respond to his. Counting the miles now. *Why wasn't Jenny here, as she ought to be? She should be driving, damn it.* But there had been words last night over Harry leaving for school. She had been unapproachable this morning, and he'd known better than to press for her to come to London with him.

There was the sign for Repton. The farm was beyond the next turning.

"I haven't died," he told himself, his voice overly loud in his ears. "I've come this far." But he couldn't have said how he got here from London.

Harry. *It isn't you, it's Harry. Something has happened to Harry—*

The motorcar turned into the drive seemingly of its own accord, and as he came into sight of the house, he blew the horn over and over again. "Jenny," he shouted, "Jenny, for God's sake, come and help me."

It was all he could do to pull on the brake and stop in the circle before the house. His hands refused to open the door, his feet refused to lift from the pedals. Fear held him in a vise, and he could do nothing for Harry, he couldn't even save his son.

His wife came running from the house.

"Walter? What's the matter? What's happened?" Jenny cried, taking in his pale, sweating face and shaking hands.

"Something's happened to Harry."

"He's in Monmouthshire, visiting the Montleighs—"

"I know—I know. Call them. Pray God it isn't too late. Tell them we'll be there as soon as possible."

But how was he to drive to Monmouthshire? He'd find a way.

She ran back into the house, and he sat there, fists clenched, eyes shut, his mind straining to hear the conversation that was going on inside the house. He felt he would stop breathing before Jenny could bring him the answer.

There she was—running toward him. He scanned her face.

"Harry's all right, Walter, he's just fine." Mollie, the housekeeper was on her heels, wiping her hands in her apron. "I've called Dr. Fielding, he's on his way. Can you come inside? Walter—what's *wrong*?"

Exhausted, he sat there, not moving. He could die now. It was all right. If that was demanded of him, he'd understand.

5

London, Early June, 1920

After several days of giving evidence in the case in Sheffield, Ian Rutledge had returned to the Yard to find Superintendent Bowles suffering from dyspepsia and a headache.

Glowering at Rutledge, Bowles had snapped, "You're late."

"There was a heavy storm in the north. Trees down, in fact, and part of the road washed away."

"If you took the train like the rest of us, you'd have been on time."

"As it happens, the train was late as well."

"And how would you know that?"

"When I came in just now, I overheard Sergeant Gibson telling someone there had been problems with tracks in the north as well as the road."

"What was the outcome in Sheffield? Well? Don't keep me waiting," Bowles snapped.

"The jury was not long in convicting. Tuttle will spend the rest of his life in prison."

"I thought the Crown hoped he'd hang."

"The jury was not for it."

"Damned county jurors. It was a hanging case if ever there was one. It would have been, in London."

Rutledge made no answer. He'd agreed with the jury. It had been, as the French would say, a crime of passion, an overwhelming grief that had ended in the death of Tuttle's ill wife. Whether by design or by accident, only God knew. For Tuttle, hanging would have in many ways been a travesty.

Bowles took out his watch and opened the case, looking at the time. "Just as well you're back. I'm informed there's trouble in Brixton, and we're shorthanded at the moment. Clarke is in Wales, and I've just sent Mickelson to Hampshire." He waited for Rutledge to raise any objection. Satisfied that none was forthcoming, he went on. "Four barrow boys in a brawl with a handful of Irishmen. But it has to be sorted out. Two are in hospital, and one could be dead by morning. And he's the brother-in-law of the constable who broke it up. There'll be hard feelings, and no end of trouble if the man dies."

And so Rutledge had taken himself off to Brixton, only to learn the fight had occurred because the men involved were out of work, gambling in an alley behind The Queen's Head, and were far too gone in drink to do more than bloody one another when one side had accused the other of cheating. The man said to be on the verge of death by his hysterical wife was nothing of the sort, merely unconscious and expected to recover his senses momentarily. And the Irishmen were as sheepish as their English counterparts. A night in gaol would sober them sufficiently to be sent home by the desk sergeant with a flea in their ear, and they had already informed Rutledge during his interview with them that they were the best of friends despite a small misunderstanding over the dice.

They swore on their mothers' graves that it wouldn't happen again. Rutledge pointed out that one of their number was still in hospital and that more serious charges would be brought if he suffered any lasting harm.

Properly chastened, the Irishmen promised to say an Ave for his swift recovery. The Englishmen were all for assuming the cost of his care.

After speaking to the desk sergeant, suggesting that the offenders be held for another twenty-four hours until the doctors were satisfied that the injured man would make a full recovery, Rutledge left the station.

He had a strong suspicion that Bowles had sent him to Brixton out of pure spite, and that feeling was confirmed by Sergeant Davis's commiserating grin when Rutledge finally walked back into the Yard.

"Wild geese are the order of the day, sir. Chasing them, that is. Inspector Mann is in Canterbury on much the same errand. And Chief Inspector Ellis is on his way to Chichester. Idle hands and all that. It's been a week of quiet, you see. That rubs the Old Bowels on the raw."

Free to leave at last, Rutledge was too tired to go home, and too angry to rest once he got there. Instead, late as it was, he had taken to the streets, trying to walk off his own mood and finding himself beset by Hamish at every turn.

He watched the last of the summer light fade from opal to rose to lavender and thence to darkness as the stars popped out above the blackness of the river. The streets around him emptied of pedestrians and wheeled traffic alike, until his footsteps on the pavement echoed in his head and kept him company.

It occurred to him at some point that today had been the anniversary of his return to the Yard. A year ago . . .

It had been a long and difficult twelve months.

Finding himself at the foot of Westminster Bridge, he went along the parapet and leaned on an elbow, watching the dark water swirl far below, mesmerized by the motion as it surged and fought its way through the arches that struggled to hold it back.

Lost in thought, he came to the conclusion that the past year was in some fashion comparable to the battle he was watching between river and stone. The implacable stone was the past, anchored forever amid the torrent of his days, redirecting, obstructing, thwarting, and frustrating him at every turn.

Hamish said, "Ye canna' resign. Ye ken, before a fortnight was out, ye'd be back in yon clinic, sunk in useless despair."

And that was the truth of it. He wouldn't be able to live with his own failure.

Or with the voice that was in his head. Hamish lay dead in a French grave. There was no disputing that. Nor did ghosts walk. But putting that voice to rest was beyond him. Working had been Rutledge's only salvation, and he knew without it, the only escape would be drinking himself into oblivion. Hamish's victory then. His own lay in the bottom of his trunk, the loaded service revolver that was more to his liking, swift, certain, without disgrace. He'd learned in France that a good soldier always left himself a sure line of retreat.

Without conscious awareness, Rutledge had registered the footsteps passing behind him—a man on crutches, a woman hurrying in shoes too tight for her tired feet, a dog trotting purposefully back to his side of the bridge. But he had missed the soft footfalls of someone creeping toward him, half hidden by the dark, jutting islands of the lamps.

Hamish said sharply, "Hark!" and Rutledge was on the point of turning when something sharp dug into the flesh of his back.

A muffled voice said, "Your money. Any other valuables. Be quick, if you want to live."

Rutledge could have laughed. Instead he said quietly, "I won't give you my watch. It was my father's. But you can have whatever money you may find in my pockets."

The point of the knife dug deeper, and he could feel it pulling at his shirt.

The man said, a nervous anxiety in his voice, "I've told you—!"

And nerves could lead to a killing.

Rutledge didn't respond for a moment. Then, without changing his tone, he said, "I saw a constable on the far side of the bridge. He'll be here soon."

"You're lying. He turned the other way."

Hamish said, " 'Ware. He's verra' young."

That too could be unpredictable and deadly.

Rutledge said, "You don't want to commit a murder. Take the money I've offered. Left pocket. I won't stop you. What's your name?"

"I'll kill you. See if I don't." He pushed hard on the knife, piercing the skin, and Rutledge could feel a trickle of blood slowly making its way down his back.

"It makes no difference to me if you do. I was in the war, my lad, and I'm not afraid of dying. But I won't give you my watch. I'll throw it in the river first. You must take my word on that."

He could smell the fear on the man behind him and listened for sounds of traffic turning into the bridge road. "What are you called?"

There was a brief hesitation. Then, "Billy."

Rutledge doubted that it was, but the name would do.

Hamish warned, "Have a care. There's no one about."

Even as he spoke the words, Big Ben behind them struck one.

Trying to reason with his assailant, Rutledge said, "You don't want to do this, Billy. I'll help you find work, if that's the problem. I give you my word." There was a distant splash. "My watch is next," he commented, taking advantage of the sound. "I won't turn you over to the police if you give me the knife now."

He could feel the boy's uncertainty in the pressure brought to bear on the blade against his back. He could feel too the twisting of the boy's body to look up and then down the bridge for witnesses. And then the pressure increased.

The time had come.

Before his attacker could shift his weight and drive the knife home, Rutledge wheeled and caught Billy's free arm in an iron grip, twisting it behind him in a single move. His other hand reached for the knife. Startled, the boy cried out, and Rutledge misjudged the swift reflexes of the young.

The knife flashed as it swung wildly in the direction of Rutledge's face. Before he could force it away and down, it sliced through his coat and into his right arm as Billy fought with the strength of fear.

Rutledge swore and ruthlessly pinned his assailant against the parapet, knocking the wind out of him for an instant as his fingers bit into the wrist of the hand with the knife. It flexed, and all at once the knife spun in the air, catching the lamplight before it clattered on the pavement. Rutledge managed to kick it out of reach, then concentrated on subduing the boy, gradually forcing his body backward until the fight went out of him.

He was just reaching for the cap that half covered Billy's face when he heard a constable's whistle and the heavy thud of his regulation boots as he came pounding over the crest of the bridge.

Startled, Rutledge sent the cap flying into the darkness.

"Here, now!" the constable exclaimed as he got closer and took in the two men, a knife lying some two yards away. From his vantage point, Rutledge appeared to be the aggressor, and Rutledge's attacker took swift advantage of it.

He screamed, "Don't let him hurt me—he's trying to kill me. Help me—"

The constable was there, catching at Rutledge's shoulder, hauling him away from his victim, and for the first time Rutledge glimpsed the flushed and frightened face of a boy who looked eighteen or nineteen but for all his size must be no more than sixteen.

And then as the constable's fist closed over Rutledge's bleeding arm, his fingers just as quickly opened again.

"What's this, then?" the constable demanded, stepping back. He was thin and middle-aged, an imposing figure with the light reflecting from the crown of his helmet, giving the impression he was taller than he was. "Is that your knife, or his?" he asked the boy.

In that split second of hesitation, Billy wriggled free of Rutledge's grip and set off over the bridge, his feet flying. The constable looked from him to Rutledge, and Rutledge said rapidly, "I'm Scotland Yard. Rutledge, Inspector. *Go after him, man.*"

But it was too late. By the time the constable had collected himself and pelted after the suspect, he had turned at the bridge abutment and was lost in the darkness on the far side of the river.

The constable came back, breathing hard, to meet Rutledge halfway. "I'm sorry, sir—"

"So am I. His next victim might not be as lucky." He gave the constable a description of the boy, including the false name, and added, "He's frightened enough to be dangerous."

"I didn't get a close look at him," the constable admitted. "But I'll see word is passed on." He gestured to Rutledge's arm. "You'd best have that seen to, sir."

The wound was beginning to hurt now. Rutledge warned, "He may not always choose this bridge."

"Yes, sir, I understand that." He shook his head as he bent to retrieve the knife. "A pity. Nothing here to tell us where it came from. Common enough, by the look of it." He ran his finger along the edge. "And sharp enough to bone a chicken."

"I'll come to the station tomorrow to make a statement," Rutledge told him. "Where are you? And what's your name?"

"Lambeth Station. Constable Bishop, sir." He grinned tentatively, adding as if it were a longstanding joke, "Though there are none in the family that I know of."

Rutledge didn't return the smile. He nodded and walked back to where he'd left his motorcar. The blood trickling down his arm to his hand left a trail behind him, and he thought cynically that it was too bad that the boy hadn't cut his own arm instead.

Dr. Lonsdale, answering the summons at his door, was in his dressing gown and still knotting the belt. "It can't wait until morning?" And then he noted the dark patch of blood on Rutledge's sleeve. "Come in, then," he said and led Rutledge directly to his surgery.

"It's not deep," the doctor informed him, turning to wash his hands after examining and then bandaging the wound, "but it will be sore enough for a few days. Be careful how you use it." Accustomed to patching up men from the Yard, he added, "Providing infection doesn't set in from the knife that did this."

It was good advice. The next morning the arm was still sore and felt heavy, but he reported to the Yard, where news of events had preceded him.

Bowles said as they crossed paths in the corridor, "Constable Walker has reported that a week ago on the Lambeth Road a boy tried to rob a doctor returning from a lying-in. Someone came along, and the boy ran. But the description is similar. He claimed he had a knife, but neither the doctor nor his rescuer actually saw it."

"So I wasn't the first victim." He had hoped that he was.

"In fact, there have been a number of robberies at knifepoint south of the river, but most victims hand over their money without any fuss. You and the doctor argued. What were you doing on the bridge at that hour, anyway?"

"A good question," Rutledge answered him shortly. And then seeing that Bowles was intent on having an answer, he went on. "Making plans of a sort."

"A mad place to go woolgathering," Bowles commented. "How's the arm?"

"It will do."

Bowles grunted. "Dr. Lonsdale tells me otherwise. You'll be on light duty for several days." He handed Rutledge the stack of folders he was carrying. "Inspector Mickelson is behind in his paperwork. You can deal with these."

He walked away without looking back.

Rutledge stood there for all of ten seconds, then strode in the direction of his office, his expression grim.

Lonsdale had said nothing about light duties. This was Rutledge's punishment for not taking his assailant into custody. And having him do Mickelson's paperwork was intended to drive the point home.

6

Jenny Teller woke from a deep sleep, disoriented. Sitting up in bed, she stared at the room. This wasn't the clinic—what was she doing *here*? And what was that strident sound in the distance?

A telephone.

This was Edwin's house, she realized, brushing back a tendril of hair that had come loose as she slept. And this was the bedchamber she and Walter always used when they were in London.

The telephone was still ringing. Should she answer it?

Rubbing her face with her hands, she tried to collect her wits. She'd had no idea how tired she was. Everyone had been kind at the clinic, but she hadn't been able to shut her eyes, her worry driving her, and only an occasional nap snatched when Walter was with the doctors or asleep himself had kept her going. Why was there no change in his condition? Why was he refusing to talk, to look at her, to eat? Why couldn't the doctors *do* something?

She remembered now: Amy and Edwin had begged her to come

away for a few hours of rest. Walter was sleeping, it would do her good. And they would bring her back in time to have dinner with him.

Oh God, had they let her oversleep? But no, sunlight was still pouring through the curtains, making bright squares on the mauve carpet. It couldn't be more than five o'clock—perhaps half past.

The telephone had stopped ringing.

She lay back against the pillows, one part of her begging to sleep a little longer, the other lashing her with guilt for leaving the clinic even for such a short time.

There was a tap at her door, and she called, "Come in, Amy. I'm awake."

But it was Rose, the housekeeper. "I'm sorry to disturb you, Mrs. Teller, but there's someone on the telephone asking for you."

"Who is it?" She swung her feet out of the bed and stuffed them into her shoes. "My sister?"

"It's the clinic, Mrs. Teller. I told them you were resting, but they said it was urgent."

She rushed past Rose, nearly tripping over her untied laces as she raced down the stairs. At the door to the telephone closet, she paused, trying to catch her breath, then she snatched up the receiver and leaned toward the mouthpiece. "Mrs. Teller here."

She listened, her mouth so dry she couldn't speak.

"I'll be there. I'm on my way."

Putting up the receiver, she called, "Edwin? Where are you?"

He opened the study door, and she hurried down the passage to meet him. And then to her surprise she saw over his shoulder that the family was gathered there. Amy, of course; Peter and his wife; Leticia, Walter's sister. Their faces, turned toward her, were strained, as if they already knew.

But of course they couldn't. She'd only just been informed herself.

"It's Walter," she told them baldly, and then, unable to say the words, afraid that to do so would make them real, she added, "Oh, please hurry, we must go—!"

There was a deafening silence, and then everyone was moving at once, and someone, Amy, she thought distractedly, was kneeling to tie her shoelaces for her.

She stood there, waiting for the motorcars to be brought around, counting the minutes, refusing to answer their questions. Her mind was filled with only one thought: what she must say to Harry, how she was going to explain.

7

Rutledge was walking out of his office at the end of the day when he encountered Bowles bearing down on him.

The Chief Superintendent waved Rutledge back into his office and sourly regarded the stack of folders beside his blotter.

"Something has come up," he said, taking the chair and forcing Rutledge to sit again behind his desk.

"Walter Teller has gone missing," he went on, as if the name should mean something to Rutledge. "Teller? Author of that book in 1914 on the reality of the missionary's life in the field?"

But Rutledge had been on the point of joining his regiment in France when the book had come out to critical acclaim. There had been no time to read it. In fact, if asked, he would have been hard-pressed to supply the name of the author.

"Gone missing? In West Africa, was it?" he asked, dredging up a memory.

"No, thank the Lord God. Here in London. He was being treated in the Belvedere Clinic. Some sort of nervous condition, as far as I can judge from what Sergeant Biggin was saying. They've searched the place from top to bottom, and there's no sign of him. They even searched among the cadavers. Ghoulish thing to have to do, but thorough."

"Sergeant Biggin is a good man."

"Yes, yes. But this is a matter for the Yard. Important man, shows we're on top of it, results quickly, and all that. If you take my meaning."

Rutledge did. He would not fail to bring in his man, this time.

"One other thing. See that you show the family every courtesy. They'll be worried. Keep them informed."

"Who made the initial report? The family or the clinic? And when?"

"The clinic. An hour ago. They sent someone around to the nearest station. When he saw the lay of the land, Sergeant Biggin contacted the Yard. And rightly so."

Bowles stood up, pacing the narrow room. "The facts are these. The clinic contacted the London police, Sergeant Biggin went to have a look, and then he contacted us. It seems Teller had come into the city from his home in Essex to speak to his bankers—there's a son off to Harrow, shortly—and took ill on the way home. His doctor—man by the name of Fielding—sent him directly to the Belvedere, hoping the medical men there could sort him out."

Rutledge nodded. "They have a good reputation."

"That was last week. And according to Biggin, Teller was not showing any improvement at all. In fact his paralysis was progressing. And then as quickly as it came on, it apparently disappeared, because in the middle of the afternoon, today, Teller dressed himself and walked out of the clinic on his own. The clinic's porter never saw him leave. So they searched the place, then called the police and summoned Mrs. Teller. She'd been resting at the home of her brother-in-law in Marlborough Street, and the family came to the clinic at once."

It was a measure of Bowles's personal interest in the matter that he had briefed Rutledge so thoroughly.

"That's all I can give you." Bowles turned to leave. "My compliments to Mrs. Teller, and we'll do everything in our power to bring this matter to a happy conclusion." With a nod, he was out the door.

Rutledge sat where he was for a moment. Missing persons were seldom brought to the attention of the Yard, unless the search ended in a suspicious death. Or the person in question was important or well known. Many of the cases were closed by the recovery of the pitiful body downriver, others with a trial for kidnapping or murder. He had a feeling that none of these applied to Teller's disappearance.

But something had caused the man to leave his sickbed. And it was the sort of puzzle that appealed to him.

"Ye ken," Hamish was pointing out, "that yon puffed-up Chief Superintendent is looking for a scapegoat."

Suddenly Bowles was there again, poking his head around Rutledge's door.

"Good. You're still here," Bowles said. "Another thought to carry with you. Teller was in the field for quite a few years. For all we know, he may be walking around London suffering from a new plague. That would set the cat amongst the pigeons. It may be the reason why Teller's doctors are closemouthed about his condition."

The terrible epidemic of Spanish flu, as it was called at the time, that killed more people around the world in 1918 than the war had done, was still fresh in the public mind.

"I thought you said that he'd recovered—"

"Don't confuse issues, Rutledge. There's no telling how long these things might fester. Talk to his doctors and discover if you can what the risks are."

"When was he last in the field?" Rutledge asked.

"What difference does that make?" Bowles demanded irritably. He pulled out his watch. "You should have been on your way a quarter of an hour ago."

"And Inspector Mickelson's reports?" Rutledge asked blandly, unable to stop himself. He gestured to the half dozen folders still on his desk.

"Damn it, man, hand them over to Gibson. Someone else will see to them. This is urgent business."

Leaving the Yard, Rutledge drove to the Belvedere Clinic. It was housed in what had been the offices of a large Canadian firm that had returned to Ottawa with the end of the war, ironically enough because it had suffered severely in the Spanish flu and the depressed state of business after the Armistice. The clinic, looking for new quarters, had taken it over because they were expanding. It was not far from the British Museum, and traffic on the busy thoroughfare it faced was heavy at this hour.

When Rutledge went up the steps to the ornate entrance the clinic had kept during renovations, a porter in a dark blue uniform nodded to him and opened the door for him. Inside was a high-ceilinged foyer, and his footsteps echoed on the patterned marble floor as he crossed it. The orderly seated at the reception desk greeted him and asked how he might help.

Rutledge had intended to ask for Mrs. Teller, but at the last moment he changed his mind. "Matron, please. Inspector Rutledge, Scotland Yard."

"Indeed, sir." The orderly pressed one of six buttons on a pad to one side of his desk. "A sister will be here shortly to take you to Matron's office."

"Were you on duty this afternoon when Mr. Teller left the clinic?"

"Yes, sir, I was." He cleared his throat, his fingers fidgeting with the panel of buttons. "Our visitors leave at four o'clock, you see. It's quite busy for several minutes. Mr. Teller must have been amongst them, but how was I to know? I had no reason to notice him in particular."

"You don't recall anyone who could fit his description?"

"No, sir. They're mostly relatives, discussing their visit. It's the usual pattern, I see it every day."

"And today?"

The porter squinted at the ceiling. "There was a man and a woman. Three sisters—they visit nearly every afternoon, it's their father who is ill. Another man with grown daughters. A priest. A woman alone. An elderly woman in a chair, with her son. A larger family, five or six of them." He returned his gaze to Rutledge. "I'm sorry, sir, it's the best I can do. We're more careful about who comes in, not who goes out. If they're very ill, I'm to summon Matron directly."

If Teller had come out this door, he had been clever enough to pretend to be with others. A comment before opening the door, and a response that appeared to be a part of normal conversation.

How was your visit today?

Thank you for asking. Mama is a little better, I think. And you?

Not much change, I'm afraid, but the doctors are more optimistic now—they feel my brother will recover—

Face turned slightly away, listening to what was being said.

It could have happened that way.

If indeed Teller had left of his own volition and knew what he was doing.

"Which means," Rutledge pointed out, "that Mr. Teller must have been able to dress himself properly, or you'd have noticed."

"That's right, sir."

A young probationer opened the inner door and came forward to greet Rutledge.

He said to the orderly, "This is the only public exit?"

"Indeed, sir."

The young woman said to Rutledge, "Matron will see you now.

Are you the man from Scotland Yard? She was told to expect you."

Rutledge thanked the orderly for his help and accompanied the probationer into a busy passage where nurses were coming and going with a minimum of conversation.

"Is this area always busy?"

"Yes, sir. The doctors have their offices here. The wards are through the door at the far end, and upstairs." She stopped at a door to her left and tapped lightly before entering.

Matron was coming around her desk to hold out a cool hand to Rutledge as he identified himself. She shook his with firmness and gestured to a chair.

She was a tall woman with erect bearing, her hair already showing more gray than blond, her eyes a blue that brooked no nonsense. Her voice when she spoke was cool as well. "Good afternoon, Inspector. Thank you for coming so promptly."

"She doesna' care for the police," Hamish said.

And she corroborated that almost at once. "It is distressing that your presence here is necessary at all. But Mrs. Teller has been quite worried, and although the local police are doing all they can, it will reassure her that the resources of Scotland Yard are now involved in finding her husband."

The sister who had brought him had quietly shut the door behind him.

He found himself thinking that Matron had had a very difficult few hours, first searching the clinic and dealing with the police, and then answering the questions of Teller's agitated family.

"Do you have any reason to think Mr. Teller was intending to do himself harm?" he asked her. "He's been very ill, I'm told."

"We haven't been able to diagnose his illness," she said. "But there's reason to believe he was disturbed about something and his distress took a physical form. The fact that he recovered so quickly leads us to hope that his mental state was also restored to normal."

She hadn't answered his question.

"Is he likely to kill himself?"

She looked at him directly. "We can't answer that."

The door behind him opened again, and the same probationer ushered in a tall, slim woman with fair hair who was wearing a dark blue walking dress. Her eyes were red with crying, her face pale.

Rutledge guessed at once who she was. Rising, he went to her and took her hand, identifying himself.

"Mrs. Teller? I'm so sorry to learn of your husband's disappearance. The Yard will do everything in its power to return him to you as soon as possible."

"Thank you," Jenny Teller replied, her voice still thick with tears. He led her to the second chair, which was already placed to one side of Matron's desk. In doing so, he glimpsed Matron's face. She was not happy that he had so quickly taken the interview away from her.

Jenny Teller took a breath. "Has there been any news?" she asked, hope in her voice.

"That's why I'm here, to collect more information to aid in our search."

"But I've told the sergeant—"

"Sergeant Biggin has noted it in his report. But sometimes as we ask our questions, we are able to elicit new details that could be useful. Would you mind telling me a little more about your husband's illness?"

She began haltingly to describe her husband's journey to London and how it had ended, with their family doctor sending him to the Belvedere Clinic for further examination. "I didn't want to go to London with him. We'd had words the night before—about Harry going to school so soon—and now I blame myself for not being there when he became ill. We might have found help for him sooner—and perhaps he would have recovered sooner—and none of this would have happened." She found a handkerchief in her pocket and pressed it to her eyes, then took a deep breath, giving Rutledge a watery smile. "This has been the worst five days of my life—"

"And there was nothing wrong with your son? Then or later?"

"No, he was and is perfectly fine. I can't imagine what the Montleighs thought of me, but I'd caught some of Walter's fear, and I'm afraid I sounded rather—*hovering*."

"Did you have any idea what was wrong with your husband?"

"My first thought was that his malaria was returning. But after I'd told him that Harry was all right, Walter tried to step out of the motorcar, and he *couldn't*. It took three of us—my housekeeper was the third person—to get him into the house, where Dr. Fielding could examine him properly."

"What was his opinion?"

"Walter's heart was racing, and Dr. Fielding asked me if he'd had a shock or bad news—that sort of thing—but of course I didn't know, and Walter couldn't remember anything happening to him. And the motorcar was all right, there hadn't been a crash."

Rutledge turned to Matron. "And the doctors here examined him as soon as he was brought in?"

"Yes. Mr. Teller had a history of malaria, and he'd lived abroad. We had several specialists in to see him, and one was concerned about parasites. But Mr. Teller hadn't returned to the field since before the war, and therefore parasites weren't likely. Dr. Sheldon, an expert in tropical medicine, came to examine him, and he could find no evidence of disease."

She glanced at Jenny Teller and then went on. "We asked another specialist to speak with Mr. Teller, to see if his problems were more likely to be the result of some illness of the mind. But Mr. Teller was quite rational in his answers. And then that night—the second day of his having come to the Belvedere—he refused his dinner, turned his face to the wall, and was unresponsive to the staff or to Mrs. Teller. And he was that way for the remainder of the week. We could see that his paralysis was growing steadily worse, and we had to do everything for him—from lifting a glass of water to his lips to helping him turn in bed."

Hamish said, "Ye ken, there was something on his mind."

Rutledge nearly answered him aloud. Instead, he said to Jenny Teller, "Do you know of anything that was troubling your husband?"

"No. I'd have told the doctors straightaway." She sniffed. "I was the one in distress, over Harry going to school. Walter was insistent that we carry out his father's wishes. And his father has been dead for six years!"

"Why was Mr. Teller so determined to send your son away? Did he and the boy get along?"

She stared at him. "Of course they got along. They're very close. It's his father's fault. Harry is the only heir, you see. Neither of Walter's brothers have children, and his sister isn't married. There's hemophilia in the family. Edwin suffers from it, and Peter's wife, Susannah, is his first cousin, his mother's sister's child. So when Harry was born, Walter's father put his name down for Harrow, where all the heirs have gone for generations. It's a family tradition. And I have nothing to say about that. I just didn't want Harry to go so soon."

"Where is your husband's family now?"

"Driving around, searching for Walter. They spoke to the police, and then hurried away. They believed he must still be in the vicinity."

"And your son?"

"My sister Mary has been caring for him. We've tried not to worry him. And he enjoys staying with her. She spoils him so."

There was nothing more he could ask her, and so Rutledge, assuring her that everything possible was being done, took his leave.

He went next to look at Teller's room, but it offered nothing. The cupboard where patients kept their street clothes was empty, and nothing in the drawer by the bed or even under the mattress offered any clues to the man's state of mind or his intentions.

He spent the next half hour meeting with Teller's physicians, and found that they were reluctant to admit that they had no idea what had struck the man down. The general opinion was that he was in mental distress.

Thanking them, Rutledge remembered Bowles's fear that Teller might be carrying a new plague and asked if there was any possibility that Teller was contagious.

There was immediate assurance that he was not. But Rutledge wouldn't have been surprised to learn that they had crossed their fingers behind their backs.

Dr. Harmon said, "The mind is a curious thing, Mr. Rutledge. It can create demons where there are none and remember events that never happened, and it can cause the body to fall ill." He smiled. "My son is sick whenever he has an appointment with the dentist. Quite sick, with a fever. That's a simple example, but it illustrates the power of the mind."

Rutledge knew all too well how powerful the mind was, and how, once it had fixed itself on a course, altering it was nearly impossible. He wondered what the good doctor would make of Hamish.

He asked, "Would this lead Mr. Teller to harm himself?"

"That's unfortunately a strong possibility. I think he willed himself to die. And when that didn't happen, he came to the conclusion that other measures would be necessary. I'd keep a watch on the river, if I were you."

Rutledge thanked him and left. Sergeant Biggin was just coming in the clinic door as he was walking out, and he stopped to speak to Rutledge.

"We've found no sign of him, sir. I've had men searching the streets for the past hour or more and we're circulating Mr. Teller's description and that of the clothing he was wearing as well. Mrs. Teller was kind enough to help us there. You wouldn't think that a man who had been as ill as Mr. Teller was said to be could disappear so quickly. We've even had a man walking through the rooms at the museum, on the unlikely chance that he wandered in there."

"Are you also watching the river?"

"I've put out the word, sir. But that's some distance away. Do you think he could have got that far, ill and on his own?"

"I think he could do whatever he put his mind to. Keep me informed, Biggin. There is nothing more I can do here. Did you meet the rest of the family?"

"Yes, sir, I did. They were angry. Well, you'd expect that. But it seemed to me they were as angry with Teller as they were with the clinic. Though that's an odd thing to say."

"All the same, I'll keep it in mind."

The next morning, Rutledge returned early to the clinic. He found Mrs. Teller in Matron's small sitting room, and again she was alone except for Matron. She was on her feet and asking him for news as soon as he stepped through the door, but he had none to give her. He found himself apologizing, as if it were his fault that her husband hadn't been found.

To distract her, he asked if her family was with her this morning.

Jenny Teller sighed and shook her head. "They came back close to eight o'clock and they weren't at all satisfied that the police were doing everything they could to find Walter. I told them you'd come to see me, but they were still upset. And then this morning, Amy—she's Edwin's wife—came to tell me that Edwin and Peter weren't convinced that Walter is still in London. And so they have each gone to look for Walter where they felt he might be. I know that Susannah, Peter's wife, went to Cornwall, because his family often summered there when he was a boy. I think it's nonsense, but they're as worried as I am." She turned away, so that Rutledge couldn't see her face. "I asked Amy if she could stay here with me. But she wanted to drive down to Witch Hazel Farm on the off chance that Walter might have decided to go home to heal. He knows I'm here in London—he wouldn't go to Essex, knowing that."

"He might have awoken to find you weren't here, and he may have gone to Essex to seek you," Rutledge pointed out.

"But he knew I wouldn't go that far. As for his family, I feel let down, somehow. As if his brothers are more worried about Walter than about me. That sounds selfish, doesn't it? But they were here last night, badgering the police, and I could see that they could hardly sit still."

"Do you think they might know something they haven't told the police? About your husband's illness or his disappearance?"

"What *could* they know?" She considered that for a moment, and then said, "Walter is a good man, he's tried to live up to his calling, and he takes his responsibilities seriously. He's kind and considerate, and not the sort of person who has secrets. He wouldn't leave me to worry like this if he were in his right mind. I'm sure of it. I don't believe for a moment that he knew what he was doing yesterday, and that's what's so frightful to think about—that he's ill and not able to judge things properly and can't care for himself."

"I understand." Rutledge glanced at Matron, to see if she had anything more to add, but she was watching Mrs. Teller with concern for her distress. Feeling his gaze, she turned to look at him.

"I can add very little to that, except to say that Mr. Teller was very depressed by his illness. I had wondered if he feared his condition was permanent."

"Then when it changed for the better," Rutledge pointed out, "it should have been very reassuring. And it was not. Which leads me to believe that something else was on his mind." He turned again to Mrs. Teller. "Where would he be likely to turn, if he were troubled?"

"Why should he turn anywhere? He only needed to ask one of the sisters where I had gone. They would have told him." She blinked back tears. "It was the first and only time I left him. I hadn't slept at all—I was so afraid he would *die*."

Matron said, "When Sister Agnes looked in on him shortly before three o'clock, he appeared to be asleep. When she returned at twenty past four, he was gone. In little more than an hour, he recovered the use of his limbs and dressed himself. It seems hardly possible."

"Someone might have helped him dress. Helped him to leave."

"Who? To what end?" Jenny Teller put in quickly. "Everyone was at Edwin's house—they were all *there*."

Hamish said, "Did he wait for her to go?"

It was a good point. Jenny herself had just said that she had never left her husband's side. And he could hardly dress and slip away with her there in the room.

Rutledge left Mrs. Teller in Matron's care and searched the clinic himself, as the staff and then the police had done the night before.

Sister Vivian accompanied him and answered his questions. But it was clear that a patient would have found it difficult to slip out the staff entrance or the door where supplies came in and the dead were carried out.

One fact was certain. Walter Teller was no longer in the Belvedere Clinic.

"Aye," Hamish said. "But for his grieving wife, it's as if he never existed at all."

8

As Rutledge was leaving Teller's room, he found Sergeant Biggin looking for him.

Biggin said, "I didn't want to disturb the wife. But there's a body. You'll have to come and see."

"I can't recognize Teller. And I won't put Mrs. Teller through this until I know whether or not you've found her husband."

"Fair enough."

"Wait here."

Rutledge went back into the sitting room where Mrs. Teller was just joining Matron in a morning cup of tea. It was painful to see hope flaring in her eyes at the sight of him, then watch it dashed again.

"Mrs. Teller, would there be a photograph of your husband at your brother-in-law's house that the police could use to help them search for witnesses, anyone who might have seen him? I'll be glad to send someone around for it."

"A photograph?" She opened her purse and brought out a small velvet case. "I have this. But it's very precious—"

"I'll see no harm comes to it," he promised, and took out the silver frame inside the case.

"He was younger, then," she warned him. "He gave me this before we were married."

Looking down at the likeness of Walter Teller, Rutledge saw a strong face, marked by something he couldn't define. The years in the field? Possibly. It was there in the eyes, a shadow that belied the smile for the camera.

He thanked Mrs. Teller, and went back to where Biggin was waiting.

"Let's go," he said.

"He's not wearing the clothing Mrs. Teller described for us when he first went missing," Biggin told him as they walked out to the motorcar. "But the physical description fits. Height, weight, coloring."

"What happened to him?" Rutledge asked.

"He was stabbed. On Westminster Bridge. He was found shortly after dawn."

Rutledge's heart sank. Had Billy killed him? Bowles would have an apoplexy if the boy's first victim was Walter Teller.

They drove in silence to the morgue, where the body had been undressed and the man's clothing had been put in a cardboard box.

"Do you care to examine his belongings first?" the attendant asked.

"Was he robbed?"

"I expect he was. No watch or rings. No money."

"Then I'll see the body now."

He was accustomed to looking at the dead. Sometimes he was surprised at how much he could read in the dead face. At other times there was nothing but a blankness. As if the substance of the living being had been wiped away with his death.

Biggin was right. The victim was of the same general height and build as Walter Teller, his fair hair parted on the left side. But one look told Rutledge that this was not Teller. Even given the changes over the years, it was not. In fact, the dead man resembled Rutledge in size and weight, as well.

Rutledge asked that the body be turned so that he could examine the wound in the man's back. The knife had been shoved in hard, just where Rutledge had felt the faint prick of the blade against his own skin. He'd found, after he left Lonsdale, that small blood-encrusted spot in his own back.

He had had the boy pinned against the parapet. He should have brought him in, in spite of the constable's interference. He should have stopped him before he killed.

Now it was too late.

Nodding to the attendant to cover the body again, Rutledge said to Biggin, "It isn't Teller. But I can probably identify the person who did this. If you bring in a suspect, send for me."

"Fair enough," Biggin said.

Rutledge left the morgue in grim spirits, and after dropping Biggin at his station, he drove back to the Belvedere Clinic.

Mrs. Teller had gone again to her husband's empty room, and he found her there, staring out the window, lost in her own thoughts.

She turned as Rutledge stepped through the door. He could see the worry in her face, and he wondered again at the family's abandoning her at such a time.

It didn't make sense.

He said nothing about the dead man, smiling instead and telling her, "No news, I'm afraid, but the police have been bringing me up-to-date on their activities." He had spoken to Biggin at length in the motorcar. "The search has been expanded to include the river—"

She cried out at that, but he said, "Mrs.Teller, we must be realistic. Your husband has been under some stress. He may have left the clinic with the intent to do himself a harm, and if we're to find him in time we must try to understand his state of mind."

"No," she said forcefully. "Walter wouldn't kill himself. I know my husband, he has no reason to want to die and every reason to want to live. I won't listen to this."

He spent another ten minutes trying to make a dent in her certainty.

Finally he asked, "If we knew what had caused your husband's extraordinary illness, we might be better able to judge where he has gone and why. What happened to him between the bank and your house that changed him and brought on his paralysis?"

"Don't you think I'd have told Dr. Fielding—or the doctors here—if I had any idea at all?" She was angry with him. "My sister was here earlier this morning. I asked *her* if she knew anything that would help. Sometimes Walter talked to her about his mission work. Mary has always strongly supported missions, and she has no illusions about the hardships people in the field endure. She couldn't think of any reason either. And I could see that she was as worried as I was. So I didn't have the heart to ask her what I really wanted to know. I wondered if someone could have cursed Walter out there. I've heard about such things. I mean, I don't really believe in them, and I'm sure Walter doesn't either. Still, you never know—"

Her voice broke and she put her hands over her eyes, partly ashamed of her fears and partly afraid to speak them aloud, to give them a reality.

Rutledge had nothing to say in response. It had hardly been twenty-four hours since her husband left, but irrational fears were already supplying answers to questions that had none.

He summoned a nursing sister to come and sit with her, then left.

9

Rutledge found the London addresses for Edwin and Peter Teller, and drove to each house, but he was informed by the maids who answered the door that the family was away.

Wherever they were searching, he had a feeling that they were having no better luck than he had had in finding their brother.

The second day of Walter Teller's disappearance brought no new information. It was as if he'd never existed.

Hamish said, "If he were wandering about—truly lost—someone would ha' noticed him and brought him to a hospital or the police."

It was what had been on Rutledge's mind all morning.

"He might not wish to be found," he replied. "An alternative to suicide."

"There's that, aye," Hamish agreed.

It made a certain kind of sense. If one can't face the nightmare, one can try to avoid it. But what sort of nightmare haunted a man like Teller?

He went back to question Teller's doctors.

They had failed to unlock their patient's secrets.

He said, "Teller's wife has been casting about for answers as well. She has even considered a curse on her husband, from his time in places like West Africa."

"Curses are interesting things," Dr. Davies replied. "They work when people believe that they will work. In short, the curse is effective because the victim accepts that it will happen, and that nothing can be done to prevent it from happening as foretold. In my view, Teller was far too intelligent—and knowledgeable about the people with whom he worked—to be taken in by such a threat. I've talked to several other missionaries who told me that a curse had been put on them by a tribal shaman, a way of discouraging competition, one might say. And of course it failed, which caused no end of trouble for the shaman. His power was seen to be weak."

"What would be a modern equivalent of a curse?" Rutledge asked.

"Ah," Davies answered him. "That's an even more interesting question. I expect it would take the form of something happening once and the fear that it could happen again. If one finds an intruder in one's house on a dark night, it might well be something one would fear, coming into that same house on another dark night." He smiled. "Guilt can produce irrational fears as well."

"Was Teller likely to die of his illness? Was that on his mind?"

"At a guess, no, it wouldn't have killed him. The fact that he recovered so quickly points to the same conclusion."

Dr. Sheldon put in, "I can tell you this. Walter Teller wasn't afraid of dying. When he turned his face to the wall, it was his acceptance that death was preferable."

"Preferable to what?" But they had no suggestions in Teller's case.

He said, "Do you have any reason to think that Walter Teller was being poisoned?"

"No. We considered poisoning. We found no evidence of it. Is there any reason to believe—"

Rutledge cut in quickly, "No. It's something a policeman must bear in mind."

Hamish said as they left the clinic, "It isna' likely that he went away to die. He could ha' hanged himself in his room while his wife was resting at his brother's house."

"He didn't want his wife to find his body."

Rutledge spent much of that day and well into the early evening going to police stations all across London, showing the photograph he'd been given to each shift of constables coming in or going out.

They studied the photograph, but no one had seen anyone resembling Teller. And as a rule, constables on the street could be counted on to remember the faces of people not normally seen on their patch, keeping an eye out for troublemakers and strangers alike. Even a well-spoken, well-dressed man like Walter Teller would be noted for future reference.

One constable, shaking his head, said to Rutledge, "It's more likely that he found a cab soon after leaving the clinic, well before the search began. He could be anywhere now. He could have taken an omnibus, a train, or cadged a lift from someone."

But Rutledge had already sent a man from the Yard to speak to any cabbie who had taken up custom near the clinic at four o'clock on the afternoon in question. No one remembered seeing Walter Teller or even someone who looked like him.

"Ye're searching for a needle in a haystack," Hamish told Rutledge.

"Or for one man when there might well have been two, if someone had come for him, or was there to help him dress and leave."

The clinic had had no record of visits to Walter Teller, other than the immediate family. Still, it was possible to use another patient's name to pass the porter and gain access. But that led him nowhere, either.

Rutledge had even driven to Essex, to the house of Dr. Fielding, arriving there just as Fielding was preparing for his first patient of the afternoon.

The man reluctantly put aside the pipe he'd been smoking and addressed himself to Rutledge's questions about Walter Teller.

"I can give you a brief sketch of his background. Missionary for many years, and then he married Jenny Brittingham. Rather than returning to the field, he chose to write a book about his experiences."

"And this was . . . ?"

"Just a year or so before the war—1911? 1912?"

Rutledge thought how the war had defined time—before the war—after the war. As if that great cataclysmic event that had interrupted and ended so many lives was still with them like a personal watershed.

"And of course there is Harry, the son. Quite a nice child, and not at all spoiled, as you'd expect with doting aunts and uncles surrounding him. Jenny—Mrs. Teller has seen to that. She's a very good mother."

"Did Teller serve in the war?"

"As a matter of fact he did. Chaplain. But he was struck down with malaria in that rainy spring before the Somme and was sent home to recover. It was decided not to send him back to France, and so he worked among the wounded here."

"Was there anything in his war years that might have affected what happened to him last week?"

Fielding raised his eyebrows. "Not to my knowledge. In fact, I remember Teller commenting that he'd seen death in so many guises that he'd lost his fear of it long before going to France. There was something about a famine in West Africa—people dying by the droves. And of course in China death was as common as flies, he said. No, you're barking up the wrong tree there."

"Then what caused his illness?"

"That I can't tell you. Which is why I sent Teller to the Belvedere

Clinic. And the last progress report I received was rather grim. He was showing no improvement, and in fact was beginning to feel paralysis in his arms and hands as well as in his legs."

"Do you think this paralysis was genuine?"

Fielding said, "Are you asking me if his illness was feigned? No, of course not! I'd take my oath on that."

"Then how would you account for the fact that three days ago, Walter Teller got out of his sickbed while his wife was resting, dressed himself, and walked out of the clinic?"

"He did what? You're saying there was a *full* recovery? And what did his doctors make of that?" Leaning forward, Fielding stared hard at Rutledge.

"They had no better understanding of events than you do. But Teller is missing, and there's been no word from him since he walked away."

"My God. He's still missing? How is Jenny? She must be distraught."

"She's taken it very hard, as you'd expect. Now, I repeat my earlier question—can you shed any light on his illness? Or his miraculous recovery?"

"If that's what it was. I can't imagine—look, Inspector, the man was ill. I saw that for myself. It was all I could do, with Mrs. Teller's assistance and that of their maid, Mollie, to get him into their house, so I could examine him properly. He was a dead weight. And that's not easy to fake. I'd look on the road between his banker's and Essex for my answers. As for his recovery, someone else must have been there when he dressed and left the clinic. I can't see how it was managed any other way."

"Why should anyone help him leave the clinic, and not inform Mrs. Teller that he was safe and well elsewhere?"

Fielding said, "You aren't—do you think there was foul play? No, that's not possible." He shook his head. "Walter had no enemies.

Except perhaps himself. Because if this illness is in his mind, the reasons must go deep into something none of us is aware of."

From Fielding's surgery, Rutledge drove on to Witch Hazel Farm, and knocked at the door.

The housekeeper, Mollie, answered the summons, and as Rutledge introduced himself, she said quickly, "Don't tell me something has happened to Mr. Teller!"

"Why should you think something has happened to him?" Rutledge asked, misunderstanding the direction of her question.

"Because you're a policeman. And he wasn't himself at all that day when he came home from London so ill."

"His doctors are still uncertain about the cause of his illness. Tell me, was he in pain, when you were helping Mrs. Teller work with him?"

"Pain?" she repeated. "No, I'd not call it that. He was more fearful. I heard him ask Mrs. Teller twice if she thought it was his heart."

"Were there any visitors to the house before he went to London? Any letters or telegrams?"

"No visitors since the party for Mr. Teller's birthday," Mollie told him. "And I don't remember any letters in particular. I'm not in the habit of looking at the post when it's brought. I just set it on the salver there." She turned slightly to point to a long, narrow silver tray on the polished table in the large hall behind her. And then she frowned, as if the act of pointing out the salver had reminded her. "I do know there was a letter from the missionary society the morning of the party. I heard him say, under his breath, that God had remembered him at last. It was an odd thing to say, wasn't it?"

"Did he receive letters from the society on a regular basis?"

"I don't make a habit of looking at the post," she repeated.

But Rutledge said, "You may not look at it, but you can't help but see what's there. This could be important."

"If I was to guess," she said after a moment's hesitation, "then I'd say it had been some time since he'd had a letter from them. It was my understanding, with the war and all, not to speak of his malaria, that he was on what Mrs. Teller called extended leave."

Had the letter been a recall to duty? It could explain Teller's distress. Rutledge said, "Has any of the family come to the house since Mr. Teller was taken to the hospital in London?"

"Mr. Edwin and Mrs. Amy came to look through his papers last week. I think they were hoping to find a reason for Mr. Teller's illness."

That would have been before his disappearance. "Did they find what they were after?"

"I can't say. I didn't see them leave. I was in the kitchen making tea, and when I came up with the tray, the study was empty and the motorcar was no longer in front of the door."

"Anyone else?"

"Mrs. Amy came back two days ago. She said she was collecting fresh clothes for Mrs. Teller. I helped her choose what she thought was suitable."

"Did she go anywhere else in the house, besides Mrs. Teller's bedroom? She didn't for instance return to the study?"

"No, sir. I'd have known if she had."

"And all she took from the house was clothing?"

"Yes, sir. I did ask her how Mr. Teller fared. She told me that Mrs. Teller would be staying on in London for the time being, while the doctors came to a conclusion about him. I could judge from her face that she was worried. Come to think of it, the clothing she took was mostly black. Now that's distressing."

And, Rutledge thought, two days ago Amy Teller had known that Walter Teller was missing.

Back in London, Rutledge went again to Marlborough Street and to Bolingbroke Street to call on Edwin Teller and his brother Peter. But neither of them had returned to the city.

He stopped by his own flat afterward for a change of clothing and found a telegram on his doorstep.

The early darkness of an approaching storm had settled over the streets, and a wind was picking up, lifting bits of papers from the gutter and tossing the flower heads in the garden next but one to his flat.

The war had taught so many people that telegrams brought bad news. Someone missing. A death. The end of hope. He reached down to pick it up and had the strongest premonition that he shouldn't open it.

Hamish said, "The war is o'er. There's no one left to kill." Bitterness deepened the familiar voice.

Rutledge lifted the telegram from the doorstep and shoved it in his pocket as the storm broke overhead, lightning flaring through the darkness like the flashes of shells, followed by thunder so close it was like the guns of France pounding in his head.

He poured himself a drink, forcing the images that were crowding his mind back into the blackness whence they'd come, and this time succeeded in breaking the spell. Or was it only the storm's fury moving on downriver and fading safely into the distance that erased the memories of the fighting? He couldn't be sure. He found a clean shirt and put it on, then reached into his pocket for the telegram.

The skies were just clearing enough that he could read it without lighting the lamp. He recognized the name below the message and realized that his premonition had been right.

The telegram had been sent by David Trevor.

A surge of guilt swept through him. Too many letters from his godfather had gone unanswered. This was surely a summons to appear in Scotland and explain himself.

Trevor had written plaintively in his last letter, "The press of an inquiry? What, are you killing off the good citizens of London at such a rate that there's not a minute to spare for us? I find that hard to believe." And Rutledge could almost hear the amusement in his words, as well as the uncertainty and the sadness.

He scanned the brief message.

Arriving tomorrow. Stop. Meet us at station.

And the time of the train followed.

For an instant of panic, Rutledge considered that *us*.

Oh, God, surely not the entire household!

But no, Trevor must have meant himself and his grandson. And that was bad enough.

Rutledge swore with feeling, trapped and without any excuse or escape.

He found an umbrella and went back out to his motorcar, driving through the wet streets to his sister's house. For a mercy, she was at home, and he came through the door almost shouting for her.

"Ian. I'm neither deaf nor in the attics. What's the matter?" she demanded, coming down the stairs.

He held up the telegram. "Trevor's coming. Did you know? He'll have to stay with you, I'm afraid, there's no hope that the flat can be made habitable in time." The thought of Trevor being there, in the same flat, hearing Rutledge scream in the night, was unbearable. Explaining *why* he screamed at night would be beyond him. And Trevor—Trevor would speak to Frances, and ask if she knew.

"Habitable? Don't be silly. When has your flat been anything but scrupulously tidy? I sometimes wonder if you ever really live there. But yes, he's staying here." She laughed at the panic in his eyes. "Darling, this is your godfather. Not your Colonel in Chief. He's bringing the little boy. He told me that Morag was turning out the cupboards and beating the mattresses, and it was no place for sane men to linger." But the panic hadn't subsided in her brother's eyes, and she said, her laughter vanishing, "Ian. Surely you don't mind giving up a day or two to spend with David? I'll see to his comfort, of course I will. But he'll want to talk to you, dine with you, that sort of thing. He's been worried, if you must know. You haven't written in ages, and he needs to be reassured that all's well." She paused, still considering him. "All is well, isn't it, Ian? It's just been the press of work, hasn't it?"

He was well and truly caught.

The trouble was, David Trevor was an insightful man, and he would see too much. What if Hamish sent him into darkness in the middle of a dinner—a drink at Trevor's club—during a walk in St. James's Park? And there had been insufficient warning, not enough time to prepare himself. He'd be on parade, as surely as if he were in the Army again, and in the end he'd betray himself out of sheer witless nerves. Something would slip, a word, a hesitation, an instant's lapse in concentration. Trevor would *know*.

Frances said gently, "It's David, my dear, and he's lost his son. He's still grieving."

"I can't replace Ross. No one can." Rutledge stood there helplessly, with nowhere to turn.

"He isn't asking you to replace him. I think he merely wants to hear your voice and see your face and laugh with you at some bit of foolishness, the way you and he did before the war. A little space in time where there's neither past nor future, where he can *pretend*. Do you understand what I'm trying to say?"

He did. All too well. The question was, could he provide the strength and the ease someone else required, and not find himself mourning too?

Rutledge took a deep breath. "He should have given me a little time to arrange matters at the Yard . . ." His voice trailed off. There was the inquiry into Teller's disappearance. It was taking up all his time—

"And you'd have put him off. I suspect he knew that. Meanwhile, I'm the one with the preparations to see to. We've aired the spare bedroom and the nursery, and there's food for meals and an invitation for his old partner in the architectural firm to lunch with David at his club, and there's even a lady who wants him to come to tea."

That got his attention. He looked up. "A lady?"

"Melinda Crawford, of course." She smiled. "We're going to Kent the day after tomorrow. It's arranged."

He could see how much had been planned without his knowledge. But if there was a luncheon and a visit to Kent, as well as the zoo, or whatever else a small restless boy might wish to see, he might—just— make it through.

"Ian?"

"All right. But you must go to the station, I can't take—"

"But you can take a half an hour," she said gently. "And bring them here to me."

And so it was that he found himself at St. Pancreas the next morning, waiting for the train from Edinburgh, Hamish ringing in his ears and his mouth dry as bone.

IO

For nearly eight months, Rutledge had refused every invitation from his godfather, David Trevor, to come back to Scotland. What had happened there in September of the previous year had left him physically near death and emotionally shattered. He needed no reminder of that time—events were still etched in his memory, and Hamish had seen to it that every detail remained crystal clear. For he had entered Hamish's world without any warning to prepare either of them, and the price had nearly been too high.

He could not tell his godfather why the very thought of traveling north was still anathema. Because of Fiona, the woman Hamish should have lived to marry. Because too many young Scots like Hamish had died under his command. All the same, he sometimes felt that Trevor already understood much of the story, at least the part that had taken place in Scotland. Please God, no one would ever learn the whole truth about Hamish, and what had happened in France.

He was grateful now for the inquiry that was presently taking up so much of his time—it would give him the excuse to absent himself from his visitors when the strain of pretense was too much.

Rutledge met the travelers at the station, as promised, and as the train came into view, he felt tension invest his body, like steel rods.

Hamish said derisively, "It willna' help."

Rutledge said nothing in reply, swallowing the bitter taste that rose in his throat.

And then the carriages were passing him, slowing as the train came to a halt, and it was too late to run. His godfather was at the window waving to him before the carriage door opened, and then Trevor was stepping out, holding the small boy named for Rutledge by the hand. He said something to the child, and reached back into the carriage for the leather valise he'd left on the seat. Rutledge had a few seconds in which to realize that his godfather looked better than when he had last seen him. Some of the strain was gone from his face, and his step was lighter. The boy's doing, at a guess.

The two crossed to where Rutledge was waiting, rooted to the spot.

"Hallo, Ian, it's good to see you!" Trevor said heartily, taking his outstretched hand. "Everyone sends their love. And here is the young chatterbox, as we call him. My lad, do you remember your honorary uncle? He knew your father very well once upon a time."

The boy shyly held out his hand and said, "How do you do, Uncle Ian?"

As Rutledge took the small hand in his, the boy added, "I rode the train. All the way from Scotland. And I was very good, wasn't I?" He turned to look up at his grandfather. "And I shall have the pick of the litter of pups in the barn, if I mind my manners while I'm in London."

His slight Scottish accent came as a surprise, though it shouldn't have done. Rutledge searched for words of welcome and found none.

"And so you shall," Trevor said, filling the awkward silence. As they turned to go, Trevor added, "Well, then. Are we to stay with you at the flat or with Frances at the house?"

The relief that this first encounter had gone off well enough was nearly intolerable. Yet after all his apprehension, the week's visit had turned out to be an unexpectedly happy one. Nothing was said about the more recent past—nothing was said about anyone who had stayed at home, though Morag had sent him the Dundee cake she had made for him at Christmas in the hope that he might have come north after all. "It's past its prime, she says," Trevor warned him, "but the fault is no one's but yours."

Rutledge had taken it with apologies and promised to send Trevor's housekeeper something in return.

He knew, none better, that Trevor refrained from saying that she would have preferred to see him, that she was getting no younger and still doted on him. The thought was there in Trevor's eyes.

When Rutledge arrived at the Yard after settling his godfather with Frances, a patient Sergeant Biggin was waiting for him in his office. He rose as Rutledge walked through the door and wished him a good morning.

"There's news?" he asked the sergeant. "Good—or bad?"

"It appears to be bad news," Biggin reported. "We'd like to have you come with us, sir, and have a look at what we've found. It appears Mr. Teller's clothing has come to light—on the back of a costermonger near Covent Garden. An alert constable spotted the man and is keeping him in sight."

Rutledge said only, "I'll drive," and he led the way to his motorcar. As they turned toward Covent Garden, Rutledge asked, "Do the clothes appear to be damaged in any way? Torn? Bloodstains washed out?"

"No, sir, according to the constable they only appeared to be a little soiled from pushing a barrow through wet streets. But that was at a distance."

They found a place to leave the motorcar and walked the rest of the way. Covent Garden was quiet, the frenetic life of the dawn fruit and produce market in the Piazza had finished for the day, only the sweepers busy cleaning up the last of the debris and gossiping among themselves, their voices loud in the silence after the morning bustle. The opera house looked like a great ship stranded on a foreign shore.

Sergeant Biggin found his constable on a street corner, his back to the doorway of a tobacco shop. He nodded to Biggin and then acknowledged Rutledge just behind the sergeant.

"Morning, sir. That tea shop down the street. The costermonger is in there. That's his barrow—the one with the red handles—just outside."

"Has he seen you?" Rutledge asked. The barrow wasn't evidence. The man's clothing was.

"I think not, sir. Wait—the shop door is opening—"

They watched as a heavyset man sauntered through the door, but instead of the light-colored suit of clothes that Jenny Teller had told the police her husband had worn to the clinic, and presumably out of it as well, he was wearing a pair of coveralls and Wellingtons, a flat cap on his head.

"Damn!" the constable said grimly. "Beg pardon, sir, but that's him. The costermonger. But where's his clothing?"

"He's just sold it to someone else. Come on!" Rutledge strode swiftly down the street toward the tea shop. The costermonger looked up, and then his gaze sharpened as he recognized that one of the men bearing down on him was a uniformed constable, the other a sergeant, moving fast in the wake of a man in street clothes.

They could see the changing expressions on his face—alarm, the debate over whether to flee or stay where he was. Outnumbered, he chose to stay, bracing himself as Biggin said, "Good morning."

Their quarry said nothing.

"I've been told that you were seen wearing different clothing earlier in the day," Biggin went on. "We'd like to have a look at it."

They could see the man weighing any profit he might have made against trouble with the police. He chose a middle course.

"What's wrong with an honest man making a living out of old clothes that have come into his possession?" he demanded grudgingly.

"Nothing," Biggin retorted. "Except they aren't old, and it's the gentleman who was once wearing those items that we're interested in hearing about."

"I know nothing about *him*. I found the suit of clothes in a neat pile by the river, just below Tower Bridge. I hung about, to see if anyone was to come along and claim them, and when no one did, I thought I ought not to look a gift horse in the mouth, as the saying goes."

It was interesting, Rutledge observed, that the costermonger knew precisely which clothing the police were after. They would have been a windfall, worth as much as he might earn in a week's time selling old clothes and boots and men's hats. There had been no pretense of ignorance, no denials. It was possible he was telling the truth.

"And where would the items in question be now?" Biggin asked.

The costermonger reluctantly answered, "I sold them to a gent in the tea shop. He fancied the cut of them, he said."

The constable was already reaching for the door latch and disappeared inside the shop. He came out shortly thereafter with a known pickpocket, one Sammy Underwood, a well-spoken man of forty-five, who could pass for a gentleman in Teller's suit of clothes. Rutledge had seen him at flat races, hobnobbing with rich punters and readily accepted in his pressed castoffs. A better sort of purse to pick there than the casual encounter at a street crossing.

Underwood demanded his own apparel back before he would consent to give up Teller's clothing. The exchange made, he scuttled off before the police took an interest in his activities.

They spoke to the costermonger for another quarter of an hour, but he refused to change his story, although he claimed that he had not found shoes or hat with the trousers, shirt, and coat.

Sergeant Biggin turned to Rutledge. "A man doesn't leap into the river wearing his hat and shoes."

"For all we know, they were taken away before the costermonger found the rest of Teller's belongings."

Rutledge made a brief examination of the clothing. The labels had been removed.

The costermonger said quickly, "They were that way when I found them."

"Yes," Biggin retorted, "and the moon's the sun's daughter."

"It's true," the man exclaimed. "I'll swear to it, if you like."

Rutledge tended to believe him, although the sergeant remained dubious. But if it wasn't the costermonger—then who had taken the time to remove them? Someone intent on throwing dust in the eyes of the police? But if it hadn't been for the vigilance of a constable, the clothing would have disappeared into the backstreets of East London, never to come to light.

"Ye canna' find a man sae easily in different clothes," Hamish pointed out.

To buy a little time, perhaps. Or travel.

In the end, the costermonger lost his sale, and Rutledge, after complimenting the constable for his good eye, left with a box under his arm containing what appeared to be Walter Teller's clothing.

He went directly to Bond Street, and walked up and down, looking in shop windows. And then he saw what he was after. Grantwell & Sons specialized in dressing men who spent much of their time in the country, and displayed over a handsome chair in the window was a man's suit of similar style and cut.

The shop was not busy at that hour, and Rutledge had the full attention of the owner. Bolts of fine cloth, trays of buttons and collars, and an array of hats indicated a clientele with the resources and taste to dress well. Sammy Underwood had found himself a bargain.

Mr. Grantwell recognized his workmanship at once, though he deplored the missing labels and the condition of the items he was scrutinizing. After consulting his client book with its diagrams and lists and measurements, he identified the owner of the clothing.

Looking up, he asked quietly, "May I inquire why you are bringing these to me? Does it mean that some harm has come to Mr. Walter
Teller?"

"We haven't spoken to Mr. Teller. These were found in the possession of a costermonger, and we are trying to discover who they
belonged to and how they came into his hands," Rutledge answered
him. It was the truth, as far as it went, and Mr. Grantwell could make
of it what he chose.

The tailor nodded. "Indeed. Which of course explains their state.
I must say, I've always admired Mr. Teller," he went on. "In his book,
he described his years in the field. It was quite shocking. Accustomed
as he was to the life of a gentleman, it was remarkable how well he
coped with hardship and deprivation. It is a tribute to his upbringing
that he had the resources of spirit to fall back on."

Rutledge was struck by Grantwell's remark. Jenny Teller had also
mentioned the terrible conditions of her husband's fieldwork, but from
a police point of view, Rutledge had considered them as a possible
explanation for Teller's disappearance: events that could have preyed
on his mind years afterward. But now he could see another point of
view—that if Walter Teller had deliberately disappeared, for whatever
reason, he was better prepared than most to deal with a completely
different way of life. Sleeping rough, for one, and for another, disappearing into the London scene not as Walter Teller, Gentleman, but as
an ordinary man of the streets, invisible to police eyes. And a first step
would have been altering his appearance—including ridding himself
of the clothing that would identify him.

Hamish, silent for some time, told him, "If ye're right, he's no'
coming back."

Grantwell was saying, "My father had the pleasure of serving
Mr. Teller's father before him, and I'd like to think we'll serve young
Master Harry in the years to come."

He was fishing, an experienced angler in search of information.

And it occurred to Rutledge that a man's tailor knew nearly as much about him as his servants, tidbits garnered in fitting sessions or the type of cloth ordered. Military, funeral, wedding, baptism, riding, a weekend in the country or a shooting party in Scotland, receptions at the Palace or a day at Ascot. His own tailor, solicitous of the gaunt, haunted man who walked into his shop a year ago in need of new suits of clothing for his return to the Yard, had asked if his wounds were healing well and if there was to be a happy event in the near future.

Rutledge hadn't been able to tell him the truth, the words refusing to form in his mind, and so he had murmured something about no date had been set, and then barely heard what followed as the man prattled on about his own son's marriage in the winter.

He said now, "Mr. Teller's brothers are among your clients as well?"

"Yes, indeed. Mr. Edwin Teller has never enjoyed good health, but during the war he was engaged in work for the Admiralty, serving with distinction, I'm told. He was for many years a designer of boats and often traveled to Scotland to oversee their construction. He was given a private railway carriage. Captain Teller was severely wounded a few months before the Armistice. I understand there was some concern that he might never walk again."

The shop door opened and an elderly man stepped in. A clerk hurried from the back of the shop to greet him, and Mr. Grantwell said to Rutledge, "Is there any other way I can help you? My next appointment . . ." His voice trailed off, and Rutledge took the hint, thanking him and leaving.

Now came the unpleasant duty of showing the items of clothing to Mrs. Teller, to confirm what the tailor had said, that they did indeed belong to her husband.

Leaving the sergeant with the box, Rutledge looked first in Teller's private room, and then went to Matron's sitting room.

There he found Jenny Teller in conversation with another couple. The atmosphere was unexpectedly tense. And as he opened the door, he'd caught a fleeting expression of relief on Jenny's face, as if she were glad of the interruption.

Then her expression changed to alarm as she realized that it was Rutledge and not a member of Matron's staff.

"Is there news?" she asked quickly.

"We haven't found your husband, no," he answered her.

She nodded. She was beginning to cope with her shock and her fear. Her husband's disappearance, coming on the heels of his mysterious illness, had shaken her badly, her emotions raw, her tears not far below the surface. Now Rutledge could see changes in her face, a new strength and determination, an unwilling acceptance of the unacceptable: that her life had changed.

She turned to present her companions.

"My brother and sister-in-law. Edwin Teller and his wife, Amy."

Amy Teller came forward with her hand outstretched. "Yes, Jenny was just telling us that the Yard had joined in the search. We're very grateful."

Rutledge was struck by Edwin's wife. She was well dressed, attractive in the way she held herself, and had clear, intelligent eyes. But there was something behind that intelligence that spoke of worry, and a sleepless night.

Edwin, pale and showing signs of an even deeper fatigue, was a rather handsome man with an Edwardian beard. He stood to greet Rutledge and said, "We've just come back from searching, ourselves. I'm afraid we've had no better luck. I was hoping . . ." He shrugged eloquently, unwilling to finish the sentence in the presence of Walter's wife.

Rutledge said, "You were looking for your brother. May I ask where?"

"We've only just got back," Amy answered for her husband. "I thought he might have gone to the house in Essex. I know, Jenny disagreed, but I did look. Edwin and Peter went to Cambridge on the odd chance Walter had gone to see someone there. Edwin seemed to remember being told that a colleague had retired there."

Jenny said, "I didn't know that. Was it Percy? I thought he had gone back to Northumberland."

"As it turned out, Percy is there for the summer," Amy told her. "He wasn't at home when Edwin called, he was meeting with someone at the college."

Edwin said to Rutledge, "My brother was severely wounded in the war and is still recovering. He kept me company."

It was an unnecessary clarification, and Amy spoke quickly to cover it. Indeed, Amy Teller appeared to answer for her husband almost as if uncertain that he knew his lines on cue.

"Susannah—she's Peter's wife, Inspector—drove to Cornwall, where the family often went on holiday. And Leticia, Edwin's sister, was in Portsmouth, on the off chance that Walter might have"—she hesitated, glancing uncertainly toward Jenny—"where he might in his confusion have thought he was returning to the field."

Edwin said, "We didn't find him, but it was better than waiting for the police to get around to looking beyond London. And we might have got lucky. There's always that." He sounded defeated but smiled for Jenny's sake and added, "We could count on Jenny here at the clinic, if the police came through."

Jenny glanced from one to the other, and said, "Portsmouth was a waste of time. Leticia should have stayed here. Walter wouldn't have left the country without telling me. He wouldn't have left Harry without a word. No matter how confused he might be."

"Do you know for a fact that he didn't try to contact his son?" Rutledge asked.

"Well—no. But Mary would have sent word at once if he had." Edwin replied.

"You should have informed the police before leaving London," Rutledge told them. "It would have been helpful."

"It wasn't a Yard matter, then," Amy answered. "And there's something else. Jenny was just telling us that a watch is being kept on the river. Surely these men could be put to better use searching the city. None of us can believe that Walter intended to do away with himself."

Rutledge said, "I don't think any of us can say with certainty what was in Teller's mind when he left the clinic."

Jenny Teller said stubbornly, "I've told you. Walter won't kill himself."

"With respect, Mrs. Teller, he hasn't been seen for days. He hasn't contacted you, he hasn't come back to the clinic. Your husband's family seems to feel he left London almost at once. I'd like to know why they were so certain of that?"

Edwin said, "Because we know him. Because he's our brother."

"And so you believed that he would visit a colleague—or his childhood holiday home—as soon as he came to himself again?"

Edwin said shortly, "Don't be absurd. That's not what we believed. It's just—look, we were clutching at straws. We drove around London searching for him that first afternoon, and then we tried to think where he might go if he needed to talk to someone or remember where he was happy as a child."

"You think, then, that he isn't fully cured?"

"Damn it, I don't know," Edwin told him. "You're the policeman, what do you think?"

"The evidence we have is circumstantial. He was able to walk out of the clinic. All well and good. He was able to dress himself presentably, so that he wouldn't attract attention leaving with the afternoon's visitors. That argues a certain awareness, an ability to think ahead. With respect, Mrs. Teller," he went on, "he chose a time when no one was here to stop him or ask questions. That tells us he knew where he wanted to go and why, and perhaps it didn't necessarily march with your opinion on the subject. And you, Mr. Teller, weren't here pacing the floor, your sister wasn't here demanding that something be done and quickly, making a nuisance of herself with the staff and the police. That's what generally happens, you see. Instead, the family left London with almost indecent haste. Mrs. Teller, unable to reach any of you, was left to cope on her own.

What, I wonder, was so urgent in your minds that it took precedence over every other consideration? And don't talk to me again about old friends and childhood holidays."

Bowles had urged Rutledge to be careful in his handling of the Teller family. But if they were withholding information, he needed to know now.

"I won't listen to this," Edwin said, getting to his feet.

Rutledge said, "The only alternative, sir, is that someone came here for your brother and spirited him out of the clinic."

The consternation on the face of Edwin Teller was a reflection of his wife's expression. Rutledge couldn't tell whether they accepted the possibility or were shocked by it. But he was nearly certain that it had never occurred to them.

Jenny said, "This is nonsense. I won't listen to any more. We need to concentrate on what's important now, and that's finding Walter."

"There's one other piece of business to attend to." Rutledge turned from her brother-in-law to her as he spoke. "Give me a moment."

He went out to find Sergeant Biggin and retrieve the box.

Returning to the room, he crossed to the table where Matron served tea to her guests and set the box carefully on the polished surface.

Jenny's gaze hadn't left the box from the moment Rutledge came through the door with his burden. It was almost as if she had a premonition of what lay inside.

Without a word, he removed the lid.

He thought at first that Jenny was going to faint, and he moved to help her, but she shook her head and resolutely looked into the box. Edwin followed her, and then Amy looked over his shoulder.

One glance was enough. Jenny's gaze lifted to Rutledge's face, and then she reached out her hand and caressed the cloth of her husband's coat.

"It's not very clean," she began, then stopped, as if afraid to hear why.

"I must ask you to make a formal identification of the clothing. If you like, I'll remove each item and hold it up for you."

"You needn't do that," she said huskily. "It's Walter's."

But he lifted out the coat, the shirt, and the trousers, all the same, along with a necktie.

"Where are his shoes and stockings?" she asked.

"We haven't found them so far."

"Where did these come from?" Amy asked, moving to Jenny's side and linking arms with her. "How did you find them?"

"The clothing was in the possession of a costermonger near Covent Garden. He claims—I'm sorry, but I must tell you this—he discovered them neatly folded by the river not far from Tower Bridge. But no undergarments. And not his wallet. That can mean one of two things. That Mr. Teller is alive and still wearing them. Or they were taken away—or went into the river—to keep us guessing about what happened to him."

"No, that's not possible!" Amy said. "It's a trick. Walter was playing a trick on us." She had lost her veneer of helpfulness, anger replacing it.

Rutledge turned to her, surprised. "What makes you feel it was a trick?"

"It—it stands to reason! Walter hasn't killed himself, he only wants us to think so. So we'll stop looking." She was very upset. "Show me his body, and then I'll believe you."

Jenny said, "Amy—"

But she turned away. "I'm tired," she said. "You mustn't pay any attention to me. I'm just—tired."

Edwin had said nothing, staring at the clothing as if waiting for it to speak and explain itself. But now he said quietly to Rutledge, "Put those things back in the box where we can't see them. You've made your point."

II

As Rutledge was refolding the clothing and settling it into the box again, Jenny Teller said thoughtfully, "The mission station in West Africa was by a river. I remember Walter telling us that he couldn't wear his English clothing there—the damp ruined everything. And so he put them in a tin box and left them behind. He didn't have a tin box just now, but he left his clothing behind as he was accustomed to doing."

Edwin said, "Jenny—don't."

"No, I think it's true. It's oddly—comforting, somehow. It means he's still alive. I've said from the beginning that he was."

Edwin swore under his breath and cast a glance at his wife. She was watching Jenny, a look of anguish in her eyes.

Rutledge set the lid back on the box.

"We don't know what he might be wearing now," he warned them. "The search will be all that much more difficult."

"I understand," Jenny said. She took a deep breath. "He'll come back when he's ready."

Rutledge was halfway to the door when Jenny called to him, "There's something I should tell you. I hadn't before. It was very—personal, and Walter has always been a very private man."

He turned and waited.

"Matron very kindly had a cot put in my husband's room for me, so that I might stay with him. The night before he disappeared, I woke up because I could hear him talking. It was only a murmur, I couldn't make out the words, and at first I thought he must be talking in his sleep. But then I remembered another time when I'd heard him doing the same thing. It was when he was writing his book. And he had come to a chapter that disturbed him—he kept putting off working on it, and I told him that he should just write—you know, like getting back on a horse after it's thrown you. It might not be the best material, but it would be a start, and he could revise it when he was finished. And so he did. And it was that night I heard him talking to himself. Or to someone. I never knew for certain what it was."

"And you think there's a connection?"

"Yes. I think Walter has made his decision. I think he's decided he's going back into the field. There must be something that he feels he's left undone, and what's sent him away is that he doesn't know how to tell me. Edwin and Peter must have guessed. It's why they went looking for him where they did."

In the passage, Rutledge met Matron coming toward him.

"There is no news?" she asked.

"I'm afraid not."

"What do you have there? May I know?"

"We've found Mr. Teller's clothing. I brought it here for Mrs. Teller to identify."

Matron was silent a moment, and then she said, "But you don't know yet that he's dead? You haven't found *him*? Mr. Teller?"

"No. As I've just explained to his family, if he's wearing different clothes, it will make spotting him all that much more difficult. And we don't know what other changes he has made. Unless finding these by the river is an indication that he took his own life."

She said, "I think he wanted to die while he was here. But wanting something and having the opportunity to achieve it can be two very different things." She gazed down the passage, the way she'd come. "I must tell you that I had the oddest feeling that Mr. Teller had lost his faith. Perhaps that's what he's trying so hard to find."

"His wife feels he's made the decision to return to mission work."

"Perhaps that's why," she said, and walked away.

Rutledge looked after her, considering her words. He was turning to go when he nearly collided with a well-dressed man just stepping out of one of the doctors' offices, pushing an invalid chair. The woman swathed in shawls and a motorcar rug looked up and smiled at Rutledge, her thin, illness-ravaged face still attractive and sweet. He smiled in return and held the door for the man.

From the clinic, Rutledge drove directly to Bolingbroke Street, intending to speak to Captain Teller before either Edwin or his wife could describe their conversation with Scotland Yard.

Hamish said, "Do you believe what yon missionary's wife told you?"

"It could be true. It would explain many of the loose ends. For instance, why Teller is so insistent that he enroll his son in Harrow."

"But why take the boy fra' his mother at sich a time?"

And that was the sticking point.

It might be well to have a word with the family solicitors.

The house in Bolingbroke Street was a corner property, trees overhanging the tall fence that enclosed the back gardens, giving it privacy.

When Rutledge knocked at the door, the maid who answered told him that Captain Teller was in the garden.

He noted as he passed through the house to the study where French doors gave onto the garden, that it had been tastefully decorated, with an air of old money that was unmistakable. There were two or three landscape paintings of the Dutch school, and one portrait of a woman in a white gown with rich blue sleeves and ribbons. She was of another generation, and dressed for a ball, but her stance and her dark blue eyes, which matched her sleeves, suggested intelligence and humor. A half smile lurked at the corners of her mouth.

When Rutledge stepped out onto the terrace, he could see Peter Teller sitting in a chair by the small pond, his left leg pillowed on a hassock.

Captain Teller had stronger features than those shown in the photograph of his brother that Rutledge still carried. There was already a touch of gray at his temples, and his blue-gray eyes were bloodshot.

For the captain was very drunk.

"Who are you?" he demanded. "I told Iris I wasn't at home today."

"Inspector Rutledge, Scotland Yard. I'm looking into the disappearance of your brother."

"Are you, indeed. Well, I hope you have better luck than we have had. Any news?"

"Nothing promising."

As Rutledge crossed the lawn, Teller indicated the chair opposite him. "Sit down. It strains my back when I have to look up at you."

Rutledge took the chair.

Teller went on, "I'm not usually drunk at this hour. The last three days have been hellish. I do my best, but sometimes the medicines my doctor prescribes can't touch the pain. I'd have been better if I'd let them take the damned leg when they wanted to."

"Is there nothing more to be done?" Rutledge asked sympathetically.

"The doctors have washed their hands of me. After two or three surgeries and endless treatments with heat and massage and the like, they can't think of anything else to do. I'm told that I'm fortunate. The sort of treatments now available didn't exist in the past. They took your leg, and you went home on crutches or a wooden limb. And that was that. But you haven't come to discuss my leg, I take it."

"I'm hoping that you can shed some light on your brother's disappearance, or if not, on his state of mind the last time you saw him."

Peter Teller was very still for a moment. Then he said, "His state of mind the last time I spoke with him was worrying. I said something to my brother Edwin about it. Walter seemed to have lost the will to live. I expect it was the thought of being paralyzed for the rest of his life. And I couldn't blame him there. The doctors were doing damn all. Well, to be fair, they couldn't tell what should be done. I think the consensus was some unknown disease. Or else Walter was losing his mind."

"Do you know how his will stands, by any chance?"

"His will? Damned if I know. But I should think there would be the usual bequests to Mollie—his housekeeper—and the church, and the rest left to Jenny in trust for Harry." He frowned, trying to clear his head. "Are you suggesting that we ought to be prepared?"

"We found your brother's clothing early this morning, in possession of a costermonger who claimed he'd found them neatly folded close by the river just south of the Tower."

"Good God," Peter said blankly. "Is the man telling the truth? Or do you think something has happened to Walter? Did you speak to Edwin? What did he have to say?"

"We're not sure what to think," Rutledge said. "That's why I'm here. Why did your brother walk out of the clinic without a word to anyone? Why has he made no effort to reassure his wife that he's alive and well? Has the marriage been a happy one? Or is it troubled?"

"I—I have no answer to give you. There's been a disagreement over Harry's future, but it was bound to come at some point. In my opinion, Walter is wrong on that subject, but Jenny is Jenny—she'll be angry for a time, and then find a way to cope."

"Where did you go when you left London to look for your brother?"

"Where?" For an instant Peter Teller seemed to be at a loss. And then he asked, "Didn't Edwin tell you?"

"I had rather hear your version of events."

"Damn it, I've nothing to add to what he said. We went looking for Walter's old adviser. He'd left Cambridge and moved to Scotland. It was a wild goose chase."

Which wasn't what Amy Teller had told Rutledge.

"Can you give me the direction of Walter's solicitors? I'd like to speak to them."

Peter Teller moved so quickly he knocked his glass from the table at his elbow, and he swore, as the sudden movement hurt his back. "The man is still alive as far as we know. I think it's obscene to read his will before he's dead. I've told you, as far as I know, it's straightforward. When you find his body, come to me and I'll give you the name of the firm."

There was nothing more to be gained from Peter Teller. Rutledge thanked him and left.

Walking back through the house, he encountered an attractive young woman with hair the color of honey and dark brown eyes. She started, and said, "Oh—I didn't know we had guests."

Rutledge apologized, then identified himself.

"Scotland Yard?" Her gaze shifted to the passage behind him, then back again. "You've—were you speaking to my husband?"

Susannah Teller, then. He said, "I've just come from the garden."

"He's a little—under the weather," she told him. "I hope you'll consider anything he said with that in mind."

What, he wondered, had she thought her husband might have said?

"I would like to ask you the same questions, if you don't mind. I've been put in charge of the search for your brother-in-law. Apparently you went to Cornwall on the off chance that he might be there."

"It was hardly an off chance, as you put it. His family had a summer cottage just north of St. Ives, and they often spent holidays there. The cottage was sold at his father's death, but he might not have remembered that. He might have wanted a quiet sanctuary."

"Why? Why leave his wife to worry? If he'd recovered, why not take her with him?"

She was watching his face. "We were trying to think where he might have gone. That's all. Cornwall was a place of happy memories."

"What would you have done if you'd found him in Cornwall, confused and difficult to handle?"

"I—I don't believe I considered that possibility. I thought he might be grateful that someone was there, and come back with me without fuss."

Rutledge let it go. Whatever motivations the Teller family had had for going off on their own, they weren't about to confide in the police. Until Walter Teller was found dead, there was no way to persuade his family otherwise.

"Has Teller had a history of such disappearances?"

"Good heavens, no! Nor has he ever been this ill, except of course for his bouts of malaria. That's what was so worrying."

Was, not *is*.

As if the solution was already known to them.

Rutledge said, "Early this morning, the police discovered Teller's clothing in the possession of a man who claims he found them beside the Thames."

"But he couldn't have—" She caught herself and added, "Surely you don't believe Walter drowned himself? I won't, for one."

"Mrs. Teller, the man's been missing for several days. Half of London is searching for him. And he's nowhere to be found. Suicide, to put it bluntly, remains an option."

With that he thanked her and wished her a good day. But he had the strongest feeling that a good day was not in the cards for the Teller family.

It had been a long morning. He changed his mind about going on to the Yard and instead turned toward Frances's house.

Rutledge had spent as much time as he could spare from the Yard with his godfather. During the day, Trevor entertained the boy with the swans in St. James's Park, the ravens at the Tower, and the giraffes at the Regent's Park Zoo. And in the evenings, after the child had been put to bed, the two men sat in the garden, talking as they had once done before the war and the loss it had brought in its wake.

Trevor had been a very fine architect before the death of his son had sent him into early retirement. He said one night, "I remember when your parents lived here in this house, and the parties they gave. Nothing elaborate, you understand, but we always enjoyed those evenings. Sometimes your mother would sit in the drawing room and play the piano while your father and I took our brandy out here after dinner. She was such a fine pianist. Your father was very proud of that."

Rutledge said, "I remember her playing. I wish Frances would use the piano from time to time. But it sits closed from one year to the next."

"Yes." Trevor sighed. "Tell me about Frances. She hasn't married. Was there someone in particular?"

"I always thought she might marry Ross. But there was someone else she loved for a time. Nothing came of it. Nothing could. Lately there was another man who seemed to take her fancy. I thought she was in love with *him*. But she hasn't mentioned him for some weeks."

"And what about you?"

Rutledge moved uneasily in his chair. "I don't think I've healed sufficiently from the war to think about marrying anyone."

"You aren't still grieving for Jean, are you?"

Rutledge looked away, watching the twilight fade to night. "No. I grieve for her, but not out of love. Out of sadness that her life wasn't filled with the happiness she was searching for so hard."

"Yes, the war to end all war hasn't turned out to be the blessing they promised us it would be. I look back at King Edward's reign, and I think to myself, we were blissfully unaware of what was to come. Although there had been some talk about the Kaiser's ambitions, no one took it seriously. I remember those days as sunlit and untrammeled by shadows."

Rutledge replied, "At a guess, half of Britain feels the same."

They laughed quietly in the darkness, and Frances said, as she stepped out into the garden, "Have I missed something?"

Trevor held out a hand. "We were longing for the past. A sign we're growing old. Come and sit here, next to me. What time do we leave tomorrow to drive down to Kent?"

And she told him as she came to join them.

In the back of Rutledge's mind, Hamish said softly, the Scots accent pronounced, "And the day after, they leave. Are ye no' glad of that?"

Rutledge found that he wasn't.

12

The next morning Constable Evans ran Rutledge to ground at his sister's house just as he was seeing his godfather and Frances off on their excursion to Kent to call on Melinda Crawford. They were trying to persuade Rutledge to join them after all, when Evans appeared.

Rutledge was not loathe to miss the journey, and the reminder of pressing business at the Yard was timely. While he was very fond of Melinda, Rutledge wasn't comfortable spending so many hours in the company of three people who knew him entirely too well. Melinda, who had survived the Lucknow massacre during the Great Mutiny in India, knew more than most about the scars war could leave behind, and for far too long now, he'd been hard-pressed to avoid her sharp questions about the shadows under his eyes and the thinness that came from tension and long sleepless nights.

Expecting to be told that there was fresh information about Walter Teller, he went to his office, summoned Sergeant Gibson, and said, "Evans told me it was urgent. What do you have for me?"

"The Chief Superintendent sent Evans along to fetch you. You'd best hear it from him."

Rutledge went along the passage to find Bowles fuming in his office. He looked up as Rutledge appeared in the open doorway and said, "What kept you?"

"I'm sorry, sir. I came as quickly as I could."

"There's been another stabbing. Are you quite sure there's nothing more you can tell us about this man you call Billy?"

"I saw him only briefly. Who is the victim this time?"

"That's the trouble. This time it was the secretary to an MP, just leaving the House and walking along the Embankment to clear his head. Bynum, his name is. There's going to be one hell of an uproar over this. If you'd held on to the young bastard while you had him, we'd not be facing the wrath of Parliament. And there's no break on the Teller inquiry. What have you been doing with your time?"

"I've spoken to everyone but the sister, Leticia Teller. I was planning to drive to Suffolk today."

"See that you deal with this latest knifing first. There may be something you can learn from the only witness. As for the Tellers, mind how you go. I don't want them on my doorstep complaining that you aren't handling the matter to their satisfaction. Do you understand me?"

"Yes, I do understand. But I have a feeling that there isn't going to be a happy solution to this case. If we find Teller alive, he may be in a worse state than he was in the hospital."

"Then the sooner you find him the better."

By the time Rutledge arrived at the Embankment, the body had been taken away, but the police were still combing the area, looking for evidence. The sergeant in charge, by the name of Walker, greeted Rutledge and said, "We aren't certain why the assailant was lurking on this side of the bridge, sir. He wasn't likely to find a target at that hour of the night, and with dawn coming as early as it does this time of year, he could well have been spotted."

Hamish said quietly, "He was looking for you."

Rutledge nearly answered him aloud, catching himself only just in time.

"Why?" he demanded silently.

"Because ye've seen his face."

But Rutledge wasn't sure that he agreed. To Walker he said, "Which way did he go? Did your witness see that?"

"Back across the bridge, sir."

"Then it's likely it's the same man I encountered."

"So I understand, sir. There's been a rash of robberies at knife-point. Did they tell you that at the Yard? But in most cases, the victim handed over his money without a struggle, and then was instructed to count to one hundred before turning around. Most did as they were told, and of course he was gone by the time they looked behind them. We think it must be the same person as killed this Mr. Bynum." Walker shook his head. "Sad, isn't? He was only just having a breath of fresh air, because his wallet and his coat were still in his office. He had nothing to give his murderer."

"I'd only been told about the one other attempt, which had ended in death. And that was on Westminster Bridge. Where have these rob-beries occurred?"

"Mostly south of the river, sir. He doesn't venture this far often. But there are fatter purses on this side of the bridge. All told, he's got no more than forty pounds so far."

"He's too young to have a family to feed. Unless it's his mother he's supporting. There may be brothers and sisters younger than he is."

"As to that, sir, we'd only be guessing. But he's killed twice now."

One of the constables searching along the path looked up and called, "Here, sir!"

Walker and Rutledge hurried to where he was standing.

"A man's coat button, sir," he said, pointing it out.

"Anyone walking along here could have lost it," the sergeant told him. "But we'll have it anyway. In case."

Rutledge took it from the constable's hand. It was a very ordinary button, dark brown and with four holes in it. For a coat, as the constable had said. Remembering the drawers of buttons to choose from in the tailor's shop, he said, "You're right. It would be hard to prove either way. But we might be lucky."

On the river a boat swept by, and bursts of laughter carried over the water.

"Where's this witness you spoke of?"

"A constable took him along for a bite to eat. The man looked half starved."

"How much did he see?"

"He said he was coming from the direction of the Abbey, walking toward the bridge, when he heard something that sounded like someone choking. He turned toward the sound in time to see one man falling down and another bending over him, as if trying to help. But then he saw that the second man was rifling the pockets of the first, and he shouted for him to stop. The second man turned and stared at him for several seconds, then turned and ran. By the time our witness reached the victim, he was dying. But there was nothing anyone could do. The witness stayed with him, then saw a motorcar on the road, coming toward the bridge, and shouted for help."

"And you're certain this witness wasn't the killer?"

"He was in the clear. He needn't have hailed the motorcar. And he'd made an effort to staunch the bleeding."

"Yes, you're right, it sounds as if he's exactly what he claims to be."

Walker was looking toward the road. "Here he comes now, sir. With the constable."

Rutledge turned. The constable was walking beside a vagrant, a man in shabby clothes, unshaven and thin. He moved with a limp, as if footsore, his eyes cast down, as if searching the pavement for lost coins.

Rutledge went to meet them and greeted the constable before speaking to his companion.

"I understand you witnessed what happened here last night?"

"I did. It was murder, right enough. There were two men, struggling together, and one fell. The other knelt beside him, and I thought at first he was trying to help. But then I saw he was going through the other man's pockets. He ran as I came up." The man's voice was rough, a workingman's accent.

"Did you get a good look at the one who ran away?" Rutledge asked.

"It was too dark. But he ran like a young person. Quick, and with ease. I thought he must be wearing padded shoes. He made almost no sound."

Rutledge remembered how easily Billy had crept up on him. "Yes, that's quite possible. Anything else? His size? His age?"

"He looked to be about eighteen or nineteen. Well set up. He was wearing a cap. I couldn't see his hair. Dark?" He squinted, as if in thought. "I can't remember anything more. It happened very quickly, and then I was more concerned for the victim." He seemed ill at ease now, eager to be off.

"How long did he live after you got to him?"

"A matter of seconds? I couldn't tell in the dark."

"Then he wasn't able to speak?"

"No. Who was he? Do you know?" The man glanced toward where the body had lain.

"They've just identified him," Walker said. "One of the constables happened to recognize him. George Bynum. He'd stayed late to finish a paper he was preparing for debate in the next session. A bit of bad luck, that."

"And your name?" Rutledge asked the witness.

"Hood. Charlie Hood." The words were clipped, unwillingly given.

"Thank you for coming forward, Mr. Hood. If you'll go with the constable now, someone will take your statement, and you can sign it."

Hood hesitated. "I don't have a regular place to live."

"That's all right. Just so we can find you, if we need to have you identify the man, once we have him in custody," Rutledge told him.

Hood bobbed his head in acknowledgment, and turned to follow the constable.

Someone was calling to them again, and Rutledge went with Walker to see what the constable had found.

This was more promising—a small scrap of paper that had an address scribbled on it in pencil. It was off the Lambeth Road.

"We can't be sure it's his," Walker said, examining it. "But it could have fallen from his pocket when he pulled out the knife."

"Send someone there at once," Rutledge advised Walker. "The sooner the better."

Walker nodded to the constable who had found the scrap. "Right you are, son, see what you can discover."

The constable hurried away toward the bridge.

Half an hour later, the search by the bridge was called off. Rutledge, his mind on the long drive to Suffolk and back, said, "I've got to go. If anything comes of the address, leave word with Sergeant Gibson at the Yard. He'll see that I get it."

Rutledge was halfway to his motorcar when he stopped short and swore.

Setting out at a dead run, he went back to find Walker, who was just leaving the scene of the crime himself.

"Where did your constable take Hood? The Yard, or the station?"

"To the station. Is anything wrong?"

"I hope to God there isn't," Rutledge responded and hurried in the direction of Trafalgar Square.

With any luck at all, he told himself, he'd reach the station in time.

But he didn't. Hood had given his statement and gone. Rutledge asked for the address he'd used, and drove there next.

It was a stationer's shop near St. Paul's. Rutledge left his motorcar in the street and went inside. The woman behind the counter greeted him with a smile that faded quickly as he asked if she knew of anyone by the name of Hood. Charlie Hood.

But she didn't. He described Hood, and she told him that such a person was not likely to be among the shop's clientele.

Rutledge thanked her and left while the voice of Hamish MacLeod drummed in his head.

He drove back to the police station and circled the blocks as best he could, on the off chance that he could spot Hood again. But by this time the streets were busy, people hurrying about their business, and one man could be anywhere, coming out of a pub just after he'd passed, walking into a shop just before he arrived. It was a waste of time, but he gave it an hour anyway.

He couldn't be sure. But something about the shabby, scruffy-bearded man had struck him, and he wanted to speak to him again. What had Walker said? That the man was coming from the direction of the Abbey, and that a constable had taken him to find something to eat.

He told himself it couldn't be Walter Teller.

But there was a good chance that it might have been.

Rutledge drove on to Suffolk, to a small village not far from the Essex border. The house he was searching for was down a lane beyond the high steepled church, a winding stretch of road bordered by wildflowers that meandered another quarter of a mile before he saw the stone gates. The house itself was not as large as Witch Hazel Farm, but set among trees as it was, he could feel the country quiet and hear birds singing as he came to a halt by the door.

He was directed to the gardens by a housekeeper, and there he found Leticia Teller entertaining a small boy who was squatting by a pool watching pollywogs swim through the murky water.

"And there's another one, Harry." She pointed one out to him. "Just there, beside the lily pad. Oh—there it goes."

Another woman sat in the shade, smiling fondly at the child.

Miss Teller looked up as Rutledge came through the hedge. She was tall, like her brothers, her face a softer version of Peter's. Attractive, with hazel eyes and a presence that some might find chilly. He gave his name and showed her his identification, and she proceeded to look him up and down.

"I didn't know the Yard had been brought into this matter."

From her tone, he thought she disapproved of such a move.

"I believe you were in Portsmouth when that decision was made," he countered. "Perhaps it might be wise to speak privately."

She turned to Harry. "Well, we'll leave the pollywogs to rest awhile, shall we? I think there might be lemonade in the kitchen, if you ask nicely. And clean your feet before you run in."

The boy straightened, a sturdy fair-haired child with a ready smile. "They won't go away, will they?"

"No, they live here, and they'll be waiting when you come back."

He nodded happily and dashed off.

"Walter's son," Leticia Teller told Rutledge. She turned to the other woman, who had risen from the bench on which she'd been sitting and come to join them. "Mary Brittingham. Jenny Teller's sister."

She was fair, like her sister, but a little shorter, a pretty woman with an air of someone who knew her own worth.

"Miss Brittingham," he acknowledged.

"Now to what has brought you here. Is there any news? You wouldn't have come all this way if there wasn't."

"Clothing that has been identified as your brother's was found by the river. Mrs. Teller recognized them."

"But there's no news of Walter?" Mary put in.

"None."

"Are you saying that the police believe he's drowned himself? While in an unsound state of mind? Nonsense. I don't believe it for a moment." Leticia Teller led them to a circle of chairs out on the terrace. "Do sit down, Inspector."

"I'm not drawing conclusions," Rutledge said, taking the chair indicated. "But the possibility is there. Why did your brother leave the hospital, Miss Teller? He chose a time when his wife was not at his side. He dressed himself—or someone helped him dress—and he walked away."

"Who helped him dress?" she asked sharply. "We—my brothers and I—were in Edwin's house when the news came of his disappearance. Who was there to help?"

"That's what we would like very much to know." He turned to Mary Brittingham. "You were not in London at the time?"

"No, I went to Monmouthshire to fetch Harry and brought him back to stay with me while Jenny was at the clinic with Walter. He's been with me ever since." She took a deep breath. "He believes his parents are visiting friends. I didn't have the heart to tell him otherwise."

"If Walter Teller dressed himself and left the clinic knowingly, where would he be likely to go?" Rutledge asked them.

Mary said, "It's possible, you know, that he left the clothing by the river himself. To buy himself a little time to think. That's probably why he left the clinic in the first place."

Leticia Teller regarded her with distaste. "Are you saying that my brother is aware of what he's doing?"

"I think it's likely that he hasn't found a solution to whatever caused him to be ill in the first place. Did you know he'd heard from his bishop? They want him back. He wrote to tell me he didn't know how to answer them."

"No, I hadn't heard that," Leticia said slowly. "He said nothing to us about it. Or to Jenny."

"He felt Jenny was distressed enough over Harry. I don't think Walter wants to go back into the field. I'm of two minds myself. I know they need good men, experienced men. But I don't think Walter is emotionally prepared to resume his work. He told Jenny before the war that he'd spent too much of his life in places where he felt he'd done very little good."

"He was praised for his honesty," Leticia said. "After the book came out, you know how people admired it. He gave the proceeds to his mission society, for good works."

"I imagine, in lieu of his physical presence in the field. You saw his book as a triumph. I saw it as an exorcism."

"That's an odd choice of words," Rutledge put in.

Mary said, "I've always believed in the importance of mission work. I think a great deal of good can be done by setting an example. And the Alcock Society has been especially fortunate in the people they've sent into the field. But Walter was a missionary by default. Because his father gave him to the church, and because he was unsuited to parish work. I know," she said, turning to Leticia, "that this is hard for you to hear. But if Walter comes through his present crisis alive and whole, it would be a travesty to send him back to Africa. Or China. You must see that."

Leticia replied, "I believe this is Walter's decision to make."

"And he's made it. By falling ill, he's made it. What other reason can there be for him to vanish as he's done? I tried to explain this to Jenny when I was in London. She doesn't want him to go abroad again, of course she doesn't, but I think she has this rather naïve belief that he's a saint and she mustn't stand in his way. He isn't a saint. He's bitter."

"I don't think his calling has anything to do with his illness." Leticia was adamant.

"Then how else would you explain it? Coming on the heels of his letter from the Society?" Mary regarded her with exasperation.

Rutledge, listening, could see that the two women had very little in common. Their relationship by marriage was their only connection. And even that was tenuous.

Interrupting again, he said, "Do either of you have any idea where he may be?"

But they didn't. And he could see that both women were far more worried than either of them was willing to admit to the other.

"I just want to see Jenny happy," Mary said, as if she'd read his thoughts. "She tries hard and she loves Walter without question. And that could lead her to heartbreak."

Leticia said grudgingly, "I must admit you're right, there. Walter is not like his brothers. He lost something out there in Africa and China. Part of himself."

"He lost it when he failed in his first living. It was the wrong church for him to be sent to, and the congregation was not prepared for an intellectual priest. They wanted someone more like themselves. A local man who understood them."

Leticia said, "You didn't even know him then. How can you judge that?"

Mary turned to Rutledge. "I met Walter when he spoke at a meeting I was attending. About his work in China. In fact, it was I who introduced him to Jenny."

The tension between the two women was interesting. Rutledge thought perhaps the root cause of it was familial. Mary was bound to protect her sister, and Leticia's loyalty was to her brother.

He said, interjecting a new question before hard feelings arose on either side, "Have you heard Mr. Teller mention anyone by the name of Charlie Hood?"

They stared at him, the question completely unexpected. It was clear that the name meant nothing at all to either of the women.

And possibly he had made too much of it as well. But there had been something in the man's face that he couldn't identify, something he felt he ought to recognize.

Harry came racing back, gleefully informing his aunts that there had indeed been lemonade.

Rutledge, watching him, could see in him the boy that Ian Trevor would be at the same age. It was an unexpected insight, and it touched him.

He took his leave, refusing Miss Teller's lukewarm invitation to stay for tea. He thought it had been in a way a suggestion that Mary Brittingham should also refuse it in her turn. That she had also outstayed her welcome.

Miss Teller walked with him through the hedge and around to where he'd left his motorcar, saying as they went, "Will he come back, do you think?"

"Your brother? When he's ready to be found. If whatever reason he left the clinic is resolved for him, in a fashion he can live with. The problem is, how lucid is he? Is he thinking clearly or still in the throes of his illness, even though the paralysis has apparently disappeared."

She nodded thoughtfully, and then stood there as he cranked the motorcar. He was on the point of driving away when she came to his side of the vehicle and put her hand on the door.

"Even as a child, Walter would take to something new with almost ferocious enthusiasm. And then he would tire of it and lose interest. Domestic life may have—palled."

"Are you telling me he's bored with his marriage?"

"No. That he may have decided to do good works among London's poor to salve his conscience. Rather than converting the heathen. If he doesn't come back, this may be of some comfort to Jenny."

"When you went to Portsmouth, you didn't actually believe that your brother would take ship without a word to anyone? Such a journey requires an enormous amount of preparation, I should think," he asked her.

Leticia Teller shrugged eloquently. "In the first shock of his disappearance, anything seemed possible. It was a chance I didn't feel I could take. And my brothers agreed, even while they disagreed."

Hamish said, "She's lying."

"I'll keep that in mind as well," he told her, and let in the clutch. She stepped back and let him go. Over her shoulder, he could see Mary Brittingham standing at the opening in the hedge, watching them.

But then Mary smiled and waved when she saw him looking in her direction.

"Twa women, ye ken, with a child holding them together," Hamish said as the boy ran up to Mary and clung to her hand. And then he darted forward, to take Leticia's hand as well and wave good-bye to the man from London who had come unexpectedly.

It was late when Rutledge reached London. He stopped by the Yard to see if there were any developments in the search for the boy he called Billy, or if Hood had been located. But like many of their ilk, they had disappeared into the dark corners of a city that knew how to keep secrets.

13

The journey to Kent had been successful, and both Frances and David Trevor were in high spirits, carrying Melinda Crawford's greeting and best love to Rutledge and telling him about the great pheasant hunt that had left them all exhausted and hurting from laughter.

A stray pheasant had wandered into Melinda's garden, and the boy had been very taken with it. He had persuaded his grandfather to let him carry it back to Scotland if he could capture it.

That had led to an afternoon of merriment as every scheme they had tried saw the pheasant still at large and mocking them from a safe distance.

In the end it was Ian who had tired first, and after one last glorious chase through the kitchen gardens had ended with the promise of cake for tea, the pheasant had been forgotten.

Listening to them, Rutledge was reminded of another child bribed by the promise of lemonade, unaware that his father was missing and possibly no longer the familiar figure the boy remembered.

He joined in the laughter, despite the day's frustrations, unwilling to spoil their high spirits, and found the tension in his mind slowly relaxing.

It wasn't until they were saying good night that Rutledge remembered that his godfather would be leaving on the morrow. The time had gone too quickly, and he'd got his wish—to be too busy to spend much of the day with Trevor and the child.

He regretted that now as he drove back to his flat, but there had been no way to change it. Even if he'd recognized the need in time.

The next morning as Rutledge collected his godfather's cases and stowed them in the boot, he wished he could find the words to ask Trevor to stay longer. But Hamish, in the back of his mind, had been a source of stressful emotions while David Trevor talked of Scotland and the war and his son Ross. Of the boy's young governess, who was being courted by a solicitor in Edinburgh. Of things best forgotten, of people left unnamed. Consequently, fatigue had racked him, and Rutledge had spent sleepless nights walking the streets in the cool summer darkness until he was too tired to stay awake.

And still Hamish reminded him over and over again of what he, a dead man lying in a French grave, had lost.

There was nothing left now except their good-byes.

Coming to the door of the house, Rutledge said to his godfather, "I think that's everything."

Frances, kissing first David and then the boy good-bye, wished them a safe journey, and sent her love to Morag, along with the gaily wrapped shawl that Rutledge had purchased for this woman who had served the Trevor household as long as he could remember. He had wanted to buy one in Tartan plaid, but Frances had told him that the sea-green Irish woolen one was a better choice. He hoped she was right.

The boy scooped up his box of toy soldiers, hugged Frances again, and ran out to the motorcar, excited to travel by train once more. He had already asked over and over whether he could come back again to London.

They reached the station in no time at all, and Rutledge had been silent most of the drive, fighting with himself and with Hamish over how to prolong the visit.

Then they were in the station, the train was coming in amidst clouds of white steam that set the boy dancing with glee, and it was time to board.

Rutledge said, hurriedly, before it was too late, "I'm glad you came."

Trevor smiled. "I'm glad I came as well. And I'll do it again, if you fail to come north to us."

Rutledge said tightly, "I can't—not yet." Not ever.

"The men you commanded and sent to their deaths have forgiven you long ago, Ian. When will you forgive yourself?"

Trevor's words were too close to the mark.

Rutledge could only answer, "Time. . ." That was as far as he could trust his voice.

"Time has a way of slipping through our fingers."

Then they were embracing, the carriage door was closing, and Rutledge could hear a whistle somewhere down the line as the engine gathered steam.

The train began to move. Trevor had dropped his window and called back to his godson, "Christmas, Ian. Come for Christmas!"

Rutledge stood there, knowing it was too late, far too late, and waved the train out of sight.

From the station, he drove to the Belvedere Clinic to inform Jenny Teller that there was no word still on her husband's whereabouts.

But when he got there, he was told that Mrs. Teller had stepped out with her sister-in-law for a cup of tea.

Matron said, "Mrs. Teller is quickly losing heart. It took some persuasion to convince her that it was all right to leave for a little while."

"Will you tell her for me that there has been no news?"

"You could probably catch them—they've only just left."

He was restless, not in the mood to sit in a tea shop and tell a wife that her husband was still missing and that the Yard couldn't find him despite all its trained personnel and experience.

"No. Let her have her brief respite. I'll only remind her of what she's trying to put out of her mind."

Matron said, "That's very generous of you. I'll see that she gets your message."

He went instead to Marlborough Street, to ask Edwin Teller if he possessed a later photograph of his brother, only to be told that Mr. Edwin Teller was resting and left orders not to be disturbed. Nor was Amy Teller available.

At the Yard, in the passage on the way to his own office, he encountered Chief Superintendent Bowles, who said in passing, "Still no trace of Teller. And that witness you wanted from Bynum's knifing hasn't been found either. Are you certain he's not the man we're after?"

"He's a witness. Nothing more. I just wanted to ask him other questions. I saw Billy, remember. More clearly even than Hood, who called him dark."

"Your priority is the Teller case. I'll put Mickelson on to finding Bynum's killer." He cleared his throat. "Are you quite certain Teller is still alive? We can't give more manpower to the search for him, with this murder case hanging over us. But I wouldn't wish the family to feel we aren't doing all we can. At least thank God there has been no plague."

"There's something wrong with this inquiry," Rutledge told him. "I sometimes feel I'm chasing a ghost."

"Nevertheless, if you know what's best, you'll find him—or what's become of him—as soon as may be. Am I understood?"

"Yes, sir."

"Have you taken the time to read Teller's book? It might be useful."

"I'll keep that in mind."

Rutledge moved on, pausing to speak briefly to Sergeant Gibson just as Constable Turner came up the stairs two at a time.

Gibson, frowning, said, "That one's in a tearing rush."

Turner reached Chief Superintendent Bowles and saluted smartly. "Sir. There's a train off the tracks up the line. Word just came in."

Rutledge called to him, "Which train?"

"The northbound to Edinburgh," Turner answered over his shoulder.

Rutledge said quickly, "Where, man, where did it derail?"

"Just to the north of a village called Waddington. Not that far—"

But Rutledge was already racing for the stairs, his mind filled with his godfather's last words: *Time has a way of slipping through our fingers.*

If he'd asked Trevor to stay, if he'd come out with the words in time, they wouldn't have been on that train—

He ran to where he'd left his motorcar. Out of breath and damning himself for not speaking up when he'd had the chance, Rutledge drove out of London at the best speed he could make, cursing the motorcars and lorries and pedestrians that held him up.

As soon as the outskirts of the city lay behind him, he gunned the motor and prayed he would be in time.

14

The train to the north had just come around a curve before it derailed, and that had slowed its speed enough to prevent a catastrophe. It was bad enough as it was.

Three of the carriages were still smoking when Rutledge got there,
a fire having started from a spark from the firebox. It was a scene of
chaos, people milling about, debris everywhere, twisted metal and
the stark white of shorn wood marking where the worst of the damage
had occurred. The great engine lay half on its side like some wounded
beast, and steam still trickled from the cooling boiler. The cars nearest it had accordioned before they derailed. As he slowed the motorcar
and looked across the flat pasture that had been scarred and torn by
the impact, he could see where a short row of bodies already lay covered in whatever was to hand: coats, a blanket, and even a tarp marked
PIERS BREWERY in block letters that someone must have carried down

from a brewery wagon left in the middle of the road, the horses standing patiently, heads down, half asleep in their traces.

He could hear people crying and shouting and a child screaming.

Hamish said, "O'er there."

Hamish had always had the keenest hearing in the company. Rutledge turned to look for a small boy and saw instead a little girl crouched beside her weeping mother, neither of them able to take in what had happened to them. He hurried across the uneven ground and knelt by the girl, and she clung to him as the mother said, "Her father—they're having to cut him out of the carriage."

Comforting both of them as best he could, he scanned over their heads, looking for a man and a boy—or come to that, either of them alone.

Then a woman from the nearest village was there to help, and he left her to it, moving past broken carriages toward the pathetic remains recovered before he'd arrived. He looked at each in turn, and felt a swift surge of hope. Trevor and his grandson weren't among the dead. It was difficult now to be sure which carriage he'd put his godfather in. And so he leaned into the wreckage of each one as he walked down the line, calling Trevor's name.

Trevor and the child were not there either.

"I should have begged him to stay," Rutledge said aloud, unaware that he'd spoken. "It's my fault."

"It's no' your fault," Hamish said. "There—yon man waving—"

He helped lift three more passengers down from damaged windows or doorways, then with another man's aid, pulled a fourth from the rubble. It was a woman, too frightened to cry, her eyes huge in her pale face. She looked around, dazed, uncertain, and then saw her husband standing to one side earnestly telling the man who was clumsily bandaging his arm that his wife was still in the carriage. With a small sound, like that of a frightened animal, she stumbled toward him, and he buried his face in her shoulder, gripping her with his good arm.

Rutledge walked on, still searching. More people were arriving to help as word spread. Among them was a doctor, who began to organize a makeshift infirmary.

Listening to Hamish, scanning faces, trying to keep his own fear at bay, Rutledge did what he could.

A woman crouched in the opening where a carriage door had once stood—the splintered remains still clinging to torn hinges—called to him. He clambered over wreckage to lift her down and then hand her over the worst of the debris. She was mumbling disjointed prayers interspersed with Hail Marys. He could see the blood in her fair hair, another cut bleeding through a tear in the sleeve of her shirtwaist. He turned to look for the doctor, urging her to come with him when she pulled free.

"No. Don't leave. There's someone still in there—I think she's dead."

"Can you walk as far as that line of trees?" he asked her gently. "Where the women are helping others like you. Do you see? I'll do what I can here."

She nodded, holding on to his arm until she had regained her balance, and then walked on. A woman in an apron came to collect her and guide her the rest of the way, offering words of encouragement and comfort.

Rutledge turned back to the task at hand. Testing his footing, he pulled himself into the compartment she'd just left.

A red-faced man, sweating from exertion, came up just then and said, "There's a doctor coming down the line, looking for the worst cases. Were you a passenger?"

"I've come to help—"

"Then follow me."

"The woman just there—the one walking to the trees—needs medical attention. And she told me someone is still trapped in here."

"Have a look, then, I'll be back as soon as I've passed the word."

The compartment he was in was a shambles, seats at an angle, door hanging ajar. He almost put his foot through a hole in the flooring, and then felt the car shift very slightly. Rutledge paused, then gingerly swung himself around the splintered door into the passage beyond. But there was no access that way. He came back again and tried to shift the splintered door. At first it wouldn't budge, then it gave way with a groan, nearly pitching him forward onto feet and a pale rose skirt. He caught himself in time, waited a moment for the carriage to settle again, and then crept through the opening he'd made.

From the far side, he was able to slide the door out of the way, then turn to the injured passenger.

It was a young woman, her trim ankles almost touching the toe of his left boot.

She lay on her side, her face hidden by a valise that had fallen next to her, and all he could see was a shoulder and dark hair. A crumpled hat lay beyond the crown of her head.

There was just room to kneel beside her. Rutledge said, "Miss? Can you hear me?"

He wasn't sure what it was that warned him. But just as she moved her head, crying out a little with the effort, he recognized her.

It was Meredith Channing.

She was dazed, her eyes not focusing right away, but then she saw him, and there was an intake of breath as her gaze sharpened.

"Ian? Were you on the train as well? Are you all right?"

"I came as soon as I heard—I was in London."

"But how did you know I was on board?"

"I didn't. I came to look for my godfather."

She tried to smile. "Is he all right?"

"I haven't found him yet," he said, making an effort to keep the worry out of his voice. "How badly are you hurt?" He was afraid to touch her. But she had trained as a nurse and he waited for her assessment.

"I don't know. My shoulder—I think it must be broken. Or dislocated."

He could see blood on her stockings, and one shoe was missing. And there was a smear of blood across her cheek.

The carriage swayed again.

"I must get you out of here. It's not safe."

"No, please, it hurts too much to move."

Glancing beyond her, he could just see a man's legs. He got to his feet and leaned forward for a better look.

The man was dead, there was no doubt of it, and suddenly he wondered if the two of them had been traveling together.

He knelt again by her side. "You're one of the lucky ones," he said, trying to divert her. "There's a man in one of the other carriages pinned where no one can get to him. And he's bleeding. Can you move your feet?"

She wiggled her toes. "They seem to be all right," she said. "A little bruised from the tossing about. It's my shoulder—my chest—that hurts."

"Your fingers now," he told her. "Move them if you can." But only her free hand could obey.

"Are you dizzy? Did you hit your head on anything?"

"I was knocked down and lost my hat. But I don't think I hit my head. It was my shoulder that took the brunt of the fall."

He looked just beyond her at the hat that matched her coat. He reached for it, and at the same time the seat against which Mrs. Channing lay shifted with a grinding noise. The dead man beyond her moved as well, sliding away as she cried out.

Rutledge sank back to his heels, reached again, and using just his fingers, he coaxed the hat toward him until it fell into his hand.

"Not too much the worse for wear," he said, putting it down beside her.

"Ian. I know what the pain most likely represents. And moving is agony. I'd have sat up long ago if it weren't for that. I can't think how I'm going to get out of here."

He smiled. "Someone said a doctor was on his way."

The red-faced man was back, leaning into the carriage. He called, "Anyone there? Did you find her?"

"Yes," Rutledge said. "A woman, broken or dislocated shoulder. We need to get her out."

"I'll find someone to help clear a way out of there." He was gone again, and Meredith Channing said lightly, "A reprieve."

"Meredith. It will take some time to clear a path for you. It might be best not to wait. This carriage could be resting on what's out there. It could be all that keeps it from sliding down onto its side. It's already halfway there. Do you understand?"

"I've been selfish. There are others who need help more than I do." She was silent for a moment. Then she said, "Do what you must. And don't mind if I beg you. Don't stop."

Someone stepped into the carriage at its far end, and it swayed again, dangerously. It was the red-faced man. "I'm afraid to move much closer in this direction."

"Stand by," Rutledge told him, then to Meredith Channing said, "First you must sit up. I'll help you brace that shoulder as best I can." He took off his belt and with her assistance drew it across her body, bringing her bad arm close to her chest. She whimpered with the pain, biting her lip and clenching her hands.

He didn't want to think how much it must have hurt, but he managed to move her into a sitting position. Her face was pale with pain, her dark hair spilling out of its pins and falling over her shoulders. Giving her a few moments to collect herself and steady her breathing, he said, "Now you must stand."

"Do you see my shoe? If I'm to walk out of here—the splinters—"

He looked around, and there was the shoe under the seat. He gave it to her, then took it back and put it on her bare foot himself, tying the laces.

"All right. Let me help with your weight. Hold on to me with your good arm, and I'll make it as painless as possible."

He tried, but she fainted before he could lift her to her feet. While she was unconscious, he carried her closer to the door of the next compartment and then through it.

But the red-faced man wasn't there. It was someone else saying sharply, "Here, what do you think you're doing?"

His shirt was torn and bloody, his trousers ripped to the knee, and blood dripped from a cut on his ear. "I'm a doctor," he went on. "She may have internal injuries, broken ribs."

"It's her shoulder," Rutledge said, "either broken or dislocated."

"Let me see." But as he stepped toward Rutledge, the car swayed again, the sound of metal rending and wood snapping. "Dear God! Is there anyone else in there?"

"I saw a man. He's dead."

"Can you be sure?"

"I'm from Scotland Yard. Yes, I'm sure."

"All right, pass her to me. We can't stand on ceremony now."

Rutledge did as he was told, lifting Meredith's limp body through the outer door, barely on its hinges, and clear of the carriage. The sun touched Meredith's face, and her eyelids fluttered. The doctor, bracing himself with the help of the red-faced man, took her from Rutledge and then, between them, lowered her safely to the ground.

The doctor knelt and felt her shoulder. "You're right. Dislocated. Let's get her away from here. We're collecting cases under that tree over there. Can you carry her that far?"

"Yes, of course."

"Then I'll keep going and come back to you."

"Have you seen a man—with a young boy? I've come to find them—"

"A good few men are all right. I haven't seen a boy among them." The doctor helped him lift Meredith Channing again, bracing her bad arm, and then disappeared into the carriage Rutledge had just left, to look at the man.

Rutledge carried her to the area where the walking wounded were being collected, and someone there spread a blanket over the bruised grass for him to lay her on. He took off his coat, rolled it, and set it under her head. Then he remembered her hat. "Stay with her," he said to the woman beside her, and jogged back to the train.

The doctor was just coming out again. "You were right, he's dead. Broke his neck from what I could see."

He wanted to ask the doctor if he had searched the man's pockets for his identification. Instead he asked, "There's a rose hat just behind you—and a small valise. The woman—"

"Yes, they all worry about such things, " he said testily but handed both out to Rutledge.

When he reached the trees again, Meredith Channing was conscious, her eyes bright with unshed tears from the pain. As he put her things beside her, she offered him a bleak smile.

"Ian," she murmured. "I thought I'd imagined you."

"There was something I had to do," he said, sitting down beside her, trying to judge whether she was comfortable enough to leave and continue his search.

She shut her eyes again, frowning a little. "I must have fainted."

"Yes. A good thing."

She tried to nod and then thought better of it. After a moment she said, "Your friend. Did you find him?"

"My godfather. Not yet."

"Oh—yes—that's right. I remember." She opened her eyes. "Go and look. I'm all right."

But she still seemed a little dazed. "After a bit," he said.

"Now. Come back and tell me when you find him, will you? I shan't be going anywhere, it seems."

He took her good hand and held it for a moment before letting it go.

Walking swiftly away, he scanned the people working around the wrecked carriages. More had appeared now, from the village and from a distance as word spread. And three more bodies had been added to the makeshift morgue, but Trevor was not among them. He found himself thinking about the man just beyond where Meredith Channing had been lying. Tall, graying, distinguished . . .

Hamish said, "It doesna' signify. Leave it."

Clearing his mind of everything else, he started back up the line, leaning in to see who might still be in each carriage, sometimes helping rescuers bring out another injured passenger, sometimes unable to see beyond the upturned seats and collapsed ceilings. And always calling Trevor's name to be sure.

And then, suddenly, there was his godfather coming toward him, a bloody handkerchief tied around one hand, a cut across his forehead, and a decided limp in his stride. The boy clung to him, still clutching the box of toy soldiers.

Rutledge was so relieved he stopped, unable to speak. The two men stared at each other, Trevor saying, "What in hell's name are you doing *here*?"

"News reached the Yard, and I came directly—"

"Well, I'm afraid you'll have to put up with us for a few days more."

Rutledge began to laugh helplessly. Then he said, "Where have you been? I must have walked up and down this train a dozen times!"

"On the far side of the engine, examining all the wheels. Where the lad couldn't see what he shouldn't. We were very lucky in our car. But they want us to give our names to a constable, and so I came round to find him."

Rutledge remembered Meredith Channing. "Do you see my motorcar there on the road? When you've given your name to the constable, go to it and wait. I won't be long. I've promised someone I'd come back."

Trevor nodded. "Go on. We'll be all right." Taking in his godson's appearance, scraped and bloody and disheveled, he added, "If you need to stay longer . . ." and let his voice trail off.

Rutledge answered the unspoken question. "Like you, she was lucky. There is the constable, I think." And then he was gone, hurrying back the way he'd come. He could feel Trevor watching him as he turned toward the trees.

He was ready to propose that he bring Meredith Channing back to London with them. But when he reached the blanket where he'd left her, she was gone. His coat was still there, and his belt. He looked around, a frown on his face, to see where she'd been moved.

A woman sitting nearby said, "Are you looking for the pretty young woman? She said someone might come. I believe they carried her to a house in the village. They've been moving the injured wherever possible. I'll be next." He realized she was clutching her arm, and saw that it was broken, the bruising already dark.

He hesitated, torn. "If you see her—tell her I found the man I was looking for. And I must take him back to London. If she needs me, she can send for me. I'll come for her."

But he had a feeling she wouldn't send for him. He had a feeling that what she had seen when he'd turned to her a few weeks earlier had shown her what was wrong with him. She'd been a nurse, she'd been at the Front. She would recognize shell shock, and know him for what he was. And he couldn't explain, he couldn't tell her about Hamish. He could never tell anyone.

In another part of his mind, he saw that she'd taken the hat and the valise with her.

No excuse then for him to follow her to the village and knock on doors. And he shouldn't leave the boy in this chaos while he searched.

Thanking the woman, he went back to his motorcar, listening to the silence that had been Hamish's response since he'd found Meredith Channing.

A constable stopped him, asking him for the names of any persons on the train he might have known.

He gave the man three names. And then thought about it and asked, "You don't happen to know where Mrs. Channing has been taken? Which house in the village?"

"No, sir, I don't. I've been given the task of collecting names. Others are seeing to the comfort of the injured."

Another thought occurred to him. He pointed to the carriage still teetering on its neighbor. "There's a dead man still in that one." He described him. "My name is Rutledge, Scotland Yard. If you learn who he is, I'll like to be told."

The constable's gaze lifted from the papers he was holding to focus on Rutledge. "Does the Yard have an interest in him, then?"

"No. It's just—I thought I recognized him. That's all."

The man nodded and moved on. Rutledge stood there, still hearing in his mind the lie he'd just told.

Hamish broke his long silence. "It doesna' signify," he said again. "He's deid."

"The dead can live on," Rutledge answered grimly. "Death is not always the end. I should know."

15

After settling Trevor and his grandson in their rooms to rest, reassuring Frances, and promising to send a telegram to Scotland informing the Trevor household that man and boy were safe and would come north again as soon as the line was cleared, Rutledge went home to change his own clothes. He thought that his godfather and the boy would sleep for a while, and cast about for something to amuse his namesake and take his mind off events. He'd been unusually quiet on the journey to London, leaning against his grandfather's shoulder in the motorcar and reluctant to let him out of his sight.

Rutledge decided a river journey to Hampton Court might suit, and stopped in Mayfair again to tell his sister.

"What a lovely thought, Ian! Will you go with us?"

"There's business at the Yard to see to. When I heard of the train crash, I simply walked out and drove straight to the site."

"It must have been dreadful. You look as if you could use a rest as well."

He laughed. "Sheer worry. It took some time to find David and the boy. I had imagined every catastrophe known to man by the time I saw them, safe and whole."

She smiled with him, understanding that he was speaking lightly of something too frightful to contemplate. "I didn't like to ask in front of David. Were many hurt?"

"Injured and killed," he told her. And then before he could stop himself, he said, "Meredith Channing was on the train as well."

"Dear God. Is she all right? Did you bring her back to London too?"

"She'd already been taken away by the time I found David. I expect the doctors were working on her shoulder. It was dislocated. I left a message for her to let me know if there was anything more I could do."

"That was kind." And then feminine curiosity took over. "Do you know where she was going?" She answered her own question. "Was it to Inverness?"

He hadn't considered that possibility. She might have been traveling alone after all. He found he wasn't as sorry as he ought to be that her journey was interrupted. "She never said. There was no time to talk about anything but finding help for the injured."

"No, of course not. I'll call on her later in the week."

He left then and drove to the Yard.

But there was no news of Walter Teller, and no one had located Charlie Hood.

Frustrated, Rutledge shut himself in his office and turned his chair to face the window.

Walter Teller, he thought, had had to survive unimaginable difficulties in the field. He had had to be clever enough as well to deal with unexpected problems facing his flock, not to speak of coping with doubters and those who clung stubbornly to their own gods, even to the point of threatening him and his converts. The climate would have been against him, the long journeys in and out of his mission post would have been trying. He'd been responsible for the lives of his converts and would have had to keep their faith fresh in spite of tribulations and setbacks—a failed harvest, an infestation of insects, plagues and natural disasters, and war, even on a tribal scale.

Then what could possibly have frightened the man between his London bank and his house in Essex?

Hamish, his voice loud in the small office, said, "His son."

And that son had been Walter Teller's first concern when he finally reached his house. Yet he had walked away from Harry as well as his wife hardly more than a week later.

Had his dead father insisted that the heir go away to school at such an early age? Rutledge had been told that, but there was no proof. He wished he'd thought to ask Leticia Teller about it. Wanting to go against his dead father's wishes was hardly reason enough to have a breakdown of the magnitude that had assailed Teller.

There was the letter from the mission society.

But Teller hadn't got ill immediately after receiving it.

Rutledge turned and reached for his hat.

It was time to find the Alcock Society and ask a few questions.

He discovered through sources at the Yard that the Society had a small house outside of Aylesford, Kent, and he drove there without waiting for an appointment.

Aylesford, with its handsome narrow bridge and narrower twisting streets, was a pretty little town on the Medway. The house Rutledge was seeking was within sight of the church. It was a Tudor building almost as narrow as it was tall.

He knocked at the door and was received by an elderly man in rusty black, his long face wrinkled with age and exposure to the sun.

Rutledge identified himself and explained his errand.

Mr. Forester, it seemed, was the secretary of the Society and handled all correspondence for it. The Alcock, he informed Rutledge, had been founded in the early part of the nineteenth century, and since that time had been very well supported by patrons who believed in the Society's work and its attempt to bring enlightenment to the forgotten parts of the world. Victoria herself had visited the tiny headquarters before she had succeeded to the throne, and above the hearth there was a small painting of the event done by Forester's predecessor. He pointed it out proudly and invited Rutledge to admire it.

He asked Rutledge to join him for tea, and they sat in the parlor on chairs Rutledge was certain the great Elizabeth would have recognized, with straight backs and seats hard as iron, discussing the Society's aims and goals and record.

"And Walter Teller?"

"He was always reliable, a steady man who was able to find common ground with the local people and work with them in projects designed to better their lives. A school, for instance, or a new well, or a market that attracted commerce to the area. Very practical things, you might say, but through them, people could be persuaded to find worth in Christianity and turn their thoughts to conversion."

"I understand," Rutledge said, "that you've only recently written to Mr. Teller."

"Yes. In fact, I have a copy there in my desk. I keep meticulous copies of all correspondence. My records are excellent." He set aside his cup and went to the desk, where he found the folder he wanted and brought it back to his chair.

"Let me see." He thumbed through several sheets before finding the one he was after. "Here it is. Mr. Teller has been some years out of the field—his book, of course, and then the war—and we are experiencing a little difficulty in finding good men to send to established missions, much less new ones." He looked up at Rutledge. "Sadly, the world has changed now. Before the war, there was a fervor for service.

We've grown sadly bitter and tired these past two years. Our missionaries are older, on the point of retiring. We'd like to see Mr. Teller return to the field. Indeed, it is more than like—there is need."

"And has he responded to your call for serving?"

"Not so far. But you told me earlier that he'd been ill. Perhaps that has been the reason?"

"Possibly," Rutledge replied, evading a direct answer. "It's Mr. Teller's illness that has brought me here. The doctors are at a loss to explain it. He seems deeply troubled by something. The family can think of nothing that would have provoked a sudden and unusual attack of paralysis."

Mr. Forester looked steadily at Rutledge. "And this has required the attention of Scotland Yard?"

Rutledge smiled. "In fact, Mr. Teller has had a miraculous recovery, and he disappeared from the clinic. I've been in charge of the search for him."

Forester shook his head. "This is very odd. I'd have never thought of Walter Teller experiencing a collapse of any kind. I do know he is very attached to his son. An only child, as I recall."

"That's correct."

"And nothing has happened to the boy?"

"He's on the point of going to public school."

"How the years fly. I remember when he was born, how proud Mr. Teller was of him, all the plans he spoke of. I have had the strongest suspicion that he didn't return to the field because of the boy. I can appreciate that, having had a son of my own late in life. The wonder of watching him grow was precious beyond words." Something in his voice as he spoke the last words alerted Rutledge.

"He was in the war?"

"Yes, how did you guess? He was lost on the Somme. I have long wanted to go to France to see his grave. But that's not to be. I'm too old for such a journey now." Clearing his throat, he said, "But to return to

Walter Teller. I shan't expect an answer any time soon. I'm grateful to know the circumstances. The Society has need of him. I hope his recovery will be complete."

Rutledge thanked him and left.

On the drive back into London, Rutledge gave some thought to Walter Teller's relationship to his son, and then stopped at Frances's house.

David Trevor was in the garden, enjoying the late evening breezes before the sun went down, and looked up with a smile when he saw his godson walk through the French doors and across the terrace.

"Ian. You've had a long day. Frances told me you'd gone back to the Yard."

Rutledge smiled, and took the chair across from Trevor's. "How are you feeling?"

"I won't lie to you, it was not the pleasantest experience. I have bruises and no recollection of how I got them. But we survived, and that's what matters." He held up his bandaged hand. "Frances saw to it. Not deep, but bruised as well. A small price to pay, considering what happened to so many. Is your friend all right?"

Rutledge was surprised that Trevor had remembered his brief absence going back to find Meredith Channing. "Yes, I have every reason to think so." He paused, then said, "I need to bring up a painful subject. How you felt about having a son. When he was born—his first few years as a child?"

"Is this to do with a case?"

"Sadly, yes."

"I don't mind talking about those years. It was a miracle, finding myself a father. I can't tell you. He was so small, and yet so real. He moved, he made sounds, he opened his eyes and stared into my face. His hands clutched at my fingers. It was unexpected, the depth of my feelings for him even then. I'd have done anything for him. Died for him if need be. Nothing I'd ever done to that point in my life seemed half so important." He smiled wryly, the late sun just touching his face and lighting his eyes. "It seems absurd, doesn't it? I don't think I've ever told anyone that before. I was embarrassed, you see, I didn't know for the longest time that what I felt was natural."

His words touched Rutledge, and he said quietly, "Thank you."

"I hope one day you'll know for yourself what having a child means."

Frances came out just then, bringing a pitcher of cold water, and Rutledge stayed a little while longer before rising to take his leave.

He spent a restless night. Hamish, ever ready to bring up memories that Rutledge could sometimes bury during the daylight hours, pressed him hard, and it was nearly four in the morning when he finally fell into a deep sleep, only to wake up an hour later, calling out to the men under his command, warning them to take cover.

He rose and dressed, grateful to be alone in the flat, and was in his office at the Yard long before anyone else had come in.

None of the reports from the night staff dealt with Walter Teller, although there was information on Bynum's murderer.

The knife used in the attack on Rutledge was too ordinary to be traced. But postmortem evidence indicated it was very likely the same kind of knife that killed Bynum. The coat button was of doubtful provenance. The address on the scrap of paper proved to be a lodging house. The woman who ran it reported that a male who appeared to be around nineteen years old, fair and with freckles, had come to ask if there was a room available in the house.

The woman told the police that although he had claimed he could pay for the room, she had her doubts that he would fit in with her other lodgers, two older men and an elderly woman.

"Restless, he was," the constable quoted from his notebook, "couldn't sit still a minute."

The man had argued with her, and then left, the report concluded, and she had no idea where he had come from or where he went after leaving her.

It was Mickelson's case now. Rutledge was a witness, nothing more. But he had taken a personal interest in Billy, and with each new victim, his own sense of responsibility grew.

He set aside the night's reports and considered his next step in the case that was his. He couldn't put a finger on what bothered him most about the disappearance of Walter Teller.

There were strong reasons why Teller might be experiencing bouts of depression and despair. His son's future, his own obligation to his calling.

But these couldn't altogether explain his disappearance.

Or why he had been paralyzed by indecision? If that was what it was.

Even the Teller family wasn't in agreement about the reasons behind what had happened. Although Rutledge had a feeling that they knew more than they were telling.

It was useless to speculate. No one was likely to solve the mystery of what lay so heavily on Walter Teller's soul until the man himself could answer the question.

And Rutledge had a feeling that that was not likely to be very soon.

How long would the Yard continue to search? When would the decision be made to call it off? It had gone on longer than the average missing persons case because Walter Teller was Walter Teller. Manpower was becoming a crucial issue in the hunt for Bynum's killer.

He was on the point of leaving his office to speak to Chief Superintendent Bowles when Sergeant Gibson stopped him. "There's a constable downstairs with a message. You'd best speak to him yourself."

Rutledge went down to the lobby to find one of Sergeant Biggin's men standing there, breathless from his bicycle ride across London.

"It's urgent, sir. Sergeant Biggin asks if you can come to the clinic at once?"

Stowing the bicycle in the boot of his motorcar, Rutledge said to the constable, "What's happened?"

"As to that, sir, you'd best wait and ask him."

They were halfway to the Belvedere Clinic when Rutledge thought he glimpsed Charlie Hood walking the other way. He swore as he lost sight of the man, but traffic was heavy, and he had to keep his attention on the motorcars, lorries, and drays that filled the street.

"Did you see that man? With the unkempt hair, and a dark brown coat?" he demanded of the constable in the seat beside him. "We just passed him. On your right."

"No, sir, I didn't," the man answered him, craning his neck to look back the way they had come. A brewery lorry was pulling in just behind them, blocking Rutledge's view as well.

It would do no good to set the constable down to follow Hood; he hadn't seen the man.

Rutledge took a deep breath and said, "Never mind."

They reached the clinic, and the constable took up his stance by the door.

Passing through the outer lobby, Rutledge nodded to the porter on duty, then walked through to Matron's sitting room.

There he was almost swept into an embrace by a joyful Jenny Teller, her face blindingly bright with happiness. Over her shoulder he saw a man stand and step away from his chair, a tentative expression on his face.

"Oh!" Jenny exclaimed. "I thought it was Edwin. Do come in, Inspector Rutledge. I want to show you that I was right all along. Here is my husband. Walter, this is the Scotland Yard inspector I've told you about."

And Walter Teller had the grace to stare sheepishly at Rutledge.

He had changed from the younger man in the photograph that his wife had let Rutledge borrow. There were deeper lines on his face, fatigue mostly, and an uncertainty, Rutledge thought, about his reception.

He needn't have worried. Despite his shabby appearance, hair that looked as if he'd combed it with his fingers, and the beginnings of a beard, Walter Teller was the most wonderful sight in the world to his wife's eyes.

Then who was Charlie Hood?

As Rutledge crossed the room, he caught the distinct odor of incense with a soupçon of cabbage on Teller's clothing. He found himself remembering what Leticia Teller had said, that her brother would salve his conscience in serving the poor of London.

"I've sent for Edwin and Peter, but the doctors want to take Walter away and examine him," Jenny was saying.

Rutledge felt an odd mixture of relief that the man was alive and a strong sense of anger at what he had put his family through.

"Mr. Teller," he said, his voice cold.

"I know," Teller admitted. "I've done a terrible thing. But I can't tell you why or even tell you where I've been. I came to my senses outside a greengrocer's shop this morning, watching as he put trays of vegetables in his window. I went inside and asked him what day it was, and where his shop was. He told me I was drunk and to get out. I'd never been spoken to like that before. On the street, I passed a milliner's shop with a mirror in the window, and I saw myself then. Small wonder the man thought I was drunk or mad."

Jenny, tears in her eyes, said, "You mustn't think about it. You're safe now, you're here."

Teller's gaze was on Rutledge, wanting him to believe, wanting him to accept what he was saying.

Rutledge was saved from answering by the appearance of one of the doctors, urging Teller to come and let them examine him, but Jenny said, "No. His brothers are on the way. Please, we've been so worried. Let them see he's safe now. Then you can have him."

But Rutledge thought it was Jenny herself who couldn't let her husband out of her sight just yet. She clung to his arm, as if still not sure this miracle was real, or if she had dreamed it.

Dr. Sheldon said, "Half an hour, and then we really must insist." He left, shutting the door behind him.

Teller said, "Jenny. Do you think Matron might arrange a cup of tea? I'm dry as a desert."

She was of two minds about leaving him. Rutledge said, "I'll be here," and finally she walked out the door, looking back at her husband, as if she expected him to vanish before her eyes.

Teller said quietly, as soon as she was out of earshot, "I left here with every intention of drowning myself. But when I got to the river, the water was filthy. Oily and with things floating in it. Paper and feathers and the odd tin. I even saw a dead seagull some twenty yards away, feathers a dirty gray, and I thought I couldn't let them find me like that. So I began walking. My God, I don't know how far I walked. Halfway to France, it seemed. At night I slept in churches. I know churches, I felt safe there. I'd wait until nearly dark, and then slip inside. There are places in the organ loft where it's not as cold, and I'm used to sleeping on the ground when I have to. I managed. Never the same church twice, for fear I'd be seen. I had money with me. I could buy enough food to keep up my strength." He smiled ruefully. "Once a constable nearly took me into custody. I'd offered to pay for my meal with a five-pound note. He thought I'd stolen it, that I was a pickpocket. I had to convince him I was down on my luck and living on the kindness of strangers. I'd bought workmen's clothes."

"Is any of this true?" Rutledge asked him.

"It's true. But I don't want to tell these things to my wife. So I'm asking you to let her believe I was dazed or ill. It will hurt her to know I was in my right mind and still let her believe the worst."

"She never accepted the possibility that you were dead."

He flinched.

"Why did you leave here?"

"I told you. I wanted to die."

"There's usually a reason for suicide. What happened on the road between London and Essex?"

"You might as well ask me what happened on the road to Damascus. I don't know. At first I thought I was dying. And then I feared for Harry. Dr. Fielding couldn't find anything wrong, and I thought he was lying."

Rutledge, judging him, could believe that, as far as it went.

Teller, seeing that Rutledge wasn't fully convinced, shrugged. "I know. I have much to live for. A fine wife, a fine son, a home I love. I have no worries about money or my health. What right have I to feel the weight of depression? But I don't think depression is measured by what you have—"

He broke off with a warning glance to Rutledge as the door opened. But it wasn't Jenny with their tea; it was Edwin Teller and his wife who came into the room and stopped stock-still, staring at the apparition before them.

"My God," Edwin said, moving as if to embrace his brother. And then he stopped. "Where the *hell* have you been? Do you know what you have put Jenny—all of us—through? If Father were alive now, he'd horsewhip you!"

Amy put her hand on her husband's arm. "No, don't, Edwin. Please—"

Walter said, "I have no excuses. No explanation. I'm sorry. More sorry than you know. More sorry than you will ever know."

Peter Teller and his wife came in just then, and Peter, recognizing his brother, glowered at him. "I hope you can explain yourself," he said through clenched teeth. "I hope there was a damned good reason for what you've done."

Susannah, her face flushed, said, "Where's Jenny?"

"I asked her to bring me a little tea. I couldn't bear her relief any longer."

"Someone should telephone Leticia. And Mary," Susannah said. And then in a burst of anger she said accusingly, "It's been a terrible week. We've driven miles, we've tried to console Jenny, we've tried to think where you might be, and then your clothes were found by the river—" She turned away, brushing angrily at the tears in her eyes.

Rutledge recalled that Peter had been drinking heavily. It explained, a little, his wife's distress.

"I know. I say again, I'm sorry. It's not enough, but it's all I can do."

The door opened, and Jenny held it wide for one of the sisters to bring in Matron's tea tray. She carried it to the table, and then turned to Walter.

"We're very happy to see you've returned safely," she said. "And Matron would appreciate a word, when you've seen the doctors."

Teller looked overwhelmed, but he said, "Yes, of course."

Jenny was saying triumphantly to his brothers, "I told you he wasn't dead. But when they brought him in to me, I couldn't believe my eyes." She laughed, trying hard to ignore the tension in the room.

Amy went to the tray and began to pour tea into cups. The practical one, Rutledge realized. Or—less involved? She carried one to Walter without a word, and then gave one to Jenny. Peter refused his, but Edwin accepted one as well, as if needing to keep his hands busy.

Matron came in, saying, "I'm so sorry to interrupt your celebration, but I'm afraid we must borrow Mr. Teller for a bit."

He followed her, almost as if he was glad of escape. Jenny started after him, then stopped at a glance from Matron.

Edwin said, when he'd gone, "I'm sorry. It's been a very difficult time for us. For Walter as well. I shouldn't have lost my temper."

Smoothing what oil she could over troubled waters, Amy said, "Jenny, you must be so happy. He looks well, doesn't he? A little tired, perhaps."

"I want to leave here as soon as the doctors will let him go," she answered. "I want to go home, and I want to have Harry back again."

"You ought to stay with us for a few days," Amy suggested, but Jenny shook her head.

"I'm sick of London."

Edwin moved to stand beside Rutledge. "Has he told you why he left? Or where he was?" he asked quietly.

"I'm not sure how much I believe," Rutledge answered. "But at a guess, I'd say he never left London."

"London?" Edwin stared at him. "Well. That most certainly is good news." He hesitated. "There are no charges, I hope, growing out of this. The inquiry, the search?"

"None." Bowles would never agree to any, Rutledge knew.

But before Rutledge left the clinic, he had a last word with Walter Teller. The doctors had pronounced him in good health and told him that he was free to return to Essex. What they really believed they kept to themselves.

Rutledge said, "This will not happen again. Is that understood?"

Walter's head reared back, as if about to challenge Rutledge. And then he said, "It wasn't deliberate. I didn't ask the police to search for me."

"What did you think would happen, when the clinic discovered you were missing? To protect themselves, the first order of business was to summon the police."

"Yes, I suppose I should have expected that. But why the Yard?"

"You're an important man, Mr. Teller. We were concerned."

Teller had the grace to look ashamed of himself. "Yes, all right. It won't happen again. For that matter, I can't think of any reason why it should."

Rutledge said as he walked to the door, "There's something else. You've put your wife through a very difficult time. The least you can do for her sake is change your mind now about your son's schooling."

Teller said, "It was my father's wish—"

"He's dead, Teller. Your wife is very much alive. Do it for her."

"I'll consider it. I can at least do that."

Rutledge nodded and went out.

Rutledge could hear Hamish before he reached his motorcar. He could feel the sunlight fading, replaced by the raw gray light of the trenches just before dawn. And then the guns picked up, their shells dropping with precision, without a break between them. It had driven more than one man mad, the shelling, and he had lived with the sound until it was almost a part of his very bones.

Somehow he managed to start the motorcar, but how he reached the Yard, he didn't know. And then the trenches faded as quickly as they had come.

Rutledge sat in his motorcar, staring through the windscreen, trying to shake off the aftermath. And then the motorcar began moving again, and almost without thinking, he found himself driving toward Chelsea.

A reasonable time had passed. It would be proper to call and see how Meredith Channing was faring. It would be expected.

But when he got there and knocked at the door, no one came to answer it.

Hamish said, "She's no' in London."

Rutledge stood there on the steps, accepting the silence beyond the closed door. And then he turned and walked back to his motorcar.

16

It was necessary to report to Bowles how the inquiry into the disappearance of Walter Teller had ended.

Rutledge braced himself and knocked at the man's door.

"Come."

It was difficult to judge his mood from the one word.

But as Rutledge walked into the office, he could see that for once Bowles was not scowling.

Rutledge said, "The Teller inquiry is closed. Teller returned to the clinic on his own, and from what the doctors have said, he's recovered and free to return to Essex."

Bowles raised his eyebrows in an expression of surprise. "Did he now? And where has he been all this time, pray?"

"Sleeping in churches. Walking the streets. Thinking. Who knows? I wasn't sure how much I could believe. He's a very private man, and

I don't expect anyone will ever know the truth about what happened. Not even his wife."

"You're the policeman. What's your opinion?"

Rutledge considered the question. "It seemed to me that the arrival of a letter from his missionary society coincided with problems with his wife, and he didn't know how to respond to the letter. At the same time, he was on the point of sending his son to Harrow early, against her wishes." That answer would serve well enough for a report. He had no idea why Walter Teller had been ill or left the clinic without a word. He rather thought, but had no intention of telling Bowles, that Teller's brothers had suspected something. Yet they hadn't confronted him. And that was decidedly odd, given their anger when he returned. Was it Jenny's presence that had stopped them?

Bowles nodded. "I should think it might be very difficult to go back to those godforsaken posts after all these years away. I wouldn't fancy it myself. But he may have felt honor bound to fulfill his commitment to the Society."

Rutledge said nothing.

"If it were anyone but Walter Teller, I'd have a word with him. Wasting police time and putting us all through the hoops. I must say, I expected better of the man."

"I already have made it clear—"

"At least you managed to keep this business out of the newspapers. With the number of police involved in the search, it's a wonder word didn't get out."

"If it had gone on much longer—or had had a different ending—we might not have escaped their attention."

"There's that. All right. Let me have your report before the day is out."

But instead of returning to his own office, Rutledge went out of the Yard and walked to Trafalgar Square and then past St. Martin-in-the-Fields, taking the streets at random while his mind was busy.

It had reached a very unsatisfactory conclusion, this inquiry, he thought, ignoring the people coming and going around him, the busy traffic of a London day.

Why had Teller returned on his own? And where was he? What had he really been doing with his time?

Hamish said, "He willna' tell anyone."

And Rutledge thought that that was probably true. He wondered if Teller had decided to return to the field. Perhaps his soul-searching had found his answer.

Suddenly he recalled what Mary Brittingham had said, that Walter Teller wasn't a saint. He was bitter. About what? It would be enlightening to know.

And that, Rutledge decided, was the best explanation of the man he'd heard.

But of course that was not something that could be expressed in a report.

17

Peter Teller sat in his garden in Bolingbroke Street and poured himself another glass of whisky. His hand was shaking, but he was far from as drunk as he wanted to be.

His brother Walter was back, greeted like the prodigal son. It was a travesty. All that was needed was the fatted calf, he told himself sourly.

What did he know? He had stared into his brother's eyes and seen nothing. And not even Walter was that cold-blooded.

Draining the glass, he sat back in his chair, moved his bad leg a little in the hope of finding a more comfortable position, and stared through the silhouetted leaves above his head at the night sky, black as he was sure his soul was.

What in God's name had he done? To make matters worse, he couldn't have said under oath what had become of his cane. It wasn't in the motorcar. In his haste he must have dropped it. In the grass? Along the road? When he got out two hours later to stretch and massage his leg?

He hadn't intended to frighten her. He had only wanted to say what he'd come to say and walk away.

He wasn't even sure now just what he *had* said—the words had spilled out, a reflection of fear and anger. He'd charged German positions under fire, he'd killed men, he'd fought for King and Country, and yet in those few seconds he'd lost his courage, and with it lost his head.

What sort of man was he? To run as he had, to leave her there, an act of such sheer cowardice that he couldn't blot it out of his mind, no matter how much he drank.

And he could tell no one. Not Edwin, not Susannah. Certainly not Leticia.

For a time he considered going inside, finding his service revolver, and putting an end to his shame and revulsion. But he couldn't do it. The same tenacity that had made him fight over and over again to keep his damaged leg when the surgeons were intent on removing it forced him to face the man he was. Perhaps, he told himself bitterly, after the shock wore off, he might even learn to stand himself again.

He was becoming a maudlin drunk, and that he despised.

Susannah came out into the garden, wrapping her dressing gown closer against the late night chill.

"Won't you come to bed? A night's rest will do you more good than this." She nodded toward the glass in his hand.

"In a little while," he said, still studying the stars, avoiding her eyes.

"You promised two hours ago. Please, won't you see the doctor tomorrow, and ask him for drops or something to help with the pain? You can't go on drinking to dull it. I blame Edwin if you want the truth, for not going himself."

There were no drops to cure this pain, he answered her silently, and then aloud, "I expect the doctor will say what he always does. That I shouldn't drive."

She regarded him for a moment, and then asked, "What's wrong, Peter? It's eating away at you. Is there something you haven't told me?"

"Go to bed, Susannah. I've had too much to drink to make any sense. We'll talk about it tomorrow."

She turned and walked back to the terrace door. There she paused and said, her voice carrying perfectly to him where he sat, "Did you kill her, Peter? Was all the rest of what you told us a lie?"

He pretended he didn't hear. Reaching for the decanter again, he poured himself another measure, concentrating on not spilling it.

The terrace door closed behind his wife, and in a sudden fury, he flung the glass of whisky against the trunk of the ginkgo overhanging the iron rail fence. It shattered, but he was already regretting what he'd done and he shoved himself to his feet to cross the lawn and pick up the shards before someone found them in the morning and read more than anger in the glittering, whisky-soaked pieces.

18

Rutledge finished his report and handed it to a constable to be typed for Chief Superintendent Bowles.

And still restless, he considered going to Frances's house and spending the remainder of the afternoon with his godfather. Then he recalled that today was the grand excursion to Hampton Court by boat.

He stopped to speak to Chief Inspector Cummins, who had just returned from Paris, where he'd been persuading the French to allow him to bring a witness back to England to testify in regard to a killing in Surrey.

Cummins greeted him, then said, "Go away for four days and my desk grows papers like the French grow grapes. What sort of mood is his lordship in?"

Rutledge smiled. "Mercurial."

"Damn. The French are being pigheaded. He's not going to like that."

Rutledge hesitated, and then in spite of himself asked, "Has the Front changed much?"

He had meant the France of the war years. The blackened ruin of a countryside. Cummins had not pretended to misunderstand him.

"Not very. It takes trees a while to grow back, although there's more grass now. I found myself feeling depressed and turned around. But the French farmers are a hardy lot. They'll not let good land go to waste for very long."

"Blood-soaked land . . ."

Rutledge shivered at Hamish's words.

They talked for several minutes, then Rutledge returned to his office.

A quarter of an hour later, Constable Ellis was at his door, saying quickly, "You're wanted, sir. Chief Superintendent."

Hamish said, " 'Ware!" as Rutledge crossed the threshold, and he guessed that Cummins had been there before him with his own bad news. And Bowles had not taken it well.

He was muttering about the French under his breath, then he looked up and said, "What the hell kept you?" But before Rutledge could frame an answer, Bowles went on testily, "I thought we were finished with these Tellers."

"Sir?"

The Chief Superintendent barked, "Now we have a request from a village in Lancashire to look into the death of a Mrs. Peter Teller. Seems she was murdered."

It required a moment for Rutledge to digest the news.

"Sir?" he repeated. "I just saw the Captain's wife. Yesterday. Surely there's some mistake?"

"Are you deaf, or is your mind wandering? I've just told you, Peter Teller's wife. Who said anything about Captain Teller? She's just been found dead by the constable in Hobson. Unusual name, all the same. Might be a relation, though it's unlikely. Lancashire?" He shook his head. In Bowles's view, the farther from London, the more benighted the place. "You'll have to deal with it, I can't spare anyone else." He closed the file and looked Rutledge in the face. "I'd counted on you to handle Walter Teller's disappearance. It would have pleased a number of people to see us successful in that quarter. Instead he came back under his own power. You reported that he slept in a church. Why didn't someone think to have a constable concealed there? Failure on your part, you know. See that we're not embarrassed a second time. Do I make myself clear?"

"I understand," Rutledge replied as Bowles searched his cluttered desk for his pen. And he did understand. Political repercussions were always uppermost in Bowles's mind. Using them or avoiding them, he had become quite adept at sensing the way the wind would blow. But to clear the record, Rutledge added, "Teller slept in different churches. Not just one. That's to say, if he was telling the truth. There are dozens of churches in London."

"He's a cleric, is he not? Someone should have taken that into account." He found his pen and uncapped it. "You're to leave for Hobson straightaway." He made a final note on the file and passed it to Rutledge.

Rutledge crossed to the door. Bowles said, "And, Rutledge . . ."

He turned.

"I shouldn't think the family would like seeing this bruited in the newspapers. For all we know, this Teller could be on the wrong side of the blanket. Might explain Hobson, if you take my meaning. The family has had a very trying time of it already."

As Rutledge walked back to his office to set his desk in order, Hamish said, "Ye willna' be here to take yon godfather to the station."

"I'll leave a note."

Sergeant Gibson, standing in the doorway, asked, "Sir?"

Rutledge had answered the voice in his head aloud, without think-ing. He turned to face Gibson and forced a smile. "A commentary on what's ahead," he answered lightly. "Do you know anything about the police in this village of Hobson?"

"The constable—Satterthwaite is his name—gives the impression he's a sound man, sir. He'll steer you right."

"Let us hope. All right, anything else I should know?"

"No witnesses. No sign of robbery. No physical assault. Nothing to go on but the woman's body found in the front passage of her house."

"What did the husband have to say about it?"

"It appears he's dead, sir."

"Indeed?"

"So the constable informed me, sir. Didn't come home from the war."

"I don't remember Hobson. Is it hard to find?"

"Satterthwaite says, look for the turning after the crossroads. It's not very well marked from this direction, but it's off the road to Thielwald."

"I'll bear that in mind."

Rutledge stopped at his sister's house and left a note for her ex-plaining his absence, and another of farewell to his godfather. He would have liked to see Trevor and the boy, to say good-bye and wish them a safe journey, but they weren't planning to return until late that evening, hoping to dine near Hampton Court. And he had a long drive ahead with no time to lose.

Half an hour later he was on the road north, facing little traffic, with Hamish unsettled in the seat just behind him, the voice close enough that sometimes over the soft purr of the motor, he could almost swear he heard Hamish breathing. He was always careful not to look in the rear seat, and he kept the small mirror turned in such a way that he couldn't see any reflection but his own. He'd made a bargain with himself four years before when he realized that he couldn't shut the voice out of his head: the day he saw Hamish MacLeod would be the day he sent both of them to the grave.

Even when he stopped for a late dinner this side of Derby, the voice followed him, a counterpoint to his own thoughts.

He had traveled this road before, coming down from Westmorland, although instead of warm breezes sweeping through the motorcar there had been a harsh wind off the winter snow, the aftermath of a blizzard that had shut down roads and cut off families from one another but not from a murderer.

And then the turning he was after appeared around a bend in the road, and he was heading in a different direction, the shadows in his mind receding with distance.

After one last turn, he found crossroads and the fingerboard pointing toward Thielwald. Some three miles beyond that, he saw the side road that bore to the left toward Hobson. He followed that through grassy pastures and a thin stand of trees, before cresting a slight hill and coming down to the first of Hobson's houses, sturdy and uncompromisingly independent, like the people who lived in them. A milking barn in the distance to his left caught the last long rays of sunlight, and ahead of him, just leaving the muddy lane that led to it, a line of cows made their way down the High Street, heading for their night's grazing on the other side of the village, their udders flaccid after milking. The bell on the leather strap around the neck of their leader clanked rhythmically as she swayed from side to side, paying no attention to the motorcar in her wake.

Rutledge could see the police station just beyond the herd and waited patiently for the last of the cows to pass. Constable Satterthwaite had just come out the door and was standing there on the point of filling his pipe.

He was a heavyset man of middle years, with an air of knowing his patch well. As Rutledge pulled up, he greeted him. "Inspector Rutledge? You've made good time, sir. The light's still good. Would you like to go on out to the Teller house, or wait until morning?"

Rutledge considered the sky. "Now is best. I'll drive."

Constable Satterthwaite shoved his pipe back into his pocket and got in, giving directions to the scene of the crime. Then he settled back and said, "I'm that happy to see you, sir. This is a puzzle I can't fathom. Florence Teller is the last person I'd have expected to find murdered. We're a quiet village, not a place where there's been much in the way of violence over the years. We know one another fairly well, and for the most part, that's a good thing. If someone is in need, we try to help. No one needs to go stealing from his neighbor."

"Murder isn't always to do with need," Rutledge told him. "There's passion and greed and anger and jealousy—and sometimes just sheer cruelty."

"I understand, sir. But I don't know how any of those things might touch Florence Teller. Why someone would come to her door, and then strike her down and leave her for dead where she fell is beyond me. The doctor says it would have done no good if she'd got help straightaway. The damage was done. But how was her killer to know that? She might have lain there suffering for hours. And no one to help her. That was a cruelty."

"She lived alone?"

"Yes, sir. The aunt who brought her up when she lost her parents died about fifteen years ago. Maybe more. And her son died some twelve years back. Then her husband didn't come home from France. That took the heart out of her, though I never heard her complain. And she more or less kept to herself afterward. Gardening was always her joy, you might say, and even that couldn't make a difference."

Rutledge glanced his way. "You seem to know her well."

"I know all my people well," Satterthwaite said with dignity. "But yes, I kept an eye on her. To be sure she didn't fall ill or lack for anything."

He could hear the pain in the other man's voice as he tried to keep his feelings in check. Not love, precisely, but a protective fondness all the same.

"She would do anything for anyone," Satterthwaite went on, when

Rutledge made no comment. "She stayed up three nights with the Burtons' little girl when she had typhoid, and the mother was too ill to nurse her. All of us knew what sort of person she was. So where was the need to kill her?"

"What was her maiden name?"

"Marshall. Her parents lived in Cheshire. The father was originally from Cheshire as I recall."

The village had straggled along the High Street and then, as if tired of trying to grow any larger, it simply stopped. Beyond Hobson, the land spread out in a carpet of early summer green, rising a little to show where plowed fields and pastures intersected, and flocks of shorn sheep cropped the grass.

Save for the sheep and a man on a bicycle passing them, there was no other sign of life. Yet the emptiness was friendly, not like the great haunted barren sweeps of the Highlands. Rutledge could hear Hamish making the comparison in his mind.

"Where is Mrs. Teller's body?"

"Over to the doctor's surgery in Thielwald. It was a single blow, he says, delivered with some force from behind. Looking at her face, you'd never guess she'd been killed. I was that surprised to see a peaceful expression, as if she had been put out of her pain, like. That's an odd thing to say, but it was my feeling."

"Yes, I understand."

They made two more turnings and came up a slight rise to meet a hedge that surrounded the front of a two-story white house. The land continued to rise about fifty yards behind it but sloped away from the road at the front, giving a long view across a high stand of grass down toward what to Rutledge appeared to be a distant line of the bay.

"That's the cottage," Constable Satterthwaite told Rutledge. "You can see how isolated it is, from the point of view of finding any witnesses. There's a farm just down this road a bit, but the owner was trying to save a sick ram, and he doesn't know if anyone passed this way or not. And just over the shoulder of the rise is where the Widow Blaine lives. Mrs. Blaine still keeps the farm but has given up running sheep and planting corn. A small dairy herd is all that's left. She's short and square, with a temper to match her red hair. If the killer had gone there, she'd have taken her broom to him. Or her." He smiled at Rutledge. "Village gossip says she's twice the man her husband was."

"And she saw nothing unusual here either."

"No, sir. She has to milk the cows twice a day, and muck out the milking barn, but she comes into Hobson once a fortnight, for whatever goods she wants. That's how she came to find the body. She stopped to ask Mrs. Teller if there was anything she needed."

"There appears to be a good bit of fallow land around the cottage. Did Mrs. Teller farm it?" They had come to a white gate set into the hedge. It led up a grassy walk to a painted door, weathered a soft rose. Rutledge drew up just past the gate.

"She hasn't since the war years. No help. Not with all the men we lost. And probably no heart for it either. She didn't need the money."

They left the motorcar and opened the gate.

Rutledge noted the sign on the front of it, with the name: SUN-RISE COTTAGE. Then he stood there, looking up at the house. It was typical of farmhouses out in this rolling country, tall and square and open to the buffeting of the wind, as if daring it to do its worst. There were no trees to shelter it and no fuss about the architecture. Guessing the age of Sunrise Cottage was nearly impossible, built as it was to withstand whatever the seasons or the years brought. A hundred years old? Fifty?

He followed the constable up the path, taking in the flowers that gave the walk and the door a little touch of color, a softness that belied what had happened here.

"There was no indication of a struggle? Or that Mrs. Teller had tried to run from her killer?"

"Nothing to tell us anything. She was just lying there, face to one side, as if she had decided to have a little nap. There wasn't much blood. She must have died very quickly."

"And no sign of the murder weapon?"

"He must have taken it with him. A walking stick? There are enough visitors in the summer on walking holidays. A hammer or tool from a motorcar?"

"If it was a summer visitor, he had his walking stick with him. If the weapon came from a motorcar or a lorry, the killer carried it to the door with him, with the intent of committing murder."

"That's very likely," Satterthwaite agreed.

They had reached the door.

"It's not locked. We never lock our doors."

"She might still be alive if she had."

The constable said, "She opened it to whoever was on the doorstep. She was never afraid out here. I've wondered, you know, if he had stopped for a drink of water or the like, and recognized her. But that would mean she had a past, and that's not in the character of Florence Teller."

"What did she do before she married?"

"She came here to live with her aunt when she was very young, and later taught school over in Thielwald. She was a good schoolmistress, by all accounts. But not two years after she'd begun teaching, she met and married Peter Teller."

"What about his family? Is there any? Is he by any chance related to the Teller family in London?"

"I wouldn't know, sir, but I doubt it. There was never anything said about family in London."

Rutledge remembered what Bowles had suggested, that this Peter was from the wrong side of the blanket.

He reached out to open the door. It swung back on its hinges quietly, without disturbing the evensong of a robin somewhere on the other side of the hedge.

"Who inherits the house?"

"Now there's a good question. I don't know who her solicitor is. We haven't come across a will."

The passage was narrow, a second door just beyond where they were standing, opening into the house itself. In this tiny hall, a small shelf of trinkets on one side faced a framed photograph of Morecambe Bay on the other. And only a small stain on the scrubbed wood flooring marked where a woman had died.

Rutledge examined the walls and the floor, even glancing at the ceiling above his head. But there were no scuff marks, nothing to show that a struggle had taken place.

"She must ha' turned to go into the ither part of the house," Hamish said.

"Her back to him," Rutledge said, too late to catch himself from answering Hamish aloud.

"Yes, very likely," Constable Satterthwaite agreed. "She might have known him, or if not, liked the look of him enough to invite him in. A good many of the university lads come walking hereabout, and some of them couldn't be much older than her Timmy would have been if he'd lived. She had a soft spot for them. We're a trusting lot, but not foolish. She wasn't afraid of him."

"A priest. A schoolboy on holiday. A woman in distress."

"I hadn't thought of it in that way," Satterthwaite admitted. "But yes."

"What's beyond this entry?"

"There are three rooms downstairs, and three bedrooms above. Her aunt lived in one of them, the boy Timmy in another. I don't think, from the look of them, that she used either room after they died."

Rutledge crossed the entry and went through the open door beyond. He could see the short passage continued, with the stairs to one side, the kitchen straight ahead, the parlor to his left, and a small dining room or sitting room to the right.

As he walked through the rooms, he found himself thinking that the parlor appeared to be frozen in time, intended for the use of guests of another generation, who never came. A settee and two chairs, a worn but handsome carpet, small tables with little treasures on them. There was another framed photograph, this time from Keswick in the Lake District, surely a souvenir of a visit. A tall blue vase intended for summer flowers took pride of place on one table, beside it a well-thumbed book of verse with no inscription. Just above the table hung a sandalwood fan in a case, spread to show the lacquered painting on parchment and the carved sticks. Handsomely embroidered pillow slips with Chinese scenes of mountains rising about a misty river set off the plainness of the dark furniture.

They were unusual pieces to find here in Hobson.

"What did her husband do before the war? Was he a farmer?"

"A career soldier. He was always sending her gifts from all over the world. I sometimes brought the packages out here, on my rounds. Her face would light up, and she'd smile as if it were her birthday."

The dining room had been turned into a sitting room cum work-room, with a tabletop easel. On it was a watercolor of a cat curled up on a windowsill. It was only half finished. There was also a book of accounts on the table, a low bookshelf of leather-bound classics by the chair that was obviously her favorite. The cushions were worn, and the padded back had taken on a comfortable shape.

The kitchen was tidy, telling Rutledge that she had not expected guests, for the teapot and the cups and saucers were in their proper places in the cupboard.

"Or ha' been washed and put away again," Hamish suggested.

The square, footed dish on the table, covered by a linen handker-chief, held honey, and there was bread in the tin box by the stone sink. Looking out at the kitchen yard, he could see that flowers and herbs grew in profusion, turning the silvery wood of the shed into a back-drop for beauty and using the rough stone foundations of what must have been the ancient barn and other outbuildings as a sheltered place to grow more delicate plants.

Upstairs the two unused rooms yielded nothing of interest. In one there were a boy's playthings in a wooden chest, an armoire, a coverlet with appliqués of animals—a cat, a dog, a duck, a sheep, and a cow—against a forest green background. The animals were cleverly sewn, with cotton wadding behind the figures to give them a three-dimensional quality. On the wall were shelves with birds' eggs, a cattail nearly gone to seed, and other small things that might catch a boy's eye, including a conch shell. In the aunt's bedroom, the bed was neatly made with a tufted coverlet and flowers embroidered on the pillow slips. The armoire, like the one in the boy's room, was empty of clothing, as if these had long since been donated where they might do more good.

Florence Teller's bedroom was equally simple. But the same hand had embroidered a picture on the wall, entitled OUR HAPPY HOME, with a house that looked remarkably like this one, save for the black door. On the bedside table was a single photograph of a small boy holding a football, his face tilted toward the photographer with a shy smile just touching his lips. A handsome child, but a frail one.

The tall oval mirror standing in the corner was the only unexpected furnishing. Crossing to look at it more closely, he thought the dark wood was either cherry or rosewood, and it was finely made. At the top of the frame was a small bouquet of roses tied by a ribbon, carved in a piece with the wood of the frame itself.

He could picture Florence Teller standing before it, admiring a new dress, smiling up at the man she'd married, pleased with the gift he'd brought her.

Hamish said, "It's no' like the rest of the furniture."

And that was true. While everything from the dining room table to the high bed frames was of good workmanship, it was from another generation, late Victorian pieces, dark and solid, the polish deep enough to reflect the light. Inherited? He thought they might have been. The sort of pieces a young couple, just at the start of their mar-

riage, might have been offered by an aunt or mother or cousin. Pieces
stored in the attic until they were needed again.

There was little of a personal nature here, and he wondered about
the sort of life this woman had led. Had her husband written to her,
his letters the high marks of her world? Although the constable
frowned in disapproval, Rutledge opened drawers but found nothing
to indicate that something was missing.

Aside from her gardening, her needlework was clearly her main interest, but as one's needle clicked in and out of the cloth, even following the most intricate pattern, what did her mind dwell on? Or as she
pulled weeds and deadheaded flowers, what occupied her thoughts
while her hands were busy?

She must have been a woman of extraordinary patience, he thought
all at once. Always waiting, like the faithful Penelope. Why had she accepted such a life? And what in the end had it brought her?

But he thought he had found the answer to her acceptance in one
small thing—there must have been a pet here at one time, something
to keep her company. A cat, a small dog for safety and for friendship? From the upstairs window he could see a little graveyard with
whitewashed headstones, four or five of them, as if over the years she
had lost her companions as well as her son, and laid them to rest in a
garden of remembrance. For around the stones grew pansies in profusion, and forget-me-nots.

He went back down the stairs, feeling depression settling over him,
and walked out to the little graveyard. Three cats, two dogs, judging
from the names painted in dark blue script on the whitewash. And one
marked only MR. G.

"Do you want to speak to the farmer?" Constable Satterthwaite
asked as Rutledge turned back to the house.

"If he was busy with a sick animal, he's probably right, he saw
nothing. What about his family?"

"His wife had gone to visit their daughter. The son is married and helps out at the farm on most days, but he walks over from where he lives." He gestured toward the distance. "On the far side of his father's land."

"Therefore, nobody from his household came this way. All right, let's speak to Mrs. Blaine. If something is missing here, we have no way of guessing what it is." But downstairs again he paused long enough to flip the pages of the books by Mrs. Teller's favorite chair, to see what might have been secreted among them. She had good taste in reading, he thought as he scanned.

Nothing but an occasional starched and embroidered bookmark fell out.

Rutledge stood in the passage for a moment, listening to the sounds of the house around him, trying to feel the presence of the woman who had spent most of her life here, and left so little of herself behind. But she was elusive, and he wished there had been a photograph of her in better times.

Then he followed Satterthwaite outside. The sky was a bright rose fading to shades of gray and lavender as the sun crept over the far horizon, and in the east the lavender deepened to purple. They closed the door on the silent house and walked back to the motorcar.

While the roof of Mrs. Blaine's farmhouse could just be seen from the Teller house, the way there was not as direct. They turned down a rutted lane and bounced along it to the house nestled in the curve of the hill.

It was very much like the one they'd just left, but the barns and outbuildings were still very much in use, and the yard was muddy with the hoof marks of cattle.

They tapped at the front door, and it opened to a small, compact woman with dark red hair and a grievance.

"There you are!" she said at once to Constable Satterthwaite, ignoring the man from London. Clutching the startled constable's arm, she dragged him toward her kitchen, all the while complaining over the earsplitting screams of something in great pain somewhere in the house. "You've got to rid me of that thing, do you hear? She told me it was thirty years old, and I can't even cook it, it'll be stringy as an old shoe. I tried to shove him out the door, but he won't leave. I can't sleep for this racket. All day, all night. There's no peace!"

Rutledge had followed them to the kitchen and saw nothing as he crossed the threshold. But he nearly backed into the passage again to save his ears from whatever was shrieking with such high-pitched horror.

Hamish, silent in the face of what could only be called a cacophony, was as speechless as Rutledge himself.

He'd heard the Irish speak of banshees, but until now he'd never given these harbingers of death much thought. He found himself remembering what old Michael Flaherty, once a jockey, had talked about in his cups. "A sound beyond any other. It tears at the soul, it wails like a lost spirit, and it can't be seen except by someone in the family."

And then something moved, and for the first time Rutledge could see the source of the incredible noise. It was a small dove gray parrot with a flash of red on its tail, and it was clinging to a plate on the top of the dresser against the far wall, almost invisible in the last rays of sunset outlining the open kitchen door. Its bright eyes were fixed on the newcomers as if expecting them to attack.

"There, you see," Mrs. Blaine said, pointing excitedly. "All day, I tell you, and all night. I don't see how she stood it. I'd shoot it if it weren't for my best Staffordshire ware. He was always sending her gifts, Lieutenant Teller was, but what possessed him to send her that thing I don't know. They can live a hundred years, she said."

Rutledge remembered the little pet graveyard, and the animals resting there. A hundred years—she would never have to weep over a lost love again. A lonely woman given something to talk to.

The parrot shrieked again. Hardly talking, as Hamish was pointing out.

"I couldn't leave it, could I?" Mrs. Blaine went on, her sense of injustice still strong. "She'd been dead for days, I could see that much, the flies on her face, and it hadn't been fed nor watered. So I took pity on it for her sake, little knowing quiet as it was, what was in store for me. I surely didn't bargain for *this*!"

Rutledge stepped into the room, moving quietly, and went to the overturned cage that was on the floor on the far side of the kitchen table. He picked it up and held it high. Tall as he was, he could bring the cage nearly to the level of the bird. And to his own astonishment, after a long moment, it stopped squawking and hopped into the open door, made for one of the swings, and sat there bobbing back and forth, plucking at the feathers of its breast.

He shut the door carefully, then reached down for the cloth covering Mrs. Blaine's kitchen table. She hurriedly caught the sugar bowl and the saltcellar before he pulled at the cloth, then lifted it over the cage, shutting the bird into darkness.

Even the frantic creaking of the swing stopped, and a blessed quiet descended over the kitchen.

"Well, I'll be damned," the constable said into the silence.

Mrs. Blaine stared from the covered cage to the man from London.

And then the bird said in a very human voice, "Good night, Peter. Wherever you may be."

In a hushed whisper, Mrs. Blaine said, "That's *her* voice. For all the world. As if she were still alive."

"You'd never heard it speak?" Rutledge asked.

"Lord, no. Never in her house and not in mine, either. He was quiet as a lamb there, and here he's done naught but to scream like a creature in pain."

"I didn't know you'd taken anything from the house—this bird," the constable was saying accusingly. "I asked if you'd touched anything."

"It's a live bird, I thought it would be like a canary. I took it out of kindness," she said, defending herself. "You're not telling me it could name her murderer!"

"No, it's just that you said—was there anything else?"

"Did she ever ask you to burn some letters for her, if something happened to her?" Rutledge asked. "Or take a photograph and post it to her late husband's family? You were her nearest neighbor, she might have confided in you," he added, though he couldn't see a strong friendship springing up between two such different women. Still, needs must, and two widows alone on isolated farms could have turned to each other to carry out last wishes.

Incensed, Mrs. Blaine said, "Look here, I never touched a thing in that house. I took pity on this creature, as I would on a stray cat. And look how it's repaid me, I ask you."

"It could have been evidence," Constable Satterthwaite pointed out, trying to keep his own temper.

"A bird's not evidence," she retorted. "I'll wring its neck and be done with it, and bury it up there in her little graveyard. See if I don't." She marched around the table toward the cage.

Rutledge said, "Constable—"

"I've got a cat," he said, as if that absolved him of all responsibility.

Rutledge stepped forward. He could hear Hamish. It was clear that the voice in his head was trying to tell him something, but he reached for the cage and said, "I'll take possession of it. The bird may not have seen who killed her, or watched if the killer searched the house. But until we know differently, it's a ward of the court."

Constable Satterthwaite turned to him as if he'd taken leave of his mind.

Mrs. Blaine said, "Ward or not, I'll thank you to remove it from my house."

"Did she have any enemies? Anyone who had had a falling-out with her, anyone who might have held a grudge against her?" he asked, gingerly lifting the bird—cage, cloth, and all.

"I'll have my tablecloth back," she told him. "As for enemies, you might as well ask if I have any. She wasn't the sort to make people angry. She never asked for much, and it was just as well, she was never given much in this life but great sorrows to bear. She had nothing to steal, though she never lacked for what she needed. It was people who'd failed her. And I can't think why anyone would have wished to see her dead."

Rutledge looked around the kitchen and saw nothing he could use to cover the bird. He set the cage down again and took off his coat, wrapping it around the cage in place of the tablecloth. The bird had his head tucked under his wing, and hardly stirred.

"You're a right fool," Mrs. Blaine said to Rutledge as he handed her the tablecloth, "but I'll thank you all the same for ridding my house of this nuisance."

"What can you tell us about Mrs. Teller's husband?" he asked.

"Only that he never came back from the war. They said there was a collection being taken up in London for a monument to the men gone missing. I've no doubt Lieutenant Teller's name will be on it. I asked her if she was going to make a contribution, but she said that would be like walking over his grave. As long as she held him to be alive, he was. Though in the last months, I think even she had begun to give up all hope. She painted that door red to welcome him, and she'd set a dress aside for the day. Well, if he's in heaven, she's found him now and is at peace."

She walked with them to the door. "She told me once that she'd read a story about a man who had gone on the crusades, and he lost his memory, and it was years before he came home again. She asked if I thought it was a true story. And I told her I did, because I couldn't say, could I, that some writer had made it up out of whole cloth to make women readers cry. I was never one for that sort of thing myself."

"If you can think of anything that would be helpful," Constable Satterthwaite told her, "you'll let me know, first thing?"

"I will. And I'm locking my door at night, and bringing in the dog. I don't want to be found dead like she was. How long do you think she lay there? It was a cruel thing to do, kill her and leave her to the flies."

They thanked her and left. For a second, Rutledge didn't know what to do with the bird, standing there looking at the motorcar and unwilling to put it on the floor by what would be Hamish's feet. But the constable took it from him and set it there, saying, "Here's a travel rug. Shall I put it around the cage instead of your coat?"

"Oh—yes, thank you." Rutledge took his coat back and pulled it on as he opened the door of the driver's side.

As the constable cranked the motorcar, he said to Rutledge, "What will you do with that thing? You can't be serious about taking it to London."

"Why not?" Rutledge asked. "For the time being at least. Who knows what else it might say."

"Aye, and I'd give much to see the judge's face when you offer a parrot in evidence."

Rutledge laughed. "What matters is whether or not someone else thinks the bird can talk. That could be interesting."

The motor caught, and the constable got in. All color had gone from the sky now, and the first stars were growing brighter. "Shall we go and see the body, sir? I think the doctor would like it released as soon as possible for burial."

"Released to whom?" Rutledge asked. "There's no family. You said as much yourself."

"What else are we to do? I'll be there. And some of the village women, no doubt. She won't be put in the ground without someone by her."

They drove through the dark streets of Thielwald, light from house windows making bright patches on the road. Satterthwaite pointed out the doctor's surgery, and they knocked at the door. Dr. Blake answered the summons himself, nodding to Rutledge and saying to the constable, "Another five minutes and I'd have gone up to my bed. But I'm glad you've come. Any word on her killer?" He was a short man, graying at the temples, perhaps fifty-five, with pale, heavy-lidded eyes.

"No, sir. But this is Inspector Rutledge from Scotland Yard. He'll be looking into her death."

Dr. Blake took them back to the room where Florence Teller was being kept, and lighted the lamps. He carried one to the sheet-draped figure and held it high so that Rutledge could see her clearly.

In the flickering light, Rutledge studied the body. A slim, trim woman of perhaps forty, he thought, older than the Teller wives he'd just dealt with. The doctor was pointing out the location of the wound, but Rutledge only half heard him, seeing the look of peace that Constable Satterthwaite had spoken of. With the lines that sorrow had put in her face smoothed away, she looked young again.

"Is there anything more you can tell me?" Rutledge asked.

"I'm afraid not. That one blow on the back of the head, near the base of the skull, was enough. I should think the killer was right-handed, considering the direction of the blow, and possibly on a level with her, rather than shorter or taller. And he was either very strong or very angry. No one interfered with her, no one moved the body from where it fell. There were no other wounds." He shook his head. "A tragedy. I knew her," he added to Rutledge. "She was seldom ill, but her son was my patient. He had measles when he was very young and never fully recovered. He died of typhoid fever, and I thought she would go mad with grief. There was nothing I could do. There are times when I curse my profession for its ignorance."

After a few more questions and a promise to release the body for burial, they thanked him and left.

Rutledge drove the constable back to Hobson and asked where he might spend the night. There was no hotel in the little town, and after the long day of driving, the thought of going another ten miles or more to find lodging was daunting.

The constable sent him to the house of a Mrs. Greeley, who sometimes took in summer walkers. The room was at the back of the house, and as she led him there, she said, "I was just putting the kettle on for my tea. There's bread and butter, creamed eggs, and some slices of ham, if you'd care for it."

He thanked her and offered to pay for the meal as well as the room. She accepted his offer, and he could tell that she was pleased to have the money.

She insisted on serving him at the small table in her sitting room, though he was perfectly willing to sit in her kitchen. But Mrs. Greeley was agreeable to talking as she laid out his cutlery and brought in a soup that she had made with beans from a tin and bits of bacon.

"Did you know Mrs. Teller very well?" he asked, after complimenting her on the soup.

"None of us knew her really well," she said. "She was a quiet sort, kept to herself. I remember she met the lieutenant in Morecambe, where she had gone for a few days by the sea after a chest cough lingered beyond the winter. He was on a walking tour, but he came back later in the summer and called on her. Then back again he came before the end of October. I could tell she liked him. And he was very taken with her. They were married two years later. He liked the Army, he said. It gave him the opportunity to travel. But he couldn't take her with him. Not then, and later, with the boy being sickly, he never wanted to take her to his postings. I always thought she must be very lonely, out there on the West Road, as they called it then. But she seemed to be happy there."

Over the flan, he asked if she could think of anyone who held a grudge against Mrs. Teller.

"Her? Never. She wasn't one to attract trouble, if you know what I mean. I don't know what's got into folks these days. The war changed everything, didn't it? People could live anywhere and be safe, no one would think of any harm coming to them. I've taken in strangers, young men on holiday, and never feared for my life."

"I understand she painted her door red to welcome her husband back from the war."

"It was a seven days' wonder, that red door. Everyone found an excuse to walk out that way, just to see it. Afterward, when he didn't come home, I thought it must be a daily reminder of her loss. But she wouldn't hear of having it painted something else. I even offered one of the lads who stayed with me. He'd caught himself a chill, and was at his wits' end for something to do until he could move on. He would have painted it any color she liked."

He waited until she had gone to bed before bringing the bird in and settling it in a corner of his room. He gave it some sunflower seeds he'd seen in Mrs. Greeley's kitchen and filled up its water bowl. And then as he covered it again, it said softly, "Good night, Peter. Wherever you may be."

19

The next morning Rutledge could hear the parrot mumbling to itself, and so could Mrs. Greeley.

"I see you've got Jake. Lord, I'd forgotten all about that poor bird, or I'd have gone up myself to see to him."

"I understand Mrs. Teller's husband brought him to her on one of his leaves."

"He did, and I could have laughed myself silly when I heard Florence say Jake could speak. I didn't believe a word of it; he was silent as the grave whenever I called. They say it's possible to teach a magpie to speak, but I don't believe that either. All the same, Jake was company for her, and that's what mattered. She'd just lost Callie Sue, her cat, when Jake arrived, and I was glad she had something to take her mind off her loss. Callie Sue had been Timmy's cat, you see."

Rutledge left the parrot to Mrs. Greeley's tender care—she appeared to know what the bird ate—and spent the morning walking around the village, asking residents about Mrs. Teller. But most of the answers to his questions were a variation on what he'd already learned from Mrs. Blaine, the constable, and Mrs. Greeley. And no one could offer any explanation for her murder. When they spoke of Peter Teller, it was with warmth, but it was also clear that they had never quite felt he was one of them. For one thing, he'd never been in Hobson long enough to put down deep roots.

The ironmonger, Mr. Taylor, told Rutledge, "When he came in for this or that bit of hardware for the house or outbuildings, he talked about Dorset more often than not. That's where he lived before he went into the Army."

"Did he say anything to you about his family—brothers—sisters?"

"Not directly, no, though when Timmy was born, he told me he hoped the boy wouldn't be an only child, as he was."

"What did his father do? Was he in the Army as well?"

"His father was a rector, and Teller mentioned that he'd regretted it all his life. That he'd have been an Army man if the choice had been his. Like his son."

Sam Jordan, the man who owned what was the closest thing to a pub that Hobson possessed, could add very little more to what Rutledge already knew. But he made one remark in passing that was helpful.

"I'd ask him sometimes about his regiment and where he was stationed. I never got a clear answer to that. I expect on leave he didn't want to think about going back. Then Jack Blaine said he thought Teller was in the Buffs. Florence told my wife he was in a Hampshire regiment."

"Did he come home on leave during the war?"

"As I remember, he didn't. Well, it's a long way from London, and the trains were carrying troops and the wounded. My own boy came to London twice, and there was no way to travel down to see him. Upset my wife no end."

Mrs. Greeley's neighbor commented that Teller had brought her a box of cherries from the tree that grew out beyond the Teller barn, and she had made preserves with the last of her sugar. "I wasn't to know the war was coming and we'd see no more. I sent a bottle up to Mrs. Teller—I sometimes did the heavy washing for her when Mr. Teller was at home—and she said they were the best cherry preserves she'd ever tasted. I remember it as if it were yesterday, her standing there in her doorway, praising my preserves, and then the Jordan boy come up on his bicycle to say we were at war. Mr. Teller came to the door and said, 'It will be over by Christmas.' But it wasn't, was it? Nor for four more Christmases to come. I asked Mr. Teller if he must join his regiment straightaway. And Mrs. Teller, poor thing, looked as if I'd struck her. Her face went all white, then flushed, as if she was about to cry. It was the last time I saw him. Two days later and he was gone at first light, to make the train."

Mr. Kerr, the curate of the small church, told Rutledge, "He never came to services, which I thought was sad. Not even after Timmy died. But Florence was here every Sunday until near the end of the war. I think she must have had a feeling, you know—a premonition—that he wasn't coming back." The curate rubbed his bald head thoughtfully. "Of course, I talked to Mr. Teller whenever I saw him in Hobson. And I wondered if he'd lost his faith. Soldiers do, sometimes, you know."

Rutledge understood that all too well.

The curate added with a smile, "Of course, attending services here at St. Bart's was never compulsory."

Rutledge found he was learning as much about Peter Teller as he was about the man's widow. She was well liked, people had known her as a child and accepted her as one of their own. But her husband apparently had kept to himself when he was in Hobson, making very little effort to fit into his wife's social life. Which of course had made the local people more curious about him than they would have been if he'd attended church services and spent an evening in the pub. It was in a way very selfish.

Hamish said, "Selfish? Or secretive?"

Or perhaps Peter Teller—like Chief Superintendent Bowles—

felt he was a cut above the local people, unwilling to sink to their level?

Then why had he chosen to live here? He didn't make his living in Hobson, he was free to go. Or was it his wife's choice, because he was away so often and she preferred familiar surroundings to Dorset or London?

A little silence had fallen. Rutledge said, "I'm curious about Teller's background. Did you marry them? Did any of his family come to Hobson for the ceremony?"

"It was my predecessor who officiated. I wouldn't know who was or wasn't among the guests, or who stood up for him."

"What attracted Peter Teller to Florence Marshall? Was it money, do you think?"

"You never met Florence. There was something about her that drew people to her. As for money, she'd inherited from her aunt, and I understood that Peter's late father had left him well-to-do. It was never an issue, as far as I know."

"Can we find the date of their marriage in the church records?"

"I needn't consult them. They were married in the early spring of 1903. My sister was married in May of that same year. In 1913, when I happened to mention to Mrs. Teller that I was taking a few days to go and celebrate Katie and Ralph's tenth anniversary, she told me it was her tenth as well. I brought her a small gift from Katie, on my return. She was that pleased. I don't believe her husband was here to mark the occasion. A pity."

Rutledge, walking back to the High Street, paused at the Great War Memorial just at the turning into Church Lane. He always spared a moment to acknowledge the dead. The Hobson men who had gone off to fight had served together. It was a common practice, for these men who had never been as far as Carlisle or Chester, much less London, felt more comfortable in one another's company. And consequently, they often died together.

He could see that it was the case here. For every surname there was a list of Christian names. Under Satterthwaite he saw three, and under Greeley five. There was a Taylor, a Blaine, and two Jordans. He could see them in his mind's eye, marching together out of Hobson to find the nearest recruitment office, then returning together in new uniforms where the crease was still sharp and their caps sat at a jaunty angle. Off to kill the Hun . . . And die themselves, whether they shot a Hun or not.

He was turning away when the elderly man walking past stopped to speak to him. Although graying and distinguished, with a trim white mustache, his shoulders were beginning to stoop with age. His voice was educated and strong, without the heavy local accent.

"That's from the fields," he said, using the tip of his cane to point to the irregular stone some three feet high that was the centerpiece of the memorial. "We thought that fitting. They came from this land, and many of them never returned to it. And so they still have a part of it."

"Yes, it's moving," Rutledge answered.

The man lowered his cane to marble tablets encircling the stone. "My sons are there, both of them. My nephews too." The cane moved on to point to the name of Cobb, and the long list beneath it. "My elder son, Browning, and his brother, Tennyson. A schoolmaster's folly, those names. I come by every morning to greet them and every evening to say good night."

"It's a quiet place to be remembered."

"You served in the war?"

"France. The Somme."

"You saw some of the worst fighting. Though I daresay none of it was better than any other."

Rutledge could only nod.

"You're here, I think, because of Mrs. Teller. A sad thing. There's no one in Hobson who would have hurt her. I can't think why a stranger might."

"No one has been able to offer the police any useful information.

Yet I've discovered in places barely as large as Hobson that grudges can run deep. And in the end, they often surface in violence."

Cobb shook his head. "I repeat. Not here."

"Apparently her husband was with his regiment more often than he was here in Hobson," Rutledge said, changing the subject. "It must have been a lonely life for her. Waiting for him to return. And not knowing, throughout the war, if he would."

"She was orphaned as a child and brought up by an elderly aunt. Well meaning, of course, but not precisely accustomed to children and their needs. I expect that's why Florence became a teacher, to surround herself with children. But they weren't hers, were they? They went home every day to their own families. It was on the first holiday she'd taken from teaching that she met Peter Teller and fell in love. I don't believe she had high expectations of it turning into something more. Not from the start, knowing he was in the Army."

"Did you meet Teller, talk to him?"

"I'd see him on occasion on the High Street. He didn't frequent the pub and he wasn't gregarious. But I found myself thinking sometimes that he was a tormented man. I don't know precisely why—he was a cheerful sort in a brief conversation about the weather, where he'd be serving next, or what plans he might have for his son's education. Alas, Timmy died young. It was a devastating blow to both parents. As you'd expect. No one should have to endure such tragedy."

Hamish said, "He speaks for himsel'."

"Was Teller eager to see his son follow him into the Army?"

"Not at all. In fact, he told me once that the only bright spot in the coming war was that Timmy would never have to go off and fight. A war to end all wars, they claimed. But it will be forgotten in a generation, and there will be another."

And then Cobb hesitated. "Perhaps I should tell you. My nephew, Lawrence Cobb, worked on Mrs. Teller's farm when she needed help. He was glad to do it. I think he'd have married her if word had come that Teller had been killed. But of course he was missing, and that's very different."

"Was she in love with your nephew?"

"No. Loneliness might have, in the end, brought them together. But it was not to be. Lawrence married Mrs. Blaine's daughter instead. Only last year."

"I'd like to speak to Lawrence," Rutledge said. "If you'll give me your nephew's direction?"

Cobb did, after a moment's hesitation.

Hamish said, "He's no' pleased now. He wishes he hadna' telt ye about his nephew."

Rutledge thanked him, and Cobb nodded, then walked on without looking back, leaning heavily on his cane.

Rutledge drove out of Hobson to the northwest, and after two false starts he found the farm where Lawrence Cobb lived.

A man was in the barn, working on a steam tractor. Rutledge could hear the clang of a hammer on metal. He walked back there, and as he came through the door, the man yelled, "Damn!" and began to suck his thumb where the hammer had struck a glancing blow.

"Lawrence Cobb?" Rutledge asked, and identified himself when the man nodded. "I've come from Hobson. Your uncle suggested I might speak to you about Florence Teller."

Suddenly wary, Cobb set down his hammer, glanced briefly at his bruised thumb, and then said, "You're here about her death. Well, I had nothing to do with it, but if I ever lay hands on the bastard who did it, I'll finish with him before the police can touch him."

"Do you still care that much for Florence Teller?"

Cobb shot a look toward the house. "What if I do? She was married, I couldn't speak to her. It came to nothing. She guessed what I was feeling, and we decided it was best that I move on. I did. My wife and I are happy."

But Rutledge thought it was not true. Content, perhaps, but at least on Cobb's part, not happy.

"Do you know who might have wanted to kill her?"

"No one in Hobson. I'd have torn out their throats if anyone touched her. I think if it hadn't been for Timmy, she might have turned to me when Teller went missing. But she loved her son, and she loved his father. Never mind how he treated her."

"What do you mean, treated her?"

"If I'd had a wife like that, I wouldn't have stayed away so many years at a time. I'd have written more often. He sent gifts, but it wasn't the same as being there. After Timmy died, she needed him more than ever. But I think coming here hurt too much, and his visits got fewer and farther between. Or so it seemed to me."

"There were letters?"

"She kept them in a little rosewood chest on the table beside her favorite chair. When I was working there and came in for a cup of tea or mug of water, I sometimes saw her putting one away, as if she'd just read it again. Her lifeline, she called that chest."

But there had been no such chest by the chair nor anywhere else in the house, as Hamish was remarking.

"You worked for her as a handyman, when you might have done far better for yourself," Rutledge told him.

"My mother left me her money. And I'd have wanted to be there, helping out, rather than in some position in Carlisle or Chester where I couldn't see her every day. I'm not ashamed that I loved her. But I'll thank you not to pass that on to my wife. Betsy is jealous. I found that out too late." He picked up the hammer and struck the frozen nut around a screw. This time the blow broke the rusty bond that had locked the two together, and he could spin the nut. "How can you be so wrong about a woman's smile? But I was lonely, and I wanted a son. I've not had even him yet."

Hamish said, "Ye ken, he was more likely to kill his ain wife than the lass in the cottage."

Rutledge had got the same feeling. He thanked Lawrence Cobb and left. But not before Cobb said, "I'll tell you this, and then deny I ever said it. But it's crossed my mind a time or two since I heard Florence was dead. It's possible her husband didn't want her anymore, that he'd met someone else he wanted to marry, and he couldn't find a decent way out of his dilemma. And so he killed her. Ask Jake. He might know."

But how did you ask a parrot about a murder?

Rutledge reported his conversations to Constable Satterthwaite, who said, "I expect that tallies with what I've been told. It's sad that Lawrence Cobb couldn't have married her. He would have done his best to make her happy."

"And you don't think he might have come to her, been turned away, and lashed out? He's a strong man. I found him working on his tractor and wielding his hammer with some force. An angry force."

But Satterthwaite shook his head. "I've known Lawrence since he was a boy. And I'll tell you this, if he killed her, he wouldn't have left her there in the doorway for anyone to find. Well. We've got word out for people to watch for a walker. That may be our only hope now. If he didn't get the wind up and leave this part of the country."

"Why would a walker kill her?" he asked for the second time.

"That's puzzled me too, but I'm used to puzzles and answers that make no more sense than the puzzle did. Unless of course he was here on purpose, to take that chest of letters. And she caught him at it. That makes a certain sense, now."

"Why would he want to steal old letters? It's a matter of record that they were married, she and Teller. At the church."

Satterthwaite laughed. "When it comes to money, people change. It's amazing how quickly distant relatives come out of the woodwork when someone dies, wanting their share. Never gave the poor soul the time of day when he was alive, but now he's dead, he's their dearest cousin, however many times removed. They arrive to present their case. Then they stumble over a wife in some dark corner of Lancashire, and something has to be done about her, doesn't it? For all we know, Peter Teller's last will and testament was among those letters, and someone wanted it destroyed. That'ud toss the cat amongst the pigeons, wouldn't it?"

An interesting explanation for the missing letters as well as the murder. "Is the farm all that valuable?"

"The farm is hers, not his. But how do we know what else he might have owned elsewhere that was valuable? Florence might not have been told about that. Or never wanted to face up to the fact that he was dead and the will ought to be taken to a solicitor. She had everything she needed right here."

It was possible, but a stretch of the imagination. Still, Rutledge found himself considering it again over his dinner, losing track of Mrs. Greeley's gossip.

He stayed one more night with Mrs. Greeley, and then left early to make the journey back to London.

Speaking to Satterthwaite the night before his departure, he said, "I want to see if I can find Teller's relatives. They may be able to shed more light on who inherits. Did Florence Teller have a solicitor?"

"She never had cause to need one," the constable told him. "As far as I know."

"Then perhaps Peter Teller did. Meanwhile, if you find any information on a walker, call me at the Yard. If I'm not there, ask for Sergeant Gibson."

On the drive south, the bird Jake, in the cage set in the passenger's seat, was quiet, almost, Rutledge thought, as if he understood he would never go back to Sunrise Cottage. He sat on one of his perches, sometimes plucking listlessly at his feathers, occasionally muttering to himself, and showing no interest in his surroundings.

Rutledge spoke to him from time to time, as he would have spoken to a dog traveling with him. But except for that one moment in Mrs. Blaine's kitchen and again when the rug was put over the cage last night, he'd said nothing remotely resembling human speech.

Hamish said, "He remembers what he hears o'er and o'er again."

And that was just as sad.

Arriving in London, Rutledge stopped at the Yard and handed the cage and parrot to a startled Sergeant Gibson. "Find out what to feed him, and see that he's kept quiet until I come back for him."

"What to feed him?" the sergeant repeated. "I don't know anyone who has a parrot."

"Try the zoo," Rutledge suggested. "And look to see if we have any information on a Peter Teller, other than the one related to Walter Teller." And he was gone.

Traveling through Dorset in search of Peter Teller's family would take time. But there was a possible shortcut. Edwin Teller might know of a connection there, a distant cousin or an unrelated family of the same name.

It was late in the evening when Rutledge found himself in Marlborough Street, drawing up in front of the Teller residence.

The house, white and three storied, stood among others very like it, a street speaking of old money and long bloodlines. It was quiet, almost no one about, and Rutledge was prepared to find that it was too late for him to speak to anyone.

He lifted the brass knocker and let it fall.

The maid who opened the door informed him that Mr. Teller had left for the country.

"And Mrs. Teller?"

"She accompanied him."

"Will you tell him on his return that Inspector Rutledge from Scotland Yard has called, and I'd like to speak to him at his earliest convenience."

Uncertain, she said, "You may call on Mrs. Teller in the morning. If it's important?"

"I thought she was in the country as well."

"This Mrs. Teller is Mr. Edwin Teller's grandmother."

"Then I'll speak to her tonight, if I may."

"I'll inquire, sir."

The maid returned very quickly and showed him into the parlor overlooking the street.

The woman sitting there in a brocade-covered chair looked up as he came into the room. Her hair was completely white, her face deeply lined, but her blue eyes swept him as she greeted him with a smile. "You're the handsome young man who just passed my window."

"My apologies, Mrs. Teller, for the lateness of my call. I've just returned to London, and this is a matter of some urgency."

"I'm told you're from Scotland Yard."

"Yes, that's true." He realized she was the woman in the portrait in Captain Teller's house.

"You haven't come to tell me that Walter is missing again, have you? It's really entirely too much. I've been in the country visiting, and I arrived here to find everything at sixes and sevens. In fact, I'm hardly in the door before Edwin and Amy were out of it on their way to Essex."

"As far as I know, Mr. Teller is with his wife and son, recovering."

"Recovering from what, I'd like to know? Nice people don't disappear without a word and upset the entire family. I hardly knew what to say to George when I was asked to stay a week longer with him. It was thoughtless of Walter, that's all I have to say. Do sit down, young man. You're quite tall, and it hurts my neck to look up at you."

He took the chair across from hers.

"Now tell me why you are here, if it isn't Walter you're looking for."

"I'm here to ask about another member of the family. I'm aware that you have a grandson called Peter, but I wonder if perhaps you have a nephew by the same name."

"Not that I know of. Why should I?"

"We're trying to find a Lieutenant Peter Teller who served in France, and was reported missing around the end of the war."

"Our Peter did come home. He was a captain, you know."

"The Peter Teller I'm looking for apparently came from Dorset, although he lived in Lancashire after his marriage. His wife's name was Florence."

"What is this catechism in aid of?" she demanded irritably. "I don't care to be questioned in this way."

"We are trying to locate members of Lieutenant Teller's family."

"Peter's wife was a Darley before her marriage. Susannah Darley. My grandniece."

"Yes, I understand that. How long have they been married?"

She frowned. "I'm not quite sure. Twelve years? Yes, that sounds about right. Now, young man, I've answered your questions. You must answer mine."

"Willingly," he told her.

"Did you know that my grandson Walter went missing?"

They had already spoken of that. But he humored her. "Yes. I was at the clinic shortly after he returned."

"Then explain to me, if you will, why he disappeared. It's bothering me, and no one will satisfy my curiosity. It's not something our family does, you know. Causing a scandal. It was really selfish of Walter, in my view. I wish I could understand it."

"Perhaps you should ask him," Rutledge answered gently. "The police were pleased that he was safe and unharmed. Now I'm trying to find one Peter Teller, whose wife Florence lived in Lancashire."

"Is he missing as well? Such a pity. When did he go missing?"

"I'm told he never returned from the war."

"How sad. Walter was in the war, of course. A chaplain. Peter was with the Army, and he still has shrapnel in his hip and leg. Nearly died of his wounds. Edwin couldn't be in the fighting, of course, but he was in charge of shipping and materiel. I couldn't sleep at night, worrying about Peter. And then the Zeppelins came, and I was sent to the country to stay with George and Annie. But I still couldn't sleep."

Hamish said, "She doesna' ken what you're asking."

Rutledge asked, "Who are George and Annie?"

"George Darley is my sister Evelyn's grandson. Susannah's brother.

Annie is his wife. Evelyn and I were twins. I still miss her terribly. They say that twins do."

Another thread that went nowhere.

"When was Peter wounded?"

"The spring before the Armistice. I remember that well. The eleventh hour of the eleventh day of the eleventh month. The Germans must have chosen that. It's very like them. They have quite orderly minds, you know. We still observe two minutes of silence on that date."

"Does Peter have a namesake in the family?"

"Oh, no, dear. Walter's son is named for his great-grandfather. My husband."

Rutledge found himself at a loss.

"Of course, my husband's grandfather was the black sheep in the family. He killed three men in duels and had to flee to the Continent for several years. My mother-in-law told me that it was feared he'd come home with an Italian wife, because he appeared to spend so much time in Venice. But in the end, he was sensible and married a girl from Dorset. Quite a good family too. Everyone was amazed that she'd accept the proposal of such a scoundrel."

"Then the connection with Dorset was on your mother-in-law's side, not the Tellers?"

"Didn't I just tell you? You must pay attention, young man. My husband's people were from Essex."

"Thank you for your help, Mrs. Teller," he said, rising. "I apologize again for disturbing you at this late hour."

"But you haven't had your tea, my boy. Surely you'll stay for tea?" She reached for the small silver bell by her chair. "I like having someone call on me. Not many people do, these days. And Evelyn is dead, you know. I miss her so."

The maid appeared at the door.

"Could we have tea, do you think?" Mrs. Teller asked, turning to speak to her.

"It's late," Rutledge said. "I was just on the point of leaving."

The old woman's face clouded. "Must you go? It's lovely to have a guest for tea, and Rose was just on the point of bringing it in, weren't you, my dear?"

She came forward and said to Mrs. Teller, "Of course I'll bring it, but wouldn't you prefer a nice warm bath first, and then your tea? There's a flan left from your dinner."

Rutledge forgotten, the old woman got to her feet and said, "That sounds quite nice. Thank you, dear." She followed Rose to the door.

Rutledge said quietly to the maid, "I'll see myself out."

Suddenly aware of him again, Mrs. Teller turned and said, "You were asking about Peter, weren't you? How odd. It was Walter who was missing, I'm sure of that. Peter went looking for Walter, you know. All of them did. They must have been out of their minds with worry. I can't think what Walter might have done that was scandalous. He was a missionary, you know. My son was wrong, choosing professions for *his* sons. Peter was never right for the Army, and Edwin hated taking over the estate. He let Walter have the use of the house and spent his time in London. Walter protested, saying that his congregation in West Africa didn't live so grandly. But Jenny loved it, and he gave in. Walter wasn't suited to the church, he never had a true calling, if you ask me. I heard him say once that he'd seen such shocking things his very soul was scarred. A dreadful thing for a man of God to say, don't you think? If Walter could have escaped from that life, I think he would have. But like his brothers, he was a dutiful son. I find that very sad. Of course Leticia never minded anyone. She went her own way from childhood. I never trusted her. I don't know why. She had no smooth edges. Only sharp ones. I expect that's why she's never married. I'm rather tired now. Thank you for coming. We'll visit again another day, I hope. It's been very pleasant."

And she walked out of the room with the maid and never looked back.

20

An old woman on the verge of senility had told him more about the Teller family than she'd realized. Driving to his flat, Rutledge considered the small pieces of information she'd supplied.

That the family had connections to Dorset, though not in the Teller line. That there was no other member in the extended Teller family by the name of Peter. That her son—the father of three sons—had chosen their professions—and the school for his grandson as well.

These were echoes of what Rutledge had heard in Lancashire.

Florence's husband had claimed his family was from Dorset. That his father had chosen his profession for him. He'd also claimed to be an only child—but that could have been the reason given for never taking his bride south to meet his family and never being visited in turn by anyone from Dorset.

Hamish said, "Captain Teller has a wife."

"So he does. And he wasn't always a captain. I'll have a word with him in the morning."

Undressing for bed, Rutledge stood by his window where a very faint breeze was stirring. The day had been hot, nearly breathlessly so.

Chief Superintendent Bowles was likely to have an apoplexy if he was presented with a possibility of bigamy in the Teller family.

It was nine o'clock when Rutledge reached Bolingbroke Street and knocked on the door of Peter Teller's house.

The housemaid who had admitted him before took him this time to the study and left him to stare at the books lining the walls as hunting trophies stared back with glassy eyes. Even though it was a warm day, the doors into the garden were closed.

Peter Teller came in shortly afterward, and Rutledge noted that he was sober, although he looked very tired. And he was limping heavily, walking without crutches or cane. He regarded Rutledge with a mixture of surprise and apprehension but said only, "Don't tell me my tiresome brother has gone missing again?"

"As far as I know, he's in Essex and safe as houses. No, I've come to speak to you this time. About a murder in Lancashire."

There was a sudden strain in Peter Teller's face. "I don't know why anything in Lancashire should concern me. Certainly not a murder."

"The interesting thing is that the victim was married to a Peter Teller."

Teller's lips tightened. "I'm sure she was. But she was not married to me."

"Are you aware of another Peter Teller in your family?"

"Are you aware of all the Rutledges in England who may or may not be related to you?" he countered.

"I have only to match the dates of your leaves with your namesake's appearances in Hobson. It may take some time, but it can be done."

"Then come back and talk to me when you've done that."

Rutledge considered the man. Was it bluster, or was he speaking the truth? If he had to guess, it was a little of both. The question was, where did the truth end and the lies begin?

Hamish said in Rutledge's ear, "And who in Lancashire will remember the exact dates?"

In truth, someone had removed the letters that might go a long way toward proving those dates.

Perhaps it wasn't a matter of inheritance after all, but of a man's handwriting.

But why kill Florence Teller now, when the secret had been kept safe all these years?

"Don't stare at me like that," Teller said irritably. "I don't even know who you're talking about. Pray, who is this woman I'm said to have married?"

"Florence Teller, née Marshall."

"And she married a Peter Teller."

"Lieutenant Peter Teller. A career Army officer who was posted all over the empire at various times. As, I believe, you were."

"My grandfather—you have only to ask my grandmother—was a man who liked women. How do I know that your Lieutenant Peter Teller isn't one of his bastards?"

"I did speak to your grandmother. Last night. It appears her side of the family came from Dorset, not the Tellers. They were an Essex family. As your brother is now."

That shook Teller. "Indeed." He strove to recover and said, "You had no business speaking to my grandmother without Edwin or I being in attendance. Her mind is slipping."

"It was clear enough on the important issue, last night."

"You're barking up the wrong tree, Rutledge."

"I daresay we could compare the handwriting where that Peter Teller signed the church register to yours. There's your desk, if you care to write a brief sample for me. And then I'll take my leave."

"I'm writing down nothing. I'll speak to my solicitor about this business. We'll see what he has to say. Because I'm innocent, you know. And I won't be dragged into another man's folly, just because I share a similar name."

He gestured to the door. "I think you ought to leave now. I've made my position clear. There's nothing more to discuss."

Rutledge left. But as he was shutting the door, he glanced back into the study.

Peter Teller was dragging his bad leg in the direction of the whisky decanter on a tray by the desk.

I f Peter Teller was at home, the chances were his brother Edwin had returned as well.

Rutledge left his motorcar outside the Captain's house in Bolingbroke Street and walked the short distance to Marlborough Street.

Amy Teller was at her door, just bidding a woman good-bye. She was on the point of shutting the door after her guest, when she happened to see Rutledge coming toward her down the pavement.

She froze, uncertain what to do, and finally as the motorcar with her guest inside drove away, she called to him, "I didn't expect to see you again, Inspector. What have we done now?"

He smiled. He'd had time to do some thinking on his walk, and he said, "I hope, nothing. No, it's information I'm after." He'd reached the steps to the house door, and she moved aside to let him enter the cool hall.

"There's been a murder," he began and watched her eyes widen at the words. "No one you know, I shouldn't think. But she happened to be married to a Peter Teller, who died in the war. We're in search of any family he might have had, here in London or perhaps in Dorset."

"Edwin has cousins in Dorset. On his mother's side." She hesitated. "Does— Was the murder in Dorset?"

"No. The dead woman's name was Florence Teller. She lived in Lancashire." He watched her face and then said, "There's the matter of a will. We can't seem to locate one, and it's rather important that we do. We need to know her wishes in regard to her burial as well as the disposition of her property. That could lead us to her murderer."

"You'd better come into the sitting room," she told him and led the way to a small, very feminine parlor with a desk and several comfortable chairs. "You think her husband's family might have killed her for her property?" she went on when they were seated.

"We won't know, will we, until we find the will and contact them."

"What about her own famiy?"

"Sadly she had none."

"And—and there were no children to the marriage?"

"A son," he said, and she bit her lip.

"Doesn't he know where the will might be?"

"We have no way of asking him that."

"He wasn't—was he harmed when his mother was killed?"

"He wasn't in the house at the time."

She nodded. "Of course you would need to find her will. But I'm afraid I don't know any other Peter Teller. Which doesn't mean there isn't one. Or half a dozen of them for that matter."

"We wondered—forgive me, but the police must consider all possibilities—if perhaps this Peter Teller was not an—er—recognized member of the family."

Amy stared at him. "Are you suggesting that my husband—or his brothers—might have a child out of wedlock? But you met Edwin, and he's the eldest. It's not possible that he could have had a child old enough to serve in the war." She was deliberately misconstruing his words.

"It would have been his father, I should think," he corrected her patiently.

She laughed outright. "You never met the man. I could believe Edwin had an affair before I could see his father with another woman."

"You knew the man when he was older and had grown children. You can't judge what he might or might not have done as a young man. These things happen in the best families."

Amy shook her head. "He could have matched Prince Albert in rectitude," she told him, and then suddenly seemed to realize that she had closed a door that the police were willing to walk through. Rutledge could almost read her thoughts as they flicked across her face. And he wasn't surprised when after a moment she said, "Of course, you're right. I can't say with certainty."

"Perhaps your grandmother might be in a position to know."

"*Gran?*" she all but squeaked in her astonishment. "But she's—I mean to say, you couldn't possibly expect a woman of her age and her diminished mental capacity to remember something like that."

She was right. But then, as if to prove her wrong after all, the sitting room door opened, and the elder Mrs. Teller stepped in, her face anxious.

"Amy, dear, has that awful woman gone—" She stopped, frowned, and then said, "Oh. It's that handsome young man I was telling Edwin about. The one who came to call last evening." Crossing the room with the aplomb of a duchess, she held out her hand. "How nice of you to come again."

Amy said, "Gran . . ."

But Mrs. Teller was seating herself in the chair next to Rutledge and saying, "Are you staying for luncheon, Mr. . . ." Her voice trailed off, and her eyes were suddenly filled with tears. "I am so sorry. I can't recall your name. I have troubles with names sometimes. It's a terrible affliction, getting old."

"Rutledge, Ian Rutledge," he told her, omitting his title.

"Ah yes, Mr. Rutledge." She smiled, the tears vanishing. "It's so nice to see you again," she repeated. "You've met Amy, I see. She's my favorite granddaughter. Of course, I love Jenny as well. Everyone loves Jenny. Have you met Jenny? She's Walter's wife."

"Do you have a granddaughter by the name of Florence? She was married to the man I was looking to find last night." Amy was about to protest, but he glanced at her, warning her not to interfere. "The other Peter Teller."

"There's only one Peter, dear," she told him. "Our Peter. A very brave man during the war, you know. Decorated and all that. But his leg is bad, he walks with a cane."

"I was thinking perhaps that your son—Peter's father—might have had a child. By someone else. And that son was also called Peter."

"Peter's father? Oh, no, dear, that's not likely. The Teller men are extraordinarily faithful. It's part of their charm. They love only once. Besides," she said as she glanced at Amy's stricken face, "it would be bad form to name a child on the wrong side of the blanket for one of your own. It brings bad luck, you see. Like a curse, you know. One of them will surely die."

Rutledge's eyes met Amy's. "One of them has," he said. "In the war."

He stood up, adding, "I've taken enough of your time. I'd like to speak to Mr. Edwin Teller, if I may. And then I must go."

Amy was on the point of saying that her husband was resting, when Mrs. Teller said brightly, "I saw him stepping into the study as I was coming here. Shall I take you to him?"

He accepted her offer and said a formal good-bye to Amy Teller, preventing her from following him to the study. "If there's anything more you can think of that would be helpful, you know where to reach me."

She glared at him. Why had he thought she was less involved?

Gran conducted him into the passage and, without knocking,

opened the door to the study and walked straight in. This had been her house as a wife and then as the dowager of the family, and she stood on no ceremony. Her appearance caught Edwin Teller by surprise, and when he saw who was just behind her in the passage, his smile of welcome turned grim.

"Hullo, Gran," he said. "Thank you for bringing Mr. Rutledge to me. If you'll excuse us, we have some business to conduct, I'm afraid."

She looked at her grandson, disappointment clouding her face. "He was staying for luncheon . . ."

Rutledge took her hand and said gently, "I'm afraid it must be another day," he told her. "After your grandson and I have conducted our business, I must return to the Yard."

"Yes, of course," she said smiling and shaking Rutledge's hand. "I shall look forward to it."

And she took her leave, with the dignity of a woman who had all her life been accustomed to the niceties of social interaction. Business was business, and women were not a part of that world.

As the door shut behind her, Edwin said through clenched teeth, "What the bloody hell do you mean, coming here and interrogating my grandmother when I'm not present?"

Rutledge said, "Your wife was present during today's interview."

"But not last night's. Walter is in Essex, where he is supposed to be. The search for him is over. He did nothing during the period when he was missing that would interest Scotland Yard. You have no business here. I'll take this up with your superior, if you continue to harass my family."

"Hardly harassment. I've come to ask if you could help me locate one Peter Teller."

"You've met my brother," Edwin said shortly. "As far as I know, he's in Bolingbroke Street, where he lives."

"*This* Peter Teller," Rutledge said, "is being sought because we can't find the last will and testament of one Florence Marshall Teller, his wife. Or I should say, his late wife. She was murdered several days ago."

Edwin opened his mouth and shut it again. After a moment he asked in a very different tone of voice, "Where was she murdered? Here in London?"

"In Lancashire. Where she had lived almost all of her life."

Teller was making quick calculations. He said, "The day Walter returned to the clinic?"

"Two days before that. Someone came to her door and, when she answered it, struck her down and left her lying there. A passerby finally saw her lying there, and summoned the police."

Edwin Teller said, before he could stop himself, "My God." And then he continued quickly, "I don't see why any of us should know anything about this murder. Walter was missing. The rest of us were searching for him."

"I wasn't suggesting that you might know anything that would help the police," Rutledge responded mildly. "Lieutenant Teller wasn't from Lancashire. He came from Dorset, or so he said. We're trying to trace his family. We've been unable to find Mrs. Teller's will. The police are always interested in who inherits property. Greed can be a powerful impetus to murder."

"A pity we can't help you. My brother is the only person in the family whose Christian name is Peter." Edwin was doing his best in a rearguard action, but he was not the strongest of the three brothers.

"We aren't sure that the murderer knew Mrs. Teller was dead," Rutledge persisted. "But it appears that all her husband's letters—which she kept in a box in her sitting room—were taken at the same time. He stepped over her once, walked into the house, and stepped over her again, on his way out. It suggests a rather cold-blooded person, in the view of the Yard."

Teller cleared his throat. "What—do you know what sort of weapon was used in the murder?"

Rutledge said, "We aren't releasing that information at the moment." Then, changing his line of questioning without warning, Rutledge asked, "When was your brother promoted to captain?"

"I—as far as I remember, it was shortly before war was declared. They were bringing the regiment up to strength in the event the Kaiser caused any trouble over the situation in the Balkans. You said that Mrs. Teller's husband was in the war?"

"He never came home from France. So I've been led to believe. Which is why we must find his family. His wife's will could very well be among his papers or in the hands of his solicitor."

"We would have no way of knowing who that might be," Teller said shortly. "A pity we can't help you," he added a second time, as an afterthought.

"Which is why I was speaking to your grandmother, in the event she might know more about other branches of the Teller family."

"You didn't tell her of the murder, did you? Damn it, she's nearly eighty years old."

"There was no need to tell her about the murder. She understood that we were looking for information on the other Peter Teller, who is believed to have come from Dorset."

"Make certain you leave it that way." Edwin got up from his desk and came around it, standing face-to-face with Rutledge. "Now if you will show yourself to the door, I have other matters to attend to."

Rutledge crossed to the door and, with his hand on the knob, he said, "I understand that before the war you were often in Scotland building private boats. I wonder if in your comings and goings you might have stopped off in Lancashire or walked in that vicinity. It's said to be a very popular spot for walking."

Edwin, alarmed, said, "I have never been to Hobson in my life. In the first place I was too busy, and the second, because of my health, I always traveled by private rail carriage."

Rutledge thanked him and went out, closing the door behind him.

Hamish was battering at the back of his mind, and as Rutledge cranked his motorcar to continue his rounds, he said, "Ye never telt him yon woman lived in Hobson."

Rutledge pulled the crank, listened to the motor turn over softly, and came around to the driver's side to open his door.

"Interesting, isn't it? That family knows about Florence Teller—I'll give you any odds you like. And who her husband is. But which of the brothers married her? And which of them killed her?"

Leaving London, Rutledge drove to Essex. The telephone could outpace him, but there was still the possibility that whatever the rest of the family knew—or thought they knew—about Florence Teller, their brother Walter had not been a party to it.

Hamish said, "His brothers were fashed wi' him, when he came back."

That was true. They had been very angry. For vanishing, instead of playing his part in whatever was happening during those crucial days?

"Ye ken," Hamish pointed out, "yon doctors believed he'd had a great shock after leaving the bank."

Was that it? Had he been drawn into something that he couldn't face?

But why now? Why had Florence Teller suddenly become a problem, if any of this speculation was true? She had not seen her husband since the war. She thought he was dead. She had lived for years, as far as anyone in Hobson could testify, perfectly quietly in Sunrise Cottage, making no demands on anyone. Who then had felt threatened by her?

"But ye havena' asked the person in the post office if there were ither letters."

He hadn't. It was an important oversight. The only excuse was, at that early stage of the inquiry, he hadn't been sure who Peter Teller really was. A member of the family that Chief Superintendent Bowles had demanded that he treat with circumspection and courtesy, or an outsider who happened in a bizarre twist of fate to be christened with the name of Peter.

That rosewood box—what had it contained besides letters from a soldier on the other side of the world to a lonely wife waiting for him to be given another leave? A will? An exchange of correspondence of a different sort that had gone unnoticed in a tiny village like Hobson where the business of everyone was everyone's business? Hardly likely.

"There's the ither town . . ."

And Hamish was right, there was Thielwald. But how would Florence Teller have got there and back, to fetch her mail? It was too far to walk.

Still, the farmer with the sick ram might occasionally have given her a lift.

Rutledge couldn't accept that the woman he'd seen lying dead on a table in Dr. Blake's office was a blackmailer.

"Or ye do na' wish to believe."

The main road forked, and Rutledge followed the sign to Repton. Not five miles on, he came to the turning into Witch Hazel Farm.

As the drive meandered toward the house, it passed a bed of handsome roses just now in their prime that gave off a sweet perfume in the warm air and filled the car with their spicy scent all the way to the door of the house.

He lifted the knocker and let it fall. After a moment or two Mollie, the housekeeper, answered the door.

"Mr. Teller, please. Inspector Rutledge to see him."

"Inspector." She repeated the word cautiously. "I'll see if he's in," she said finally and disappeared, leaving him to admire the white roses in stone tubs by the door. They hadn't been here when last he called, he thought.

Mollie had come back, and she led him to the study, whose windows looked out toward the drive. Teller had seen him coming, Rutledge suspected.

Walter Teller was sitting in a chair, an open book in his lap, and he said as Rutledge came in, "One of my brothers has disappeared?"

It was dark humor, not intended as a jest.

He offered Rutledge a chair and then went on, "Do people always suspect the worst when a policeman knocks at their door? Or do you sometimes bring joy in your wake?"

"We seldom have the opportunity to bring joy. But yes, sometimes."

"Did you come from London? May I offer you some refreshment?"

"Yes, I drove here from London. And no thank you."

Teller marked his place, closed his book, and set it to one side, as if preparing himself.

Rutledge said, "There's been a murder, and I'm trying to find the family of a man who died in the war. They may be able to cast some light on the last wishes of the victim and who is to inherit."

Teller frowned. "A death in Repton? Why wasn't I told?" He got to his feet. "I'll come at once."

Rutledge said, "Not here in Repton, no. The man I'm after is Lieutenant Peter Teller—"

Walter Teller had turned at his words and walked to the window.

"The only Peter Teller I'm aware of is my brother. And he survived the war." There was a silence, and when Rutledge didn't carry on, Teller said tensely, "Who was murdered? Surely you can tell me that."

"A woman in Lancashire, by the name of Florence Teller."

"Flor—" He broke off. And then, as if the words were torn from him, he said, "I don't know anyone by that name, I'm sorry."

"But I think you do," Rutledge said. "Your brothers know who she was."

Teller wheeled. "Don't lie to me. Ask me what you want to ask, and get out of here. But don't lie." His face was ravaged, aged.

"I'm not lying. I've just come from asking them the same questions. And while they deny all knowledge of this woman or the Peter Teller who married her, there's something they're both concealing, and Edwin Teller's wife, Amy, as well."

"I don't believe you. It's a ruse, and I'm not stupid, Rutledge. Get out of here. I won't hear any more of this."

"You aren't even curious about how Florence Teller died?"

Rutledge could see that he was torn between asking and giving himself away.

Finally he said, "I don't know her. I'm sorry to hear that she has died, but I can do nothing about it. I hope you find the husband you're looking for."

Standing his ground, Rutledge said, "She was struck over the head and left lying in her own doorway for two days until someone passing by the house happened to see her there and called the police. It's a murder inquiry, Mr. Teller, and you'd be wise to tell me what you know."

"I can prove I have not left this house since my wife and I returned from London. Now get out."

"It happened while you went missing from the clinic. Your brothers and your sister are unaccounted for as well. You may have been sleeping in churches or you may not have. They may have been searching in Cambridge and Cornwall and Portsmouth. Or they may not have. Unless I can find this Lieutenant Teller and prove beyond a doubt that he is no connection of yours, I have no choice but to consider you all as suspects in Mrs. Teller's murder."

Walter Teller crossed the room, took up the book from the table beside his chair, and in one motion, heaved it at Rutledge.

It missed his head by inches and clattered against the door before falling hard to the floorboards.

"I'll assume that was a reflection of your distress," Rutledge told him coldly. "But I'll advise you now never to try that again."

And he opened the door and left the study.

As he walked out of the house, shutting the outer door behind him as well, Hamish said to Rutledge, "He kens the lass."

"But did he kill her?"

Back in London, Rutledge was met with a message left at the Yard by Edwin Teller.

He drove to Marlborough Street and found Teller waiting for him in the study.

Teller said, without preamble, "I've sent for you because I need to know when this woman will be buried?"

"I've given permission for the body to be released," Rutledge said and watched Teller wince at the word *body*. "I should think services will be held in Hobson tomorrow or the next day."

"I should like to attend."

Teller saw the surprise on Rutledge's face and said, "She was married to a man by the name of Teller, is that not so?"

"As far as we know."

"And you haven't found his family, I take it."

"No."

"Then I feel honor bound, as the present head of the family, to be there when she is interred. As a gesture. You may discover that her husband has no connection to my family. It's what I expect. But I have a duty all the same."

"Then be there day after tomorrow. If you are serious about this."

"I've never been more so. But I shall also tell you in no uncertain terms that it is a duty on my part, entered into freely. And it has nothing to do with her life or her death. It is merely a show of respect."

"I understand," Rutledge said, and he thought he very likely did.

But he thought there might be as well a measure of curiosity mixed in with that sense of duty.

And he wondered who else might decide to come to Hobson out of curiosity.

Rutledge was driving back to the Yard and was nearly there, when he saw a woman walking along the street and stopping at the next corner to cross over. She looked up at the same time, and he realized it was Susannah Teller.

Pulling over just beyond the crossing, he said, "Mrs. Teller?"

"Mr. Rutledge? I was just on my way to see you."

"Let me drive you the rest of the way," he said. "Or would you prefer to talk to me somewhere else?"

"Perhaps we could walk to the bridge. What I have to say is—rather private."

He took her to the Yard, left his motorcar there, and then accompanied her to the river, where a slight, cooling breeze moved across the water.

She paused to look at the river, and he realized she was not more than five feet from where Bynum had been murdered.

"Shall we?" he said, and gestured in the opposite direction.

It seemed that whatever she had to tell him was weighing on her mind, but she was not certain how to begin, or possibly where to begin. He kept in step with her and let her take her time.

Finally she said, "My husband—Peter has told me about this poor woman—in Lancashire, is it? The one who was murdered. And he told me as well that you can't seem to find her husband's family. He was from Dorset, I believe?"

"Apparently, yes. It's what we were told in Hobson."

"Yes, well, I may have an explanation for this mystery." She paused again and watched a small boat pulling upriver. "There was a young subaltern in my husband's regiment. Burrows was his name, and he was from a good family. He had connections to Dorset, but I believe his family lived outside Worcester."

She glanced up at him and looked away again.

"He was a very nice young man. We saw a good bit of him. And I'm afraid my husband and I made fun of him behind his back. It was unkind, but Thomas admired my husband no end. He had no older brothers, and I think he saw Peter as a role model, in a way. And he emulated Peter at every turn. When Peter showed an interest in golf, it became Thomas's enthusiasm. When Peter bought himself a pair of matched blacks to pull his carriage, the next month Thomas sported a pair that was almost identical. Peter grew a mustache, and Thomas must have one as well. Peter shaved his, and soon after, so did Thomas. It would have been very trying, except for the fact that we knew it was harmless."

"And what has this to do with the dead woman in Hobson?"

"I don't know anything at all about Hobson," Susannah Teller said. "But I should imagine it was a very small place, and that the dead woman—"

"Her name," he said, "was Florence."

"—Florence, then. That Florence was not from a wealthy, influential family, however nice she might have been?"

"If you are trying to say she wasn't of his class, she was a schoolteacher and not an heiress, although she had property of her own."

"Oh." Her face flushed. "This is difficult enough for me, Inspector. I'm not trying to disparage this—Florence Teller. But I wonder if perhaps Thomas fell in love with her and married her under a false name. Or perhaps felt obligated to marry her, and knew his mother and father would not approve of the match. In fact, they might well have cut him off without a penny. I have no way of guessing his reasons. But he might have been desperate enough to marry her not as Thomas Burrows, the nephew of a member of Parliament and the grandson of a baronet, though the title went to his mother's brother, but as the man he most admired. Peter."

It was, Rutledge thought, as likely to be true as the possibility that her own husband was a bigamist. And possibly a murderer as well.

"I'll look into it. Where is Thomas Burrows now?"

"Lieutenant Burrows died in the war. He was shot leading his men across No Man's Land. Peter saw it happen. By the time Lieutenant Burrows could be brought in, he was dying and never reached an aid post."

"And he never told his family about his marriage? I find that difficult to believe."

"I don't know whether he did or not. But if he did, they surely disowned him. All I can tell you is that Thomas Burrows was a very different man when the war began. The brash young subaltern striving so hard to please ten years before was by that time a very good officer, but he had lost his illusions. About the Army and about himself. He seldom spoke of his family, nothing more was said about the Army as a stepping-stone to his uncle's seat in Parliament."

Her voice rang true, and yet he found it interesting that Susannah Teller had come to tell him this story, and not her husband. But sometimes women were more perceptive than men. They caught undertones and nuances that were lost to male ears, and drew conclusions that depended as much on intuition and instinct as on solid fact.

"Does your husband know that you've come to give me this information?"

She blinked. "You can ask him if you like. About Thomas Burrows. He'll tell you that Thomas did all those things, and perhaps more than even I can recall. But I think he will be less willing to accept the fact that Thomas could have married without his family's knowledge and consent. And yet Peter had to fight for me. I was his cousin on his mother's side, you see. The family was against it from the start. It was very likely that my children would have the same blood disorder that afflicts Edwin. They were right, actually. We lost two before we gave up. It might color his feelings about Thomas, you see. The fact that *he* never fought for that—for Florence."

And there he knew she was telling the truth. But how much of it?

"Thank you, Mrs. Teller. I'll look into this matter. May I drive you home?"

"No, thank you. I'll just walk up to Trafalgar and find a cab."

But he accompanied her that far anyway and hailed the cab for her. As he was about to shut the door, she put her hand out to stop him and said, "You won't tell Peter where you heard this? He'll be very angry with me."

"Not," he said, "unless it's absolutely necessary."

"Thank you." She spoke to the driver, and the cab pulled away. The last sight he had of her was a handkerchief in her hand, pressed against her eyes when she thought he could no longer see her.

Rutledge had asked the Yard for information on any other Peter Teller, and Gibson had answers for him, though from the sergeant's terse manner, Rutledge knew that Jake had been troublesome.

Gibson said, "As to that infernal bird, sir. We've a list of things he's likely to eat. I've put that on your desk. Along with a box of samples to see you through until you can decide what to do with the creature."

"Thank you, Sergeant. Is there anything else?"

"We've come up empty-handed in our search for one Peter Teller."

"You haven't found one? In all of England?"

"Oh, we've found them right enough. One lives in Gloucester, and he's just on the point of celebrating his seventy-sixth birthday. The other is one of a pair of twins, Peter and Helen Mowbray Teller, who are seven. There was another Peter Teller in Ely, who died in 1910 of pneumonia. The constable there believes he was about thirteen at the time. The man outside New Castle on Tyne, lost both his legs in a mining accident in 1908. He was a supervisor, went down with his men to look at a troublesome face, and there was an explosion. The last one was the son of Peter and Susannah Teller, died age two of bleeding internally. The list is also on your desk."

"Thank you, Sergeant. I'll relieve you of the infernal bird. Meanwhile, if you will, I need to know more about one Lieutenant Thomas Burrows who didn't survive the war." Rutledge gave the particulars of his regiment and added, "Uncle is an MP. Or was. I believe his mother still lives somewhere outside Worcester."

"I'll see to it, sir. And if I may make a suggestion, I'd take the bird out covered before the Chief Super learns he was here. We were able to blame one squawk on a baby whose mother had come in to complain of her neighbors."

Rutledge laughed, and went to recover Jake.

Not knowing what else to do at this time of day—it was well past his dinnertime and possibly Jake's as well—Rutledge took the bird home with him.

It was silent as the tomb on the journey in the motorcar, but Jake took an instant dislike to a jackdaw outside the flat window where Rutledge set him at first, and the loud denunciation of Rutledge's choice of accommodation was nearly deafening.

Moving Jake's cage to another window, he took note of that beak and the condition of the papers inside the cage, and wondered how to manage cleaning them without losing a finger or two in the process.

As a last resort, Rutledge put a little food on the table across from the cage and left the door open while he went to change his clothes and find something cool to drink. When he came back, Jake didn't appear to have budged. But the food Rutledge had left out for him was gone.

He was tired and said to Jake, "We'll deal with you tomorrow, my lad." Shutting the cage door, he sat down across from the bird and considered the day's events. But he found himself on the edge of sleep instead.

Hamish said, "It wasna' a verra' profitable day."

"But a beginning," Rutledge answered him drowsily. "The question now is how to put the pieces together. And what we'll have, when we've done it."

And then he had a horrible thought.

What if Jake could hear Hamish, and began to speak in his voice?

That brought him wide awake. A solution eluded him, but he got up and flung a cloth over the birdcage and listened silently as Jake began his nightly ritual of saying good night to Peter.

21

The parrot had finished its seeds and taken a bath in the water Rutledge had left in the cage.

In the gray light of a misty morning Rutledge showed the fatigue of a long drive and a short night's sleep. He looked down at the stained newspapers in the bottom of the cage. He'd just watched Jake crack a nut with ease, and he had no intention of testing that beak against bone. But something had to be done.

He was collecting fresh newspaper when there was a knock at the door of his flat, and Frances came in, calling, "Ian? Are you here? I saw your motorcar. Shouldn't you be at the Yard?"

"I'm in here," he told her, and she walked through to his bedroom, where the bird was ensconced on a table by the double windows.

"What possessed you to buy a parrot?" she asked, stopping in astonishment. "But what a pretty creature. Does it have a name? Surely you don't have the time to care for it properly."

Rutledge straightened and gazed fondly at his sister.

"Frances, this is Jake. The bird is presently a ward of the court. Sergeant Gibson has already cursed my offspring, my hope of promotion, and my mental capacity. And so it's here. But you're right, I don't have time to care for it properly. You do. Would you like to be its guardian for the next several days?"

"Ian, you must be out of your mind. What am I to do with a bird?"

"That's exactly what Sergeant Gibson said to me. Although he called me Inspector Rutledge. You have a lovely window looking out onto the gardens. It would be very happy there. And all you have to do is feed it, water it, and—er—keep the newspapers at the bottom of the cage fresh."

She had come over to the cage. The bird was sitting on a swing, regarding her with a fixed gaze, then it blinked and ducked its head down in a shy motion.

"I think it's flirting with me," she told her brother, laughing. "Look."

Rutledge had wisely stepped aside. "Yes, I think it actually is."

The bird ducked its head down again, and Frances touched the wires of the cage with her fingers. "Does it talk?"

"I've heard it say good night. That's all. So far."

"Pretty birdie," she said lightly, and then, "Good morning, Jake."

To her surprise, Jake sidled over to her fingers and tucked his head down close to them. "I think he wants to be petted." She moved her fingers through the wire and touched his feathers, first on his shoulder and then his bent head. "He likes it." She was smiling with that fondness women reserve for small children and baby animals. "Oh, you are a sweet boy."

Rutledge had been on the point of warning her to watch the bird's beak but stopped just in time.

Hamish said, "Ye ken, it belonged to a woman."

Jake was leaning into Frances's fingers, clearly enjoying the personal contact. Then it shook itself and flew to the door of the cage.

"He wants to come out."

"Not on your life," Rutledge told her.

"But, Ian . . ." She was already unclasping the cage latch, and she put her hand in. The bird hopped on her fingers like a hawk perching on a falconer's glove. Frances lifted her hand out of the cage, then held it in the air, looking at Jake. They stared at each other, and then he flew to her shoulder, moving back and forth across it in a bobbing motion.

"If men were as malleable as this," she said, smiling at her brother, "women would be happy as larks."

"Frances," he began.

"No. I can't imagine having to mind it all day. No."

"It likes you. Look at the feathers in the bottom of his cage. He's been plucking them out. I think in mourning. His owner is dead. But he likes you. And he may be a witness. Who knows? I need to see to it that he's safe and comfortable."

"Do you think he saw a murder? Is that it?"

"I doubt if he did. But it's possible that someone might confess, if the killer thought Jake knew something."

She held up two fingers, and Jake stepped passively on them.

"No, don't put him back. Not until I've cleaned out those newspapers."

Frances talked quietly to the bird as her brother worked. Jake cocked his head, as if trying to understand, then ducked it for more petting.

"Was his owner a woman?"

"Yes. He lived with her for quite a few years. They must have grown close." He thought of that touching good night that Jake must have heard week in and week out.

"I believe he understands that I'm not his mistress, but he knows I'm a woman."

"The woman who had temporary care of him threatened to wring his neck. He was screeching like a wild thing."

"That's terrible."

"Will you take him? If only for a few days?"

Frances took a deep breath. "I will not keep him, Ian. Are we clear on that? But I'll take him for your few days."

"Wonderful. Er—why was it you stopped by?"

"For one thing, David and little Ian arrived home safely. I thought you'd like to know."

"That's good to hear."

"And," she went on, "I must admit, I miss the company. I came to see if you could arrange a few days of leave. We might go down to Cornwall or somewhere for a bit. Just to get away. And now I'm saddled with a parrot." But she smiled wryly.

Rutledge had cleaned the bottom of the cage and put in fresh newspaper. Washing his hands, he said, "It won't be for long. I promise you. As for leave, it's just not possible at the moment. In fact, I'm driving north again this morning. I can't say with any certainty when I'll come back."

He followed her back to her house and settled Jake in the breakfast room, where sunlight, breaking through the clouds, promised a better day. Through an open window, the scent of roses came wafting by on the light breeze.

Jake bobbed as he gazed with interest out the open window.

"Roses," he said, quite clearly.

"His owner," Rutledge told Frances, "had a garden outside the kitchen windows. This must remind him of his home."

"It was a verra' clever thing to do, bringing him here," Hamish said.

Rutledge left his sister coaxing Jake to speak to her, crooning softly and letting her fingers brush the bird's feathers.

He was very grateful to make his escape before she changed her mind.

At the station, he spoke to Gibson, who had no news of Thomas Burrows, and then went to see the Chief Superintendent.

He filled Bowles in on the direction he felt the case was taking, and got in return a tongue-lashing for disturbing the Teller family without permission.

"You're mad if you believe they have had any hand in this business. I'll be hearing complaints next, and what am I to say? That you've taken leave of your senses? And why aren't you in the north? It makes no sense to be frittering your time away in London. She wasn't murdered here, this Teller woman, and there must be a dozen Peter Tellers out there. Find him."

"Gibson has given me a list of those he found. Not one of them is of the same age as we believe Teller would have been now."

"Then tell Sergeant Gibson to look again."

Rutledge went in search of Gibson.

The sergeant said in resignation, "I'll be bound I found every one there is. But I'll look again."

Rutledge left him muttering to himself about time wasted.

He headed north, picking up rain showers halfway. And then it cleared as he turned toward Thielwald and Hobson.

Constable Satterthwaite had nothing to report when Rutledge walked into the station and greeted him.

"But I'm that glad to see you again. Any luck in the south?"

"The Yard is still searching for Lieutenant Peter Teller's family. I'm beginning to think we have already found it. The Chief Superintendent disagrees. Here are the facts. There's a Teller family in London. Three brothers, one of them presently a captain in the Army. There's no reason they should even know Florence Teller's name, but her death came as a shock to them. I'm beginning to wonder if her killer realized she was dead."

"He made no effort to find it out," Satterthwaite responded angrily. "Which in my book is still murder. What brought him here?"

Rutledge said, "That's why I've come back. That and the funeral. Do you think Mrs. Greeley will have a room for me again?"

"Indeed, sir. She was asking just yesterday if I was expecting to see you."

"No sign of the murder weapon?"

"As to that, he must have taken it with him."

"The services for Florence Teller?"

"They're tomorrow," Satterthwaite told him. "I'm glad you'll be here for them."

"So am I," Rutledge said, and went to find Mrs. Greeley.

To his surprise, the next morning Edwin and Amy Teller arrived in good time for the service.

They found Rutledge just coming out of the police station and asked if he could give them directions to the house where Florence Teller had lived.

"You can't go inside," he warned them. "This is still an active murder inquiry." What he wanted to say was that it wasn't a spectacle for the Teller family. How Florence Teller had lived and died was now police business.

"I understand," Edwin said. And Rutledge was surprised to realize that the man did. "It just seemed—the right thing to do."

"Then I'll go with you."

He could tell it wasn't what they wanted, but he got into the motorcar and told Edwin to follow the High Street out of Hobson.

As they went, Amy commented on how empty the landscape was, and how lonely. Rutledge thought it was a reflection of someone brought up in the south, where the roads seldom lacked some form of habitation for very long.

Edwin was silent, concentrating on driving. When at last they began to crest the rise before the house, Rutledge said, "Ahead you'll see a hedge. Stop at the gate."

He could feel the tension in the two people in the front seat. And he thought, *Is this how Hamish knows what's on my mind?*

But there was no time to consider that as Edwin came to a halt in front of the house.

"Sunrise Cottage," Amy read, then looking up the path to the house, she said, "A red door. Once."

Rutledge said, "Mrs. Teller painted it to celebrate her husband's homecoming. Only he never returned. She left it, perhaps in the hope that someday he would. Or because she couldn't bear to give up all hope."

Edwin sat there, looking up at the house. "It's not a very pleasing house, is it?" he mused aloud. "Small and plain and isolated. She lived here alone? That's sad. He could have done better by her."

"Perhaps it was what she wanted," Amy said after a moment. "What she was used to. She took pride in it—you can see that."

"Still . . ."

The silence lengthened. Finally Edwin let in the clutch and said, "I must find somewhere to turn around."

"There's a farmyard just down the road," Rutledge told them.

Edwin found it and was soon headed back into Hobson.

When they reached the police station, Rutledge said, "Mrs. Greeley's house is just there. I'm sure she will let you have a room to freshen up. She needs the money."

Edwin thanked him and drove on.

Rutledge could see them speaking together, but not even Hamish's sharp hearing could discern what was being said.

Satterthwaite had come out and was looking after them. "And who might they be, when they're at home?"

"Edwin Teller and his wife, from London. He considers himself the head of the Essex branch of the family. He felt it was his duty to be here, to represent the family that we haven't found. His brother is Captain Peter Teller."

"Kind of him," Satterthwaite said shortly. "Where's his brother, then?"

"Does he resemble Peter Teller, do you think?"

Satterthwaite considered the question. "In a vague way. Hard to judge with yon beard. Remember, I've not seen the man for years. I don't know how the war changed him." After a moment, he said, "Does the wife know about Florence?"

"Amy? Yes. She must." Rutledge, looking back to his first meeting with her, nodded. "But it's Peter's wife who has taken the news the hardest."

St. Bartholomew's bell, rather more tinny than deep throated, had begun tolling the age of the departed.

Satterthwaite nodded. "It's time."

They walked down the High Street, turning up Church Lane at the war memorial. Rutledge saw Cobb pausing there for his morning greeting to his sons, then move on, his cane supporting him over the uneven ruts of the lane.

Watching him, Rutledge said thoughtfully, "Edwin Teller's brother was badly wounded in the war. He's in need of a cane as well. But he doesn't always have it to hand."

"I'm told Mr. Cobb sleeps with his on the bed, on his wife's side."

"You've looked into his nephew Lawrence? Anything more on that front, since I left?"

"I've kept my eye on him. But there's nothing there."

"I saw him wielding a hammer in anger."

"We'll see, shall we, if there's any guilt shown today."

"Fair enough."

People from the village were also walking up the lane, and among them Rutledge saw the Tellers in mourning black that was stylishly cut and out of place here among the rusty black of ordinary clothes that hung unused from Monday to Saturday.

St. Bart's was as plain inside as it was on the outside. Built for sturdiness, built to last, built to worship and not adore. Rutledge had the fleeting thought that Cromwell would have approved. But the people of Hobson had probably not approved of Cromwell or King Charles. Their independence came from the land they farmed, not from London, and it was a hard life, short as well.

The service was brief and as plain as the surroundings in which it was held. The curate spoke simply about our dear departed sister, listing the major events of her life and commenting only once about her death, as an undeserved tragedy. He read several Psalms, and the choir led the mourners in three hymns, including "Rock of Ages."

And then they moved to the churchyard, watching the plain coffin being lowered into the ground. Next to the open grave was the small patch of grass, slightly lower than its surroundings, that marked her son's resting place. A rosebush bloomed where a stone should have been, the small pink blossoms reminding Rutledge of one very much like it he'd seen in Florence Teller's garden.

Beyond Timmy's grave was a third, the sod flat and untouched.

No one stepped forward at first to throw in the first handful of earth until the constable came up, did his duty, and said under his breath, "I hope you've found peace, now."

Edwin walked up, stared for a moment into the grave, as if he were praying, and then took a firm handful of earth and scattered it gently. It dropped like the first sounds of a heavy rain on the roof as it struck the wooden coffin. Amy Teller followed him, and others came up as well, among them Mrs. Greeley and then Sam Jordan. Lawrence Cobb, watched by his uncle, paused for a moment looking up at the cloudless sky, then gently dropped a yellow rose into the grave. It landed at the broadest part of the coffin, and he nodded, as if that was what he'd intended. Without a word, he walked on, ignoring the red-haired woman just behind him. Rutledge could see her resemblance to Mrs. Blaine, but Betsy was slimmer, prettier. Her mouth was drawn tight now, and he noticed that she didn't look into the grave or reach for a handful of earth. Instead her eyes were fixed on her husband.

Hamish said, "He'll no' spend a restful night."

Rutledge was the last of the mourners to step forward. Mr. Kerr gave the benediction, and then Florence Marshall Teller was left to the attentions of the gravediggers and the sexton.

Rutledge stood there for a moment longer, then went to join Edwin and Amy Teller as they walked back to their motorcar.

"I'm glad we came," Edwin said with conviction. "It was the right thing to do."

"A very simple service," Rutledge said. "But I think it suited her."

"I've always liked that psalm," Amy said. "'I will lift mine eyes unto the hills . . .'"

Edwin said, "The curate spoke of a child. A boy. Were there any other children?"

"Only the one son. I'm told he died of illness many years ago."

"But you told me—I thought you said he was still alive," Amy accused him.

"I said I was unable to ask his views," Rutledge answered her.

"How sad," Edwin Teller said. The words sounded sincere, rather than a conventional expression of sympathy. "For her."

"Was she your sister-in-law?" Rutledge asked without emphasis.

Edwin Teller stared at him. "This is neither the time nor the place," he snapped.

Rutledge replied, "Where then is the proper place?"

But there was no answer to that. Even Amy Teller looked away, her face pale.

They had nearly reached the Teller motorcar. Before he could press the issue, Rutledge was distracted by a boy running toward the churchyard, in the direction of Constable Satterthwaite. Rutledge excused himself and left the Tellers standing there.

By the time he'd reached the spot where Satterthwaite was standing listening to the boy, the constable looked up.

He said in a low voice, "A message from the police in Thielwald. They've found a walker who admits to being in the vicinity around the time Mrs. Teller was killed. He can't be sure of the exact day, but it fits well enough. He's being held there. Are you coming, sir?"

"Yes. My motorcar is at Mrs. Greeley's house."

"I'll meet you there in five minutes," Satterthwaite said. He thanked the boy and turned to speak to the curate, commenting on the service.

Thielwald had ancient roots, but the town itself looked as if it had been born in the last century and had no recollection of any past before that.

Rutledge had only seen it in late evening, the night he and Constable Satterthwaite had called on Dr. Blake, whose surgery was in a side street before they had reached the High Street.

He could see now that Thielwald's gray stone houses were crowded along the main road, which was bisected by a few cross streets. In the town center there were the usual shops and a busy pub called The Viking's Head. The church was just beyond the center, as plain as the one in Hobson but slightly larger, its churchyard clustered around it like lost souls on the windswept rise.

Hamish, who had been quiet during the service and the drive here, said, "It's no' a place I'd like to live."

Rutledge had been thinking the same thing—no character to set it off, no natural features to make it more attractive. A small town with no pretensions.

Seeing the post office set in a corner of an ironmonger's shop, Rutledge said, "Ah. I'd like to make a brief stop here before we see this walker. I want to ask the postmistress a question."

"Can it wait?"

"No." He halted the motorcar, and leaving it running, he said to the constable, "Wait here. I shouldn't be more than five minutes."

Striding into the ironmonger's, he turned to the left and found the tiny square of space that was Thielwald's post office. The middle-aged woman behind the counter smiled as he approached and said, "What can I do for you today, sir?"

Rutledge identified himself and asked if she handled the mail for Hobson as well.

"Oh, yes, sir. It's carried up to the village once a day and delivered. Not that there's much of it, now the war's over. Business was quite brisk then, you know, everyone writing to a soldier son or father or brother. Quite brisk."

"Do you recall mail for Mrs. Florence Teller?"

"Yes, sir, that's Florence Marshall that was. She got the most exotic packets sometimes, covered with foreign stamps. I always wondered what was inside, you know. Mrs. Greeley told me once there were silk pillow slips from China. I hardly know where to find China on the map, and here's silk pillow slips coming to my own post office."

"It must have been quite exciting," he agreed. "Did Mrs. Teller write to her family or her husband's family in England?"

"Letters, you mean."

"Yes. Was there an exchange of letters with members of her husband's family? We're trying to locate them. It's the matter of her will."

"I don't believe she ever did. No, nothing like that. She wrote to Lieutenant Teller and he wrote to her. And that was the end of it."

"Where did she send the letters to Lieutenant Teller? What regiment? Do you remember?"

"But they didn't go to his regiment, sir. They were mailed to an address in Dorset. Lieutenant Teller had told her it was faster than waiting for the Army to send them on. Still and all, it was sometimes many months before a reply came."

"Where in Dorset? Do you remember?" He tried not to sound eager.

She frowned. "A place called Sedley, I think it was. Peter Teller, in care of A. R.—no, I believe it was A. P. Repton, Mistletoe Cottage, Sedley, Dorset," she finished triumphantly, and smiled at him. "I rather liked Mistletoe Cottage."

Repton was the name of the village outside Witch Hazel Farm, where the Teller family had lived for generations. In Essex, not Dorset.

He thanked her and left.

So much for the theory of blackmail.

"Any luck, sir?" the constable asked when Rutledge came back to the motorcar and they drove on.

"Another dead end, most likely. At least there was no correspondence between Mrs. Teller and her husband's family."

Satterthwaite said, "Just there," and pointed out the police station, which looked as if it had once been a shop itself, the front window overwhelming the door set to the side. Inspector Hadden was waiting for them with a scruffy-looking young man who was, Rutledge thought, an undergraduate student somewhere.

He was introduced as Benjamin Larkin, who stood to shake hands with Rutledge and the constable. His voice, when he spoke, was educated, and he said at once, "I was in a pub south of Morecambe when I heard there was a murder over by Hobson. A woman in an isolated farmhouse. So I got in touch with the police. It appears to be the same one I passed several days back. I was going to stop in and ask to refill my water bottle, but there was a motorcar on the far side of the hedge, and so I moved on."

"A motorcar? Did you see anyone in it?" Hadden asked.

But Rutledge said, "Start at the beginning if you will."

"It was mid-afternoon, I think. I was coming over the rise, taking in the view, and there was a house to my left. I saw a pump in the kitchen yard and I thought I might stop and refill my bottle. But no one was about, so I thought perhaps I'd come around the front and knock, rather than help myself. The view was rather nice, and I moved toward my right to see more of it, when I realized there was a road below the house, not just a lane. I didn't remember that being on the rough map I had, so I stopped and dug in my gear for it, to be sure I wasn't in the wrong place. I was walking and looking at the map when I saw a motorcar was stopped at the end of the high hedge surrounding the front garden. It seemed to me that the owner might have come up from Morecambe—it was that kind of motor, and it occurred to me that it would do no harm to ask for a lift. No one was around, so I sat down by a small shrub and ate the last of my biscuits, hoping he wouldn't be long. I was just putting away my map when I could hear footsteps. And there he was, hurrying back to the motorcar. He was lame, finding it difficult to deal with the crank, but before I could collect my gear and hail him, the motor turned over, and he hobbled around to haul himself in. I didn't like the look of the situation—he appeared to be angry or upset, not the time to ask favors. I just walked on, and thought no more about it, until I heard talk in the pub where I spent last night."

"Did he see you?" Hadden asked.

"I have no idea. Probably not. I did notice that he glanced around, as if looking for something, but it all happened rather fast."

"Where did he go from there?" Rutledge asked.

"He was driving east."

"What can you tell me about the motorcar?"

"It was a black Rolls, well kept and quite clean. I hadn't expected to see that out here." He turned to Inspector Hadden, adding, "With no disrespect. But it was more the sort of vehicle you'd find in a city. It hadn't been used to haul cabbages or saddles or hens."

"And the man?" Rutledge said. He had more or less taken over the questioning, Hadden deferring to him.

"Lame, as I told you. Tall, slim. Darkish hair, military cut. Well dressed. Like the car, he seemed out of place here."

"Was there a quarrel, do you think? Was that what had upset him?"

"I can't say. I wasn't close enough to hear if there was. But no one was shouting, if that's what you're asking. Still, not the time to be knocking on doors or asking for a lift."

"Did he have a cane? Or some sort of tool in his hand—did you see him toss anything into the motorcar, like a box?"

"I don't know—no, actually I do." Larkin squinted, as if bringing back the scene in his memory. "He was empty-handed when he went to crank the car. But if I'd seen a cane, I wouldn't have been surprised, given the problem with his legs."

"Describe the Rolls, if you will."

"Black, well polished, 1914 Ghost, touring car. Rather like the one you drove up in, save for the color."

And very like the one Edwin Teller had just driven away in.

Hamish said, "Do ye believe the lad?"

All things considered, Rutledge thought he did. Larkin needn't have come forward, for one thing. He'd already disappeared into the landscape. But sometimes cases turned on unexpected evidence like this.

"Where are you studying?" Rutledge asked, curious.

"Cambridge," Larkin answered and named his college. "Which is why this was a walking tour and not two weeks in Italy. I couldn't afford it," he added with a grin.

"Did you see anyone at the house? A woman? Or notice that the house had a red door?"

"I never saw the door. No one was in the kitchen yard. I don't know about the front garden. There was the hedge, you see. Nearly as tall as I was."

Rutledge turned to Hadden and Satterthwaite. "Anything else?"

They had no further questions. Rutledge thanked Larkin and told him he could go. And then he said as Larkin reached behind the desk and lifted his haversack, "Would you mind if I looked in that?"

Larkin slung it off his shoulder and said, "Help yourself. Mind the dirty wash."

But there was nothing in the pack that could have been used for a weapon. And nothing that could have come from Florence Teller's house. Only spare clothes, a tarp for wet weather, a hairbrush, a toothbrush, a comb, a block of soap, a razor, a book on English wildflowers and another on birds, a heavy bottle for water, and a small sack of dried fruit, biscuits, sweets, and a heel of cheese. Nothing, in fact, that a walker shouldn't have, and everything he should.

Hamish said, "He could ha' left behind anything he didna' want you to see."

It was true. But the very compactness of the haversack, intended to minimize weight and maximize comfort in a small space, didn't allow for extras.

Rutledge nodded, asked for his address at Cambridge, and when that was done, thanked him again. Larkin went out the door.

"What do you think?" Inspector Hadden asked, echoing Hamish.

"I'll ask the Yard to be sure he's who he says he is. But I expect he's telling the truth."

"Was it Teller coming home?" Satterthwaite asked. "If it was, he has money now. I never thought he did before. He had enough that he wasn't looking to live on Florence's money from her aunt. But not rich."

"A good point," Rutledge acknowledged. "Pass the word to keep an eye on Larkin while he's in the district. He might be able to identify the driver, if we find him."

Turning to Satterthwaite, Rutledge said, "Did you look at that hedge around the front of the house? If I wanted to rid myself of a murder weapon, I might consider sticking it deep in there. It's thick enough."

Satterthwaite said slowly, "No, we did not. Under it, yes. But we'd have seen anything in the branches, wouldn't we?"

"It won't hurt to have another go at it."

By the time they reached Sunrise Cottage, clouds were building far out over the water, and Satterthwaite, scanning them, said, "Looks like this fine weather is about to break. I'm glad the service was dry."

Rutledge agreed with him. But he thought they had another hour.

They searched the hedge carefully, together pulling at the thickest parts of it and then letting them fall back into place. Inch by inch, they worked one side and across the front. As they came round to the corner closest to the house, Rutledge had to step into the hedge to make it easier to part the thick branches there, and grunting, Satterthwaite pushed and shoved at them. Rutledge nearly lost his footing and caught the constable's shoulder to steady himself. He turned to look down.

The earth under the hedge was thick with last winter's fallen leaves and possibly those of winters before that. They formed a light bed perhaps a good inch or so deep.

Cobb, the schoolmaster, had told Rutledge that since the war, there had been no one but his nephew to help with the farm. And this was proof of it.

"What's the matter?" Satterthwaite asked as Rutledge knelt to run his fingers through the damp and rotting mass.

He had to dig deep into the soil below, but it was loose enough and damp enough for him to wedge his fingers behind something there.

He found what he was after and pulled it toward him. He could hear the constable's indrawn breath as he realized what was coming to light.

Not a walking stick as the doctor had first suggested, but the remains of a Malacca cane. Rutledge stood up with it in his hands.

Although filthy, with leaves still clinging to it, it was not an old and rotting thing. It had been hidden here fairly recently, buried just deep enough that a policeman searching among the sparse hedge trunks close to the ground would have seen only what he expected to see—the carpet of leaves. But someone had taken the sharp end and used it to thrust the length of the cane out of sight well below that layer.

"If I hadn't felt it under my sole, I wouldn't have thought to dig," Rutledge said, running his hands along the wood, gently brushing off the debris.

"There's no head," Satterthwaite pointed out.

The head had been broken off, and the smooth dark red shaft was still raw where the wood had been splintered.

"It would match the wound in Florence Teller's head—or at least the murderer thought it might." He frowned. "It wouldn't be easy to snap off the head. Rattan palm canes are very strong. There must have been a weakness—where the cane had dried and cracked around the knob that served as a handle."

"Why leave the rest? Why not take the cane and throw it off a bridge far from here?"

"The killer wouldn't have wanted to be seen with it in his possession."

"But if he brought it here—"

"Yes, that's the point. But it only became a weapon once Florence Teller was killed. Before that it was simply someone's cane."

He looked around. The tidy bit of lawn, the flowers on the path, the step and the street door . . . They hadn't been disturbed.

Hamish said, "The step."

It was a long, rectangular slab of stone, smoothed to serve the doorway. Rutledge walked over to it and ran his hands along the edge. Someone could have shoved the head of the cane under the slab, and with the force of anger or of fear, managed to snap it off. Brush the earth back again, where the head had dug in, and who would notice what had been done. If the police hadn't found the cane, the slab of step would hold no significance. Someone, having just killed, had taken the time to think through what to do with the weapon.

That was an interesting look into his state of mind, whoever he was.

Rutledge began to sift the earth very gently through his fingers, moving aside a plant and reaching down under the stone. The head of the cane wasn't there. He hadn't expected it to be, but he'd had to be sure.

He was just smoothing the earth back into place when Hamish said, "There!"

Rutledge stopped. There was nothing he could see at first, and then he recognized what was caught in the roots of the pansy.

It was not as big as a toothpick. Just a fine splinter of wood, like the proverbial needle in a haystack. It was, in fact, more like a needle than anything else, one that had been held to a flame and tarnished.

He dug it out carefully, blew away the earth that smothered it, and put up his hand for the broken end of the cane that Satterthwaite was still holding.

There was no match, of course, but there was no doubt that it was the same wood.

Satterthwaite said, "It was savagely done."

"He'd have liked to hit her a second time, I expect. One blow was not enough to satisfy him. I wonder why? Because she died so easily? Or would her battered head give him away?"

"The walker. Larkin."

"I doubt it. The only thing taken was a box of letters."

"I wonder where the head of the cane might be? Was it valuable, do you think? Larkin indicated he had no money to speak of, this summer."

"He might have found the cane here, and stolen the head. But that would be after the murder, and her body would have been lying here in plain sight. Still—" Rutledge turned to stare beyond the gate, in the direction of Thielwald. "It's just as well we're keeping an eye on him." He returned to the cane in hand. "It will be a miracle if we ever find the rest." *It must have been distinctive,* he thought, this head. They were usually ivory or gold, with initials or a figure that could easily be identified and therefore was equally damning. He wondered if Edwin Teller would be willing to describe his brother's cane.

Teller's motorcar? Teller's cane? But none of these was proof of murder. Only that he was here on the day that Florence Teller died. Or one of his brothers was here . . .

"The man in the motorcar. He didna' have a cane when he left," Hamish pointed out.

"But we don't know if he carried one with him when he arrived. For all we know, he found the body and panicked."

He'd spoken aloud.

Satterthwaite said, "The man in the motorcar? That could be. He didn't have the casket of letters either."

"What if he'd already put them in the boot? He might have returned to the house to destroy the cane."

"True enough. I'd sworn we'd searched that hedge carefully."

"I'm sure you did. But not the ground below it. Only for something caught in it." Rutledge put the splinter of wood carefully away in his handkerchief and then dusted his hands.

Looking up at the sky, at the heavy dark clouds drawing closer, he said, "We'll be caught yet." Turning to Satterthwaite, he said, "Did you sift the ashes in the stove? In the event anything was burned in there?"

"We did. And nothing came to light. Of course, it might not have, if there were no hinges on that box. Or clasp. It'ud burned right up. But that would take time. In my mind, he took the box with him."

"All right then. I think we should be on our way to Hobson, before that storm gets here."

As it happened, they had only just reached the police station when the dark clouds, heavy with rain, rolled in on their heels. Satterthwaite thanked Rutledge, and said, "You're staying the night?"

"I want to take the cane to London as quickly as I can. I'll see that you know what we found out."

"You think the answer is in London then? One of those brothers."

"I don't know," Rutledge told him. "But you and I have run out of suspects here. Let me try in London."

Satterthwaite grinned. "You'll drown before you get there." And he made a fast dash for the door of the station just as the first heavy drops of rain became a raging downpour.

Backed with wind, it was a cold rain for June. And it followed Rutledge nearly as far as Chester. He ran out of it there and considered staying the night another fifty miles down the road. But his mind was busy with new directions, and he was in a hurry to test them.

22

Edwin Teller drove through the night after leaving Hobson, intent on getting as far from Hobson as possible. They had discussed stopping halfway, as they had done coming up. And he had overruled the idea. London was home, it was sanctuary. It was not on the north road, where every mile was a reminder. At home he could forget.

Amy was asleep in the seat beside him, and he felt more lonely than he could ever remember feeling in his life.

He had done the right thing, attending the services for Florence Teller. They had all tried to dissuade him, Amy and Susannah and Peter. He hadn't asked Walter's opinion. It wasn't important to him.

Given the circumstances, he wasn't sure why he had felt such an urgent need to be there. She wasn't what the others called her—the woman. As if she had no identity that mattered, someone who had caused more trouble with her death than she had ever caused in her lifetime.

Florence Marshall Teller. He whispered the words, and the night wind whipped them away. *Florence Marshall Teller.*

He recalled reading somewhere that as long as someone living still remembered one's name, one was never truly dead.

Florence Marshall Teller.

Beside him Amy stirred, then settled herself again without waking. He envied her.

He thought that of all of them Inspector Rutledge had understood his need. A member of the family—even if she had no family to call her own and was only a Teller by marriage. There was a dignity in that. And something in the policeman's face as he stood by the graveside reflected what he himself was feeling, that she had deserved better.

He didn't want to remember that plain house on its windswept knoll. He didn't want to think about the plain wooden coffin, and the plain little churchyard. It had made him want to lash out at all of them, and tell them the truth. But it would have hurt too many people. And so it had had to be buried with her, next to the boy she must have loved beyond bearing, alone as she was.

Edwin shook his head, trying to clear it and concentrate on the road ahead. His duty to the family.

That meant all of them. Divided though his loyalties were, the duty remained, and he would say nothing. He would go to his grave in silence if need be. But if he did, he would carry it on his conscience beyond his last breath.

God bless you.

Florence Marshall Teller . . .

23

Rutledge reached London in the small hours of the night and went to his flat to sleep.

He was in a quandary over the cane. Peter Teller, of course, would deny any knowledge of it. But Edwin would have made the journey back to London in easy stages and would reach Marlborough Street tomorrow at the earliest.

Walter Teller, then.

Leaving London for the trunk road, he caught sight of Charlie Hood again, this time walking briskly along the pavement, head down and buried in his thoughts. Rutledge pulled over and called to him.

Hood turned around, stared at Rutledge for a moment, then placed him. Reluctantly he came toward the motorcar, saying, "You don't have that man's murderer in custody, do you?" There was a mixture of emotions in his voice. Fear uppermost.

"Not yet. I don't think he's killed again."

"No. He's lying low somewhere, I'll be bound. He didn't expect to stir up a hornet's nest, now did he?"

"Do you know a Walter Teller?" Rutledge asked, still trying to place that vague sense of having seen Hood before.

"Teller? Should I? Is that what you're calling the boy?"

"We still don't have a name for him. I have a feeling the one he gave me was not his."

"Stands to reason. He was committing a crime, wasn't he?"

"Is your name Charlie Hood?" Rutledge countered.

"It's as good a one as any." Hood straightened up. Then he said, "Watch yourself, mate."

With that he walked off, ignoring Rutledge, who called to him to come back and finish the conversation. Turning a corner, Hood was quickly out of sight.

Hood had heard something, Rutledge thought. In that secretive telegraph system that tied the poor and the wanted and the running together, and no policeman knew the key.

Hamish said, "He answered the question aboot Teller wi' one of his ain."

"So he did. I'll give you odds he and Teller crossed paths." He considered that. "When he gave his account of the Bynum killing, he was coming from the direction of the Abbey. I wonder if Teller slept there. Or if it was in another church."

And then he swore. In his pocket was the photograph of Walter Teller that Jenny Teller had let him borrow to help the police find her husband. He had carried it with him, first to use, and then to return to her. And he had not yet kept his promise. He could have shown it to Hood. Who knew what name—if any—Teller had been using while he was invisible in London?

People behind Rutledge were sounding their horns, telling him to move on. He did, for a moment, consider returning to the Yard, but by the time he could send anyone to search for Hood the man would have been lost to sight again.

He drove on to Essex, and found Teller deadheading his roses after the night's rain.

Teller looked up when he saw the motorcar coming up the drive and straightened, as if preparing himself for what was to come.

Rutledge left the motorcar on the drive and walked across the lawns toward the roses. "They've done well this year," he said.

"You haven't come all this way to praise our roses."

"No. But they reminded me that Lawrence Cobb had put one in Florence Teller's grave. I think he was in love with her."

Teller's face tightened. "I don't know a Lawrence Cobb."

"No, that's probably true. Did you know a Charlie Hood? No? Then can you describe the cane that your brother Peter uses for his leg?"

"His cane?" The swift change in direction caught Teller unprepared.

"Yes. Was it ash, by any chance?"

"As I remember," Teller said, frowning, "it was Malacca. I've seen it so often, to tell you the truth I don't heed it anymore."

"The knob at the end?"

Teller was wary now. "Ivory, I think. A Gorgon's head. Why?"

Was he lying? Or telling the truth? It was hard to read his face.

"We have reason to believe it was a cane that killed Florence Teller. We found part of it in the hedge surrounding the front garden. I haven't seen your brother using his of late. Instead, he struggles to get around without one."

"I suspect he's trying to wean himself from the use of it."

"I doubt that. From the type of wound he suffered, I should think he will need a cane for the rest of his life."

"That may be—"

"It's likely," Rutledge said harshly, "that he used that cane to kill

Florence Teller. His motorcar was seen outside the house that same day. We've found that cane. And we have a witness who can describe both the driver and the vehicle."

Teller said, "Peter would have no reason to kill the woman. What's she to him?" He went back to the roses, his face turned away.

"His first wife, very likely," Rutledge said. "I think you've suspected that all along. She had a child, you know. A boy. If Timmy had lived, he would have displaced your son as heir."

"This is arrant supposition. My brother was in love with Susannah, and it was three years before he could win the family's approval to wed her. Why would he take another wife in the meantime?"

"Lawrence Cobb wanted to marry Florence Teller. I've told you. And when he couldn't, he married Mrs. Blaine's daughter. Your brother may have acted in haste and disappointment and then lived to regret it."

The strain on Teller's face was plain to see as he looked up. "Do you think I'd have countenanced that? Do you think I'd have let him wed Susannah, if I'd known there was an impediment to the marriage?"

"I don't know. Did you attend their wedding?"

"I was in West Africa. I didn't learn of it until months later."

"And so you let it stand by default. But he continued to visit Hobson, in fact. Even after his marriage. I have witnesses to that too. After the war, when his leg was so badly damaged he couldn't travel north, he let her believe he was dead. An easy solution."

"I won't listen to any more of this. It's a hodgepodge of wishful thinking and make-believe. There's not a grain of truth in it!" It was more a cry of pain than of denial.

Rutledge nodded and walked back to his motorcar. He turned it and then drove back up the drive. When he was nearly out of sight of the rose bed, he glanced in his rearview mirror.

Walter Teller was bent over, his arms wrapped around his body, as if he were in pain, his head down. Rutledge was too far away to see his face, but he carried with him the image of a man in agony.

He decided to drive on to Leticia Teller's house, and when he got there, he found that once more Mary Brittingham was ahead of him.

When the maid showed him into the garden, he realized that the two women had been having words. They hadn't heard his approach.

Their faces flushed, their eyes bright, they were confronting each other, standing several feet apart, as if any closer might lead to blows.

As he stepped through the gate from the shrubbery, they turned to stare at him, as if he'd dropped down from the moon, a creature they had never seen before and dangerous.

Leticia forced herself to smile. "Inspector Rutledge," she said. "Mary is just leaving."

"On the contrary, I want to hear what he's got to say."

Leticia's mouth tightened. "It's nothing to do with you, this business. I'd be grateful if you leave."

Mary said, "My sister is married to your brother. I'm here to protect her. She's not as strong as I am."

Leticia said through clenched teeth, "That can wait. Until we see what the Inspector has come to say." Turning to him, she added, "I must assume we owe the pleasure of your company to Yard business?"

He said, "I've come to ask you what you know about Florence Teller."

"Yes, that woman in Lancashire? I understand she was found murdered. It's a tragedy, of course, but nothing to do with us. I don't understand how we can help you," Leticia said.

"Your brother felt it had enough to do with your family that he attended her funeral yesterday."

The two women, their quarrel forgotten, were giving him their undivided attention now.

"Which brother?" Leticia demanded finally. "It's the first I've heard of this. Not Peter, surely?"

"Edwin Teller. As we haven't yet been able to locate her husband's relations, he felt it was his duty to represent the Teller family there."

"Was Amy with him?" Leticia asked as Mary's voice cut across hers.

"Duty?"

"There's damning evidence piling up against Peter Teller," he told them. "I have a shard of cane in my motorcar, part of the murder weapon, if I'm not mistaken. I have not seen your brother use a cane since I've met him. But I'm sure Sergeant Biggin in London will remember if there was one before I came on the scene. A witness saw what we believe was your brother's motorcar in front of the victim's house the day she died, and then watched a lame man matching your brother's description hobbling out to crank it and drive away in some haste. He was angry—upset, according to the witness. And if we take a sample of your brother's handwriting, I'm sure it will match the signature in the records of St. Bartholomew's Church in Hobson, where Florence Marshall and Peter Teller were married. For that matter, I could bring a dozen or more witnesses from Hobson, who knew Teller well enough to recognize him if they saw him now."

Leticia said, "Then why haven't your arrested him?"

"There are one or two loose ends to tie up. For instance, when you were in Portsmouth looking for your brother Walter, where was Peter?"

"He was with Edwin," she said immediately. "They went together. To share the driving, since both of them have had health problems. It was agreed."

"But that makes very little sense. The four of you left Jenny Teller in London, at the clinic alone. Why didn't Peter, since he found it so difficult to drive, stay with her and cope with the police? Cambridge was not so great a distance for Edwin."

"We did what we thought was most useful. We might well have found Walter, if he'd left London. We were fairly sure we would. And Peter was there to spell Edwin, if he were too tired to carry on." Leticia's eyes were hard.

"Peter couldn't have been in two places at once," he pointed out. "I suggest to you that he went to Lancashire under cover of his brother's disappearance, because he knew Walter would try to stop him. Whether Edwin knew at the time what it was Peter was intending to do, I can't say. But it would explain, very well, why Edwin felt compelled to attend Florence Teller's funeral. It wasn't a kind gesture to another of his name; it was a guilty conscience because he lied to protect Peter."

Mary said with interest, "You've worked out all the details. But what if they aren't true? What if it's all circumstantial evidence? It could be, you know. I've known Peter for a good many years. I can't believe he would have married someone else when he was so devoted to Susannah. That's the human evidence, Mr. Rutledge. However beautiful or exotic or wealthy or socially prominent this woman was, he was waiting to marry Susannah."

"She was none of those things."

"And that may be the key. An opportunist. Perhaps he met her on a walking tour. And there was a child. He might have had no choice but to marry her. But this child," Leticia added. "He's older than Harry? Or was he never born, because he didn't exist? What's become of him?"

"He was the elder. He's dead."

"Well, then," she countered, "if the child is dead, there was no longer a tie. He would have divorced the woman as soon as he uncovered her lie."

"We have it on good authority that he was still involved with Florence Teller until the war. I don't think he could make up his mind."

Mary said, "I'm glad I stayed. This is nonsense, but it will upset Jenny no end. She's very fond of Peter and Susannah." She turned to Leticia. "We're all invited to the farm, to celebrate Jenny's birthday on Friday. It's going to be a very uncomfortable state of affairs."

"I must contact our solicitor. The time to stop this ridiculous

business is now, before the police act on what they consider their
'evidence.' Thank you for your information, Inspector. I hope you
will come to your senses and realize that you are about to take a step
that will seriously jeopardize your career. I suggest you look into the
background of this woman. The solution to her murder is there. Not
with my family."

He accepted his dismissal. There was other information he needed
to collect now. A. P. Repton for one. That would explain why Florence Teller had never tried to contact Peter through the Army or at his
London house at the war's end.

Rutledge stopped in Cambridge and asked the porter at King's for
information about one Benjamin Larkin.

The porter looked him up and down. "And who might be inquir-
ing about one of our young gentlemen, sir?"

"Rutledge, Scotland Yard." Rutledge produced his identification,
and the porter scanned it closely.

Then, satisfied, he said, "He's one of our brighter lads. Never been
in trouble. Comes of a good family. I've seen his father visit a time or
two. A doctor, I'm told." He hesitated. "And what's he done, if I may
ask, to draw the attention of the Yard?"

"He's helping us with an inquiry."

"I would expect no less of him. Very fine young lad, is Larkin."

Rutledge digested this as he drove west and then south toward
Dorset.

He found Sedley in the middle of the county, a village with houses
directly on the road, some of them whitewashed, others of local stone.
There was a small but handsome church, a pub, and a green where
geese swam in the warm waters of a shallow pond. In the pub, he
paused for a late lunch and information.

"Mistletoe Cottage," the man who brought his meal repeated. "It's
just on your left as you go out of Sedley."

"Does A. P. Repton still live there?"

"A. P.—oh you'll be meaning Alice Preston. Not Repton. She died in the summer of 1918 and is buried along there in the churchyard. A strange old bird. She came into money some years ago and told Rector she had only to receive and mail letters to earn it. Rector thought she was going dotty, but she traveled to Shaftesbury every week on the baker's cart, to the post office there. Faithfully, rain or shine. If you want the truth, I expect she was just having us on."

"What else did she do? To earn this windfall?"

"That was it."

Then how did this woman in Dorset come to know Peter Teller?

"Did she have a son or nephew in the Army, by any chance?"

"Not that any of us knew about," the man told him.

"What did she do with her free time? When not traveling to the post office?"

"She knitted for a missionary society. She'd collect odd bits of yarn around the village, and then she'd make these scarves and gloves and hats for children in faraway places. Quite colorful, some of them. She said foreign children liked bright colors."

"Which mission society, do you know?"

"One in Oxford, I think it was."

"Not Kent?"

"No, I'm sure it was Oxford. They have missions amongst the Eskimos."

A dead end. Circumstantial evidence with no way to learn if she was the same woman the postmistress had described. Likely, yes, but that was as far as it went. All the same, when he'd finished his lunch, Rutledge went to Shaftesbury and inquired at the post office there. But all the postmistress could tell him was that Miss Preston sent and received letters sporadically, although she didn't recall the name Peter Teller. "I remember her only because she was eccentric," she told him apologetically.

And then, just as Rutledge reached the post office door, the postmistress said, "Oh—there's something else. Alice told me once she was nursery maid in the household of Evelyn Darley. My mother remembered Evelyn and her twin sister when they came out. She said they were the prettiest girls she's ever seen. I asked Alice if it was true, and she said it was."

Rutledge stared at her in disbelief, then smiled and thanked her.

This was the connection he'd hoped for and very nearly missed.

Evelyn Darley's twin sister was Gran, the Teller grandmother.

Peter Teller had paid Alice Preston, onetime nursery maid to his great-aunt Evelyn, long since retired to Sedley, in Dorset, to act as go-between, so that Florence Teller never wrote directly to him through his regiment. And his letters back to her never gave away whether he was on leave or with the Army. He'd told her, according to the postmistress in Thielwald, that it was the safest, surest way to reach him.

And when Alice Preston died in the summer of 1918, Peter let this only link to Florence die with her.

Lieutenant Teller never came home from the war.

Rutledge went to find a telephone.

He could just see the mellow stone of the church from where he was standing in the hotel lounge, asking to be connected to the Yard. When Gibson was brought to the telephone, Rutledge asked if there was any more news about one Lieutenant Burrows, whom Susannah Teller had told him about.

"It's true enough, he was killed in the war. The only son. Widowed mother lives in Worcester, off the Milton Road. The family's well connected, Army and politics. I've also had the Army looking for another Peter Teller. They move like treacle, but they searched the regimental records where our Captain Teller served, and he's the only one of that name they could find, going back a generation."

"Any reason to believe that a widow turning up would distress the Burrows family?"

"That's the interesting bit, sir. The lieutenant married on his last leave and leaves a widow. No children. She has married again and now lives in Scotland."

Hamish said, "It wouldna' signify. Yon lass didna' ken how to find her husband's family."

But Rutledge was prepared for anything. He thanked Gibson and put up the receiver.

No stone unturned . . .

Hamish said again, "It doesna' signify."

"It was important enough for Susannah Teller to bring it to my attention."

"Aye, with lies. To throw you off the track of her ain husband."

He drove on toward Worcester, tired now and ready to end the game of chase he'd been playing. But it was the last of the outstanding questions, and when it came to trial, Rutledge preferred not to leave anything to chance.

The house where the Burrows family lived was on the southern outskirts of Worcester, with a river view. It was a large and comfortable estate set back from the road. The house was of the same stone as the famous cathedral, with a portico and white pillars leading up two steps to the door. A fountain featuring a statue of Neptune, a conch held to his lips, and water horses at each corner spouting streams of water formed the centerpiece of the circular drive. From the age of the fountain, Rutledge thought it might have been shipped home from a Grand Tour a generation ago.

Wisteria climbed the wall of one wing of the house, and an old climbing rose set off the stonework on the opposite side.

When Rutledge lifted the knocker, he could hear the sound echoing through the house, and expected to find it was empty for the summer. But a maid in crisp black came to answer his summons, and he asked to speak to Mrs. Burrows.

She wanted to know his business, and he identified himself.

After a time she came back and escorted him to a sitting room overlooking a shrubbery, where a woman of perhaps sixty-five waited to greet him. Her graying hair was put up in the older style, and her clothing was rather old-fashioned as well. But her blue eyes were alert and wary.

"What brings the Yard to my door?" she asked, after asking him to sit down.

"A wild-goose chase, at a guess," he said, smiling. "Your son Thomas was, I'm told, lost in the war."

"Yes. Such a promising future lost with him as well. It was a pity. Does this have to do with Thomas? I can't think why!"

"I understand that his widow has remarried and lives in Scotland."

"Yes, Elizabeth was the sweetest girl. A perfect match. My husband and I were terribly pleased."

"Can you tell me where your son might have been in 1902? I'm sorry, I can't give you the month. Summer, I should think."

"Of 1902?" She smiled. "That's very easy to do. He contracted rheumatic fever and nearly died. It was something of a miracle that he lived. We had him with us for almost fifteen more years. The doctor warned us there might be lasting effects, but thank God, he sprang back to health with the vigor of youth and was chafing at the bit to rejoin his regiment."

"Did he walk as a way of recovering his strength? For instance, in Lancashire, which isn't as demanding as the Lake Country or Derbyshire. Or perhaps he took the sea air in Morecambe?"

"I don't believe anyone in this family has ever been to Morecambe? I'm beginning to think you must have the wrong Burrows, Inspector."

"We're trying to find anyone who might have been in that vicinity in 1902 and into 1903."

"It couldn't have been our Thomas. He was very ill for weeks, and then there were weeks of recovery after that. Walking tours would have been impossible." She frowned. "I've always had the feeling that Thomas knew he was living on borrowed time. He grasped life with such eagerness after that. I was surprised his regiment allowed him to sail with them for India. But of course the long sea journey was good for him."

Rutledge hadn't intended to name names, but he could see no other choice.

"Do you perhaps know Peter Teller, who was in your son's regiment?"

"Yes, we met him at a regimental affair. Quite a handsome young man in his dress uniform, and his wife was charming. Susannah? Was that her name? Imagine remembering it after all these years. But I couldn't help but think watching her that I hoped Thomas would find someone just as loving. I heard from friends that Captain Teller was severely wounded and is still recovering. Is there better news now?"

"He's walking again," Rutledge told her, "though still with great difficulty."

"I'm glad. Thomas admired him so. I must say that if my son had to emulate anyone, Peter Teller was as fine a choice as I could wish for."

Susannah Teller had been right about the imitation, then. But either she'd forgotten or didn't know about Thomas Burrows's illness.

Hamish said, "Ye ken, he'd ha' put it behind him. It was no' something to bring up."

And that was true. Stiff upper lip and all that for a young subaltern just learning to fit in.

Rutledge took his leave, thanking her for her help.

"But I've given you very little," she said. "I hope your inquiry prospers."

In the motorcar once more, Rutledge said as he let out the clutch, "I don't think Susannah Teller expected her story to collapse so quickly."

"Aye. That's verra' likely. But she's afraid her husband is a murderer."

"And she may be right." He took a deep breath. "It's time to go to

Hobson. Constable Satterthwaite and his superiors have the right to know where we're looking, and what the evidence is."

"He will be verra' angry," Hamish warned. "It was a cruel thing to do to such a lass."

He stayed the night in Cheshire and drove the rest of the way to Hobson just after first light.

The village was awake and the shops busy when he got there. Constable Satterthwaite was pleased to see him, standing in the police station doorway with a packet of tea biscuits in his hand and smiling.

"Did you learn anything more about Larkin?"

"I went to his college in Cambridge. The porter there vouched for him. Meanwhile, I've been searching for the real Peter Teller. Not the man you thought you knew. That man never existed."

"I met him—we saw him time and again here in Hobson," the constable argued. "He wasn't a figment of her imagination. Or ours. Besides, there's the boy."

"He was someone else. There's much to tell you," Rutledge said, taking the chair across the desk, as they reached the office.

"The man in London, then," Satterthwaite said with resignation.

Rutledge proceeded to outline what he had learned so far, and how he believed it all fit together. Satterthwaite listened in silence, but his face reddened as the evidence against Peter Teller mounted.

"Why did he have to kill her, then?" he asked finally. "She thought he was dead. It was finished."

"I don't know. Yet," Rutledge admitted.

"Damn the man!" he said heavily, and then to Rutledge, "I'm sorry, sir, but you weren't here, I was. I'd like very much to watch him hang for what he's done. Not just the murder, you understand, although that was bad enough. But for her empty life, for not being there when Timmy died and she was half out of her mind with grief, wanting to bury him at the farm, and not in the churchyard. We had all we could do to convince her to let us take him away. She wanted him there, where she could see him every day."

Rutledge was reminded of Mr. Cobb, who spoke to the memorial to his sons, every morning and every evening. He could understand her need.

Satterthwaite got up and paced the floor, his feet heavy on the boards as he traced the same line back and forth, back and forth.

Then he stopped and looked at Rutledge. "It all fits together. I must say it does. But in spite of what I feel about the bastard—begging your pardon, sir—it's hard to believe, isn't it? That someone could be that cruel? I never got to know Teller well, of course, but I wouldn't have put him down as that cold-blooded. Selfish, yes, he was that." He shook his head. "It'ull take a little getting used to. You'll bring him back to Hobson to face charges?"

"Yes. On Monday."

"I'd like to be with you when you take him to Thielwald."

"I'll see that it's arranged."

"Thank you, sir. And thank you for telling me. It means more than I can say. I'll keep it to myself until you bring the man here." He cleared his throat. "Will you be staying the night?"

"I might as well. And get an early start tomorrow."

"Mrs. Greeley will be that pleased to see you. She was asking only yesterday if there was word of Jake."

"He's with my sister," Rutledge told him. "In good hands."

Satterthwaite nodded.

Rutledge went back to Sunrise Cottage in the late afternoon. He couldn't have said why he was drawn there. Satterthwaite offered to go with him, but Rutledge thanked him and shook his head.

The day was fair, with a stiff breeze that cooled the air and made it feel more like early spring than June. Fat lambs followed slow-grazing ewes in the pastures along the road.

As he drove, he asked himself again, as he had on the journey to Lancashire, what had become of the cane's head? It was the last piece of crucial evidence, and he wanted very badly to find it.

If it had been taken away and dropped from a bridge, as Satterthwaite had suggested, it would never come to light. Which meant that the rest of the evidence against Peter Teller had to be damning.

"He'll have a verra' good defense," Hamish agreed.

The house was just ahead, first the roof and then the hedge coming into sight on its knoll. He left the motorcar on the road and walked through the gate, intending to dig around in the flower beds with his fingers, to see if the cane's knob was there. It was hopeless, he knew that very well, but he had to try.

But someone had watered the plants, and pulled out any weeds that would mar their appearance. He bent down to touch a leaf.

It was still wet.

Instead of opening the door, he went out the gate again and walked around the house to the gardens by the kitchen door.

The man squatting beside one of the beds leapt to his feet with surprise as Rutledge suddenly appeared, braced for anything that might come at him.

It was Lawrence Cobb, his trousers stained from working the earth and pulling weeds. A pile of wilting debris lay on the grassy path next to his boots.

"Oh—it's only you, then," Cobb said in relief. "I've come here to keep the gardens for her. Until someone knows what's to happen to this place. It's the least I can do. Her flowers shouldn't die too."

Rutledge could read the unspoken words in his eyes—*and it brings her closer, as if she were still alive and somewhere inside.*

"I see nothing wrong with it," Rutledge answered him. "A pity you weren't out here working on the day she was attacked."

"Don't you think I dream about it at night?"

"If your wife hears of it, it will be on your head."

Cobb said, "If I had been here, she might still be alive. But that's hindsight. I hear you found that walker. Was he the man?"

"As it turned out, he was a witness and a very helpful one. He saw the motorcar by the hedge and the man who was driving it."

Cobb dusted his hands, nodding. "I knew it. Someone from his family, most likely, with an eye to the property."

"Someone from his family, yes, but I don't think this property entered into it. I think he'd come to see her, and decide what to do about her. What I don't know is whether or not she invited him in. It must have been a shock to her to see him there. She wouldn't have known what to say."

Cobb stared up at the bedroom windows, as if he could see the answer written there on the glass. "She stopped looking for him—waiting, listening for the door—over a year ago. She told me he must be dead, but you could tell she hadn't really started to believe even then. I think she expected some miracle, and then when it never happened, she lost hope. The logic in her head told her one thing, her heart something else."

"Was he good to her?"

Cobb brought his gaze back to Rutledge. "It depends on how you define good, of course. She never wanted for anything—food on the table, wood for the fire in the winter, clothes to keep her warm. He never struck her or called her names. This was the place she wanted to live in and bring up her son. Just as she'd grown up here with her aunt. And he made no objection. Of course, if he'd asked her to go wherever his regiment was sent, she would have, just to be with him. No matter what the hardships were. But the truth is, he wasn't here as often as he should have been. There's the Army, I understand that, of course I do. But I'd have moved heaven and earth to come home if she'd been mine. I'd left the Army and found other work to do, digging ditches if I had to, anything to be near her."

"You knew her well," Rutledge said quietly.

"I loved her. And so I listened to her, and read between the lines sometimes. But she saw me as her friend. And I was scrupulous about keeping it that way. I'd have lost her, otherwise."

"I think you would have," Rutledge said.

He rubbed his forehead with his gloved hand and left behind a long streak of rich earth. "I was here when Timmy died. Not in the house. I meant, in Hobson. I thought she'd lose her mind. She stopped coming into town, stopped eating, stopped looking out for herself. But some of us saw to it that she had whatever she needed. Mrs. Greeley. Satterthwaite. Others. People would bring her food, for fear she wasn't cooking. I chopped wood that winter and piled it outside the kitchen door there, within reach even on the worst days, and kept it covered with a tarp. When she didn't milk the cow, because it reminded her too much of feeding the boy those last days, I took it down to Mrs. Greeley to keep until she was ready to have it back. I've never seen so much grief as she felt."

"I saw the photograph of her son in her room."

"That was the only photograph she had. And I took that for her. She said that Teller never cared for pictures set about. But she was glad of it. You'd have thought Teller would have understood something like that."

"There was never a photograph of her husband? Not even a wedding picture?"

"There was a small one of the wedding couple. She kept it safe somewhere, out of sight and out of mind."

With his letters very likely, Rutledge thought. And gone with them.

Cobb took off his gloves and swatted at an insect busy about his ears. "I want to know. Have you found her killer? Don't lie to me, I want to know. I can't sleep nights, sometimes, thinking about everyone who knew her, anyone who could have done such a thing, and I need to *know*. I come into Hobson sometimes and look at the faces of people I meet on the street or in a shop or sitting next to me on a Sunday. And I think, could that be him? Or that one? My uncle tells me I'll drive myself mad doing that, but it's the only way I'll have any peace, finding him before the police do."

"I can't tell you how the inquiry is progressing. I will say that it's possible that we know who it was."

"And the bird? He's been no help? My mother-in-law told me you'd taken Jake. I was glad. I thought she might do it a mischief with its squawking so loud she couldn't sleep. And Betsy wanted no part of it."

"The bird hasn't said much. So far." He hesitated, then said, "If you found something unusual—out of place—tell Satterthwaite, will you?"

He left Cobb there and went into the house, walking through the empty rooms, listening to the sounds of his own footsteps in the silence. Hamish, in the back of his mind, was busy, but he could find nothing to trigger a sudden thought or offer a glimmer of light.

Nothing had changed. He hadn't expected it to.

And that was the problem. Nothing *had* changed, he could see only what he had before. With the eyes of the past, not the present.

He considered what to do about Cobb coming to tend the flowers, and decided he was doing no harm. And it gave him something to think about besides taking the head off whoever had killed Florence Teller.

Without speaking to Cobb again, he left the house and drove back to Hobson.

Rutledge and Satterthwaite ate their dinner together at a pub in Thielwald. The food was heavy, suitable for men who did physical labor, filling and satisfying. As Satterthwaite promised, the pudding was excellent, and as they were finishing it, he said to Rutledge, "You're quiet."

"I was thinking about a birthday celebration. Tonight in Essex."

"Did you want to be there?"

"I wasn't invited. I just have a feeling that I shouldn't have stayed over. I should have gone directly back to London."

"One day won't matter."

24

Rutledge was putting his valise and a packet of sandwiches prepared by Mrs. Greeley into his motorcar, when Lawrence Cobb came down the High Street and nodded as he walked up to Mrs. Greeley's door.

It was then that Rutledge saw the left side of his face. There was an angry welt along his cheekbone. It was oozing a thin line of fluid and blood.

Shutting the driver's door, Rutledge said swiftly, "What's happened?"

"Nothing. I'm leaving Betsy. I told her as much last night. That this marriage is a pretense and we're both better off out of it. I came to see if Mrs. Greeley will give me a room for a few days, just until I can make arrangements."

"Why not stay with your uncle?"

"He's old. I don't want him caught up in my troubles."

Rutledge said, "Work it out. Florence Teller is dead."

"Look, I'm tired. Working in Florence's—Mrs. Teller's garden yesterday I could see my way for the first time. I'm still mourning her. I will be for a very long while. It's not fair to Betsy, it's not fair to me, pretending I have deep feelings for her. We've no children. That's a blessing. And so I've told her. I also told her that she could have the farm. I won't send her back to her mother. They don't get on." He smiled grimly. "I should have waited until she'd set down the hot bread tray. The corner of it clipped me. She's gone home to her mother. But she'll be back. She likes the house. It will matter more than I do before very long."

He'd thought it all out, just as he said.

But Rutledge persisted. "You're doing to Betsy what Teller did to his wife."

"No. I married a Betsy who didn't exist. The true woman is nothing like the one I courted. She's not sweet and loving and caring. She's like her mother, mean-spirited, discontented, selfish. The day after I married her, I knew it was a mistake. This has nothing to do with Florence. I was expecting to be happy. I really believed we could be happy." He shook his head. "You can't make love happen when there are lies to start with."

Hamish said, "It willna' do any guid. He's made up his mind."

Rutledge silently acknowledged that. "I'm just leaving. Mrs. Greeley will be glad to offer you my room, I'm sure."

Cobb looked sharply at Rutledge. "You aren't coming back. What about her killer?"

"I'm going to take the killer into custody. I won't be needing the room again."

Cobb thanked him and was about to turn away. Then he said, "What becomes of Jake? When you've made your arrest? I'm offering to take him. I can now. He sometimes speaks with her voice. It would be a comfort."

"Even when that voice says good night to her husband?"

"That doesn't matter to me. It's her voice. Close enough. I'll hear it again."

"I'll see what can be done," Rutledge promised, thinking that Frances would be delighted to hear that Jake had a permanent home.

And with that, Lawrence Cobb opened the door to Mrs. Greeley's house as Rutledge turned the bonnet of his motorcar toward the south.

25

On his way into London, Rutledge made a detour to Chelsea, but the Channing house was quiet, the drapes still pulled across the windows, as they had been for days. The long golden rays of the setting sun touched them with brightness, but it was only a shallow reflection, not the lamplight he had hoped to see. He couldn't bring himself to walk up to the door.

She was in good hands, wherever she was. He could only wish her a speedy recovery. And time would see to that. He could still remember the shock of recognition as she lay there injured in the broken and twisted wreckage of her carriage. He'd been too busy then to deal with the image that was burned into his memory. Seeing her whole again would change that.

"Aye," Hamish said. "But she isna' coming back to London straightaway. She was already leaving it, ye ken."

Analyzing his own feelings, he realized that the uppermost emotion that day had been fear. Fear that she was terribly injured. Not pity or compassion or anger at the waste of a life.

He had been in love once. And it hadn't worked out. Just as Lawrence Cobb had said. He'd seen the look on Jean's face when she finally visited him in hospital and realized what he'd become. He had done the only thing he could do in that single appalling moment: he'd released her from her promise to marry him, so that he wouldn't have to face her rejection. The relief on her face as he spoke the words had stayed with him long after her first horrified view of him sitting there, a broken man, had begun to fade.

Once was enough. He said as much to Hamish, his voice sounding overly loud in the cacophony of traffic as he turned toward the Yard.

Gibson greeted him with the news that Billy had killed again.

"There's been another murder. Of the same ilk. And this time Billy has cut his throat. The victim was on the bridge, walking, minding his own business. And he was robbed."

"How can you be sure it's our friend Billy?"

"The past week, we've had constables in street clothes walking over the bridge and along the river late at night, and we've been watching them with field glasses. But nothing happened." He paused. "None of them looked like you from a distance. They were a different shape. Different height. And nothing happened to them. And then this poor sod was attacked."

"Billy was elsewhere. Or recognized them for policemen."

Gibson said, "We don't think so. His victims are usually near the bridge. And out late at night. They could have passed for you, walking off a mood. You do that, you know."

Rutledge hadn't realized that he was so predictable. "All right. Go on."

"You nearly caught him. He's afraid of you. And he wants you dead, for luck."

It wasn't unheard of.

"He won't come back tonight. Not with the police everywhere, looking for evidence."

"No, sir. I suggest you get a good night's sleep. Tomorrow night you'll be on that bridge, and we'll be watching you."

"Whose idea was this?" Rutledge asked, curious.

"Inspector Mickelson, sir," Gibson replied, his voice neutral. "But we have to catch him, sir. There's no other way."

"Yes, I understand. All right. But only tomorrow night, Gibson. I must drive to Essex on Monday morning, unless Captain Teller returns to London sooner. "

"I hope you'll be taking someone into custody soon. Old Bowels is getting impatient."

"Bowles isn't going to like it when we do. Peter Teller, Walter Teller's elder brother, seems to be our man."

"My dear lord." Gibson whistled softly. "I hope your evidence is rock solid. Or none of us will have any peace."

Rutledge left, intending to visit his sister. If Jake hadn't said anything of importance—and he was not anticipating hearing that he had—then he would carry the bird back to Lancashire and give it to Lawrence Cobb.

He caught Frances just returning from dinner with friends and hailed her as she was going inside. She turned and smiled at him.

"Ian. Come in. I've had a lovely evening. What brings you here? Don't tell me it's Jake. I'll be jealous."

He laughed. "I expected to find the lights on, Jake on the loose, and myself in bad odor for bringing him to you."

"He's been a dear. I've tried to write down everything he says, but it's mostly wishing her husband Peter a good night, or something ordinary. He says 'My dearest wife' in her voice, but I know it's a letter he must have heard a hundred times. And 'Shall we have tea, my dear?' He always answers that with 'What will Jake have?' Hardly useful in a courtroom, I'm afraid."

"I didn't expect an enlightening conversation with a murderer," he said as Frances turned on the light in the small breakfast room and then lifted the covering from Jake's cage.

He was asleep, head tucked beneath his wing, but he looked at them, blinking the second lid on his eye, and said, "Shall we have tea, my dear?"

"It's not teatime, Jake. In the morning."

He began to swing, and Frances said, "I can see that he must have been wonderful company for a woman alone, but my maid is terrified of him and won't come near him. He squawks at her, as if she's an interloper. It's either Jake or Nell. And I must choose Nell."

"There's someone who wants him. If it works out, it will be the right choice for him."

"You look tired."

"Much on my mind."

"I'm sure. Well, go home, Ian, and let me go to bed."

He wished her a good night, and left.

Sunday morning was misty and gray as Rutledge returned to the Yard early. There was a report to write and then preparations to be made for the night's promenade along the river. He had debated asking for a weapon, to even the odds, and then thought better of it. Sitting in his office, staring out the window and listening to Big Ben chime the hour, Mickelson's plan seemed workable. But Billy was becoming an accomplished killer now. And in the dark, many things could happen. What had driven the boy to this point in his life? Not that it mattered. He had crossed the boundary; he was going to hang when caught.

Rutledge was just turning around to begin his report when Sergeant Gibson burst into the small office with only a cursory knock.

"I think you'd better know, sir. We've just had a telephone call from Essex, sir. There's been a death at Witch Hazel Farm. The Teller house."

"What happened?" Rutledge asked, getting to his feet. "When?"

"Someone fell down the stairs. Just before breakfast. Chief Superintendent Bowles isn't in, nor is Inspector Mickelson. I think, if you hurry, you can be on your way before they arrive. It's still your inquiry, after all."

Rutledge reached for his hat. "It will take no more than fifteen minutes to pack a valise."

He was down the passage and in the stairwell when he remembered the rendezvous with Billy. Mickelson could deal with it.

Sunday morning traffic was light, and he made good time, going directly to the house at Witch Hazel Farm.

The drive was crowded with vehicles, and he could see that the police from Waddington were there, already taking over from the constable in Repton. Dr. Fielding, the Tellers' Essex physician, was standing by the door in the watery sunlight, an unlit pipe in his hands.

He saw Rutledge pull up and hailed him. "Inspector. Good, you've come."

"I've had no briefing," he told Fielding. "There wasn't time."

"It's Captain Teller. He tripped coming down the stairs this morning."

"Gentle God," Rutledge said blankly. And then, "What can you tell me?"

"It was a family weekend. Mrs. Jenny Teller's birthday. There was a party on Friday, and my wife and I were invited. Rather a nice party, actually. I did notice that Captain Teller was drinking a little more than usual. But he carried it well, there was no disturbance. My wife and I left just before eleven, and that's all I can tell you until the summons came this morning. Amy Teller called to say there had been an accident and to hurry. But by the time I got here, Captain Teller was dead. Amy Teller was the first to reach him. She said he was alive then. He spoke her name. She distinctly heard him say 'Mee' as she bent over him."

"Considering his injuries, was that possible?"

"I should think so. I've examined him as best I can on the floor at the foot of the stairs. I'll know more when I've got him in the surgery. If you want my best opinion at this time, I'd say his bad leg gave way, pitching him down the stairs. According to his brother Edwin, Peter has been avoiding using his cane of late. He may just have paid for his stubbornness with his life."

Rutledge thanked him and walked into the house.

Captain Teller lay where he'd fallen, his body sprawled at the foot of the stairs, his bad leg still on the first step behind him. Just coming down the passage was a man of slender build with a pockmarked face.

"Good morning. Who let you in? There should have been a constable on the door."

"My name is Rutledge, Scotland Yard. I believe someone sent for me, since I was just involved in Walter Teller's disappearance."

"Inspector Jessup. Waddington." They shook hands. "Disappearance? When was this? I wasn't told about it."

"You wouldn't have been. It happened in London, and Teller returned unharmed, after giving his wife a hellish four days of worry."

"Indeed. Well, this one—Captain Peter Teller—fell down the stairs, as you can see. He's quite lame, I'm told, and wasn't using his cane, as he should have done. Straightforward. Accidental death. A waste of the Yard's time."

Rutledge said nothing, kneeling by the dead man, close enough now to smell the stale whisky on his skin and in his hair.

"He was drinking. Last night, I should think. It wouldn't have helped him manage the stairs," he commented, straightening up. "What does the family have to say?"

"They're in the breakfast room. I haven't interviewed them. Mrs. Susannah Teller, the victim's wife, insisted that we touch nothing until you'd arrived." Rutledge could tell that Jessup wasn't especially happy to be second-guessed by the Yard. Not in what he clearly believed was an accidental death on his patch.

And Rutledge would have agreed with him, if it weren't for the other case in Lancashire. A fall down the stairs was easier to face than the hangman, and Teller had been drinking enough of late to indicate something was troubling him.

"I'd like to speak to Mrs. Susannah Teller in the study. Do you think that could be arranged? I'd like to know why she sent for me."

Inspector Jessup said, "I'd like to be present."

"Not immediately, if you don't mind," Rutledge said, keeping to the formalities of refusal. "She may speak more freely to me."

He stood there looking down at Teller's body, thinking that Constable Satterthwaite would be disappointed, and Lawrence Cobb jubilant. Then he nodded to Jessup. The body could be taken away.

Jessup went outside to find his men, and Rutledge waited until the door had closed behind him. Then he squatted by the body and lifted the legs of Teller's trousers. But there was no mark that he could see to indicate that Teller had been tripped. And so, accident—or suicide.

Just as Rutledge was stepping back, Fielding came in, preparatory to the removal. He said, looking at Teller as Rutledge had done, "A tragedy, this. The leg he fought so hard to save betrayed him in the end. He might have been better off if he'd allowed them to take it."

Rutledge said, "In a way you're right. But I think, knowing Captain Teller as I did, I'd venture to say he'd have wanted it that way, even so."

As a blanket was spread over the body before lifting it onto the stretcher, Fielding said, "Unless I find evidence to the contrary, gentlemen, I'll consider this an accidental death."

Jessup said, "I'd agree with that finding."

And then Peter Teller was carried out into the gray morning, leaving only a small spot of blood to mark his passage. Rutledge, thinking about Monday morning's expected arrest, was of two minds. When he closed this case, there would be very little justice for Florence Teller now.

In some fashion, it might be for the best. It would save the Teller family endless publicity and sorrow. Chief Superintendent Bowles would be pleased about that.

When the house door closed behind the dead man, Rutledge walked down the passage and into the study where once he'd spoken to Walter Teller about his brother.

Five minutes later, the study door opened and Susannah Teller was ushered in, her face pale with shock and grief, her eyes red from crying. She had tried very hard to protect her husband. Even knowing what he had done.

She looked Rutledge straight in the face and said as the door swung shut behind her, "You're to treat this as a murder investigation, do you hear me? They killed him. With their unspoken accusations, their finger-pointing when Jenny wasn't in the room, their snubs. He told them he hadn't killed Florence Teller. He tried to explain. But the evidence was against him, and he drank himself into oblivion Friday night and last night. I told him we shouldn't have come. But he said he must do it for Jenny's sake. It's always for Jenny's sake, isn't it? The innocent victim, Jenny Teller. Well, I'm having them pay for my losing Peter, do you understand me?" she ended fiercely.

"Mrs. Teller—"

"No, don't tell me it was just a horrible accident because he'd been drinking and couldn't find his cane. And don't try to tell me he killed himself out of a guilty conscience. He didn't murder that woman in Lancashire. If you want to know the truth, it was either Walter or Edwin. Take your pick. Because when Peter was there, when Peter just wanted to speak to her, he could hear Walter in the house some-where out of sight. Or Edwin. I don't know. I don't care. They both sound very much alike. Have you noticed? One of them was there, and after Peter left, whichever one it was seized the opportunity to kill her and let Peter take the blame."

She turned on her heel and walked out of the room, slamming the door behind her. But she didn't go up the stairs. He heard the front door slam as well, and when he went to look out the window, she was running across the lawn to the rose garden, as if trying to flee her own thoughts.

Susannah Teller had tried to throw him off the scent once before.

Hamish said, "She loved him verra' much."

"Yes." He took a deep breath and went out to find the rest of the family.

They were a grim and silent lot when Rutledge walked into the dining room. Walter Teller was standing at the window, his back to his family. Leticia was also standing, staring down at the cold hearth. Amy and Edwin sat together at one end of the table, and at the other, Mary Brittingham was trying to calm her weeping sister.

Mary said, "Has he been taken away?"

"Yes. Just now."

"Then if you will allow it, I'll take my sister to her room and sit with her. It's been frightful for her."

"I must begin by asking each of you where you were when Captain Teller fell. Miss Teller?"

"I was just coming down the passage. I'd been in the kitchen, helping Mollie. I generally do when all of us are here. It's a great deal of work, and finding suitable help from the village isn't always possible on a Sunday morning."

"Thank you. Miss Brittingham?"

"I was upstairs. I'd overslept and was late coming down for breakfast."

"Could you see Captain Teller fall?"

"I was still in my room. Two minutes—less—later, and I'd have been in the passage."

He turned to Jenny.

"I was outside, I'd taken my tea outside this morning. I—I wanted to walk a little."

"It was misting here? Raining?"

"A soft mist. I don't mind that. It was cooler after a string of warm days." She broke down again.

Rutledge turned to Amy Teller. "I was in the study, looking for a book. I'd finished the one I'd been reading last night. I was the first to reach Peter. They may have told you. He was still alive, and he said my name. And then he died. It was awful. I think I screamed for Susannah."

"Where was she?"

"I believe she'd already come down and was in the dining room. She appeared from that direction, anyway."

Her husband looked up at Rutledge, his face grim, his eyes red. "I was in my room. Like Mary, a few seconds more and I'd have been with him. I might have saved him from falling. I can't seem to get that out of my mind."

Rutledge waited for Walter Teller to give his whereabouts. He didn't turn. Finally he said, his voice muffled, "I was in the drawing room. I wanted to be by myself."

And so no one had been on the scene. Or at least no one admitted to it.

He nodded to Mary Brittingham, and she rose, saying to Jenny, "Come on, love, you'll be better off lying down."

Jenny shook her head. "I won't go up those stairs. I don't think I ever shall again."

"Then we'll use the back stairs," Mary told her.

Jenny said, rising from her chair, "I'm to blame. I told Walter I wanted to have a party, as I did last year. With everyone here. If I hadn't, Peter would still be in London this morning, and not dead."

"Don't be silly," her husband said roughly from the window. "Accidents happen. He could have fallen down his own stairs, for that matter. He was drunk enough last night."

She looked at him, hurt clear in her face. And then without answering him, she turned and walked from the dining room. Mary followed her.

The covered dishes of the family breakfast were still on the sideboard. Rutledge could smell the bacon and see a dish of boiled eggs.

Used plates had been set on the small table to one side. By his account, four of the family had already eaten their breakfast. It fit with their statements.

When Jenny was well out of hearing, Rutledge said, "Your sister-in-law has just told me that Peter Teller was shunned all weekend. Miss Teller, did either you or Mary say anything to the family about the evidence against Captain Teller?"

"I told Edwin. You had already spoken to Walter. I imagine Amy learned of it from Edwin. It was Jenny's birthday, and we had agreed not to upset her. She'd been through enough, and it would make for a very unpleasant party. As it was, we were all struggling to put up a good front. In the end even Jenny felt the tension and wanted to know what was wrong. We all lied through our teeth. It might have been better if we'd told her the truth and been done with it. Peter was moody, he could read between the lines. Walter hardly spoke to him. Edwin was not himself either. He hadn't been since he came back from that woman's funeral—"

"Florence Teller. She had a name," Edwin said sharply. "Use it."

Leticia closed her mouth firmly and stared at him.

Edwin said, "Oh, to hell with it. Inspector Rutledge, when can we leave? It will be better for everyone if we just go home and stop pretending."

"I don't know. We'll need statements from all of you, telling me where you were, and what if anything was said, what your reading was of Captain Teller's state of mind."

Amy said, "You aren't suggesting it was suicide—" She broke off.

"Don't be ridiculous," Walter said from the window. "I don't think Peter had that much sense."

Rutledge cut across Amy Teller's retort. "It might interest you to know that the Captain's wife—widow—has just told me that she feels he was murdered."

There was a sharply indrawn breath from the people looking up at him. A collective reaction to his suggestion.

"She's upset," Walter said.

Edwin added, "I don't think she knows what she's talking about."

Leticia said, "Yes, she does. She doesn't see this as a blessing in disguise, that Peter—and the rest of us—will be spared the nightmare of a trial. It doesn't matter how it ends—in full acquittal or a conviction. The damage will have been done."

Amy said, "That's an awful thing to say. No one is rejoicing."

Leticia crossed the room and poured herself another cup of tea.

"It's time we all faced some very unpleasant facts. And one of them is that Jenny will have to face them as well. We can't go on lying to her. It's not fair to Peter or his wife."

"Oh, do shut up, Leticia," Walter Teller told her. "I'll deal with Jenny in my own way."

"If we could have thrashed this business out amongst ourselves on Friday, none of this might have happened," Leticia retorted. "And what about Harry? What is Harry to be told?"

There was a strained silence.

"Harry," Walter began. "Oh, my God, we've forgotten Harry."

"He's all right," Amy said. "He's gone to the church services at Repton. He asked if he could. I told him yes. I thought it would be a good idea. And so he wasn't here when—when it happened."

"Surely not alone?" Walter demanded. "You must have taken leave of your senses."

"He went with the rector and his family," Amy said curtly. "I went over and asked politely. They were delighted to have him. There's some sort of blessing of the animals today. He likes that. And he's staying for lunch."

"I'd forgot," Walter said. "Jenny was to take him. When Peter fell, everything else went out of my mind."

"There's Gran to be thought of. What are we to tell her?"

"Why wasn't she invited to the birthday celebration?" Rutledge asked.

"It's distressing for her to travel. It's confusing," Edwin said.

But she had traveled to visit her dead sister's grandchildren.

Rutledge waited until they had finished dealing with the unforeseen problems brought on by a death.

And when there was a lull in the conversation, he said, "Now that that's settled to your satisfaction, there's something I should like very much to know."

They turned to face him, wary, their eyes waiting for the blow to fall.

Rutledge said into the tense silence, "What did Susannah Teller mean when she told me that it wasn't Peter who had killed Florence Teller. That one of you was in the house when Peter came there, and used the opportunity he'd given you to kill her?"

26

It was as if, collectively, they had lost their tongues.

"She was upset," Leticia said finally. "And imagining things. All the blame for whatever happened to that woman in Lancashire had fallen on Peter's head. She was trying to clear his name. To give him dignity in his death. I think she believes that he must have fallen deliberately, because everyone had seemed to turn against him. People do lash out in grief," she ended. "I've seen it myself. And so must you have, Mr. Rutledge."

He had. But he'd heard the pain and anger in Susannah's voice, and he'd almost believed her.

He turned to Walter and said, "What was the real reason for not calling off the party?"

"I've told you. We didn't, for Jenny's sake. She was looking forward to it. It meant more to her than we realized. A family healing, if you will. After my disastrous disappearance."

"I think," Rutledge said, "you went ahead with the party to gauge just how much of my evidence was true. To shame your brother into telling you what happened in Hobson that day. He hadn't, had he? He'd been tormented by his own knowledge—even I could see that he'd begun to drink heavily. And once I'd outlined my own evidence, you knew he was very likely to be taken into custody very soon. And you wanted to make him tell you before the police came, so that you could band together to protect him. Only he didn't quite see it that way. I think he felt you'd abandoned him. In which case he might well have chosen to fall down the stairs. His only way to punish you for what you'd done to him."

They stared at him, nothing in their gazes telling him whether his guesses were right or not.

"I can't force any of you to confess. But I'd give a great deal to know why Peter Teller suddenly felt compelled to rectify the situation in Hobson in regard to Florence Teller after all these years. I want to know for her sake where all of this began."

Amy Teller said, "You can't expect us to answer that, when we were left not knowing the truth ourselves."

"Was it suicide?" Edwin Teller asked. "Do you believe he killed himself?"

"There's not sufficient evidence either way," Rutledge said. "It will depend on what the police and the inquest have to say about his state of mind. There will be an inquest. Make no mistake about that."

"Dear God," Edwin said under his breath. "Will it have to come out that my brother was suspected of murder?"

"All the essential facts will have to be presented."

"It was a fall," Leticia said. "I know my brother. He would no more kill himself than Walter here would have done. It's not in the nature of our family to run away from anything."

"Oh, do shut up, Leticia," Edwin said. "This is not the time to be pompous. Of course Peter didn't kill himself. Walter?"

"No."

"Then there you are, Inspector. The family, who knew Peter Teller better than anyone else, have given you their considered opinion. There was nothing on his conscience. Your so-called evidence was entirely circumstantial. Your witness can hardly identify a dead man. There is no case. There never was."

"There's still a dead woman in Lancashire. What about her?"

"I have no idea. I leave such matters to the police."

There was a knock at the door.

"Come," Rutledge said, expecting to see Inspector Jessup walk into the room.

But it was Mollie.

She said, "Beg pardon, sir. Scotland Yard is on the telephone. They want to speak with you. It's urgent. They said."

"Thank you. Tell the Yard I'll be there directly," Rutledge told her.

He looked around the room, seeing relief in the eyes of his captive audience.

"You will all remain here at the farm until further notice while your brother's death is being investigated. When Inspector Jessup is willing to release the body, you may proceed with burial arrangements. I'll arrange for the inquest as soon as possible. You won't find it pleasant, enduring one another's company for a few more days, but there it is."

"There's Gran," Edwin said. "We need to go to London."

"And what about Harry?" Walter said. "What are we to tell him?"

"The truth," Leticia said. "That his uncle met with a terrible accident, and we must all grieve for him."

Rutledge said, "I'm sorry. I must go. There's another case in London that is demanding my attention."

He turned and walked out of the room.

Mollie was waiting in the passage and took him to the room where the telephone had been put in.

Rutledge had expected to hear Sergeant Gibson's voice on the telephone. He had expected a summons to London to carry out Inspector

Mickelson's plan. Once the Chief Superintendent was set upon a course of action, there was really no good way to deflect him.

He thanked Mollie, picked up the receiver, and waited until she was out of earshot. Then he said, "Rutledge," and waited for Gibson to speak.

The voice traveling down the line was Gibson's. He said, without preamble, "It's Lancashire, sir. You're to go there at once. If you need someone in Essex to deal with the situation there, the Chief Superintendent will send someone else from the Yard."

"It's stable at the moment," Rutledge answered, unwilling to turn the inquiry into Peter Teller's death over to anyone else at this stage. There were secrets here that he would have to get to the bottom of before the final verdict on Peter Teller's fall was handed down. And he wasn't prepared for anyone else to muddy the waters.

"That's good news, sir. You'll be leaving from there?"

"As soon as I speak to Inspector Jessup, the local man."

"To be sure," Gibson agreed. "A very wise decision, if I may say so, sir."

Rutledge swiftly translated that to mean that avoiding London at the moment was a good thing.

"And Mr. Rutledge, sir?" Gibson was saying, his voice lowered and barely audible.

"Yes? What is it, Gibson?"

"Inspector Mickelson has just informed the Chief Superintendent that he feels the trap cannot be sprung by anyone else. Just a friendly warning, sir."

27

Sunday evening had been nearly insupportable. Leticia, complaining of a headache, had excused herself early and gone up to bed. But not to sleep.

She lay awake, her windows open, the cries of an owl in the distance loud in her ears. She had always disliked owls. Their haunting calls spoke to her of grief and sadness and something to be feared. As a child, she'd run to her nanny's bed and flung herself under the covers, to shut out the sound.

Her mother had always maintained that Leticia must have overheard one of the servants claiming that owls were omens of ill fortune. Leticia herself didn't know if it was true or not. She just knew she had always felt that way.

And, of course, with Peter only newly dead, the cries of the owl were particularly appropriate. She got up once to close the windows, but the room still held the heavy closeness of the day and she could hardly breathe in the resulting stuffiness.

She couldn't stop herself from thinking about her brothers. They had always been a close family. Edwin's illness had brought them all together in a pact to keep him safe. When their parents died, it had fallen to her lot to watch over Edwin while Peter went off to the Army and Walter had gone into the mission field.

Now Peter was accused of cold-blooded murder, Walter had been different ever since his mysterious disappearance, never satisfactorily explaining it to anyone except perhaps to Jenny. And Edwin was withdrawing even from her.

She turned to one side, trying to shut out the sounds from the wood in the distance.

It was odd that now there was still a conspiracy to protect Jenny. The mother of the heir. The youngest of them. They hadn't told her about Florence Teller. It had seemed the right thing to do. But it would all come out at the inquest anyway. Someone would have to tell her before the questions of the police aroused her suspicions, before she found herself hearing in public what Peter had been accused of and why.

And there was Susannah as well. Something would have to be done about her. Her distress and anger were understandable—natural. But she couldn't be allowed to upset everyone by involving the Yard and trying to clear Peter's name. She'd stood by him, even when Leticia had told her what the man from London had said about the evidence. All the same, Leticia had had the sneaking suspicion that Susannah was already worried about Peter. Something in her eyes . . .

She sighed, and turned over again, and finally got up to walk to the window, defying the owls.

She was the eldest. It was up to her to straighten out this tangle. Damn Edwin for going to the funeral. Damn Peter for losing his head. Damn Susannah for not keeping her mouth shut so that all this could be smoothed away. And damn Jenny, for being naïve and for walking into rooms at just the wrong moment, never mind that it was her house. Every time the rest of them had tried to confront Peter, he was either drunk or he was protected, unwittingly, by Jenny's presence.

She had another thought. If it hadn't been for Jenny, Peter might not have died. They could have cleared the air, got through to whatever it was that was tormenting him, and come up with a solution.

Her hands over her face, she pressed cold fingers against her closed eyelids.

What could she do? What should she do? What would her father, who was never at a loss about anything, have done about an accusation of murder against one of his sons?

She could almost hear her father's answer.

Protect Harry. Keep the family intact. Preserve the Teller name. At any price.

She took a deep breath, pulling in the cooler night air until her lungs hurt.

It was too bad Susannah hadn't fallen down the stairs instead of Peter. It would have made her task easier. But there it was.

And if Jenny's innocence had to be sacrificed, so be it. Walter would just have to live with her decision.

After a while she went back to bed. The owls had stopped. But she still couldn't sleep.

28

Rutledge drove to Lancashire without stopping, save for petrol.

The misting rain kept him company, the windscreen wipers almost hypnotic in their sweep, clearing his vision and then blurring the landscape.

What was the truth about Peter Teller's death? he asked himself, coming out of St. Albans.

Accident, suicide, murder?

In spite of Susannah Teller's angry claims, he could see no conceivable motive for murdering the man. To keep the family's name from being dragged through a courtroom drama that would have London agog? A very poor reason for murdering one's own flesh and blood.

Suicide, then, to spare his family the onus of a convicted murderer turned over to the hangman?

Or just a simple, horrible, unbelievable accident because the man's leg was weak and his cane lay in the boot of Rutledge's car?

"Why did he no' buy anither one?" Hamish asked.

Rutledge answered, "It would have drawn attention to the missing one. If it had a special head, that would have to be ordered. Time wasn't on his side."

There was no immediate solution to the problem of Captain Teller's death, he decided finally. It could wait until he returned from Hobson.

He had a fairly decent idea of why Satterthwaite had summoned him in such haste. A simpler solution, that. The head of the cane had been in the gardens after all. He hadn't looked long enough. Or Cobb had stumbled on it.

Satterthwaite was waiting in the station for him, late as it was. He could just see the glow of lamplight through the window. He walked in, pulling off his driving gloves. The single lamp on the constable's desk guided Rutledge through the outer office and down the dark passage.

A Thermos of tea stood on the desk in front of Satterthwaite, and in the lamp's flickering glow, he appeared to be bone tired, as if he hadn't slept, the deep hollows and bony ridges of his face stark as he looked up to greet Rutledge.

His own fatigue forgotten, Rutledge studied the man. He was under great strain.

"I'm sorry, sir, for the abrupt summons," Satterthwaite began. "But I didn't know what else to do, given the circumstances."

"What circumstances?"

"I thought it best you didn't take Peter Teller into custody tomorrow. And I wasn't ready to tell the world and his uncle what I believed you ought to hear first." He gestured to the Thermos. "There's a clean cup just behind you on that shelf. It's likely to be a long night."

Rutledge found the cup and filled it with the steaming liquid. He drank half of it to clear the rest of the cobwebs out of his head, and then set it aside.

"All right. Where's the cane's head?"

Satterthwaite smiled. "You do take all the wind out of a man's sails," he said grimly. But he reached into his drawer and pulled out a round object wrapped in a clean handkerchief. He passed it to Rutledge with distaste, handkerchief and all, as if he couldn't bear to touch it.

Rutledge glanced at him, then looked down, unwrapping the linen to reveal a gold knob that caught the light and flashed dully in his hand.

It was indeed the head of a cane, broken off the Malaccan stick.

With one finger he rolled the knob toward the light, and sat there for a moment, absorbing what it represented. Satterthwaite said nothing, watching him.

Damning was the best word for it. Small wonder Walter Teller had lied, telling Rutledge the cane was of ivory.

Embedded in the heavy gold head was an enameled button or plaque. A black scum obscured part of the design, but even so, Rutledge knew what it was.

He glanced at Satterthwaite.

"Captain Peter Teller's regimental badge," he said. "It leaves us in no doubt. Very likely a gift from his father or his wife. Such things often are. We can find the maker—there should be a record of such an expensive item." The knob winked as he turned it again in the light. "And there's still a little blood pooled at the edge of the enamel."

"Yes." Satterthwaite stirred. "I didn't like to look at it. Put it away." He took a deep breath, then said, "It's what you wanted. I wouldn't have given any odds that it would ever turn up."

Rutledge rewrapped it and set it aside, then finished his tea.

"I should be heading back to London. There's a small problem. Peter Teller fell down the stairs early this morning at his brother's house and died on the spot. We'll never know now why he came north or why he killed her."

"Accident or suicide?" Satterthwaite asked, watching Rutledge's face closely.

"Hard to say."

"Yes, well, in that case, perhaps you ought to hear where this came from."

Rutledge realized that with his mind already on Peter Teller and the problems he faced resolving the issues of the man's guilt and the cause of his death, he'd accepted this last bit of evidence without the enthusiasm it deserved.

Good police work on Satterthwaite's part, even though the cane's head was almost moot now. Still, there must be an inquest into Florence Teller's death. And her killer must be identified. She deserved that.

He dragged his thoughts back to the present. "Well done. Finding this." He couldn't put his finger on what was bothering Satterthwaite—the blood on the cane's knob or something else. He thrust the handkerchief holding the knob into his pocket, out of sight. As he did, his gaze locked with the constable's.

He didn't need Hamish's soft warning. Fully alert now, he waited.

Satterthwaite spun the cap back onto the neck of the Thermos and set it aside. "First, to give you a little news. I don't think you were here when it happened."

"All right."

"After an altercation with a cooking pan, Lawrence Cobb walked out on his wife, Betsy, and took your old room at Mrs. Greeley's for the time being."

"Yes, I met him coming into town just as I was leaving that day. I tried to persuade him to rethink his decision. To see if the marriage could be saved. I don't think Florence Teller would have liked being the root cause of the breakup. Although having seen Betsy Cobb, I could understand the battle ahead. She appears to be as domineering as her mother."

"Worse, from all reports. She likes her way. Well, Lawrence Cobb would have done better to listen to you."

Rutledge saw that the conversation wasn't taking the direction he'd expected. "What happened?"

"Betsy Cobb came in to see me very early this morning. She couldn't sleep after their quarrel on Friday, she said. So she began clearing out her husband's belongings, putting them in a pile in the passage—tools, clothes, watch, everything she could lay hand to that he'd not had time to snatch up in his haste to go. This morning before first light she even went out into the barn, where he'd been working. And she tossed the contents of the tool chest into a wooden crate. She said the chest had belonged to her father."

Rutledge knew now where this was heading. He waited for Satterthwaite's strained voice to finish the account.

"To make a long story short, as she was sorting through to make sure he got only his things, she shifted a pair of working gloves, and this knob fell to the barn floor. She didn't know what it was at first. And then she realized it was gold and that Lawrence had purposely hidden it where she wouldn't find it. So to make trouble for him, she brought it in to me. She was still furious with him, you could see it in her face."

"What did you do?"

"I told her I'd look into it. And after she left for the farm, I went to Mrs. Greeley's, rousted Lawrence Cobb out of his bed, and confronted him. He swore he knew nothing about the knob, but you could read in his eyes that he knew how it had been used. He's not slow, is Cobb. I told him to dress and come with me to the station. He argued, but I wouldn't take no for an answer. Some of Betsy's anger had rubbed off on me. I was looking for an opening, so to speak."

He started to get up, as if he needed to walk, then he sank back into his chair, defeated. "By this time, Betsy Cobb had gone straight to her mother. You'll recall Mrs. Blaine had found Florence lying there in the doorway. She came into the station looking like the wrath of God, telling me I must take Cobb into custody, to protect her daughter. That he'd do her a harm for telling the truth. And she swore he'd been working there at Florence Teller's house that day. I thought Cobb was going to strike her. He called her a liar, and there was a shouting match you wouldn't believe. Mrs. Blaine reached for the paperweight, and I had to push Cobb back to the only cell and slam the door."

Rutledge could picture the scene.

"I came back to speak to the two women while Cobb was shouting something at them and at me. Mrs. Blaine claimed he'd read too much in Mrs. Teller letting him help her about the gardens. He must have said something to her, and Mrs. Teller told him he was a married man and she wanted nothing to do with him." Satterthwaite paused. "So he killed her." He examined the Thermos as if it had just appeared on his desk and he'd never seen it before, avoiding Rutledge's eyes. "I'd have liked five minutes alone with him. It would have been worth it." Then he looked up. "I could never understand Peter Teller walking away from her at the war's end. That's if he wasn't dead. She was sure he was. We all believed it. So it made sense that he'd come back, finally, to make his peace and tell her his reasons. His lame leg, for one. And she sent him away with a flea in his ear, because she had a pride of her own, did Florence Teller."

He set the Thermos aside and moved a little in his chair.

"She must have told Cobb when he came to do a little work what had happened between herself and Teller. And he killed her then, because he knew that whatever she was saying now in the heat of anger and hurt, in the end Florence would go back to her husband." Looking away at the square of window, seeing the darkness no longer pitch-black, he went on. "I didn't want her killer to be one of us. I wanted it to be Teller. But it wasn't."

"That's a very good reconstruction," Rutledge said after a moment. "It makes a strong case for Lawrence Cobb as the murderer. But it doesn't explain the cane."

"That must have been what Cobb saw as he came up the walk. How he knew Teller had been there. Where Teller had dropped it when she cast him off. And she must have left it there, in the event Teller came back for it. She wouldn't have to see him again."

"And what does Cobb have to say to this? Does he still deny he killed her, or has he admitted what he'd done?"

"By the time his wife and her mother had left, he was in a state. He demanded I send for you, but I told him it was no use, the evidence was there, and we had to go forward. The truth was, I couldn't bear the sight of him, I wanted him out of Hobson where I couldn't lay hands to him. I think he must have seen that in my face, because when I told him he was going to Thielwald, he came quietly and gave me no trouble."

A silence fell.

Rutledge was trying to test the information that Satterthwaite had given him. Had all the evidence pointing to Peter Teller been circumstantial? The man was on the scene. He'd been spotted by an independent witness. His cane had been used as the murder weapon. But there was an equally strong case now against Lawrence Cobb. Furthermore, it fit the facts—that Teller had indeed come to Hobson and spoken to Florence Teller. His cane had been missing since then. And he'd left in a hurry, according to the witness, Benjamin Larkin. It also explained why Lawrence Cobb had possession of the cane's knob.

He knew the decision that Chief Superintendent Bowles would come to: charge Cobb and leave the Tellers out of it—they'd suffered enough, and Peter Teller was now out of reach of the law. Guilty or not. If a jury found Cobb guilty, then he was.

But Florence Teller deserved to have her killer punished. And not a surrogate.

Rutledge took a deep breath. Somehow he'd been very sure of Cobb's innocence.

As if the constable had heard his thoughts, he said, "Remember? Larkin heard no shouting, no one crying out when the Teller motorcar was there."

"Because by the time Larkin came down the hill, she was already dead."

"I never could understand why Teller broke up that cane," Satterthwaite went on. "If he'd taken it with him, we'd been none the wiser. Two minutes under a pump or dangled in a stream, and it would have been clean. But I can see Cobb killing her and then destroying the cane afterward. The cane was Teller's, and he'd have liked to break it over the man himself. But he couldn't. So he took his frustration and anger out on Teller's possession. And Cobb is strong enough, he could have snapped off that knob."

And that was the irrefutable fact. As Hamish was pointing out, even if Teller had hated himself for what he'd done, even if he'd broken his own cane out of self-loathing, he'd surely have had the sense to take the head of the cane with him. Even the drunken Peter Teller was far from stupid.

"Ye said yoursel', it's damning," Hamish told him.

He should have been satisfied. But he wasn't.

"Why did Cobb leave the rest of the cane for us to find?"

"To protect himself, if suspicion fell on him." Satterthwaite stood up, collecting his own cup, intending to wash up. "I've had hours to think, waiting for you to come back. Hours."

Fighting a rearguard action, Rutledge said, "And the box of letters?"

Satterthwaite replied, "Cobb said he never touched them. He had no reason to do it, and he couldn't have taken them home with him. Teller must have put them in the boot. We'll have to ask Larkin if he could see the boot of the motorcar from where he was."

"No," said Rutledge. "If she'd been alive, she would never have allowed that. Not her letters. She'd have fought him every step of the way."

"Even if she was disillusioned?"

Satterthwaite scowled. "Then it was Cobb. Bound to have been. To hurt her more? Or maybe he wanted to read them. Who knows?"

"You said Cobb was in Thielwald?"

"I told you. I didn't want him here. He's safer there. And so am I."

"I want to see him."

"I know how much time you've given to this inquiry. I know how well you'd put together the case against Teller. I know how I'd said all along that no one here in Hobson would touch her. We were both *wrong*."

Rutledge kept his cup, reached for the Thermos, uncapped it, and poured himself more tea. Then he said, "All right. I still must speak to Cobb. I want to judge him for myself. Let's go."

"Now? At this hour of the night?" Satterthwaite demanded as Rutledge drained his cup and handed back it to him.

"I have to be back in London as quickly as I can. There's Teller's death."

They drove to Thielwald in an uncomfortable silence. Satterthwaite had said what he knew he must say. And Rutledge could think of no way to prove him wrong.

Hamish, a third in the motorcar, his voice at Rutledge's ear, was trying to make himself heard, but Rutledge shut him out.

Concentrating on the dark winding road ahead, Rutledge tried to find holes in Satterthwaite's arguments, weighing Teller against Cobb. He'd liked Cobb. He'd believed the man when he said that he couldn't have killed Florence Teller. But then Teller himself had denied touching his wife. And that had rung true as well.

The sky was just brightening as the rain clouds scudded away, already thinning enough to offer the promise of sun to take their place.

Satterthwaite broke the silence. "A fair day . . ." And then his voice trailed off as Rutledge brought the motorcar to a halt in front of Thielwald's police station. "I was thinking," he went on as they got out. "If Cobb hadn't walked out on her, I wonder if Betsy would have come to me. Even if she'd found a dozen bloody canes lying about in the barn.

I think she'd have kept her mouth shut, and lived with a murderer, if it meant she could keep Cobb. After all, he'd rid her of her rival, whatever the reason behind it. Still, in the end, he'd have been brought under her thumb with the threat of exposure. That's in her nature, to want to rule the roost. And he might have killed her then, to escape."

"The only surprise is the fact that she didn't wait longer than she did, on the off chance that he might come back. Now he's out of reach for good."

Rutledge went to the boot and took out the pieces of cane, wrapped in an oiled cloth. Changing his mind, he left them there and led the way to the door.

The sleepy constable on duty picked up the lamp on his desk and showed them to the cell where Cobb was sitting on the edge of his cot, his head in his hands. From the drained, empty look in his eyes as the door swung open and he saw Rutledge standing there, it was evident he'd not slept since he'd been arrested. He got slowly to his feet, and in the light from the constable's lamp, Cobb's eyes gleamed like those of a trapped animal.

Rutledge had seen that look before—nearly as often in the innocent as in the guilty. That fear of things getting out of hand, of wanting to fight back when flight was no longer an option, and that blindingly helpless feeling of knowing the odds are set against you because the evidence is overwhelming.

He was prepared for argument, for Cobb appealing to him over Satterthwaite's head, expecting the man from London wouldn't know Hobson or its people as well as the constable did.

Instead Cobb said, "Am I to be taken to London, then?" The words came out more harshly than the man intended.

Rutledge said, "That hasn't been decided."

"You'll have to find another home for Jake, you know," he went on, striving to conceal the anxiety that had kept him awake.

"He seems to prefer women."

"There was no one else in the house with them year after year. It's not surprising. I'd have had to win his trust. Or not. But I'd have kept him," he added wistfully. Then with a spark of his old self, "He didn't get along all that well with my mother-in-law. My mother-in-law heard him speaking once and swore I was in that house somewhere. Florence told me that."

A thought struck Rutledge. Peter would have known the difference between Jake's voice and his brothers' . . .

"What do you have to say for yourself, Cobb? You swore to me you hadn't killed her. You told me you wanted to get your hands on the man who did."

"I never expected Betsy to turn against me," he said. "Not that I blamed her. But it was a stab in the back, all the same."

"You walked away from her and your marriage."

"After great provocation. It was that or strike her back. All I can do is wonder how long she'd have kept that cane's head hidden, if I'd stayed. Or begged to come home again." It was what Rutledge himself had wondered.

"Why did you keep the head of the cane?"

"I didn't. If I'd found it, I'd have come to the police."

"Then how did it wind up among your tools? Your wife has sworn in her statement that she'd found it there."

"I don't think it bothered her to swear to a falsehood. She was that angry. At a guess, the knob came from Mrs. Blaine, Betsy's mother. She found the body. If she'd seen the cane and realized that the head was gold, she'd have taken it. She's like a magpie. Always had an eye for herself, or anything to her advantage. She'll offer to buy Florence's land. See if she doesn't. I hope Teller tells her to go whistle up the wind."

"All the same, it was interfering with the scene of a murder." He paused. "Peter Teller is dead."

"What? How? By his own hand?"

"We don't know yet. Early days."

"My God." Cobb shook his head in disbelief. "She'd have been a widow after all. As for the cane, I wouldn't have kept it, gold or not. There's blood on it. Constable Satterthwaite made certain to point it out."

"We'd like to ask you one last thing. What became of the rosewood box with Mrs. Teller's letters in it?"

"I wouldn't have taken them. What good were they to me? But they meant a lot to her. It would be like taking Timmy's photograph. A cruelty."

"What else was in that box? The deed to the house?"

"How do I know? I never saw the contents. Only her reading a letter to Jake." He frowned. "Even my mother-in-law saw her reading them. She thought it was a love letter from me. And didn't I get a flea in my ear! But I could look her in the face and tell her it wasn't true. The only time I'd ever written Florence Teller was when Timmy died, to tell her how sorry I was over his loss. I doubt she kept it."

Into the brief silence, he said to Rutledge, "You haven't asked me if I killed her. Only what I had to say for myself."

"Did you kill Florence Teller?"

Beside him he could feel Satterthwaite stir and then be still again.

"I did not. If I hang, I will tell the hangman I never touched her."

"Then who did? Teller?"

"He must have done."

Rutledge turned away.

The constable holding the lamp said, "Will that be all, then?" He shifted it to his other hand, preparing to close and lock the cell's door.

"No. Not yet." Rutledge walked away, through the gloom of the station and out into the cool morning air.

Satterthwaite's silent accusation, as if Rutledge had betrayed him, kept him from thinking, and the beaten spirit of Lawrence Cobb, feeling his own sense of betrayal, clouded the issues.

And what were they? A dead woman. A broken cane with blood on the knob. A missing box of letters. Those were the facts, irrefutable, and the evidence must encompass them or it was faulty.

It was also a fact that Teller—or someone—had driven away around the same time Florence Teller was murdered. And Larkin, a walker, was a witness to that. The cane was a witness as well to Peter Teller's presence. If he'd been chary with information about his regiment while living here in Hobson, he'd never have left that at Sunrise Cottage in his absences. It hadn't been there for the killer to find ready to hand, until Teller himself brought it.

Teller—or Cobb? Where did the truth lie?

He walked on up the street, shops still closed, the milk van making its rounds, the sound of clinking bottles off in the distance, a crow calling from the church tower down another street, and wheels somewhere clattering over cobbles. A dog trotted up behind him, sniffed in his direction, and trotted on, looking for company. A cat in a house window silently meowed at him as he passed.

Go back to the evidence.

Hamish said, "It hasna' changed."

And that was true. It hadn't altered. Going back over it was fruitless.

Rutledge swore.

He needed a night's sleep, to clear his mind. But there wasn't one in the offing.

Hamish was right. The evidence was the same. What was new?

The cane's head had been found. Peter Teller's regimental crest on it showed that Peter had been in Hobson, at Sunrise Cottage, on the day of the murder.

But that was all it showed. It couldn't speak and identify who had used it.

Cobb's words came back to him: *She found the body. If she'd seen the cane and realized that the head was gold, she'd have taken it. She's like a magpie . . .*

And Satterthwaite's voice: *Mrs. Blaine reached for the paperweight, and I had to push Cobb back to the only cell.*

After that, his own: *What else was in that box? The deed to the house?*

Cobb again: *She'll offer to buy Florence's land. See if she doesn't.*

He could hear Mrs. Blaine threatening to wring Jake's neck, because he didn't talk, he only made a terrible racket.

Hamish said, "Aye, it wasna' the letters."

Rutledge turned on his heel and walked briskly back to the police station. He found that Satterthwaite had brought chairs to the cell door, and he and Cobb were staring at each other like mastiffs circling each other looking for a weakness.

Rutledge said to the Thielwald constable, "Handcuff him. I want to take him with us."

"Back to Hobson?" the constable said.

"Where?" Satterthwaite demanded.

"Just do it," Rutledge told them. "I'll be in the motorcar."

And he walked away.

His mind was on Hamish. Cobb in front, Satterthwaite in the back. And then both of them could watch Cobb.

The two constables emerged from the station with Cobb between them.

"This is most irregular. Sir?" the constable was saying.

"It's all right. He'll be back within the hour. Front, Cobb. Sit just behind him, Satterthwaite."

They did as they were told. One look at Rutledge's face, and none of them was willing to risk argument.

They drove in silence out of Thielwald to the road for Hobson, and then took the turning for Sunrise Cottage.

"We're going back to the house?" Satterthwaite asked.

Rutledge didn't answer, his mind on what was to come.

When he drove past the cottage and turned into the rutted lane to the Blaine farm, Satterthwaite said, "Here, you can't call on her at this hour!"

"She keeps a dairy farm. She was up milking at four." Drawing up at the front of the house, he said, "Cobb, stay here. And keep watch." He strode up to the door and knocked. "Let me do the talking," he told Satterthwaite.

"If you'll just tell me, sir—"

But the door was swinging open, and Mrs. Blaine was standing there, a basket of eggs under her arm.

She stared at them suspiciously. "Inspector. Constable. I was just about to candle the eggs." Then she saw Cobb in the motorcar, and said angrily, "What's he doing here? He's a dangerous man."

"If he's smart, he's doing precisely what I told him to do," Rutledge said. "May we come in?"

She was still blocking the door, but she said now, "I'll tell you flat out I found it hard to believe he was a killer. Just shows you, doesn't it, that you can't be sure about people, however well you think you know them. And so I shall say at the inquest."

"This isn't about Cobb. I've come to tell you that the parrot does talk."

Her eyes widened, but she said only, "We heard it. It said good night to Lieutenant Teller." She stepped aside. "You'd better come in, then."

"Thank you."

They followed her through to the kitchen where she set the basket of eggs to one side of the sink, then turned to face them.

"There's a witness who heard the bird exclaim 'No. No. No.' in some distress. We've come to believe that this was the moment when Mrs. Teller turned from her assailant and tried to escape."

"A witness?" Mrs. Blaine asked warily.

"The person who is presently caring for the bird."

"Did it mention a name?" She waited, her eyes on Rutledge's

face. "It would know Cobb. He was always there. Couldn't stay away."

"You found the body. Is that correct?"

"I told you—I was off to market and I often asked if there's anything Mrs. Teller needed. That's why I saw her in the doorway."

"After she'd been dead for what? Two days?"

"It's you and the constable there who said two days. I couldn't tell."

"You brought Jake here, to keep him safe, is that correct?"

She was more comfortable now. "Yes. Poor thing, someone had to have mercy on him."

"But you were prepared to wring his neck when you discovered he couldn't name her killer."

"I—who said he could name him? It was you, wanting to take him to London with you."

"You found the body. You'd taken Jake without telling the police. What else was there? Did you see that the cane had a heavy gold head? And did you think the rosewood box might hold more than letters? That the deed to the house might be in there as well? After all, there were no heirs."

"Here!" she exclaimed. "You can't prove any of that. Except that I took the parrot out of pity for it."

"There's no one else who would have taken the box. She was alive when Peter Teller saw her, and she would never have given the letters up—"

"Peter—but I was told he was dead."

"But he was there that day. It was his cane you picked up. And he owns the house with the red door, now that his wife is dead."

Her face flushed. "If it was Teller who came back, why didn't he stay? Why did he leave? I don't believe you."

"I don't know the answer to that. Still, he must have spoken to Florence. She must have turned him out. Perhaps she decided that she preferred Lawrence Cobb after all."

"She did. Betsy—"

She stopped.

"Betsy asked her?"

"I was about to say—"

"Mrs. Blaine. Was it you or your daughter who murdered Florence Teller?"

Satterthwaite's breath came out in a hiss, but he said nothing.

"Murdered her? It was that husband of hers, I tell you. You've seen the proof."

"I don't think it was Cobb. Teller came to see his wife, and she sent him away. Or he said what he'd come to say and left. We'll never know. And someone came along just after that. Was Mrs. Teller sitting on her step crying? Or standing at the door looking as if she'd seen a ghost? Someone stopped. A woman. And misunderstanding what was said when Florence was asked what was wrong, one of you suggested she go back inside, and as she turned, one of you picked up the cane her husband had dropped in his own shock and grief, and struck Mrs. Teller with it, then panicked and left her there."

"There's not a word of truth—"

"And then," he went on inexorably, "when no one found her, you had to be the one to call the police. You couldn't wait any longer."

"It's Cobb—"

"Cobb didn't have the box of letters. Teller didn't have them. That left you. Which means you went inside that house, stepping over the body, to see if Cobb was in the back weeding. And because he wasn't, you helped yourself to the bird, to the box where you knew Mrs. Teller had kept her personal papers, and then the head of the cane, which was gold. Putting it all together, I can see now that it was Betsy who killed her. And you went there as soon as she told you, to make sure there was no evidence against her."

Mrs. Blaine, fighting for control, said, "I'll tell them in the court-room that you're a filthy liar, that you came here from London and couldn't see your nose in front of your face. I'll tell them that because I did a good deed, you want to blame me, to cover up your incompetence. They won't like you when I've finished with them, and they won't believe a word you say."

"Betsy thought it was Cobb, didn't she, who had brought Florence Teller to tears? She didn't wait to hear all of it. She acted in a fury."

Mrs. Blaine moved away from the sink. "You'll not hang my daughter. She's the victim here. Betrayed by her own husband, watching that woman suck him dry of any feeling for her, and not satisfied with that, he turned my daughter out of her own house. The constable will tell you, he saw Cobb coming into Hobson with the mark on his face where my daughter had to defend herself from his brutality. He said straight out that he'd kill her if she touched Florence Teller. Do you think she'd dare?"

"Cobb walked out, he didn't turn her out."

"He's a murderer. He'd have come back in the night and stabbed her in her sleep. That bit of cane was found in his things. Not hers."

"The parrot. The head of the cane. The box of letters," Rutledge said again. "You took them all. Shall I bring the parrot back to Hobson?"

"I thought I was protecting her. It turned out I was protecting her worthless husband. And who will listen to a bird?"

"If you'd believed it was Cobb, you wouldn't have needed the parrot or the box. And you'd have left the cane where it was. Didn't it bother you that she lay there two days while you hoped someone else would find her? *Two days*—I call that inhuman."

She whirled, her hands closing over the heavy whetstone that was used to sharpen knives, and she flung it at Rutledge with deadly aim.

But he was expecting it, and she narrowly missed him. With a cry of fury, she turned and was on her way out the door, just as her daughter came into the kitchen from the yard.

Mrs. Blaine burst into tears. "I'm a mother. I had to protect my daughter. I killed her, not Betsy. It was *never* Betsy."

Betsy, barging into her mother, spun her out of the way. "I heard all of it," she said, her face flushed and her eyes bright with her fury. "I heard what you were saying. Well, I'd do it again. *If I had the chance, I'd do it again!* You don't have any idea how much I hated her."

29

It took some time to arrange matters. The two women were shut up in the pantry by the kitchen door, where the windows were too small to allow either of them to escape. Satterthwaite was left to guard them while Cobb and Rutledge went back to Thielwald to bring back help.

On the way, Cobb said, "How did you know?"

"Betsy wouldn't throw a handful of earth on the coffin. You left her a rose."

"You knew then?" Cobb asked in disbelief.

"No. But it occurred to me on the way to the Blaine Farm. You said yourself Mrs. Blaine was like a magpie. The gold knob for a rainy day. The letter box in the event a deed was in there as well. Jake, in the event he could name her daughter. If Betsy had been glad someone else had killed Florence Teller, she'd have wished her to rest in peace. And to leave you in peace."

"I'd told her I'd kill her if she hurt Florence."

"She was in a fury that day. She must have thought you and Mrs. Teller had had words. That you'd come to the front door of the house like a suitor, and Mrs. Teller had taken her husband's cane to you."

"If she'd turned me out, why would Betsy kill her?"

"For fear, I think, that you'd go on begging Mrs. Teller, and one day she might be lonely enough to relent and let you live with her. Or sleep with her."

"My God." Cobb took a deep breath. "I thought I'd hang. I thought that the evidence was so strong I was going to be convicted. Satterthwaite was damned good in his reasoning. And he would do his best to see me hang as well. I think there was some jealousy there."

"I'm sure there was. But he tried to be fair as well."

But Cobb was silent, as if he disagreed.

They were coming down into Thielwald when Cobb spoke again.

"I'm not sorry to hear Teller is dead. If it was by his own hand, do you think it was because Florence told him to go away and not come back?"

Rutledge thought no such thing. But he said only, "I don't suppose we'll ever know."

It was late afternoon when Rutledge had finished his last duty in Hobson.

Satterthwaite bought him a drink in Thielwald and said, "I couldn't see the forest for the trees."

"Neither could I."

"What was it about Florence Teller that attracted men like Cobb—and me—to her? And yet she couldn't keep her own husband. I think you felt a little of it too."

"It was her strength, I suppose," Rutledge said, considering it. "And her loneliness. I wanted her murderer caught. As much as you and Cobb did."

Satterthwaite nodded. "Cobb's going to live with his uncle for now. Did he tell you?"

"I think they'll deal well together."

Sighing, Satterthwaite said, "Well, I for one could use a night's sleep."

"I've to deal with the Teller family. And then there's a pressing inquiry in London."

"Was it accident or suicide? Teller's death."

Rutledge didn't answer for a time, and then he said quietly, "I wish to God I knew."

He should have slept, he knew that, but he circled around after leaving Hobson, and went back to the house with the red door.

Letting himself in, he walked through the empty rooms. Standing by the chair where Florence Teller had sat so many days and nights, waiting, he wondered if she was at peace now.

The police from Thielwald had searched the Blaine farmhouse and failed to find the rosewood letter box. Nor had they found either a deed or any other private papers belonging to Mrs. Teller.

He walked on, looking out at the garden behind the kitchen, at the flowers that had been so important to the lonely woman, and then turned and went up the stairs.

There was no way to know what the Teller family would do with this house now. Something, surely. He had a feeling Cobb wouldn't go back to the farm he'd shared with his wife. But he might end here. He had the money to buy Sunrise Cottage if he chose. And keep it as Florence Teller's shrine. All the small, painfully important memories of a woman's lifetime would be lost otherwise. Already the house felt as if she was no longer there, even in spirit.

In the bedrooms there was already a light film of dust collecting on the tops of tables and the windowsills.

He walked into her room.

There was Timmy's photograph where she could see it every night. Waiting for her to come up to bed.

He crossed to the table and picked it up, looking at it again.

It shouldn't stay here to be lost with the rest of Florence Teller's life. It belonged with the family that had never acknowledged the little boy who would have been their heir, if he'd lived.

"Shall I?" he asked the silence around him.

And then after a moment, he put it in his pocket.

He would take it home himself. A last gift to a woman he'd never seen, except in death.

And then he left the cottage, shut the red door firmly behind him, and then the gate.

If he drove through the night, as long as he could count on staying awake, he could be in Essex in the morning.

As it happened, he stopped at St. Albans out of necessity, for petrol, and he realized that he couldn't go any farther without endangering himself and anyone who got in his way. There was a room available in the inn inside the cathedral close, the sleepy clerk welcoming him and asking when he wished to have his breakfast.

Rutledge laughed. "When I'm awake," he said and went up the stairs like a drugged man, to fall into the bed by the windows over-looking the river, and after that he could remember nothing until he awoke two hours later. It was still dark outside, but he got up, shaved, and dressed, and went to find a telephone in the town.

Clouds had come in during the night, and now intermittent show-ers were cropping up. He ran through one on his way to a hotel near the railway station, and dashed in. He was shown to the telephone closet, where he put a call in to the Yard.

Gibson answered and Rutledge gave him a brief summary of what had transpired in Hobson.

"I'm going now to Essex. I'll be back in London as soon as may be."

Gibson said, "You were supposed to be on the bridge last night."

"Yes, well, a different murder took precedent." And then he paused. "No one else was killed?"

"They sent the constables out again in your place. And nothing happened. The Chief Superintendent was not best pleased."

"I don't suppose he was."

And then he was driving through the last of the darkness toward Witch Hazel Farm, chased the last five miles by a shower. As he came down the wet drive and his headlamps swept the front of the house, splintering into fragments of light against the mullioned windows, he had a premonition that all was not well.

He couldn't have said why, except that Hamish, in the back of his mind, was as moody as the weather, his voice as depressing as the rain.

As he stepped out of the car, he realized that the rain had brought a chill with it. He splashed to the door as the shower grew heavier.

He lifted the knocker and let it fall. Even though it had been draped in black crepe to mark a house of mourning, its sound echoed through the silence, startling birds taking shelter in the greenery below the windows.

No one came.

And then the door was flung open and a frantic Walter Teller cried, "Come quickly, for God's sake—"

He broke off, staring at Rutledge in bewilderment. "How did you get here so soon? The doctor isn't even here." Then looking over Rutledge's shoulder, he exclaimed, "Here he is now. Let him in, will you? I must go—" And he ran back into the house, leaving the door standing wide.

The doctor's motorcar was barreling down the drive, pulling up smartly behind Rutledge's.

"This way," Rutledge said, and Fielding nodded, preceding Rutledge into the house and taking the stairs two at a time.

Rutledge followed. On the first floor, the passage ran to the right and to the left. The doctor turned right, entered a room two doors down, and disappeared from view. Rutledge could hear someone crying.

He reached the doorway, and the first thing to meet his eyes was the great four-poster bed from another era, its bedclothes scattered and some falling onto the polished floorboards in a wild tangle.

Jenny Teller lay on the bed in her nightdress, her fair hair tumbled and uncombed, her feet bare.

Walter Teller was stepping aside to let the doctor work with her.

Fielding bent over the bed, his hands quick and sure. But after only a matter of minutes, he straightened and said, "There's nothing I can do. She's gone. I'm so sorry, Walter."

"But she was alive when you got here!" he exclaimed. "I could tell."

"I don't think she was. And if she had been, it was too late, far too late. The laudanum had done its work. She must have been dying when you found her."

"She can't have been. I won't believe it." He leaned over his wife, touching her face, calling her name, begging her to wake up. The doctor watched him for a time, then caught his shoulder and pulled him away. "There's nothing more you can do, man. Let me make her decent. She shouldn't be left like this."

It took some time to convince Teller to go out of the room. He reached the doorway, his face wet with tears, his mouth open in a silent cry of grief, then stumbled into the passage, going as far as the stairs, where he sat down on the top step, his head in his hands.

Shutting the door, Rutledge began searching the room from where he stood, his eyes roving from the armoire to the tall dresser, to the smaller chest of drawers on the far side of the bed, a desk by the windows, and a long mirror.

"There was a glass verra' like that one in Lancashire," Hamish said.

And so there was. Very like it. Even to the carved roses at the top of the oval frame. It must have come from the same manufacturer to be so alike.

Odd that both women owned the same mirror. He wouldn't have accused either of them of vanity.

He brought himself up sharply and continued to search for anything out of the ordinary.

Finishing his inspection of the room, he waited without speaking.

"What are you doing here at this hour?" the doctor demanded as he turned to see Rutledge still by the door.

"I got here not five minutes before you. I was called away before I could finish that business of Captain Teller's fall."

Fielding nodded. "I thought he might have called you. Walter, I mean." He gestured to the woman on the bed. "Well, since you're here, help me lay her out. The bed's in a state. Where's Mollie?"

"The maid? I don't think Teller summoned her." He crossed the room and helped the doctor with his work, smoothing out the bedclothes, laying the dead woman back into the center of the bed, and pulling a sheet up to her chin. He worked impersonally, and when the body had been made presentable, he could say with certainty that there was nothing unusual here, no signs of violence.

He said, when their work was done, "What happened?"

"An accidental overdose of laudanum at a guess. I prescribed it some time ago. I can't tell you why she was taking it now. Worry over that business with her husband? Or the boy going away to school? I know she took it very hard when Captain Teller fell here. She said something to me Sunday evening about not knowing how she was to sleep. She kept seeing him lying there at the bottom of the stairs."

"And you prescribed nothing then?"

"No. She wasn't asking for medical advice. I just asked how she was bearing up. I'd come back because I was worried about her and the Captain's widow. Susannah Teller. She was quite distraught. She should have been allowed to go back to London straightaway, but she said you refused to hear of it. Then the police from Waddington came back, and they told everyone they were free to go. Edwin Teller and his wife took Susannah back to London. They were concerned about his grandmother and how to break the news to her."

"And the sisters? Miss Brittingham and Miss Teller?"

"They left as well. Miss Brittingham asked the rector to keep Harry for the night, thinking it for the best. Miss Teller was very upset and had words with her brother Walter. Then she left."

Rutledge said, "The Tellers didn't share a room?"

"The master bedchamber is just through that door. This room is where Jenny stayed for her lying-in with Harry. It was where she always slept when her husband was away."

"If Walter Teller had been sleeping in there, would he have heard anything?"

"I doubt there was anything to hear. Certainly no violent death throes if that's what you mean."

Fielding stood there, looking down at Jenny Teller. "I can tell you, I wouldn't have been surprised to be summoned because Walter Teller was dead of an overdose. In his case, deliberate." He shook his head. "He's been under a terrible strain. They'd warned me at the clinic that this might be a consequence of his illness, and when I was here Sunday to pronounce the Captain dead, I was stunned to see the change in Teller. The attending doctors at the clinic felt that his recovery would depend on finding a solution to his distress."

"I thought he'd decided not to return to the field. That he was going to tell them that he had done enough."

"Yes, well, he might have been vacillating," Fielding said. "I didn't know the senior Teller very well. Walter's father. But he was a martinet, you know. Planning his children's lives without a thought to what they might like or might choose to do with themselves. Walter is a stickler for doing what's right. And it may have been more difficult than he imagined to step away from the path he'd been intended to follow all his life."

"How do I view this death?" Rutledge asked.

"I expect, like the Captain's, a tragedy that shouldn't have happened."

Rutledge nodded. And yet he wasn't satisfied. Not yet.

And he heard Hamish saying in his ear, "She doesna' look as peaceful as the other lass . . ."

Fielding turned to the door. "I'll let Teller come back. Then I'll see to it that he has something to carry him on. There's his brother's funeral. And now this. I understand he's not delivering the eulogy for his brother. Susannah Teller was adamant that it be the eldest brother. Edwin. Now we must concentrate on the living. The husband. The child. Someone ought to notify the family. I don't think Teller is up to it."

"I'll see to the family." Rutledge followed the doctor to the door and then went back into the room to look down on the woman lying on her pillow, her face pale and already losing that quality that made people real.

There was a glass on the bedside table. Milk, he thought. And a bottle that had come from a doctor's dispensary. There was no label on it.

He walked to the only other door in the room and opened it.

A dressing room, and then on the other side, as Dr. Fielding had said, the door into what must be the master bedroom. He crossed to open it, then looked back into the room where Jenny Teller lay.

"Why was she sleeping in there tonight?"

But Hamish had no answer for him.

Walter Teller's bedchamber was high-ceilinged and spacious, handsomely furnished, and with a newer bed, more modern in style than the four-poster, and a low bookcase beneath the double windows that faced the front of the house. A part of the original building, it had the wider floorboards and a prie-dieu against one wall that looked very old, a vestige of the Catholic owners before the Reformation. Someone had kept it for its beautiful lines and decorations, and it was well suited to the room.

Walking back to where Jenny lay, he closed the dressing room door. And at almost the same moment, Fielding returned with Walter Teller.

Teller crossed the room, looked down at his wife, and collapsed to his knees beside the bed, taking one of her hands in his and burying his face in it.

Fielding gestured for Rutledge to leave him there, and they walked out into the passage together.

Rutledge asked, "Did Walter Teller ever tell his wife where he was when he disappeared?"

"I'm not sure. She brought Harry in to visit the dentist on Thursday, and I was just coming out. I asked her how her husband was, if I should stop in and see him, perhaps keep him under observation for a while. And she told me he had fully recovered. I asked if he'd said anything to her about where he'd been while he was missing. I was curious, and it was important as well to add that to his file in the event it happened again. She replied that he hadn't confided in her. I could see she was unhappy about that. I suggested that she should give him a little space. That perhaps he himself was in need of time to understand his behavior. Harry had gone to speak to the vicar's son, who was coming down the street with his mother. Mrs. Teller watched him for a moment and then said that she wondered if her husband's family knew more about what had happened than she did, that they'd left her and gone in search of him, as if they knew something she didn't. I tried to make her understand that staying occupied was one of the best ways to weather a worrying time. That if they were at all like their brother, they couldn't have sat still and just waited, as she had done. That seemed to relieve her mind a little."

"Could that explain sleepless nights? Women worry about their families—if they are ill or hungry or frightened or hurt. It's their nature to care."

"I doubt it. It could be as simple as still not forgiving her husband for sending Harry away so soon. Or her guilt over her brother-in-law's fall. After all, he came down for her birthday celebration."

"Yes, I see that."

"Her death is consistent with overdose. There were no signs of struggle, only the disarrangement of the sheets while Teller strove to revive her. She drank her milk—if that's where she put the sedative— of her own free will. No marks on the lips to indicate that she was forced to swallow it."

Rutledge let it go. He went to rouse the maid, snoring deeply in her room in the attic, and asked her to prepare food for what was to come. She burst into tears when he told her that her mistress was dead, and he left her to grieve as she dressed.

His next duty was plain—to summon the police from Waddington and finally to put in a call to Edwin Teller's London residence. He got through there, and as he told an incredulous Edwin that his sister-in-law was dead, he could hear Amy's voice in the background saying, "Edwin? My dear, what is it? What's wrong?"

And Edwin shushing her as he listened to Rutledge's voice.

Leticia said, after Rutledge explained his calling her, "Don't disturb Susannah. She's been through enough. I'll deal with her later."

His call to Mary Brittingham's number rang and rang. The operator warned him that no one was at home. And then a very sleepy voice answered, "Do you know what time it is, Leticia? What could you possibly want at this hour?"

Rutledge said, "It's Scotland Yard, Miss Brittingham. I think you ought to come to Witch Hazel Farm straightaway."

Her voice was now crisp and alert. "Is it Harry? Is Walter all right?"

"It's your sister. I'm afraid she's dead."

The silence went on so long that he thought she'd hung up. Then she said, "She can't be dead. I was just there. Today. Yesterday. She was all right then. Is this Inspector Rutledge? Where are you, in London?"

"I'm at the farm. I'm sorry to break such news over the telephone, but I don't have time to come to you. It's more important that you come here."

He could hear a hiccuped breath, as if she were fighting tears. "Yes. All right." And then she was gone.

In the study, where he'd gone to wait until the police arrived, Rutledge discovered Walter Teller already sitting there with a brandy in his hand.

"Doctor's orders. It's supposed to give me the strength to cope," Teller said. He looked at his glass, holding it up to the light. "I doubt it will. I doubt anything can." He studied Rutledge for a moment and then asked, "How did you know to come? Was it Fielding?"

"I was here before I knew there was anything wrong," Rutledge said. "I've just come from Hobson. It's too late to tell your brother what happened there. But you should know. We found Mrs. Teller's murderer. It wasn't your brother. It was Mrs. Blaine's daughter. Betsy. A neighbor."

Teller repeated the name. "Betsy. Why?"

"Jealousy. She thought her husband would leave her for Florence Teller. It's a long story, and this isn't the time for it. But I felt you ought to know that your brother's name has been cleared."

"Too late for him," Teller said. "But thank you."

"When your elder brother arrives, I'll need to speak to him about disposal of the house in Hobson. I don't know that he wishes to leave that to Peter's solicitors. I don't know if they are even aware of the property."

"Leave it to me. I'll see to it. It's what Peter would have wished, I think. Edwin will have enough on his plate, with Peter dead. I'm told our grandmother took the news very hard. And now there's . . ." He cleared his throat. "Well."

Rutledge gave him time to recover, then said, "I must do my duty, however unpleasant it may be for me and for the family at such a time. The inquest will want to consider your wife's state of mind."

"Her state of mind? My God, I haven't even told my brother or sister—I haven't spoken to Mary—much less found words to tell my son his mother is dead—and you're talking about the inquest. Damn it, man, have you no decency?"

"It isn't a question of decency. Have I your permission to look into your wife's state of mind?"

"Do whatever you need to do. Just leave me alone." He got up to refill his glass, looked at the amber liquid, and put it down again with distaste. Rutledge could see that he was remembering his brother Peter's drunkenness.

Rutledge said, "Did your brother always drink as much as he did in the short time I knew him?"

The change of subject brought an irritated frown. "I—the level of pain he has—had—to endure must have been unimaginable. But no. He was more careful. What difference does it make now?"

"Would you say he drank in excess after he came back from Hobson?"

"Look, he's dead, you can't arrest a dead man. What difference do his drinking habits make now?"

"He was the catalyst for Florence Teller's death. Some of this will have to come out at the inquest into her murder. I'd like to know why he went to see his wife after such a long silence, and what she said to him when he was there that made him rush off in such a hurry that he left his cane behind. It became the murder weapon."

It was clear Walter Teller hadn't considered an inquest in Hobson or what it might reveal.

"Dear God, will it never be finished? Get out, Rutledge, do you hear me? I've lost my brother and my wife. Just leave me the hell alone."

Rutledge left him there and went in search of Mollie. She was in the kitchen, and as he came down the passage, he heard her singing hymns in a low tearful voice as she rattled the pots and pans preparing breakfast.

He made a fuss over opening the door into the kitchen, to give her time to recover.

She turned quickly, then said, "I thought it was Mr. Teller. I don't know what to say to him. First the Captain, and now Mrs. Jenny. I don't see how the poor man will survive this blow. And what will Master Harry make of it all, poor lamb? He adored his mother. It's such a tender age. Have you sent for his aunt? Miss Brittingham? She'll have to stay awhile. He'll need her. She should have stayed after the Captain's fall. Mrs. Jenny needed her then."

"Why did she leave?"

"They were all at sixes and sevens. Quarreling and slamming doors. This was after you'd left. Miss Brittingham said she'd had enough and went home. Mrs. Jenny went to bed with a headache. So she said, but I think it was an excuse to leave them to it."

"What rooms did Mrs. Teller most often use for her own purposes?"

"She liked the bedchamber where Master Harry was born. It's bright and cozy, she said, and sometimes when Mr. Teller wasn't here, she'd sleep in that room. And of course the nursery. She spent a good bit of her time there. When the nanny left two years ago, and Master Harry went to the local school, she would sit with him there and help him with his studies. The nanny's old room she made into her sitting room, with her desk and things about her. She could rest there and hear Harry playing or working. Or listen to him sleep. She said she found that the most peaceful sound in the world, a child's soft breathing."

Mollie had been working as she talked, her hands busy preparing tea and boiling eggs, making toast. She looked up now, and said, "Nobody has told me how she died."

Rutledge said, "An overdose of laudanum, apparently. In a glass of milk."

"Ah, that explains it then."

"Explains what?"

"There was a little milk spilled last night. Someone was warming it. I'd just wondered. She must have been having trouble sleeping. It just seemed odd that she'd leave the milk and the pan for me to clear away. She's—she was so tidy about things like that. She liked a gleaming kitchen, she said. It made her feel good that what Harry ate was prepared in clean surroundings." She bit back another round of tears. "Would you care for a cup of tea, sir? It has steeped long enough."

He thanked her and left, unwilling to intrude on her grief.

Going back to the bedchamber where Jenny Teller lay, he looked again at the room itself, and he could see what Mollie meant, that there was a warmth here that a woman might want to draw around her in times of great emotional need. A comfort that the master bedroom in its masculine formality lacked.

He went next to the nursery, opening doors here and there until he found what he was after. It was a large bright room filled with childhood, from a cradle to a rocking horse, a little wooden train that could be drawn about on wheels that clacked as they rolled, and a yacht that must have come from Harry's Uncle Edwin, who designed such things. It would float wonderfully, Rutledge thought, on a pond, the keel deep and the superstructure well balanced for it. Harry was a neat child, most of his possessions in good condition and not thrown about wildly. An only child, Rutledge remembered, who needn't worry that someone would snatch away his favorite toy.

The next room was his bedroom, with the narrow cot against one wall and a chair that rocked and a footstool for the one that didn't. The armoire was full of clothes, but not excessively so for a boy still growing. There were no photographs here, and he realized there had been none in Jenny's bedroom. But when he opened the next door, normally the nanny's room in the nursery suite, he found them all.

The dark blue and rose carpet was strewn with more toys—a small stuffed giraffe with green glass eyes, a sled with a toy dog sitting on it, waiting to be pulled through the snow of the carpet, and a green ball.

A desk stood under the window, in the French Provincial style, with a matching chair, but what interested him was the round table beside it, covered with a long skirted brocade and adorned with a forest of silver frames.

He crossed the room to look at them.

He could identify many of them. Jenny and her sister, Mary, as children, at the seaside and again at the Tower of London. A couple who appeared to be Jenny's parents. The three Teller sons, stair stepped beside their seated sister, shyly staring into the camera. Peter and Walter at university. Edwin with his wife just leaving the church after their wedding. Their parents with the three Teller sons and daughter sitting in front of a Christmas tree in the hall of this house. And more than a dozen photographs of a little boy, marking the various milestones of his life. A baby in his mother's arms, eyes closed, long christening gown draped across her lap. Just walking and holding his mother's hand, riding his rocking horse, playing on the lawns with the green ball Rutledge had just seen.

A record of a happy family, though seldom including the busy father.

Reaching for the Teller family grouping, he studied the senior Teller. He was tall, handsome, perfectly groomed. Not the sort to be found on a Sunday afternoon with rolled-up sleeves pruning the roses or racing his sons across the lawns in an impromptu game. His face was strong, rather more like Walter's, Rutledge thought, than Edwin's or Peter's, and more than a little stiff, as if smiling for a camera was an unpleasant duty to be borne with the best grace possible. His wife, her face upturned to his, was also surprisingly strong, as if she shared her husband's views and reinforced them. He could see where Leticia got her own strength of character. Gran, standing at her husband's shoulder, was tall and elegant, with a whimsical smile, the only one in the group who appeared to be genuine.

He had borrowed a small photograph of Walter Teller from Jenny, and he'd made a promise to return it, because it was one she cherished.

Rutledge took it from his pocket and set it among the other frames, where it belonged. He was glad he'd remembered.

What struck him about this collection of family photographs wasn't their number, nor the stages of a small child's life that they'd captured, but the similarity of this boy to the one in the single photograph that had stood by Florence Teller's bedside in Lancashire. Timothy was undoubtedly his father's son. And he belonged here.

As he set the small frame down in the midst of the family groupings, he felt an overwhelming compassion for Florence Marshall Teller.

Hamish said, as he was about to turn away to examine the contents of the desk, "Look again."

Rutledge did, frowning. At first there seemed to be nothing to see.

He'd been comparing Timmy to his cousin Harry, but now a photograph of the Teller sons taken with their sister caught his eye. In it Walter, the youngest, was about the same age Timmy was when he died. Almost Harry's age now. And the likeness, as Rutledge held them side by side, was so striking he wondered he hadn't seen it before. Harry had his mother's gentleness to soften his Teller features, but Timmy was the image of Walter at six or seven, looking into the camera with the same expression, that mixture of shyness and warmth, the same set of the eyes, the same way of tilting the head. There was a family likeness to his uncles, but anyone comparing the two photographs would think that Timmy was Walter Teller's son.

Rutledge pulled out the chair at Jenny's desk and sat down. It wasn't a trick of the light. It was there, he thought, holding the frames closer to the window so that even the dreary rain-damp natural light could reach them.

Walter Teller no longer looked like the child in the photograph with his brothers. Edwin still resembled his youthful self, but Peter too had changed. War and mission work had etched new lines where there had been none and honed down the soft fullness of a child's face to the harsher bone structure of maturity. Edwin, sheltered of necessity, had changed the least.

The resemblance didn't make Walter Teller Timmy's father. But it opened avenues of thought that gave Rutledge a different perspective on what he thought he'd understood unequivocally.

After a time, he put the frames back where he'd found them, and searched cursorily through Jenny Teller's desk. There was little of interest to him. A few letters, stationery and envelopes, stamps, and a clipped packet of paid household accounts for May.

Satisfied, he went downstairs to the study.

Walter wasn't there. Rutledge locked the door, crossed to the desk, and methodically went through it.

Nothing there to shed light on what he was asking himself.

And then he found, among folders of mission travel records and other related material, a single folder marked simply WILLS.

He took that out, opened it, and scanned Jenny Teller's last will and testament. It was, as he would have expected, very straightforward. Money inherited from her family was to be held in trust for her son, her jewelry for his wife on their wedding day, and a sum for servants past and present, another for the church in Repton. The remainder of her estate went to her husband.

Rutledge set that aside and looked at Walter Teller's will, though he had no right to do so. It too was straightforward. The greater part of his estate went to his son, with a sum set aside for his wife until she remarried or her death. Bequests to servants, to the Repton church, to the Alcock Society, and for the upkeep of the rose garden at Witch Hazel Farm in memory of his wife. But no mention of a woman in

Lancashire or St. Bartholomew's churchyard where she and her son lay buried.

Rutledge read the last bequest again. "For the perpetual upkeep of the rose garden at Witch Hazel Farm in memory of my wife."

And in his mind he could hear the parrot, Jake, pleased with his new if temporary quarters in Frances Rutledge's breakfast room, overlooking the garden. *Roses . . .*

He put the folder back where he found it, shut the desk, and unlocked the door.

Not a moment too soon. Mollie was there, telling him that breakfast was set out in the dining room, if he cared for any.

He walked with her into the passage. "There are lovely roses blooming by the drive. I'm surprised not to see them in arrangements indoors." In fact, now that he was aware of it, there were no cut flowers in the house at all. None of the displays that country houses could produce in abundance from their own gardens.

"Mr. Teller wasn't fond of cut flowers indoors. He said it reminded him of flowers for a funeral. He'd seen enough of them crowding the pulpits in churches where he preached."

"And Mrs. Teller? Was she fond of roses?"

"I don't know, sir. She never said. She did sometimes walk up to the garden by the drive. But for the most part she left the gardening to the gardener."

He thanked her and let her go. And then he opened the drive door and looked out. Even in the rain, the heavy dew-wet scent wafting on the slight breeze was pleasant.

Closing the door again, he walked into the dining room. But Teller wasn't there. A plate and silverware set to one side indicated that he'd come in and eaten a little, but the dishes were hardly touched.

Rutledge put food on a plate without thinking about what he had chosen.

He was remembering Captain Teller, when Rutledge asked about

Walter Teller's will during his disappearance, saying that it would be time enough to read it when they knew his brother was dead.

And Rutledge had never pursued the question, because Walter turned up alive and well.

He went to the telephone and gave instructions to the constable at the Yard who answered. He had just put up the telephone when there was the sound of a vehicle coming down the drive.

He waited outside for it to reach the steps. Leticia pulled up the hand brake, turned off the motor, and stepped out.

"You seem to bring trouble in your wake. I see Dr. Fielding is still here. Where is my brother?"

"I haven't seen him this past half hour."

"He'll be with Jenny, then," she said decisively and went briskly past him and up the stairs.

Fielding came down shortly afterward and said, "I asked if he'd like to speak to the rector. He said he'd prefer my company. He won't let me give him anything. He said that God was punishing him, and he couldn't escape that."

"There's breakfast in the dining room."

"Thank you. It's been a long morning for all of us. I could use some tea." He nodded and disappeared down the passage.

Rutledge was standing very close to where Peter Teller had been found at the foot of the stairs. He looked at the spot, remembering the sprawled body and the family in distress. It had seemed to be genuine distress.

Amy, first to reach Peter, had said he had tried to speak her name. *Mee* . . .

Rousing himself, Rutledge was about to walk back to the study when he heard another vehicle on the drive. It was the local police. Inspector Jessup said as Rutledge opened the door, "Dr. Fielding asked us to wait before coming. Who's here now? I see the other motor."

"Miss Teller, Walter Teller's sister."

Jessup nodded. "Was she here last night?"

"I telephoned her earlier. She arrived not five minutes before you."

Rutledge led the way into the study. "It appears to be a straightforward case of accidental overdose." He told Jessup what he had seen and about the spilled milk in the kitchen. "At this stage, I can't see a case for suicide."

"Or murder?"

"Not at this stage," Rutledge repeated.

Jessup said, "Sometimes people aren't careful enough counting out their drops. Are you comfortable with accidental death?"

"At the moment. I'll listen to what other family members have to say."

"There seems to have been a rash of them in this house. I hope this is the last. Bad things come in threes."

"Teller and his sister are upstairs. To your right, second door. Or the master bedroom, farther along the passage."

"Any marks on the body?"

"None that Fielding or I saw. He'll know more later."

Jessup nodded and went up the stairs two at a time.

Another motorcar came rapidly down the drive, and Rutledge opened the door to find a constable already standing there on duty, his cape wet with rain.

"Morning, sir."

"Good morning, constable. I think that's the deceased's sister just arriving. Let her come in."

"Thank you, sir."

Rutledge went back inside and into the study, leaving the door ajar. He could hear Mary Brittingham speaking to the constable, then hurrying up the stairs.

A moment or two later, he heard a muffled cry as she must have reached her sister's room.

It was sometime later that Walter Teller came down the stairs alone.

He walked into the study, nearly turned about as soon as he saw Rutledge there, then went to the window.

"The women are doing women things. I can't think about what she's to wear. I can't face putting her into the ground. Tomorrow it may be easier. Jessup seems to be satisfied. He's in the kitchen questioning Mollie. Something about milk spilled in the night."

"Where did your wife keep her laudanum?"

He sat down, took a deep breath, and said, "Oddly enough, on a shelf in the kitchen. She was terrified that Harry might find it. I told her he'd have better sense, but she wouldn't hear of keeping it anywhere else."

"Did she take it often?"

"She only took it once before. When she'd hurt her back and couldn't sleep. I'm surprised it hadn't dried up long since."

It made sense. Fumbling with the pan, spilling the milk, then miscounting her drops . . .

Rutledge said after a moment, "Why did she need them last night?"

"I expect it was Peter, the sound he made as he fell. She said she could still hear it. It was a shock for all of us. I don't know how Amy held up. She watched him die."

Rutledge let another silence fall. Then he said, "Do you think your brother's death might have been intentional? Rather than facing trial and the publicity that will come in its wake, affecting the whole family. He couldn't have foreseen he'd have been exonerated."

"If Peter had wanted to escape anything, he would have gone somewhere quiet and private and shot himself. There are enough grounds here at Witch Hazel Farm for him to do that."

"A good point. Who was Florence Teller? In truth?"

That brought Walter Teller out of his chair. "Now that Mary is here, we must break the news to my son. If you will excuse me?"

And he was gone.

Jessup came to say that he was ready for the body to be taken away.

But Leticia Teller had asked him to wait until her brother and his wife arrived. Pulling out his pocket watch, he stood there considering time and distance. "Another hour, at best. I've told Dr. Fielding that he can leave."

"Yes. Thank you."

Jessup said, "You're sure there's not something more I ought to know?"

Rutledge answered, "There was an inquiry in Lancashire. As it happened, Captain Teller was an unwitting witness. He called on someone there, and shortly afterward, she was murdered. The woman who killed her is now in custody. We shan't have his evidence at the trial, but I don't think we'll have any worries about a conviction. Two policemen heard the murderer confess."

"I didn't know he was recently in Lancashire."

"It was during the time when his brother was ill."

"I'm beginning to think there's much I haven't been told."

"Walter Teller's disappearance was a London matter. The murder took place in Lancashire."

"And I've got two deaths here."

"So you have."

"Fielding said something about Teller's illness worrying his wife as well as her husband's disappearance. What was the nature of his illness? Was there any diagnosis?"

"Worry," Rutledge said succinctly. "His mission society would like to see him back in the field."

"I'm sure they would. Good publicity for them, with Walter Teller back in harness, perhaps another book in the offing. What does Teller think?"

"You must ask him. He may be needed here now, with a motherless son."

"True enough. I'm not one for traveling in places where I'm not wanted. I've never seen the good in telling other people how to live and how to believe. Still, I admire those who can do such things."

Jessup was fishing, Rutledge thought, and knew his business.

"His role in the Lancashire affair didn't prey on Captain Teller's mind, did it?"

"It's more likely that a bad leg and his refusal to use a cane killed him rather than events in Lancashire."

There was the sound of new arrivals outside the study. Rutledge said, "Edwin Teller and his wife."

Jessup stood. "Let's be clear. Is this my inquiry or the Yard's."

Rutledge smiled grimly. "At this stage it's yours. I'll give your people a statement. I was here just before the doctor came. So far, I'm a witness. But I know this family better than you do, and you'll find me useful."

"As long as we understand each other."

They went out into the passage in time to see Edwin and Amy walk in and then climb the flight of stairs. Behind then was the elder Mrs. Teller. Gran's face was drawn, as if it had aged too fast.

"Who is that?" asked Jessup.

Rutledge explained, adding, "She's a little vague, but I wouldn't discount her information, if I were you."

It was not long before Amy brought a weeping Gran down the stairs and took her into the dining room.

"Don't fuss, Amy," she was saying when Rutledge walked in. "I'm quite able to put milk into my cup on my own." Looking up, she said, "It's that handsome young man who walked by my window. I didn't know you were invited for the weekend as well?"

He came to take her hand. "I'm sorry to meet you again in such sad circumstances."

"Yes, there's Peter dying, and now Jenny. I don't know what to make of it." Her face puckered again. "Two funerals. I thought the next might be my own."

"You've many years ahead of you," he assured her.

Amy said quietly, "Go away. Let her drink her tea and cry a little, if that's what she needs to do. Then I might persuade her to lie down for a bit."

He ignored her. To Gran, he said, "You must be prepared to work with Harry. He will need your support and your care."

"To be sure," she told him impatiently. "What I don't understand for the life of me is why Jenny took laudanum."

"Captain Teller's death unsettled her."

"Oh, my dear, I could hardly bring myself to walk up those stairs. I can't think what Jenny must have felt. But there are the arrangements for Peter. The flowers, the food, airing the beds. Who is to see to them now?" she demanded fretfully. "Why didn't Susannah come with us? But I expect Leticia will know what to do."

"Why would Jenny not have taken laudanum to sleep?" he pursued. "It must have seemed to her the sensible thing to do, so that she'd be rested."

"But they gave her laudanum before," Gran said, "and she didn't like it. It made her so deathly ill."

Amy started to speak, but one look from Rutledge and she held her tongue.

"When?"

"When I was here, of course. She'd hurt her back, and I came to stay. She found it hard to wake up. She felt all muzzy. She didn't like it because of the baby."

Amy said, "But Harry was away last night."

Gran took another slice of cold toast. "Is there any of that nice jam left, dear? The one I like so much."

Amy brought her the pot of strawberry jam.

"Thank you, my dear." She spread it across half a slice of toast. "Has anyone told Susannah we're here? I don't understand why she didn't come down with us."

"Mary is here. You've always liked Mary," Amy pointed out.

"No, I haven't. Just because she's Jenny's sister, she thinks she's invited everywhere. I much prefer Jenny." Frowning she began to cry again. "It's so sad, you know. First Peter, and now Jenny. It's very trying."

Rutledge prepared to go. "Mrs. Teller?" he said to Amy. "I'd like to speak with you privately, if I may."

"If it's about Jenny and the laudanum—"

"No."

With a glance at Gran, happily spreading jam on another slice of toast, Amy rose. He led her out of the dining room, but Leticia was in the study, sitting at the desk, making a list, and at the top of the stairs, he could hear Walter speaking earnestly to Mary.

As she answered him, Rutledge caught the words, " . . . your fault, Walter. You must accept that."

Rutledge said, "Will you find your coat? There's no privacy here."

"It's raining, if you haven't noticed it."

"Your coat."

She came back with it and said, "Edwin wants to know if I'll be long."

"Nothing will happen while we're gone."

Irritably, she handed him her coat to hold for her, and then together they walked out past the constable and into the rain. Rutledge opened the door of his motorcar for her, and then turned the crank. Reversing the vehicle, he drove past the rain-laden roses. Amy said, "I've just driven from London. Edwin wasn't feeling well enough to take the wheel. I'm not in the mood for a tour of Essex."

They had reached the gate, just out of sight of the house. There Rutledge stopped.

Without preamble, he said, "Florence Teller wasn't married to Captain Teller, was she?"

Amy opened her mouth, then closed it smartly.

"What I need to know is why Walter used his brother's name."

"I have no idea what you're talking about," she said, looking at the trees that overhung the road.

"Look. I've seen his will. That rose garden, the one we just passed, is to be a memorial to his wife's memory. And interestingly enough the will doesn't specify Jenny Teller. There's been a conspiracy of silence from the start. You've known the truth all along, haven't you? And helped to cover it up," he accused her.

She had turned to look at him again. "Jenny loved roses."

"No, she didn't. But Florence Teller did. Do you remember the rose that Lawrence Cobb dropped into the grave?'"

"Was that his name? Yes, I remember. I remember that day very well."

"Peter didn't kill her. Someone else did. Lawrence Cobb's wife. But I rather think I'm to blame for Walter believing he did. And it's possible that in revenge he killed his brother."

"You mean Peter's fall—no, that's ridiculous."

"What I don't know is how much he loved his wife. Or if he cared anything for his dead son. And I need to know, or my judgment will be flawed."

"It's pathetic," she said angrily. "You hounded Peter to his death with threats of taking him into custody. And so he drank too much. That meant he wasn't steady on his feet, and with that leg, it's not surprising he fell. If there's any blame in his death, it lies at your door. All you're trying to do is shift it to Walter. Well, I won't let you."

Rutledge had both hands on the wheel. Between them in the far distance, over the tops of trees, he could just see the tower of Repton's church, floating like an island in the sweeping curtains of rain.

Hamish was there too, the Scots voice loud in his ears.

Rutledge turned to look at Amy Teller.

"You aren't protecting Walter. I don't think you're even fond of him. And you let Peter take the blame without compunction. Well, Jenny is dead. Nothing can hurt her now. It's the boy. It's young Harry. It was always Harry." He turned to look at her. "As long as Peter shouldered the blame for marrying two women, Harry was safe. Even Susannah, his wife, was willing to say nothing, for Harry's sake."

She refused to answer him.

"Why did Walter Teller use his brother's name, instead of his own? Neither of them had married in 1903."

And still she sat stubbornly silent. But Rutledge could see tears bright in her eyes, tears of anger, frustration, and helplessness.

"How long have you known? At a guess, not very long. Was it during Walter's illness? Did something happen then?"

He waited, giving her a chance.

Finally he said, "Peter Teller died trying to preserve that lie. When you got to him, he said, 'It was me.' And instead, so that it wouldn't arouse any suspicion, you told everyone that he had spoken your name."

He thought for a moment she would fling open the motorcar's door and run down the drive in the rain to get away from him.

"And Leticia, you and your husband, along with Mary, tried to pry the truth from Walter on Sunday after I'd gone north. Did Jenny overhear you? Is that why she took an overdose of laudanum?"

She broke down then, her face in her hands.

It had mostly been conjecture on his part, putting together what he knew with what he suspected, and holding the two together with a tissue of guessing.

He added as he prepared to let in the clutch and start down the drive, "Peter didn't kill Florence Teller—but I tell you again it's possible Walter thought he had, and killed him. That's why I need to know how he felt about Florence Teller, and if he would avenge her when the chance presented itself." He handed Amy Teller his handkerchief, adding, "I think you can see my dilemma. Inspector Jessup is already suspicious. If I walk away, and don't do my duty, someone else will. And it will be worse. I'll do my best to protect Harry. But I will need help."

30

Amy was out of the motorcar almost before Rutledge had come to a stop. He watched her dash through the rain into the house as the constable opened the door for her.

He sat where he was, feeling distaste for what he had just done. But Amy Teller was the only one he thought might eventually tell him the whole truth.

"Ye may be wrong," Hamish warned him.

The study door was shut, and Rutledge opened it, expecting to find most of the family gathered there. But Walter Teller was sitting alone.

"If you're looking for the others, they're in the drawing room. I don't know whether they're leaving me alone to grieve or if they can't bear my company."

His voice was dispassionate, as if he had shut off his own feelings.

Rutledge said, "They're still trying to come to terms with your brother's death. And now this—"

He was interrupted by a knock at the door.

Teller said, "Tell them I'm not seeing anyone."

But it was the rector, Mr. Stedley, who stuck his head around the door. "Walter? They told me you were in here." He was tall and robust, with a deep voice. "I thought I should come. Mary is with Harry. There's nothing I can do in that quarter at the moment."

Walter, rising, said, "Ah, Stedley. Thank you for your care of Harry. It's very kind of you and Mrs. Stedley to take him in. It's been very difficult for all of us. And it will be hardest for him."

"The question is, what can I do for you? Would you like me to go to Jenny and say a prayer?"

"I—yes, if you would. I'm sure she would have wanted that. She's in the room where Harry was born."

As the rector went up the stairs, Walter said, "It's beginning. The flood of mourners. And each time I speak to them, her death becomes a little more real."

"You must have seen death many times in your work abroad."

Walter laughed without humor. "My first posting, I buried twelve people on my first day. A cholera epidemic. It was only the beginning. I should be accustomed to death. And then the war. I lost count of the number of men who died in my arms inside and outside the medical tents. Sometimes kneeling in the mud, sometimes watching shells scream over my head. Sometimes by a cot with bloody sheets, or in an ambulance, before the stretcher could even be lifted out. I was quite good at giving a dying man the comfort necessary to make the end easier. And all the while, I knew I was lying to them and to myself. I will say one thing for the King James version of the Bible, the words are sonorous and speak for themselves. All I had to do was remember my lines."

Rutledge thought about the curate reading from the Psalms for Florence Teller's service. He had seemed to speak from the heart.

"If those men were comforted, then it didn't matter what you felt."

"I wish I could believe that."

"There must have been rewarding moments in your mission work?"

"That too was a sham," he answered tersely.

"But you spoke eloquently about fieldwork in your book. So I'm told."

"That was worse than a sham, it was a fraud. But it bought me time. And that's all that mattered."

"Time for what?" Rutledge asked, but Teller ignored him.

"You have no conception of what Africa is like. There was a tribe on the far side of the river. Which was hardly more than a stream that fed into the Niger. Still, it kept them from our throats. We only had to guard the crossing. But then their crops failed in the rain. My God, I'd never seen so much rain! And then it was gone, the soil baked nearly to brick in days. I'd been frugal—thrifty. So they came for our crops, pitiful as they were. And I abandoned my flock. I stood in the pulpit and exhorted them to put their faith in a merciful and compassionate God, knowing all the while they'd be slaughtered. And I'd be dead with them if I stayed—the foreign priest who had lured them away from the old worship. I can still see their eyes, you know—looking up at me, believing me, putting their trust, their lives in my promise, and the next morning I was packed and walking out before first light. I dream of their eyes sometimes. Not the poor slaughtered bodies."

Rutledge said nothing.

As if driven, Walter went on.

"And then there was Zanzibar. We'd had a disagreement with the bishop, and we thought we knew better how to deal with the Arabs. Better than he, surely? And instead we found ourselves charged with insubordination. Zanzibar is an island—have you ever been to a spice island? My God, pepper and mace and allspice, cloves and vanilla and nutmeg—you ride down a hot sunny stretch of road where they're drying the cloves on bright cloths spread almost to your feet. Small brown spikes, thousands of them, like a carpet that moves with the wind. And vanilla pods—or tiny green seeds of pepper. Mace. That thin coating of a nutmeg is worth its weight in gold. Amazing place, and the sea so blue it hurts your eyes to look out across it. But the smell of slaves is there in the town as well. Misery and grief and pain and helpless anger. That's Zanzibar as well."

Hamish said, "You mustna' let him finish."

But Rutledge refused to halt the flow of this man's confession. He could see how the soul of the man had been scoured to the bone.

"In China we used the opium traders. They carried messages where no one else would, and sometimes were the only protection a traveling man of God had from bandits we found on the road. So we lived with the devil—quietly, mind you—while we preached that opium was evil and led to madness and death. Double standards, Rutledge. We preached and didn't live a word that came out of our mouths. Sanctimonious, self-righteous prigs, that's what we were, and I was ashamed of all of us in the end."

"Do you think you were the only missionary who felt that way?"

"I hoped I was." He laughed harshly. "I wasn't like the rest of them. I had no calling, you see. I became what my father told me to become. And Peter hated the Army as much as I hated my own work. I'd have liked being a soldier, I think. But who knows? I might have hated that too."

Which, Hamish was remarking to Rutledge, explained why he had told Florence Marshall that he was a soldier. Living a lie because it made him feel better about his lack of choice in the matter, made him appear to be dashing and romantic in the eyes of a young woman who had never seen the world beyond where she lived. And yet, cowardly enough that he used his brother's name, for fear his father would somehow learn of his rebellion.

They could hear Mr. Stedley, the vicar, coming down the stairs.

Teller shook himself, as if awakening from a reverie, as if he'd been talking more to himself than Rutledge.

"She's very peaceful," Mr. Stedley said, coming into the room.

"Yes."

"Is there any comfort I could offer you, Walter?"

"Thank you, Rector, for coming. You might wish to speak to the rest of the family. We've been overwhelmed by events. I'll be in touch about the service. I think Jenny would have liked you to conduct it."

"Yes, of course." He looked from Teller to Rutledge and back again. "If you need me, you've only to send for me."

And he was gone. Walter Teller sighed. "Next it will be the police cornering me, asking questions. And then Mary will be at me again, or Leticia. And then my brother. I'd like to lock the door and pretend I'm not here."

Rutledge rose. "I've brought Timmy's photograph from the cottage."

Walter Teller was very still. Then he said, "Perhaps his mother would have preferred to have it buried with her."

He lost his temper. "What did Timmy do? Fail his father by dying when it wasn't convenient to come home and pray for him?"

Teller's face went so white Rutledge thought for an instant his heart had stopped. And then catching his breath almost on a gasp, he said only, "Peter would be grateful to you."

R utledge went outside to walk off his anger. The rain had moved on, black clouds toward the east, the sky overhead still roiling as the weather fought for stability. He went to the other side of the house, unwilling to pass the roses, and instead crossed the lawn toward the little stream, swollen with rain and threatening to overflow into the grassy water meadows on either side. He could feel the soles of his boots sinking into the soft earth, and moved a little above the soaked banks.

Jenny Teller was well out of it, he told himself. And then he found himself thinking that she would have managed, as she had done in London, whatever she had discovered about her husband's past. She could have been married again to regularize her union, and she would have said nothing that would endanger her son's future. Whether she could bear to live with Walter Teller again was another matter. He might have had to accept the Alcock Society's next posting to the field until he and his wife could come to terms with the ghost of Florence Teller and her son, Timmy.

Hamish said, "Perhaps that's why she had to die?"

"Don't be a fool," Rutledge told him harshly.

"Ye're looking at black and white. It's a man's way of thinking, no' a woman's."

In the distance, he could hear someone calling his name. Looking up, he realized that Leticia Teller was trying to attract his attention.

He turned back toward the house, and she waited by the French doors for him. When he was within hearing, she said, "There have been two telephone calls for you. One appears to be urgent. Scotland Yard."

He thanked her and took the message she was holding out to him.

Inside, he looked at the first. From Inspector Jessup in Waddington, it read, "Mrs. Susannah Teller wishes to know when her husband's body can be released for burial."

He called the police station and left a message for Jessup: *At your earliest convenience.*

Murder, accident, or suicide—it didn't matter. The police had no reason to hold Peter Teller's remains any longer.

Next he put in a call to the Yard. When Sergeant Gibson came to the telephone, Rutledge could hear the tension in his voice.

"Sir? There have been developments. In the inquiry concerning Billy."

Bowles was growing restive.

"Go on."

"Inspector Cummins took your place last night."

"I thought you told me that the constables had tried again, with no luck."

"That's true, yes, sir. But Inspector Cummins decided he'd try his chances. Without notifying the Yard. He gave as good as he got, the Inspector did, but he's in hospital, and they're stitching him up."

"And Billy?"

"Got away, sir. There was no one posted on either end of the bridge to stop him."

Rutledge swore under his breath. "All right. What does the Chief Superintendent want?"

"You on the bridge tonight. He said to tell you that unless what you're doing is a matter of life and death, you're to be here. No later than nine this evening."

"I'll be there. I'm coming from Essex."

"Yes, sir."

Rutledge put up the receiver, then stood there for a moment thinking.

He asked himself how he would have viewed the death of Peter Teller and the death of Jenny Teller if he hadn't known the background of events in Hobson. If he'd come here as Inspector Jessup had done with nothing to color his perspective but a man with a bad leg who'd had too much to drink and simply fallen down the stairs. Or a woman distressed by a death almost literally on her doorstep and very tired but unable to sleep, miscounting the drops from a bottle of medicine that she expected to give her some relief.

Hamish said, "But ye ken, it isna' sae simple!"

Rutledge went to find Leticia.

"I'll have to leave for London later in the afternoon."

"There's a cold luncheon in the dining room. I need to speak to you."

He followed her there, and as she filled a plate and handed it to him, she asked, "What did you say to Walter?"

"What is it you think I said?" he asked.

She shook her head irritably. "He's gone up to his room and locked himself in. The dressing room door, as well. They've come to collect Jenny's body. Shall I tell them to wait?" She began putting food on her own plate with scarcely a glance at what she was choosing.

"Let them go ahead. What about Harry?"

"Mary has decided it would be too upsetting for him to see his mother's body. She's staying with him at the rectory."

"If his father finds that acceptable, the police will have no objection."

"It wouldn't matter if you did."

He smiled. "What do you really want me to say, Miss Teller? Very well. The inquiry is closed in Hobson, with the arrest of Florence Teller's killer. It was someone who knew her. And while the evidence was unequivocally pointing to your brother—Captain Teller—he was not the cause of her death."

He could hear the hiss of breath as she released it. "Then Peter was never guilty. Even though he died expecting to be arrested at any moment. Dear God. That breaks my heart."

"He couldn't see how events unfolded after he'd driven away. Until we tried to account for certain missing items, nor could we. But we might have reached our conclusions earlier if there hadn't been so many lies to cover up who Florence Teller really was."

"But I thought you knew," she said forcefully. "She was Peter's wife. The foolish mistake of a young man whose father refused to allow him to marry his cousin."

"I'm sure Florence Teller would be happy to hear she was only a foolish mistake."

Leticia had the grace to flush. "I wasn't referring—"

"Yes, you were. She's been a thorn in the side of this family since you first learned of her. Did you believe your brother Walter left the Belvedere Clinic to travel to Hobson? Is that why you sent Peter there to find out what he could?"

"Peter didn't discuss his private affairs with us."

"Come now. I was told that he'd gone to Cambridge with Edwin. And that was a lie; he was in Hobson. Susannah told me about Lieutenant Burrows, and that was a lie. She knew the truth and was trying to help conceal it. But Jenny knew nothing." He considered her for a moment. "What did you do, go through his papers looking for some clue to why Walter was ill and not responding? At a guess you found something that set off alarm bells. And you haven't put it back, have you? Because I saw the file this morning, and it held only a will."

He could read the answer in her eyes. That was precisely what someone had done.

"Was it your brother Edwin and his wife? The head of the family, with his strong sense of duty? Yes, I'm sure it was. The truth must have come as a shock. And so Peter—the real Peter Teller—was dispatched to Lancashire to see who this woman was, what she might want, and whether Walter was leaving Jenny for her."

She picked up her plate and put it on the tray for Mollie to collect. "I'll leave you to enjoy your lunch, Inspector. I'm afraid I have much to do."

Leticia walked out without looking back.

Rutledge said to the empty room, "With Florence Teller dead, and Peter, and Jenny, the past is wiped out. Except for Harry . . ."

Hamish answered him, "There's the Captain's wife."

Susannah, who refused to set foot in this house again.

"But she's loyal to the family."

"*Was* loyal."

It was a very good point. Could she be trusted to keep the secret?

He went to the telephone and put in a call to the Yard. Sergeant Gibson listened to Rutledge's request, then said, "It's going to be difficult getting it past the Chief Superintendent, but I'll see that a watch is set. You don't care to explain why it's needed?"

Rutledge said, "Early days," and let it go at that.

Edwin Teller met him in the passage and said, "I should think the Yard would have no further business with the family. I'm told you've found your murderer. I'm glad. A pity Peter couldn't hear that as well."

"Indeed," Rutledge agreed. "I'm leaving this afternoon for London, there's something there I must do. I'll be back by tomorrow morning."

"I don't know why you should return at all."

"There are loose ends."

He was about to walk on when Edwin said, "Do you mean Susannah? Peter's wife—widow?"

"I'm not sure I understand what you're asking."

"Look, I'm just concerned, I wanted to know if you're expecting to speak to Susannah. She's grieving, and in great distress. This was such an—no one can prepare for these things, can they? Peter should have lived to a great age, like my grandmother. Give her time to come to grips with her loss."

"Are you afraid she might decide, finally, to tell the truth? To clear her husband's name?"

"She hasn't been told that he's no longer under suspicion. I tried to telephone her just now, and Iris says she's not taking calls. For God's sake, let her alone."

"I'll take that under advisement, shall I?"

Leticia came out of the study. "Has anyone asked Walter if he'd like a tray? Edwin, try to persuade Gran to eat something. She says she doesn't care for Mollie's cooking, that Jenny knew what she liked."

"I'll try." Edwin excused himself and walked off.

Leticia said, "I'll see to Walter then. He ought to have something."

Rutledge, looking after her as she went up the stairs, decided to start out for London. He could hear her now knocking on Teller's door and calling to him. Turning away, he found his hat and left the house. The constable nodded to him.

"I have to return to London. I'll be back as soon as possible. Tell Inspector Jessup I'll give him a clear answer then."

The constable came forward to crank the motorcar for him. And then he was on the road. Clearing his mind of everything else, he concentrated on Billy and what might be waiting for him on Westminster Bridge.

31

Rutledge made good time to London and went to his sister's house before reporting to the Yard.

She was surprised to see him, saying as he walked through the door, "Are you coming for Jake?"

"Not yet. How is he?"

"I don't want him to grow more attached to me than he is," she said. "He likes to sit on my shoulder and walk around the house. I dare not take him outside, for fear he'll fly away. But he wants to go to every window and look out, then he searches for roses."

"His owner grew them. Bring a few inside. That might cheer him up."

"A very good idea."

"Any news of Meredith Channing?"

"I haven't seen her since she returned to London. But I'm told she's back and feeling much better. Oh, speaking of injuries and recoveries, did you hear that Chief Inspector Cummins was viciously attacked last night? I ran into his sister coming from the hotel in Marin Street. She was sent for. He was badly hurt, loss of blood, stitches. I hope they find whoever did such a vile thing."

"I'm sure the Yard has every possible man searching."

"What brought you here, if it wasn't Jake?" she asked.

He smiled. "No further word from Scotland?"

"All's well. Ian had his pick of the pups. He's excited because Fiona is allowing him to sleep with it. I don't think there's any lasting harm from the horror of the train crash."

"The resilience of youth."

Leaving, he trolled the streets toward St. Paul's, looking for Charlie Hood. But there was no sign of the man. Another loop, he thought, and then, six blocks from the cathedral, he spotted Hood.

This time Rutledge caught up with him and called, "Hood?"

The man turned, recognized Rutledge, and started toward an alley where the motorcar couldn't follow. And then he thought better of it and came forward slowly, stopping about five feet from the vehicle.

People were swarming around them at this hour of the day, weaving in and out and making any sort of conversation nearly impossible.

"What do you want?" Hood asked. And Rutledge read his lips rather than heard his words in the noisy intersection.

"A drink. A few words," Rutledge said to him.

"I don't have the time," Hood replied. Then, coming nearer, he asked, "You haven't caught your murderer, have you?"

"Not yet. He came close to killing another man last night."

Hood nodded. "Word gets about on the street." He made to go.

Rutledge said, "Have you ever had trouble with the police?"

Hood laughed harshly. "Not since I was twelve and learned my lesson. Still trying to make a connection with that other man?"

"That inquiry was successfully concluded."

"I'm glad to hear it." And he was off, moving briskly through the late afternoon crowds, then crossing the street and disappearing into a shop.

Rutledge watched him go. "I'll have you yet, my friend," he said under his breath, then turned back toward the Yard.

Instead he went to Bolingbroke Street and asked to speak to Susannah Teller.

To his surprise, she agreed to see him. The shades were drawn in the sitting room, but even in the dim light Rutledge could see that her eyes were red-rimmed from crying and lack of sleep. Yet he thought she seemed to have found some inner strength to carry her through.

Hamish said, unexpectedly, "Anger."

Rutledge thought that was very true. For she kept him standing, like a servant.

"I wanted you to know that we've released your husband's body."

"Thank you. I had a call from Inspector Jessup. I have arranged for the service to be held tomorrow afternoon."

That was very quick, but he said only, "He didn't kill anyone, Mrs. Teller. He's been completely absolved."

"How nice to know that the rector needn't mention in his eulogy that Peter was nearly arrested for murder," she said sardonically.

"If I'd had the whole truth from the start," he told her, "it might have been different."

"All I know is, you made his last days a hell on earth. I hope this knowledge will give you nights as sleepless as his were."

"I expect there are worse burdens on my conscience than this one."

"Who did kill that woman in Lancashire?" she asked him, unable to stop herself.

He told her, and she said, "Jealousy is a powerful thing."

"But you weren't jealous of Florence Teller. After all, there was no need. She wasn't Peter's wife."

"It never troubled me," she said, still keeping up the lie, "from the time I found out. We had a happy marriage, Peter and I. Whether you believe that or not."

"Have you asked your solicitor what your rights are, if you persist in this charade? Whether you are in fact the legitimately surviving spouse? Mrs. Teller is dead. Of course, the Captain must have made proper provisions for you in his will."

That visibly shook her. But she said, "Our solicitors will sort it out."

"Or perhaps they weren't informed of the necessity for provisions. Unless your husband changed his will in the last ten days."

"You're unbelievably cruel, Inspector. My husband is dead, and so is the woman in Hobson. He can't be prosecuted for bigamy, and you will only bring public shame on me if you pursue this."

"Shaming you isn't my intent, Mrs. Teller. But when people break the law—and there is a law against bigamy, I remind you—there are often repercussions that hurt the innocent. Your husband, for instance, whose name was used by Walter Teller. And Jenny Teller, who—if the truth had come to light—was about to discover that she was no one's wife and her child illegitimate. It was convenient for both of them to die when they did. Accidentally? Very likely. But if not, I want you to realize that you may also stand in some danger. You're very angry just now about your husband's death. Understandably. He bore the brunt of his brother's misdeeds. And he kept his head and fought me every step of the way. I recognize why, now. All of you are very fond of Harry. And you're protecting *him,* not his father. But when you find yourself being denied your rights as the Captain's widow, you might well see matters very differently. And if you are forced to tell the truth to protect yourself, you will break this wall of silence."

He could see she hadn't thought that far ahead, she hadn't considered the legal repercussions or the danger she might stand in. She replied slowly, as if still thinking through what he'd said, "But you've just told me that Peter's death and Jenny's were accidents."

"At this stage, we have to consider them accidental. We haven't been able to find any proof to the contrary. But they were—providential. You must see that."

She shook her head. "My murder would bring to light everything that the family has fought so hard to protect."

He let it go and told her instead, "As for the voices your husband heard in the cottage when he was speaking to Florence Teller, it might well have been the parrot, Jake, that her husband brought her. It speaks sometimes. *Mimics* may be a better word."

"I—parrot?"

"Yes. He's here in London. You can see him for yourself."

"No. You're saying I have no grounds to believe Walter or Edwin were already there in the house? Peter was so sure."

"I think Edwin can prove he was in Cambridge. And Walter was aware you'd discovered his secret. He never left London."

"Or is this a trick to see to it I withdraw my charge of murder?" she asked suspiciously. "I don't trust you, either."

Rutledge smiled. "I don't ask you to trust me. Just consider what I've said."

He turned to go.

As he reached the door, she stopped him. "What you're telling me is that you aren't finished with Walter. And you want me to leave him to you."

He turned. "I'll do my best to protect Harry. For his mother's sake. And I owe it to the Captain to protect you as well. At the same time I have a duty to the law. Until I am satisfied, neither your husband's death or Jenny Teller's will be closed."

He left her then, and she didn't call him back.

Rutledge was returning to the Yard when he saw Meredith Channing just coming out of Westminster Abbey. She still wore a sling on her arm but moved without pain as far as he could tell. He slowed the motorcar, and when she came within speaking distance, he called to her.

She looked up, recognized him, and paused, as if uncertain whether to greet him or not. And then she crossed to the motorcar.

"I see you've recovered," he said.

"And you found the people you were searching for? Were they all right?"

"Yes, thank God. I came back to look for you. I was told you'd already been moved, but no one seemed to know where."

"A very kind woman took in several of us. It was a relief to get away from such an horrific scene. And then friends came for me. I stayed a few days with them. " She paused. "Ian. I've decided to travel for a while. I think it would be good for me."

There was traffic behind him. He said, "Are you going home? Just now?"

"Yes. I sometimes come here to think. It's very lovely and very quiet."

"I'll take you, then." And he lied when he saw her hesitation. "I'm going in that direction."

"All right. Yes. Thank you."

As they pulled away from the pavement and headed for Trafalgar Square, he asked, "How long do you expect to be away? For the summer?"

"I'm not sure. A year or two, perhaps. I haven't looked ahead." After a moment, she added, "I've—become fond of someone. And I'm not sure that it's wise."

He couldn't see her face. She was looking at the passing scene as if she had never traveled this way before. He wasn't sure she was seeing it now.

"Something has upset you."

"I think the train crash upset everyone who was there," she said evasively. She turned to look at him, then looked away again.

He remembered that no one had sent him word about the name of the passenger who had died.

"Was he on the train? The man you've become fond of?"

Surprise flitted across her face as she turned back to him. "On the train? No. I was traveling alone. What made you think—"

"There was a man in your compartment. He didn't survive."

"Oh. I didn't know. I'm glad I didn't. He was very nice. We'd chatted for a time." She bit her lip. "He'd been to visit his son." Her eyes filled with tears, and she blinked to hold them back. "Well. You see. I'm still very emotional about the crash."

"It's not unusual. God knows—" He stopped.

"Like my shoulder, that will heal too," she said, trying for a lighter tone. "With time."

He said nothing, weaving his way through traffic, giving her space to recover. The tension in his mind brought the voice of Hamish to the forefront, so loud it seemed to fill the motorcar.

They had reached Chelsea. Her house was just three streets away. He was searching for words now, unable to think for the other voice, realizing that time was slipping away.

Two streets now.

He didn't know what he wanted to say. He had steeled himself against any feelings, and the wall was high, insurmountable.

One street.

"Running," he said finally, "is no solution."

She sighed. "No. But I don't know what else to do."

They had reached her house. He slowed the motorcar, stopped, was getting out to open her door, and the moment was lost.

"At least," she said, smiling brightly, "it isn't raining this time. Thank you, Ian. This was very kind of you."

And she strode up the walk, opening her door, disappearing inside.

He stood there, Hamish hammering at him, and then turned and got in his motorcar.

Afterward, he wasn't sure how he got as far as Windsor without knowing it. He had to turn around and drive back to London.

Chief Superintendent Bowles had given some thought to the trap he intended to lay for the murderer they knew only as Billy.

He said, as Rutledge reported to him, "Good, you're early."

"How is Cummins?"

"Out of the woods, but not thanks to Billy. He came damned close to severing an artery. We've got to stop this maniac, and you're to be the bait. At least that's the current thinking—that it's you he's after."

"I don't think he's a maniac."

"Stands to reason that he is. Hunting people like an animal. Then taking his knife to them."

Rutledge let it go. Instead, he asked Bowles, "Was there any information on that man Hood, who is our witness for Bynum's killing?"

"The address he gave us was false, a stationer's shop. Like many of his kind, he doesn't want to be found."

So, Rutledge thought, little more than he'd known already. "Have you spoken to Gibson or one of the older sergeants? The man may have a past. I've seen him before or dealt with him somewhere."

"It doesn't matter. We shan't need him until the trial. Here's the plan. You'll drive over to the police station in Lambeth, and speak to the sergeant on duty. It's a routine question, about one of the men Billy robbed earlier on. I want you to be seen, and then return here. At nine o'clock, I want you to dine with Mickelson, walking with him to that pub on the far side of St. Martin-in-the-Fields. Then you'll return alone on foot as darkness falls, and walk along the Embankment. Failing any sighting of our friend Billy, you'll walk to the bridge and stand where you did before."

"He's not going to fall easily into a trap," Rutledge warned. "He's seen your men, he knows he sent Cummins to hospital. Here's a better choice." And he outlined what he had in mind.

Bowles was willing to compromise, and at eight o'clock Mickelson and Rutledge left the Yard on foot for their meal. It was a stilted dinner, neither man feeling much like opening a conversation, the animosity between them making even a request for a saltcellar sound like a declaration of war.

Their dislike of each other went back to an inquiry in Westmorland, where Mickelson misjudged a volatile situation and nearly got an innocent bystander killed. Rather than acknowledge his mistake, he'd rushed to London and laid full blame at Rutledge's door. Circumstances had cleared Rutledge, but Bowles had not been swift to act on the information and still favored Mickelson.

Rutledge finished first, and went on foot back to the Yard. He felt like dozens of eyes watched his progress, but from street level he could see no one.

He went into the Yard. A quarter of an hour later, Constable Miller, dressed as a sweep, was drunkenly making a nuisance of himself in front of the House of Commons. A single constable was dispatched to deal with him, but the noise level didn't abate. Rutledge, with another constable in tow, strode down to Commons and reasoned with the drunken man. Miller, young and excited, nearly overplayed his role, but in the end, the two constables marched him back to the Yard, protesting every step of the way at the top of his considerable lungs. A small crowd gathered to watch, laughing at the spectacle, and Miller played to his audience, offering to kiss the pretty girls and bring them a sweep's luck. He dropped one of his brushes, bent over to retrieve it, and fell on his face. The two constables, one on either side, brought him to his feet and kept the bundle. By this time, Miller appeared to be turning a little green, and the onlookers moved away as he knelt and was sick in the gutter. The constables, waiting impatiently, urged the last two or three people who were lingering to see how the situation turned out, to be about their business. A decidedly uncomfortable Miller, holding his stomach, and complaining that he'd meant no harm, shambled between his captors and was soon hauled through the door at the Yard.

Rutledge, inside Commons, walked out talking to a well-dressed man who could have been as important as he looked. They stood together for a good five minutes, as the last of the light was fading from the sky, sped on by a heavy bank of clouds in the west.

The man with Rutledge finally took his leave and walked back to the Commons and disappeared through the door. Rutledge stood there looking after him for a moment, then walked back toward the Yard. Halfway there, one of the constables came out to meet him, passed on a message, and went back the way he'd come. Rutledge went down toward the water, studying the clouds that were already blotting out the western stars and moving downriver. A flash of lightning in the darkest part of the clouds lit them from within, and a cool breeze picked up to herald the storm. A roll of thunder followed.

"There's no' much time before the rain comes," Hamish said. In the distance, somewhere near Trafalgar Square, a motorcar's horn blew sharply. Rutledge started back toward the bridge and paused to watch a river skiff expertly run the gantlet of the stone arches, and voices carried to him across the water, three men as far as he could tell, and young enough to like the excitement of danger.

He had come to the bridge and stood there, as if debating what to do next. Another roll of thunder reached him and the flashes of lightning were brighter and more often. Taking off his coat and slinging it over his shoulder, he turned and walked back in the direction of the Yard.

He never knew where Billy came from. There was more thunder, a hiss of warning from Hamish, and suddenly the boy was there, arm round Rutledge's neck, jerking his head back. Rutledge fought then, with every skill at his command. The boy was strong and driven by obsession. Rutledge had his hands full. And where, he wondered in a corner of his mind, was Mickelson with a half dozen constables?

"'Ware!" Hamish yelled.

The knife flashed, and Rutledge caught the arm wielding it, twisted, and brought his weight down on it.

The boy screamed, letting Rutledge go, and then kicked out viciously with all his strength, grazing Rutledge's kneecap as he leapt back.

There was more thunder, and Rutledge could hear the German guns.

His attention on the boy, looking for an opening to bring him down once and for all, Rutledge felt arms flung around his shoulders, hauling him back. He thought it was one of his own people and relaxed his guard.

Billy hit him then with locked fists, across the face.

Behind Rutledge, someone said, "Will. For God's sake—"

"No, I'll kill him. And you as well." His face was green in the lightning.

"Listen to me, Will. I'll help you, I swear to God I will."

"I don't want your help."

Billy lunged with the knife, straight at Rutledge's exposed chest, but the man behind him shoved Rutledge to one side with such force that both went down, and the knife plunged into the man's left side.

Rebounding, Rutledge was already on his feet, and before Billy could react to what he'd done, he had the boy in a grip that brought him to his knees. Billy yelped in pain. The man lying on the pavement looked up and cried, "Don't hurt him."

Rutledge said through clenched teeth, "I'd like to throttle him."

But he was referring to Mickelson, for the sound of boots pounding belatedly in his direction was none too soon.

The first constable to reach the three men held a torch in the face of the fallen man, and Rutledge nearly lost his grip on Billy as he recognized Charlie Hood.

"Are you all right, sir? That was a very foolhardy thing to do," the constable chided him, bending over Hood. "And very brave, I must say." He was shoving something against the heavily bleeding wound as two more men came up and took Billy roughly from Rutledge's hold.

Rutledge knelt by Hood. "What the hell are you doing here?" he demanded, but Mickelson had just reached them, out of breath, saying, "Who's this other man?" Thunder cut across the rest of his words.

"Good Samaritan," the constable retorted as he worked. "We'll need help straightaway, sir. This looks bad."

Billy said nothing, standing there pale in the torch beams, looking down at Hood. Then he burst out with, "What did you want to go and do that for? Now look at what's happened."

Hood cleared his throat, and they could all see flecks of blood like black freckles on his lips. "I didn't expect to see you again quite so soon," he said to Rutledge.

"What were you doing here?" Rutledge asked again.

"My son, man. This is my son," Hood replied haltingly.

They looked nothing alike. As Rutledge glanced from Hood's face to Billy's, he could find no resemblance at all. And then in a quirk of the light as Billy turned to him, fright replacing his belligerence, he caught a similarity in expression around the eyes.

He'd seen Billy only once before, and then only fleetingly. Yet he had managed to register that expression as Billy had tried to plead his innocence to another constable, and it had stayed with him. And Charlie Hood had triggered that memory.

Hood was leaning back in the constable's arms now, his face pale, his mouth a tight line of pain.

"It's my fault," he whispered, smiling with an effort. "I should have been in time. Long before this."

They were trying to lead Billy away, but he was fighting to stay with the man on the ground. A flash of lightning illuminated all their faces briefly in a shock of white light, and then they were blinded in the aftermath of blackness. Thunder rolled, and the breeze had become a wind tearing at their clothing and pulling at their hair.

Someone had come with a motorcar, and there was an effort to get

Hood in the back before the rain fell. Already the first heavy drops accompanied the thunder just overhead, and Big Ben striking the quarter hour sounded muffled.

Mickelson said out of the darkness, "We couldn't see. There was a third person, and so we weren't sure."

Rutledge ignored him. He went to the motorcar as the rain fell and leaned in to speak to Hood. The man was breathing with some difficulty, and pain had set in. His clenched fist beat against the seat in rhythm with the throbbing.

"Why were you hunting him?" Rutledge asked urgently, bending over Hood.

"His mother and I separated years ago. I didn't know he was in trouble. I'd been working in the north. When I heard, I started looking. I nearly caught up with him the day Bynum was killed. Too late to save him. He needed a father's hand. I wasn't *there*. The men she lived with were bad for him. I didn't *know*. Criminal records."

"Why did he want to kill me?"

"I think—you got in his way. He never liked being thwarted. He tried to kill me once, when he was twelve. I made him return a stolen bicycle."

"Sir?" a constable said, and Rutledge pulled away. The motorcar gathered speed as it turned back the way it had come.

Billy too was gone, in custody.

A constable had stayed with Rutledge, rain cascading off his helmet and onto his cape. "Sir?" he said again.

"Yes, very well." And Rutledge turned with him toward the Yard. He realized he was wet to the skin and cold.

Mickelson had disappeared.

The constable said, "Are you all right, sir?"

"I'm fine," he said shortly, and the constable was wise enough not to say more.

In truth he was not fine. Tired, hurting, and angry enough to take on Mickelson and Billy at the same time, he set the pace, stride for stride with the constable.

When they reached the Yard, the constable—he realized in the light above the door that it was Miller—said, "He held us back, sir. He said he couldn't see who was with you. The other man confused him. He said."

"It doesn't matter," Rutledge told him.

"I think it does, sir."

But Rutledge refused to be led into answering. He went to his office and sat there for some time in the dark, watching the storm move downriver, thinking about Billy and the man who had called him Will.

After an hour had passed, and then most of another, Rutledge stood up and walked to the door.

Chief Superintendent Bowles had not come to find him. Not to apologize for Inspector Mickelson's disregard for orders or to congratulate Rutledge on his role in capturing the killer the newspapers had begun to call the Bridge Murderer.

He drove to his flat, bathed, and changed to dry clothes, then slept for two hours. When he woke, his face on one side was bruised, his knee ached, but on the whole no damage had been done.

He stopped at the Yard to ask the night duty sergeant for news of Hood and was told that the hospital reported he was holding his own.

"And there's a message as well from Inspector Cummins, sir."

He handed it to Rutledge.

The single word *Thanks* was written in a bold script he recognized.

Nodding to the sergeant, he left and drove to Essex.

It was very early. The storm over London hadn't cleared the air here. The clouds were heavy, the rain dismal, and he had had no breakfast

Hamish said, "It willna' improve your mood."

He waited in a lay-by until eight o'clock, and then drove the short distance to Witch Hazel Farm. He found Edwin standing in the doorway, looking out at the weather.

"It doesn't appear that this rain will stop," Edwin called as Rutledge got out of the motorcar. "Good God, man, what happened to your face?"

"An altercation with a belligerent prisoner," Rutledge said.

"Peter's funeral is today. Did you know?"

"I spoke to Mrs. Teller yesterday in London. She told me."

They walked indoors, and Edwin said, "What about Jenny? Can we go ahead there as well? I think it's not in Walter's best interests to go on brooding. We've hardly clapped eyes on him. He stays in his room. Leticia has been taking up his meals."

"I see no reason not to release the body," Rutledge said. "I've decided to agree with Inspector Jessup for now that these were accidents. I have found no evidence that they weren't."

"I don't see how anyone would gain by their deaths. Financially or otherwise."

Rutledge said, "It has nothing to do with money. What concerned me was the fact that your brother is no longer alive to deny he was married to Florence Marshall. And Jenny Teller is no longer alive to be hurt should the legitimacy of her marriage be questioned."

"I don't think—"

"No. I'm sure none of you did when first you embarked on this venture."

Edwin said, "As I was about to say, I don't think justice would be served by pursuing this."

Rutledge entered the study to find the family collected there, save for Walter. They looked tired, dispirited, and isolated in their own thoughts.

Mary said, "The funeral is at two o'clock this afternoon. Did Edwin tell you?"

He thanked her, and asked after Harry.

"He's bearing up well enough. The rector's son gave him a puppy. I don't know what Walter will say to that—he never cared for pets—but it has taken Harry's mind off death."

Rutledge was reminded of another small boy rewarded by a puppy from the litter in the barn.

Leticia said, "Did you speak to Susannah, Inspector? Is she coming?"

"I expect to see her," he said.

She started out of the room. "I'll see that her bed is made up."

Rutledge had the feeling that his very presence dampened the conversation. He followed Leticia out into the passage. "I don't believe she'll stay here," he told her.

"Well. Her choice, of course."

He went to the nanny's room that had been Jenny's sanctuary and sat there until it was time to come down for the service. It was a quiet room, serene and seemingly distant from the tense atmosphere of the study, and from its windows, Rutledge could count the motorcars and carriages arriving for the funeral.

He made a point of attending. The church was larger by far than the one in Hobson. He watched the mourners gather and listened to a well-meant eulogy by Mr. Stedley, extolling the Captain's bravery, his sense of duty to God and country, and his love for his family.

And then Peter Teller was buried in rain that pattered softly on the cluster of umbrellas struggling vainly to keep the mourners as dry as possible. But the earth that was to be sprinkled into the grave struck the coffin in muddy clumps, and he saw Susannah Teller wince at the sound.

She had held up remarkably well, greeting the guests with quiet dignity, her face nearly invisible behind the long silk veil of mourning, her feelings hidden as well. But he heard her voice tremble once or twice.

Afterward, the guests returned to Witch Hazel Farm for the funeral repast.

Mollie and her cohorts had done their best, and the family stood about in the drawing room and the dining room, making the right remarks and responding to questions that must have galled them.

Rutledge watched Susannah Teller, with Edwin at her side, as she greeted each guest and thanked them for coming.

When the last of the mourners had left, Edwin went straight to the drinks table in the study, pouring himself a whisky. He held it out to his wife, but Amy shook her head, asking for a sherry.

He brought her a glass, then turned to Rutledge.

"Nothing. Thanks."

Edwin sat on the small settee and said, "God." He looked tired and drained.

"It was a nice service," Amy said. "Everything considered. A few gawkers, there out of curiosity. Three fellow officers and their wives came. Someone who'd known Peter in school. Three women who were widows of men who served under him in the war. One of them had the handsomest boy with her. Thirteen, at a guess. She said he was the image of his father, and you could hear the grief of *his* loss still there in her voice. I can't remember who else. Oh—someone who had served in the field with Walter. He must have been close to eighty but was spry as a man ten years younger. I think that pleased Walter. At least he seemed happy to see the man. A good number of people from the village, as you'd expect. Most of them remembered Peter as a boy. I think Susannah was quite touched."

"Where is she?" Edwin asked.

"She left fifteen minutes ago. Leticia told me. She stood up very well, didn't she?" Amy went on. "Women generally do. It's expected of them not to make a fuss. I remember Walter telling us that somewhere he was sent, the women beat their breasts and tore at their hair while making the most haunting noise. An ululation, he called it. He said it made him shiver."

"Did Inspector Jessup come?"

"No. His wife was there. She said he'd been called away."

Leticia came in. "Mr. Rutledge. There is tea in the dining room, and sandwiches. Please help yourself."

He thanked her and went to find Mary sitting at the table, crumbling bits of bread from her sandwich into little pills on her plate.

He poured himself a cup of tea, then took sandwiches from the platters set out on the buffet. "May I join you?" he asked before sitting down.

"Yes, please do," she answered, whether she was pleased to see him there or not.

"Mrs. Teller felt that the service went well."

"Yes, I'm glad. And there's still Jenny's funeral to get through. Today I wished myself anywhere but there. Still, one has to support the family. As they've supported me." She got up and set her plate on the small table already piled with used dishes. "I'll come in later and help Mollie with these," she said. Then after hesitating, as if of two minds what to do, she came back and sat down. "Have you seen Walter? He was here for a bit, and then I looked for him and he was gone. I thought he might have retreated to the study."

"I was there. I haven't seen him."

"Then he's in his room," she said, nodding. "Did he kill Jenny?"

Surprised, Rutledge countered, "There's no real proof. Why should he wish to see her dead?"

"Well, that's what we've all been waiting for, isn't it, these past few days?" she said bitterly. "Proof one way or the other. About Walter's illness. About Peter. About that death in Lancashire. Then about Peter again, and now about Jenny. The other shoe dropping." She turned away. "Do you have any idea what the tension has been like, since Walter first took ill? I went through his study, trying to find out who to contact in the Alcock Society, I thought someone might come and speak to Walter at the Belvedere. I was foolish enough to believe he was worried about going back into the field and they might set his mind at rest. Imagine my shock when I learned about his other life. And all the time—it was Edwin who suggested that Florence Teller might have been here in London and Walter happened to see her. But of course she wasn't, as it turned out. So we will never know, will we, why he was ill?"

Rutledge said, "It doesn't matter now what made him ill."

"Yes, it does, because he still has to come to terms with it and choose. I think it has to do with Harry, with Walter's insistence that the boy be sent away to school. It was as if he didn't want him anymore. I couldn't for the life of me understand why. And then he recanted on Harrow, telling Jenny it would be all right to wait a few years. But now, this morning, he told me he thought it would be best for Harry to go after all, because he's motherless. I'd already promised to take him and look after him for a bit, but Walter is adamant. Harrow it is to be. I knew Walter long before Jenny met him. As a brother-in-law, he was kind and thoughtful and always willing to help me with the house where Jenny and I grew up. I couldn't have asked for better. And I could share Harry with them—they were always asking if I'd take him for a night or for a few days. I really care for the boy, I'd do anything to protect him. But I've begun to realize that Walter uses people. Not wittingly, purposely, but most certainly conveniently. I've even begun to wonder if he married Jenny to have a son again, to replace that dead one. He's capable of it, you know."

Her bluntness was almost brutal. And he found himself thinking that Mary had understood what was behind the two marriages better than anyone else, because she was so alone herself.

"I don't know, Miss Brittingham, what to say. But you may be right. As to what he intends to do, there's no impediment. Walter Teller can do as he pleases. I've every intention of closing the inquiries here, and asking the inquests to bring in a verdict of accidental death in both cases."

Before she could answer, Amy came to the door. "Inspector, Inspector Jessup is here. He wants to speak to you urgently." She turned to Mary. "Have you seen Walter? And what's become of Gran?"

"He must be in his room," Mary said. "I don't have the energy to go and see. Mr. Rutledge tells me he wasn't in the study. Your grandmother is lying down. Leticia settled her half an hour ago."

"Thanks. I'll go and look for him."

Amy closed the door again. Mary rose and said, "Needs must. I ought to join the others, whether I feel like it or not. I'm a guest, now that Jenny's gone. And so I must fit in with the wishes of others."

She went out of the room, and Rutledge followed her, in search of Jessup.

He was pacing the hall. When Rutledge came down the passage, he turned and said, "There's been an accident. Can you come at once?"

Rutledge followed him out to the waiting motorcar. "What is it? What's happened?"

"It's Mrs. Teller. Captain Teller's widow. She left here, I'm told with the last of the mourners, intending to drive to London. She's had an accident."

"Is she dead?" he asked, remembering the warning he'd given her.

"No. Badly bruised. And she wants to see you. She won't let us fetch a doctor to her until she does."

They drove on in silence, through the gray evening, and shortly after the intersection where the Repton Road and the one to Waddington met the trunk road to London they found Captain Teller's black Rolls touring car with the bonnet having run up into an ancient hedgerow topped by a wooden fence that lead into a pasture. He was out of the Inspector's vehicle before it had come to a halt and was striding to where Susannah Teller was sitting in the rain, the veil she had pulled to the back of her black hat drooping. Her coat sparkled with raindrops in the light of her motorcar's headlamps.

He came and sat down beside her, then put his arm around her shoulders. She cried out in pain, then began to weep in earnest.

Jessup was saying, "Bruising where the wheel struck her, scraped knees—" He broke off as Rutledge silently shook his head to stop him, and he moved away to speak to his men.

"What happened? I didn't know you'd left. Was the motorcar tampered with?"

"I couldn't stand being there—every time I went past the stairs or saw someone stepping on the place where he was lying, it was more than I could bear. I wanted the garden doors open instead, but Mary told me that with the rain, the lawns were too wet. I went to Walter, but he wouldn't open his door and help me. I left as soon as I could."

"Did you tell anyone you were leaving?"

"Only Gran. You don't know how much I miss Peter. It's been worse than anything I could have imagined, coming here. The funeral. And I feel so alone."

"How did this happen?"

"I was crying. I couldn't see where I was going. I did to myself what you were afraid someone else might do."

"Are you sure there was no problem with the motorcar—the steering or the brakes?"

She shook her head.

He sat with her a little longer, and then she agreed to let Inspector Jessup take her to Dr. Fielding.

He said to Jessup, "Go over this motorcar. If there is any reason for that crash other than her emotional state, I want to know."

Jessup looked at him. "Are you saying someone would like to kill that woman?"

"I told her that if there was an attempt at a third accident, we would know that the other deaths were murder."

"And she thought . . ."

"She was frightened. But it was the only way I could make her watch for trouble. She was angry with the family, she blamed them for her husband's fall."

"I don't understand how she could."

Rutledge was walking around the motorcar, but in the rainy darkness he could see nothing. "It doesn't matter. The fact is, she did. All right, let me know what you find."

He asked one of the constables to drive him back to Witch Hazel Farm, and with a nod from Jessup, one stepped forward and said, "This way, sir."

Hamish was saying something, but Rutledge wasn't listening. He went to find Amy as soon as he reached the house.

"Your sister-in-law ran off the road in the rain. Dr. Fielding is seeing her in his surgery."

"Oh, dear. I ought to go to her. She should never have been allowed to drive to London alone. Are you sure she's all right?" She clicked her tongue. "I don't know what's to become of us. It's a little frightening."

"She's all right, but I think she might prefer not to be alone."

"Of course not. But—there's another problem. We've looked everywhere, and Walter isn't here. No one has seen him since the funeral service. I telephoned the rector—he told me he hadn't seen Walter since we left the church. You don't think he's vanished again? It would be too horrible to contemplate."

"Did you look in the nursery?" Rutledge asked.

"Yes, before I called the rectory." She glanced uneasily toward the door. "You don't suppose he went for a walk?"

"Not tonight. Is his motorcar here?"

"I'm sure it is," she began doubtfully, then said, "Would you look? It's in the small barn just beyond the kitchen garden."

Rutledge went around to the shed where the motorcar was kept.

It was still there. Rutledge laid a hand on the bonnet. It was almost completely cool after driving to the service.

When he found Amy Teller and told her, she said, "I don't remember exactly when I saw him last. But then I didn't realize Susannah had left, either. There was such a number of motorcars and carriages and people, at the end." Amy turned toward the stairs. "Let me fetch my coat," she said. After a moment she was back, adding, "Perhaps we ought to go to the church. I'll feel better when we know he's all right." She bit her lip. "We let him stay to himself too much. But we were all angry still, and upset about Peter and then Jenny. We let him bear the brunt of our feelings."

"The church?" Rutledge asked. "All right, we'll have a look."

He drove with her to the church, but it was dark and empty, with no sign of Walter. They encountered Mr. Stedley just coming to return the church umbrellas, and asked him again if he'd seen Walter.

"I'm afraid not." He looked across the churchyard to the raw mound of earth that marked Peter Teller's grave. "Do you have a torch, Inspector?"

He found the one in his motorcar, but although he flashed it across the stones and beneath the yew trees, there was no sign of Teller.

Stedley, standing in the porch shivering, said, "It's grown quite chilly. I hope he's not wandered far."

Rutledge drove Amy Teller back to Witch Hazel Farm and with her searched the house again, then the outbuildings. But Teller had gone.

"He might have decided to spend a little time with Jenny," Amy said doubtfully.

She called Dr. Fielding's house, but Mrs. Fielding told her that they had not seen Teller since the service for his brother.

Edwin, coming down from his bedchamber where he'd been resting, said, "I should think he's all right. He might have just walked around, trying to clear his head." But it was like whistling in the dark. His voice betrayed his concern.

Mary said, from her corner by the fire they'd built in the hearth against the chill of the rain, "You don't suppose he went to my house? Or Leticia's? Or he may have gone back to London with Susannah.

We're all staying the night here. He may have wanted a little peace and quiet."

Leticia, who joined them, said, "On foot? The motorcar is here. No, he must have begged a lift from someone."

Edwin said, "We may be worrying prematurely. Let's give him another hour. It's foolish to panic like this."

"He wouldn't just—vanish again, would he?" Mary asked Rutledge.

But he could offer her only cold comfort. "I don't know."

"Call the Belvedere Clinic, Amy," Mary suggested.

"He couldn't have reached London this soon," Amy protested.

Mollie came in to ask if anyone would care for tea, and they asked her again if she knew where Teller might be.

But Mollie hadn't seen him since the first mourners had departed.

Hamish said, "Ye're worrying about the lass. It's possible you were fearing for the wrong person."

32

It took them some time to discover how Teller had vanished so quickly.

Amy brought Rutledge the list of attendees. It took half the night to track them down. He and Jessup dealt with the local names, while Gibson at the Yard ran the others to ground.

The former missionary had been the hardest to locate, for he was traveling about England raising funds for various charities that helped support mission work and had no particular itinerary.

He told the constable who had tracked him down in the middle of Hampshire, "Yes, Walter asked if I was coming to London. I told him I was, and he asked for a lift. There was a meeting he had to attend in the morning. He didn't want to put the family out, although Edwin had volunteered to take him. And I was happy to oblige, it was company on the road."

The constable asked where the missionary had dropped Teller. "By Scotland Yard," the constable told them.

"It was all a lie," Edwin said, angry. "You were here. Why should he go to the Yard?"

"He's going back to the field," Leticia told them. "Leaving us to deal as best we can with the problems he left behind."

Hamish said, "Lancashire."

Through Sergeant Gibson, Rutledge had already sent a telegram to Hobson, asking Constable Satterthwaite to keep a watch on the house. But would Teller go there as penance for what he'd done to Florence Teller? Or to escape from his family? He could live as a recluse there as easily as he could in Africa.

Mary Brittingham said, "He might have gone to my house. There's no one there. I'd given the staff a few days off. But Jenny still had her key. He could have taken it. I'll have a look, at least."

It was nearly dawn by that time. Rutledge said, "You should rest first."

Mary, her eyes sunken with worry, laughed without humor. "I doubt I'd sleep at all. Someone ought to look and see if Peter's revolver is here. I can't sit still. Let me drive home and look. He may have turned back, to confuse us. I'll stop at Leticia's too. I'll bring him back if I find him. If I don't, I'll take your advice and rest." She held up a Thermos. "Mollie has given me tea to keep me awake on the road. I'll be all right."

There was a light breakfast in the dining room, but no one felt like eating. Rutledge said, "I have a feeling he's not in London. He could have taken a train anywhere."

Amy, who had gone looking for the revolver, said, "It isn't there. He might well have shot himself this time. He was so depressed about Jenny. Although you'd think he would have a care for Harry."

"He may have thought Susannah had reached her house. He could be there." He went to put in yet another telephone call.

"Tiresome man," Leticia said. "He's thinking only of himself. I for one am going up to my bed." She turned on her heel to leave.

The storm had gone with the night. A pale sunlight touched the windows.

Amy said, "Shouldn't someone go to Portsmouth?"

Leticia said, "As I learned the last time, no one can simply arrive at a mission and announce his return. There are arrangements to make—travel for one, supplies, money, and so on. Details, like how long he'll be expected to remain there, what comforts he can expect—or not. Whether Bibles have been translated into that particular dialect. What his expenses are, and who will sponsor him. Enthusiasm isn't enough."

"Which is why," Hamish suggested, "he went with yon auld man."

It was a strong possibility. Except that he'd left the missionary in London.

Rutledge said, "If there's any news at the Yard, I'll make certain you hear it right away. Meanwhile, I need to return to London. I can coordinate a search from there."

"No, you aren't," Amy said. "You're going along to Hobson. Aren't you?"

It was true. He'd thought Hamish might be right, and in the silences of the house with the red door, Teller might use his brother's revolver. Who would hear the shot? Even Mrs. Blaine was gone. But he hadn't wanted to alarm them.

But on his way he detoured to speak to Inspector Jessup. The Teller motorcar had been moved from the scene of the accident, and it was now sitting in the small paved area to one side of the police station.

Inspector Jessup had gone home to bed. Rutledge was turned over to one of his constables, who gave him the report on the accident.

"Nothing anyone did caused Mrs. Teller to run off the road," he said. "But someone had tried to tamper with the brakes and failed."

He went out to have a look for himself and saw that Jessup had been right. "Any report on Mrs. Teller?"

"Dr. Fielding gave her something to calm her and kept her overnight. But he thinks she will be fine. Bruised and shaken, he said, but nothing time won't heal."

It was late when Rutledge finally arrived in Hobson, and he was tired. He debated knocking on Mrs. Greeley's door and asking if his room was available. But he was afraid that Cobb might still be staying there, and the last thing he wanted tonight was to talk to anyone.

Instead, he found his way in the dark to Sunrise Cottage, and well before he reached the house, he stopped and stared up at it. There were no lights. The house looked just as it had done when he'd left it the last time.

"You wouldn't see a change. He's asleep," Hamish said quietly.

If he was even inside.

There was a rug behind his seat of the motorcar. It was tempting to reach for it and sleep for half an hour. Neither his wits nor his reflexes were at their best.

When he didn't immediately open the door, Hamish said, "It isna' wise to stay here on the road."

"He's not likely to slip up on me."

"Aye. True enough. But ye must move the motorcar."

Walter Teller might well be twenty paces from where Rutledge sat, asleep in his wife's bed. He didn't want to risk more noise.

There was no way of knowing what the man's state of mind was. Or even if he'd come this far. Walter Teller was a man who kept his emotions close, whose feelings had been lost in a welter of events, from the day he left for Africa, or possibly even from the day he was ordained. Was he a killer? He hadn't murdered his first wife. The odds, then, discounted his murdering the second.

Hamish said, "Why did ye no' feel for the second wife what you felt for the first? The lass here?"

Caught off guard, Rutledge said, "Because no one else did."

"Aye."

"I can't help but wonder if it would have made any difference if Florence's son had been brought up in London, not here. He might have had better medical care. That might have occurred to Walter Teller as well."

But Hamish had no answer for that.

"We may never explain Walter Teller satisfactorily. Tidily and with ribbons."

He had only to open his door to find out. That is, if Walter was indeed in Sunrise Cottage—and still alive.

"Ye're no' thinking straight," Hamish said.

Rutledge could feel the darkness coming down, the sound of big guns in the distance, and closer to hand, the rattle of a Vickers gun.

No, that was at the Front. When Hamish was still living and breathing. Before he'd had to shoot him for disobeying orders . . .

His mind felt as if it were stuffed with cotton wool. But he'd come this far. Pulling his motorcar out of sight on the far side of the hedge, he listened, but nothing stirred.

Opening the motorcar door as quietly as he could, Rutledge stepped out into the night. There were stars overhead, and the looming shape of the house, rising behind the hedge, the whiteness of it almost ghostly in the ambient light.

He could still hear the guns in France, distantly echoing in his mind. Closer than they ought to be.

Shaking off the encroaching darkness, he turned toward the gate, then stopped.

He could have sworn another motorcar was coming up the rise. Moving deeper into the shadows cast by the hedge, he listened. The road was empty still.

He hadn't imagined the motorcar. Footsteps were approaching the house on the unmade road, someone trying to walk quietly.

There was a slight creak as the gate opened and closed. Rutledge stayed where he was in the deep shadow of the hedge. A shaft of lightning lit the sky like a searchlight. Peering through the hedge, he was nearly certain someone was standing on the step by the red door.

Teller, arriving? What had kept him?

Or Cobb, coming to the house because he couldn't stay away?

Hamish said, "He hated Teller."

It wouldn't do for the two of them to meet, both of them tense and under a great strain.

Either it was his imagination or someone had opened the door now and stepped inside. The front step was empty.

The silence lengthened. Rutledge shut his eyes, to hear better. But the only sound was his own breathing, and the beating of his heart.

Something fell over in the house. Rutledge moved quietly through the gate.

Hamish said, "Someone's in yon parlor."

"Yes."

And then a light bloomed in the bedroom window, a candle flame, he was sure of it.

Rutledge returned to his motorcar and collected the torch. Then crouching low so that he couldn't be seen from the windows, he made his way to the rear of the house.

He stumbled, realized that he'd tripped over one of the tiny headstones, and froze. But no one came to the windows or the door. Aware that he'd failed to gauge his approach properly, he realigned his direction to avoid the flower beds by the kitchen door.

Ducking under the kitchen windows, he glimpsed a flash of light, as if whoever was holding the candle was moving down the stairs.

Time was of the essence.

He reached the door, counting to twenty-five before putting his hand on the latch. Lifting it gently, he waited in the doorway.

No one spoke, and he stepped inside.

The candle was in the parlor. He couldn't see who was holding it, only the faint glow as it was raised to allow someone to survey the room.

It moved on to the sitting room.

Rutledge was well inside the kitchen now, letting his eyes grow accustomed to the darkness within the house.

Then there was an intake of breath, and a curse as the candle went out.

"My God, what are you doing here?" It was Teller speaking. And then the scrape of a match, and the candle bloomed into life again. Rutledge could see Teller's shadow thrown against the far wall, black and formidable, but knew he himself was invisible.

Teller raised his voice. "I asked you what you were doing here?"

A woman's low voice said, "The police said you weren't here. But I knew you were. Do you think you can make amends to *her*? Or is this sackcloth and ashes too late?"

Rutledge strained his ears. Was it Susannah? Hamish disagreed.

"Sanctuary. Of a sort. That's all."

"Men like Rutledge don't walk away. He'll find you here."

"Well. I'll think of somewhere else to go. I've lived rougher than this. At least the roof is sound, and I have a bed. Though I couldn't sleep in it. I made myself a pallet on the floor, next to Timmy's bed. I slept there many a night when he had croup or a heavy cold. It was familiar."

"Did you love him more than Harry?"

"I didn't know Harry. Even though I was there with him as he grew. Timmy kept getting in my way. I'd see his smile in the way Harry's lips quirked. The shrug of a shoulder—the way he'd kick a football. Even the way he sometimes talked with his mouth full and the way a lick of hair stood up straight after a nap. God, how I tried."

"And Jenny? Did you love her as much as you loved Florence? Or are you unable to love anyone but yourself?"

"What difference does it make to you? Yes, I thought I was in love with Florence—I was young, I wanted the world, and she thought I was everything I wanted to be. I could see myself in her eyes. Better than my father's, surely."

There was a silence, and he said, "Jenny knew nothing about Timmy. It was a relief to talk to her—to pretend this part of my past didn't exist. And then I couldn't bear not to come here and remember. You saw through me. You always have known the kind of man I was. It was like looking into my mirror, when I was with you."

"Yes. Well. It all came crashing down. You brought it down, you know. Wittingly or unwittingly."

"You haven't told me. Why did you come?" he asked.

"I brought you something."

"That's Peter's revolver."

"I thought you might like to die as Peter Teller. *This* Peter Teller."

"I won't hang, and I won't shoot myself. I disappeared before, and I can do it again. You heard Gran—what she said will still be enough to hang me about the laudanum."

"I was angry enough with you to want to see you hang," she said. "I could have told them it was nonsense about the laudanum. She could tolerate it perfectly well, mixed with warmed milk. I don't know why she was ill that other time. She might have had a miscarriage for all I knew."

"Why the hell didn't you speak up and tell Jessup what you knew?"

"Why should I make life easier for you? It would be best, really, if you just went away, but the police will find you in the end. Harry will do very well with Amy and Edwin to care for him. Put the barrel in your mouth and simply pull the trigger. Like this."

"You're wrong about me. I didn't kill anyone!"

"Of course you didn't. I did it for you."

Even from where he was standing, Rutledge could hear the hiss of Walter Teller's indrawn breath.

"It sorted out everything very nicely. Jenny died knowing she was safe and loved. Peter was the last connection with Lancashire. You of all people should appreciate the logic of that. After all, everything pointed to him. And it left Harry as the Teller heir, and that was all everyone cared about. If you're honest, you'll agree with me."

"Were you that jealous? I wasn't aware of it."

"That's because you're selfish and self-absorbed. So do the decent thing and get it over with. I loved you once—single-mindedly, blindly— but I was misled like everyone else. And now I've come to my senses."

"No. I won't touch that gun. In the morning, I'm going back to Essex. There's nothing left for me here."

"Are you so afraid to die?" she asked pityingly. "Well, then. I'll take care of that for you as well. My last gift."

And before Rutledge could move, the revolver fired. Through the echo, Rutledge heard a slight cough, then the sound of a body hitting the floor.

He reached the dining room in time to see Mary Brittingham standing over Walter Teller, the revolver down by her side, tears on her face shining in the light of the candle.

"Put down the weapon and step away from him," Rutledge said, his voice sharp.

She looked up, startled, so intent on the man lying at her feet that she hadn't heard Rutledge coming toward her.

"Why are you here?" she asked. "I'd have left him for them to find. They'd never have realized he hadn't killed himself."

Reaching Teller, he went down on one knee, feeling for a pulse. It was faint, fluttering. Rutledge swore silently. He shoved his handkerchief into the wound in Teller's chest, pressing against the warm flow of blood, willing it to stop. As the handkerchief was soaked, he flung out his other hand, trying to find something else to add to it. And Mary reached for the table's cloth and was down beside him, frantically adding the pressure of her hands to his.

They worked for several minutes, but Walter Teller's breathing slowed, caught, then stopped altogether.

Rutledge rocked back on his heels, easing his shoulders.

"No—don't *stop*," Mary cried.

"He's dead," Rutledge told her, but she wouldn't hear of it, begging him to find something else she could use, and when he wouldn't, she screamed at him, her voice a shriek that sounded like Jake's, wordless and primeval.

And then over her scream, he heard the faint choking sound that preceded a long indrawn breath, and Teller was breathing again.

Mary collapsed over Teller's body, telling him that she hadn't meant for him to die, begging his forgiveness. Rutledge picked up the revolver and put it in his pocket. He felt drained, but his mind was already setting out what had to be done next. He found sheets in the bedroom and tore them into strips, rough bandaging of a sort. And working swiftly, he moved the woman aside, leaving her huddled in a corner, crying, as he ripped the buttons from Teller's shirt and set about keeping the man alive.

The sun was just showing over the horizon when Mary Brittingham got to her feet. The first rays struck the front of Sunrise Cottage and illuminated the faded red door.

She looked down at Teller, still unconscious but alive.

Turning to Rutledge, she said, "Will you give me the revolver? I'll write anything you wish me to write. But I don't want to hang."

"You've killed two people. It was nearly three. A court will have to set this to rights. I can only do my duty."

"And if you let me be tried, Harry will be branded a bastard. Everyone will know. That's worse. We can end this here, quietly. A lover's quarrel. People will wonder at it, then forget us."

"Susannah Teller will want to see you hang if you killed Peter and tried to kill her. I've got to take you to Constable Satterthwaite, and bring a doctor back here with me. It's been a long night. Don't make it any longer."

"All right." She seemed resigned to her fate, her face lined with fatigue and grief and despair. "Will you at least let me make a cup of tea? I don't think I can endure the rest of this without it."

"No. Did you have a coat?"

"I left it in the parlor, I think." She looked down at Walter Teller. "I wish I'd never come. But I didn't want him to go to the gallows in my place. At least cover him with something. A blanket from one of the beds upstairs."

Rutledge stooped to retrieve the bloody cloth from the table to spread it over Teller. And at the same instant, Mary Brittingham made a lunge for the revolver in his pocket.

It was well out of her reach. He had seen to that. But she was driven by something stronger than muscle and bone. Her will carried her across the distance, and her hand gripped the metal just as his clamped down over it.

There was a struggle. She was unbelievably strong, and it took every bit of his own strength to turn the weapon toward the wall as she managed to pull the trigger.

The second shot went into the ceiling before he could force the revolver out of her hands and shove her hard as far away as he could.

She hit the wall with a force that knocked the wind out of her, and for an instant she stared at him with such venom he took a step backward. Before she could recover, he'd emptied the chamber and pocketed the bullets.

Taking her arm, he led her out of the house and to his motorcar. The seats were wet after the rain, but she let him put her into the passenger door. He turned the crank, got behind the wheel, and happened to see a long shaft of sunlight touch the roofline of the house where Mrs. Blaine had lived.

There would be another woman for the hangman now.

Hamish said as Rutledge backed into the road, "There's her motorcar. Down the road. 'Ware."

Rutledge saw it, and pressed hard on the accelerator. It didn't deter her. Just in time, he caught Mary Brittingham's arm as she tried to open the passenger's door and throw herself out of his vehicle as it gained speed.

"Not this time," he said.

Pulling her back, he kept a firm grip on her arm.

"I will succeed," she told him through clenched teeth. "In the end, I will cheat the hangman."

And he had a feeling that she would.

But not on his watch.

33

It was a miracle that Teller lived. Dr. Blake, who was brought out to attend him, said as much. "Lost blood, the internal damage. He'll not be up and about for weeks."

"His family is in Essex."

"They could be on the moon for all I care," the doctor snapped. "The hospital here in Thielwald will do very well."

But who, Rutledge thought, would come to sit by his side? Not Susannah. Nor would Amy leave Edwin. Leticia? Perhaps.

He sent telegrams to the Yard and to Inspector Jessup. And five days later he left Lancashire and pointed the bonnet of the motorcar south at last.

There had been a great deal of time on his hands during those five days. He had sat by Walter Teller's bed or walked the streets of Thielwald, and spent an hour or two with Lawrence Cobb one afternoon.

But when he was free to leave at last, he knew what he was going to do.

And despite the fury that was Hamish in his mind, he grimly kept his eyes on the road.

There were times when he thought about Florence Teller.

Driving all night, he came into London in a light rain, mist hanging heavy over the Thames as he turned toward his destination.

Hamish said, "Ye're no' fit to do this."

It was true. He was unshaven, his clothing wrinkled and stained with Walter Teller's blood. Mrs. Greeley had done her best with a damp cloth and an iron, but it was still there. Even if he couldn't see it, he could feel the stiffness along the edges of his cuffs.

But there was no time to worry about that. He was nearly certain he was already too late.

Pulling up in front of the house in Chelsea where Meredith Channing lived, he sat for five minutes in the motorcar, searching for some sign of life. Proof that this hadn't been a wild-goose chase.

And then he got out, feeling the cramps in his muscles, determined to know.

He had knocked at the door before he realized how early it was, how foolishly early.

But to his surprise, Meredith Channing opened the door herself. He only had time to notice that she was dressed for travel before she said, "Ian. What's wrong?"

He could think of nothing to say. And then, "I've just returned from a case in the north," he managed finally.

"I must finish my packing," she said, looking up at him, her eyes filled with an emotion he was too tired to read. "My train leaves in an hour."

"Don't go," was all he said then.

She shut the door without answering him.

As he walked back to the motorcar, he could feel her gaze on him from the window of her parlor.

He didn't turn.

He had said what he'd come to say.

The decision must be hers.